ARTIFACT OF BETRAYAL

JUNO CHASE

Juno Chase Romance

CHAPTER ONE

Claire

Claire Townsend unlocked the door and stepped inside to her very own retail shop. The centerpiece was an Old West cash register that worked. She ran her fingers across the embossed silver, feeling the ridges. A friend at an antique shop had refurbished it and given it to her as a gift. Social connections were important in this city, if not the most important thing. Connections and money. Nothing else mattered.

Usually when she walked into her boutique, there was a sense that she was pretending, but today? The air was cool, the sun was shining, the space was beautiful, and she enjoyed the moment by twirling around. Silly, she knew. Product moved quickly in the post-modern Brooklyn shop. White shelves displayed colorful dishes and uber-luxe housewares. Stand-alone racks were filled with specialty paints and signature wallpaper, antique door pulls and paper shades hand-painted by local artists.

The well-to-do liked to spend money here, but more importantly, she received invitations to exclusive events. Everything she wanted. Except that she was still single, but that didn't matter. Relationship status shouldn't be on her list. The fact that she didn't have complete financial control of her business was more important. She owed money. A lot. Until the loan, *the loan*, was paid off, the place wasn't actually hers.

Claire decided to review her finances to make sure there were no mistakes. She gathered a box of receipts under the counter before heading back. In the stock room, empty cardboard boxes were piled up against one wall. As part of a new contract with Barneys to sell her signature design wallpaper, she was asked to discontinue a similar pattern in her shop. She was proud of her design, something she'd come up with from her previous life as an anthropologist.

She had graduated with a degree in that field, but gave it up when she'd been offered a lucrative position in art sales. The job paid real money, but she hated the high stress. Even though she was surrounded by people all the time, the job made her feel unconnected, lonely. She made a cup of single-brew coffee and added nothing. She took a sip and pursed her lips. Since pulling the inventory off the shelf, she had a larger than expected loss of revenue.

She sat at her desk and turned on the computer. She should check the Excel spreadsheets to see how day to day revenue was, but instead, she wanted to review a different document. She opened her purse, pulled out a tiny key on a Las Vegas keychain and unlocked the top-right desk drawer. The only thing in there was a three-subject college notepad with lined paper. Claire placed her fingers around the edge of the notebook and lifted it gingerly, as if it were fragile.

She opened it to find the details of the loan she'd taken out with loan shark Lucia Occhipinti for one hundred thousand dollars. The only reason she'd taken the money was because every single attempt to raise capital failed. All the Small Business Loan applications had come back rejected. She tried to raise funds through angel investors, but they wanted a contract guaranteeing them fifty-one percent of the profits. She'd sold a few pieces of her investment art to finance the shop, but that wasn't enough. And one day Lucia was just there, with an offer.

The loan made her nervous. The monthly payment was thirteen thousand dollars the first Friday of each month for one year. She had agreed to the terms even though the interest was fifty-six percent. She could afford the payments with revenue from the shop and commission from her primary job at Apfel Gallery as a sales associate. She deserved this opportunity, she deserved her shop, and the only way to get ahead in this world was to take advantage of every opportunity.

Only five lines were written in the notebook: a date, an amount of thirteen thousand, and the word paid. She had to make seven more payments and Lucia would be paid off. Her dreams would come true, and she was willing to risk everything on it. In two years, she'd be making quit-your-job-and-live-on-a-yacht money. Dreaming of those days was why she worked so damn hard.

This month, though, due to revenue loss from the wallpaper sales, she was six thousand dollars short on the loan payment. She had expected to lose money in her first year as a business owner; it was why she still had a job at the Apfel Gallery. If she sold the Bromanshank painting on Friday, the thirty grand commission would cover the loss, and she'd make Lucia's payment.

The problem was she would be twelve hours late. She'd get the check Friday evening and deposit it, but her cash machine had a daily limit of six hundred dollars. She would have to wait until Saturday morning to go inside the bank and withdraw the money. The earlier joy dissipated; she almost felt faint. She placed the coffee cup on the desk and steadied herself. Lucia was not going to like that. The woman scared her, even though she'd been nothing but pleasant and polite; something underneath the formality made her anxious.

With trepidation, she picked up her cell and dialed Lucia's number. To her relief, no one answered. She left a voicemail informing her of the delay. Surely Lucia would negotiate with her; she'd proven herself to be a good client.

Claire put away the notebook and locked the drawer. Back on her computer, she switched over to inventory reporting and immersed herself in the numbers. The front door bell clanged. Startled, she sat up and listened.

"*Alo?* Is that you, Claire?" asked an accented voice from the front. Margot had arrived, her lovely sales girl from Paris who could sell GMO wheat muffins to a gluten-free hypochondriac.

"Yes, it's me. I'm in the back."

"I saw your coat," she said. "I will be up front getting the shop ready."

"Great. Don't forget to restock the wallpaper section with the new inventory." Claire heard Margot's okay and then refocused her attention on an Excel spreadsheet. She heard the front door entry bell ring again. Claire checked her watch. They weren't open yet for another hour. She was sure Margot would advise the visitor to return. A few minutes later, Margot came into the back and told her there was someone waiting for her. Claire got up from her seat and grabbed her coffee. For God's sake, she didn't have time for some uppity Brooklyn stay-at-home mom with her two kids and a nanny from Trinidad. Couldn't Margot handle the customer instead of having an "I want to speak to the manager" moment so early in the morning? Before going out front, she took a deep breath. Being late on Lucia's payment had rattled her nerves; no need to take it out on a paying customer. She didn't have the luxury to be judgmental.

The woman in her shop was no stay-at-home-mom. Lucia Occhipinti stood near the register. She had olive skin and jet-black hair. Her pixie cut was gelled back. Her fingernails were short and manicured with clear nail polish. The clothes were high end, a floral wraparound dress from Diane von Furstenberg paired with equestrian boots that would support the shop for six months. The dress was runway—a one of a kind—the pattern unused in any ready-to-wear. She wasn't textbook pretty. Her neck was too long. Her face too thin. Her lips too big. Put it all together, though, and she was stunning. Behind her was a man dressed in a black suit, his arms crossed. He stared past Claire with a hardened gaze.

"Hi, Claire." Lucia looked at Margot like she wasn't invited.

"Margot, take a break?" Claire added, "Get yourself some tea in the back."

"Of course, Ms. Townsend." Margot looked uncertain, but she left immediately.

"You are probably wondering why I'm here."

"Well, I'm…" Claire began cautiously, out of respect. The only reason Lucia was there at all was *money*. Either she had not received the phone message, or, if she had, she was there with a reminder about the penalties of late payments. The *other* penalties.

"This is a friendly reminder that your payment is due Friday."

Claire swallowed hard. Her right knee began to quiver. With an internal voice, she commanded her body to relax. When she first started selling high-end, million-dollar art at the Apfel Gallery, her body had reacted nervously, and she had learned how to calm her physical reactions. She made eye contact with Lucia, but the quivering didn't stop.

"I left a message," Claire said. She wanted to look Lucia in the eye, but instead used a sales trick by concentrating on the space between her sculpted eyebrows. The mark always thought you were looking them in the eye. "I was hoping to get your permission for a one-day extension. I won't have the cash until Saturday morning. I get the check on Friday night, but the banks won't be open to withdraw the cash. Anyway, I'm hoping my past, on-time payments will give me some allowance."

"Oh?" Lucia said.

The quiet afterwards made Claire uncomfortable. "I tried to make it happen earlier in the week, except the buyer isn't coming into town until Thursday night, so they wouldn't move the date."

"No one cares. You could have taken a bank loan to cover the payment."

Claire's shoulders slumped. Of course, she could have done that, but after being rejected so many times when she applied for small business loans to start her retail shop, it hadn't occurred to her. It was too late now.

"Normally, I don't allow delays. Everyone pays me on time."

Claire knew that she was entering dangerous territory. "I'm really sorry. You know my payment history. My shop is right here. You'll get your money."

"Cash, Claire. That's what I care about. There will be a five-thousand-dollar a day late payment."

Holy mother of… FIVE THOUSAND DOLLARS A DAY? She'd be fine, she told herself, she had no other options. "You'll get your money on Saturday. Eighteen thousand dollars. Do we need to shake on it or sign anything?"

"No need. Unless you don't trust me?"

Claire swallowed and met her gaze.

"Claire, would you please do me a favor," Lucia said.

"I, um, of course," Claire was unsettled by Lucia's tone.

"Would you open the drawer of your till and take all the money out?"

Claire looked at her strangely.

"Did you not hear me?" Lucia asked.

"Oh sure, hold on," Claire said and pushed a button on the till. The spring-loaded drawer clanged open.

"Give me the money, please."

Claire lifted the catch and dug out all the twenties, tens, fives, ones, and handed the money over.

Lucia pointed to the man behind her, who took the cash and put it into a bank bag.

"Do you want the change?" Claire swallowed hard. What a stupid question.

"No," Lucia said. She pointed to the man again and then towards the register.

He met Claire's eyes as he approached the counter. They were so void of life, so empty. He braced himself and then, with a grunt, pushed the register over the edge. Claire stepped back and threw up her hands in front of her face. It crashed onto the floor with a thud that sounded like a sawed-off shotgun. The drawer broke off and clattered into the organic rugs section. The coins sprayed out and scattered over the wood sounding like hail on a metal roof. Or a machine gun. The glass broke out of the display and lay glittering on the wooden floor.

"Look at that. What a shame. Be sure to drop off the money in the usual spot."

Claire watched Lucia leave the premises. She leaned on the counter with both her palms flat. Her heart raced; her blood pounded. Why was she freaking out? All Lucia did was have some jerkoff thug knock over her till. Her gorgeous till. She hit the countertop so hard her palms stung. No way she'd let this setback ruin everything. She was determined to sell the Bromanshank painting and get Lucia off her case.

"Claire? Are you all right? What has happened?" Margot asked, entering the sales floor. She saw the register on the floor, broken, and kneeled to pick up the quarters and dimes that had scattered on the floor.

"Be careful, there's glass," Claire said.

"Ow," Margot stood. A thin trail of blood streamed from her knee. She reached for a tissue from the countertop and pressed it against her skin.

"Do you want me to call the police?" Margot asked, her voice full of concern.

"No need to," Claire said, looking at the broken antique register. The sharp glass shimmered under the canned lights. "It was an accident."

Claire turned away, planning to head to the stockroom. What was she scared of? Why didn't she call the police? Maybe she would. That would put an end to it. The front bell dinged again. Claire twisted towards the sound, startled. Had Lucia changed her mind? She backed up, trying to escape, thinking of a way out, and ran into a stand-alone shelf. Antique door pulls clattered to the ground.

"Merde!" Margot said. "Claire?"

A young woman peered into the shop. "I saw someone leaving. Are you open early?"

Claire doubled over, breathing hard, trying to calm her heart and breath before speaking.

"Hold on a moment," Margot said to the woman. "I'll be right with you." Margot's hand touched Claire's shoulder, "Let me help you."

"No," Claire said, standing up straight, forcing herself to appear in control. "There's a customer up front. Go on."

CHAPTER TWO

Claire

Claire stood in front of a painting worth one point two million dollars that she planned to sell within three hours. The painting was half the length of the room, measuring a cool eight feet long, four feet high. The waves were green-blue and crested as a Fibonacci sequence, breaking along the shoreline. Behind the beach, rolling hills and scrubby grass waved in a gentle wind. An oncoming sunset gave the piece a rosy tint. Claire smiled pleasantly, but if there was one thing she loathed, it was natural landscape art.

Natural landscapes created unrealistic expectations. Real panoramas were marred by telephone wires and black asphalt roads, cars, garbage on the beach. A landscape without modern touches was wishful thinking, a fantasy, but she didn't dare say that to the nouveau riche Theodore Paul Frederick Champlin standing next to her. Teddy was quiet. His posture indicated serious inclination to purchase the item. She wouldn't be standing next to him if he was thinking otherwise.

The party was a special unveiling of Jaque Bromanshank's latest piece. He was a new artist brimming with possibility. He had the momentum of Basque, the style of Wyeth, the craziness of Pollack. The buzz was palpable. No photographs of the painting were allowed, although the owners, Bjorn and Annika Hermann, informed staff they would not physically stop anyone from taking pictures. The intended marketing consequence was #BroPicParty and #SnuckaBroPic achieving viral popularity among the art'ophiles on Instagram.

David Jackson, another Apfel Gallery sales associate, stood nearby with a client on his arm. David came from money and had grown up around art, selecting pieces for his parents and friend's collection since he was twelve years old. He had gone to the best schools. Knew the right people. He sold million dollar paintings as if he were selling a slice of pie. Even though the job came easy, he was fiercely competitive. Any sale Claire made had to be earned.

Teddy, her potential buyer, wore a handmade silk damask jacket of tan, gold, and yellow. The colors were understated, but the jacket was not. In getting to know him the past few days, she noticed he liked to be the center of attention, but when he considered art, he demanded quiet. His hands were clasped behind his back. He seemed mesmerized by the Fibonacci waves. That was Bromanshank's talent. He'd been able to paint the water in a way that made it seem like you were right there with the force of the waves, the strength of the ocean.

"Reminds me of my childhood growing up near the beach," he said without looking at her.

He seemed immersed in nostalgia. Back to a time when life was simple, she surmised, so she said nothing of how the painting would hang in his house. If she sold the painting, her commission as an Apfel Gallery sales associate was Pi percent (3.14159), which would equate to $37,680. If she sold the painting tonight, Bjorn and Annika Hermann would pay a ten grand bonus. In any case, the amount would easily cover the eighteen thousand dollars she owed Lucia.

Claire glanced past Teddy to check out the crowd. The gallery party was invite-only to press, serious buyers, social media "influencers" and socialites of a certain caliber. A few men dressed in polyester leisure suits (an attempt at irony, usually younger with beards and a man bun). Some men wore expensive, ready-to-wear suits (stockbrokers). For a few individuals, she could not discern gender or categorize them, which was the point. The women mostly wore high-end couture. Flowy dresses were the norm. One lady wore an outfit inspired by Broadway's Hamilton and wore men's breech pants, white hose, and a double-breasted blue jacket with bronze buttons. All this detail told Claire how much money they could spend.

The bulk of the crowd was what she called "airplane money," which meant they were wealthy enough to afford a private plane, household staff, and the Bromanshank painting. Airplane money usually came with "Get me the Manager" personality types. Teddy was airplane money.

The second type of wealth classification was called "God money," as in the person in question had more money than God. Claire noted a few people meandering around the crowd wearing jeans and Gap t-shirts. They were polite and nice. Oddly enough, these people usually had God money. The tell could be a five-hundred-thousand-dollar watch or a discreet, but exquisite, piece of jewelry. Sometimes it was the Hermes Birkin purse or handmade shoes from London that declared status. Judging people shouldn't matter to her, but it did. It mattered when you weren't one of them.

The problem was, she had to look like one of them in order to sell to them. Nice clothes, designer bags, and trendy watches did not come cheap. Buying tables at exclusive bars and memberships at private dining clubs did not come with a discount. But it always paid off when she made an art sale.

Teddy motioned for a glass of Champagne. He didn't appear introspective now; he looked bored. With a pseudo

California Girls bright smile (she was from Ohio) she explained that the painting's locale was Southern California (the truth), near the Temecula Valley (could be the truth), which happened to be where Teddy grew up (thank you Google).

She spoke up with a litany of well-timed questions: Did he know that Jaque Bromanshank made his brushes from the hair of wild mountain lions native to the area? Did he know the artist had crushed local rock for the pigment base and mixed it with desalinized ocean water and his own spit, sweat, and even blood to create the perfect blue? Even though the bulk of the painting was oil, there were aspects of watercolor mixed in. Did he know the two formats naturally resisted each other, and that was what made this painting so spectacular, a technical masterpiece? He also apprenticed with well-known artists in Europe. Couldn't he see the Impressionist influence of the brush strokes?

Teddy didn't make eye contact with her, but she could tell he was thinking. She used the moment to surreptitiously glance around the room again. Around the edges of the crowd, bloggers and an art reporter from the New York Times perused the art. There was a din of small talk. Amaya Kato (Japanese, second born immigrant), the blogger who ran ARTSPARTNY, was on her way to Claire. They had met several times, and she was probably coming over to say hi and get a few words for the record. She had a GoPro in one hand and a Champagne flute in the other. Claire gave her a brief nod. Although she wanted to greet her, she did not want to be distracted from selling the Bromanshank.

In her peripheral vision, she saw Teddy's focus—just his eyes—move from the painting to Claire. He inspected her as casually as he might a piece of art, lingering on her legs before moving up her body. Claire suppressed a shudder.

Sometimes clients—especially ones about to drop major cash—believed they had unfettered access to the staff. #Metoo had slowed the expectation, but power and money absolved them of culpability, or so they believed. The heat of his hand pressed into her waist. "How does this make you feel?" he whispered into her ear.

She had to give the impression that she was interested so he'd consider purchasing the painting, even if she was repulsed by him. Most of the time, outright rejection led to an immediate sales loss. She had sidestepped undesirable encounters before, but it was a matter of skill and tact, steel nerves and charm. She glanced over to see if Amaya was still on her way. She had stopped to chat with the NY Times editor.

Teddy's fingers dug into her skin. Claire looked at him with a slight smile, then repositioned herself. She wanted to appear as if she were evaluating the painting, when in fact, she was wondering if rejecting Teddy would harm her future prospects. His graying hair was colored blond. College football ring on his pinky, for God's sake. He called himself Teddy. Obviously, he suffered from Peter Pan syndrome. He seemed the type who knew he could get away with copping a feel; she had to figure out how much physical reciprocation he expected.

Next, she had to assess if her rejection would ruin any social contacts. He seemed to know the Hermanns personally. The Hermanns owned Apfel Gallery, in addition to a world-famous private gallery in Frankfurt. They were the one percent of the one percent in the art world. If she rejected him too harshly, she could lose her job at the Apfel Gallery. Teddy knew the purchasing agent at Barneys, and that was how he learned of the Apfel Gallery sale. If she rejected him and Teddy said something to the purchasing agent, she might lose the Barneys contract. If she rejected him and he wanted revenge, he could exact it on her with just a few words. "She isn't trustworthy. She offended me." One sentence from Theodore and her whole world would crash. Her ventures were still too delicate.

He brought her closer and nuzzled her ear. "My cock is hard."

Claire closed her eyes slowly, wishing she had stepped away earlier. He was gross. She wasn't a prostitute. The best way to handle him was to put distance between them. Best used with charm. She needed the money for Lucia's payment, though. She needed the sale. Maybe she should relax, just this one time. Claire saw Amaya waving at her. The GoPro light was blinking. Claire gave her best smile. Teddy did not step away.

"Amaya!" Claire said, moving a mere fraction of an inch away from Theodore. His fingers dug in, and he reached around her waist. She gently removed his fingers and took another step. Besides, it followed social protocol to step away when a third party approached. "I would like for you to meet someone," she said, turning to Teddy. "This is the impressive Theodore Champlin. He took six weeks to get here, having sailed up from Florida."

"Wow! That is remarkable," said Amaya, her smile turning flirtatious. "How big is your boat, darling?"

Teddy opened his mouth, presumably to say something witty, but when Amaya pointed the camera at herself and started talking, he clamped his mouth shut and glared at Claire.

"My name is Amaya, and today I am bringing you art." She pointed the camera to Claire. "I'm here at the Apfel Gallery for the premiere of Jaque Bromanshank. Say hi to the people, Claire."

"Hi," she said with a bright smile.

"Claire is one of the sales associates here. What can you tell us about the painting?" Amaya asked, keeping the camera focused on her.

Teddy took a step away, darkness shading his expression. She needed to get Amaya away so she could refocus on Teddy. She needed the sale. Claire took a sip from her

Champagne (she wanted to guzzle) and licked her lips delicately (she wanted to clench). A crowd of random people formed around them, but Amaya's camera stayed focused on her.

Claire noticed that Bjorn, the owner of the gallery, had turned toward them. He towered above the crowd with a natural towhead blond mop of hair and a regal Michelangelo Davidian nose that spoke of Roman roots in his Germanic ancestry. He stopped to return a single hello but otherwise cut conversations short as he walked in her direction.

"Welcome to Apfel. Have you seen the new #JackPic yet?"

"It's not #JackPic—it's #BroPicParty." Amaya furrowed her brows and half smiled. The look reminded Claire of mean girls in high school.

How did she forget that? She knew the hashtag. Claire saw the change in expression on Bjorn's face.

"Amaya… Hello," Bjorn said in accented English. "This, as you know, is Jaque Bromanshank's latest piece titled *Water*."

Amaya turned her camera from Claire and swept over the painting. "Why'd you tell the staff that no pictures were allowed?"

Bjorn swallowed hard and glowered at Claire. "As you can see, this painting is quite large. This format is extremely technical and difficult, to say the least. That is why Bromanshank is a genius. Videos or pictures might fail at the essence."

"Where's Jaque at?" asked Amaya, swinging her camera to Bjorn. "Big fail if you ask me."

Normally artists were at their own premiere, but Claire had suggested Jaque stay absent to create more organic PR. She had told Bjorn and Anika that it might be negative at first, but in the end, it would bear out as beneficial for the gallery. They had agreed, but now she could see Bjorn rubbing his fingers together, even though his face maintained professional courtesy. He was fuming.

"Yeah, where is Jaque?" asked someone from the crowd. "We want him here."

A single voice started up a chant. "Jaque. Jaque. Jaque." Others from the crowd began to join him. If she stopped it too soon or too late, the result would be disastrous. The NYT art critic was on her way over to see what was happening.

Amaya turned the GoPro on the crowd. They reacted, jostling each other as if they were in a sports stadium rather than an art gallery. Amaya aimed the camera back to Claire and spoke over the crowd, "Where is Jaque, Claire?"

The camera lens zoomed in on her, the red-light blinking, blinking, blinking. She lost momentum and stood there, not moving. She wasn't sure what to do. Bjorn stood still too, hypnotized by the chanting, stunned by the speed of escalation.

The volume of the chanting went up a notch. "Jaque. Jaque. Jaque."

Amaya pumped her fist in the air. "Ladies and gentlemen, this is what we call Performance Art!"

A general cheer electrified the small group. They continued to chant "Jaque." The sound grew louder with each word. Some clapped to the rhythm. Theodore grasped again at her waist, fingers pressed in, trying to pull her back, as if he were a hero trying to save her.

Claire put two fingers in her mouth to whistle and blew hard. The sound of the whistle was one that could pull a cab over during Broadway rush hour. "STOP!" she said. A hush fell over the crowd, and everyone looked at her.

Amaya's camera was focused on Claire. "And there you have it, ladies and gentlemen." The red light recording. "Claire Townsend. Apfel Gallery sales associate."

"Let's get back to a wonderful evening," Claire said with enthusiasm. "The waitstaff will have drinks for you." She pointed toward the bar station set up in a far corner.

A waiter lost his balance. His tray flew out of his hands.

Champagne glasses hit the tile and shattered. Amaya panned in on the broken glass. "Yeah," she said, "that looks chic." Amaya turned the camera to herself. "Great party," she said with a raised eyebrow and a bad Elvis half smile. "No Jaque. No party. I'm out."

On that note, a couple from the crowd agreed. "We're outta here." Amaya filmed the two as they walked out the door. For a moment, there was uncertainty, but then another person followed and then more. Someone smashed another glass, causing a woman to scream. Damn near had a rush out the front door, Amaya filming its entirety.

Theodore gave her a dirty look and shook his head at Bjorn. "Where is David?"

David. The other Apfel sales associate. No. No way was David going to steal Teddy from her, but she couldn't move. She looked from Teddy back to Bjorn and back to Teddy. *Stop this!* Her mouth remained firmly together; no words came out. She was barely even breathing.

"Just a moment, Teddy," Bjorn said and walked calmly toward Claire. He leaned in close and whispered under a forced smile, "Get out."

Claire stood back, shocked still by his words. At the most important moment in her life, she choked, and now she was being fired. *Was she still being filmed?* Claire looked up, towards the camera. The black lens like an evil eye as Amaya zoomed in on her expression. Then, she turned the camera back on herself. "You'll see it on my blog. Live in five."

CHAPTER THREE

Bruno

*B*runo Canul braked hard on his mountain bike to take in the view overlooking the southern side of the Mojave Desert. He was in the San Bernardino National Forest on a trail that wasn't well marked, but wasn't invisible, either. About seventy miles northeast from his vantage point, near a town named Twentynine Palms, California, over nine thousand different Native American artifacts had been found. Ever since the announcement, amateur archeologists had been poking around nearby, and it was his job to prevent unauthorized digging in the protected lands.

A biface blade or a piece of pottery dug up by a naïve amateur wasn't a big deal, although it bothered him. What really pissed him off were the amateurs who completely ruined a potential dig site. They dug without taking proper photographs to understand anthropological impacts, they dug without proper verification from geologists to see how deep the items were which would accurately date an item, and the wrong tools could accidentally chip an artifact. As a result, the academic community did not trust any item or relic that an amateur brought in. Any historical and cultural information that might have been learned would be discarded.

Worse than the amateur archeologists were the black-market treasure hunters. His job, along with being a college professor, was to prevent professional treasure hunters from scoring off designated federal lands. During his off hours, he worked as a consultant with the Art Crimes division of the FBI to prevent black-market trade. It was a thankless job, but he'd managed to bust one or two big digs. One of them was a colleague of his, Rex Martel, from a nearby college, whom he had busted based on a few rumors he'd heard in the classroom.

Bruno spun the bike pedal around and looked over the horizon. Someone had called in with concerns about a possible dig site just south of Twentynine Palms. So he'd come up to the mountains to take pictures. With a panoramic view, the chances of spotting something were higher. From his backpack, he pulled out a camera, a semi-fancy Canon DSLR digital. As an archeology professor at California State University, he had access to decent equipment. If anything suspicious showed up in the pictures, he'd forward the copies to James McNally, his liaison at the FBI Art Crimes division which investigated art and cultural property crimes such as fraud, theft, looting, and trafficking across state and international lines.

He planned to take a few pictures then stop in Big Bear for lunch before heading back to the campus office. He was single, so his time was his own. No wife to check in with, no girlfriend to call. Once he finished, he popped the camera into the backpack, turned his bike so that it was on the path, and pedaled hard.

The terrain wasn't technically difficult, so he moved fast, the fir trees a blur as he passed them. His instincts sharp, he handled the bike with expertise, avoiding rocks, leaning into small jumps, turning corners. All his thoughts, all his concerns, were put out of his mind as he pumped hard on the pedals.

Sweat dripped down his face, his thighs screaming; he didn't slow until he returned to trailhead, where he had parked his jeep.

In no hurry, Bruno drove twenty miles into Big Bear. Once in town, he navigated to a local brew-pub for lunch. A beer and burger sounded perfect. In the restaurant, he found a seat at the bar. A couple of chairs away, a young couple sat together, their fingers entwined. They laughed quietly over their cheese fries, unaware that anyone else was around.

He smiled sadly. He longed for someone who loved him, who looked at him like that. Bruno's girlfriend of a year and a half had broken up with him a few months ago. She said he didn't have time for her, which was true. He'd be in Mexico working on a Preclassic Mayan dig. Working with McNally. Or in Belize for the summers, working as a guide with his brother Alberto on exclusive Mayan adventures. He still owned a house there, a small rambler his mom had sold him. There was never time for a relationship. The ex was disappointed, but not mad. He picked up the menu and immersed himself in selecting a burger.

In his mid-thirties, he wasn't exactly old, but he had never found a woman who could deal with his schedule. Bruno had tried to date women within his professional field, but he didn't like mixing business with pleasure. Would that life, having a girlfriend, becoming a husband and a father, ever be his? A waitress came up and set a beer on the table.

"The usual, Bruno?" she asked cheerfully.

"Yeah, can you give me an extra side of that curry sauce for my fries?"

"Sure, Mr. Canul," she said, scribbling words on her pad. "Anything for you."

He opened up his phone and saw a new email from a random address ArtifactsForYouToo@google.com. The handle didn't jog his memory, but it didn't matter; he got emails like this all the time. There was an open req for an archeologist and guide, anthropologist, and program manager for the American Museum of Natural History out of New York City.

Without thinking, he forwarded the email to Xander Moore. Xander was his peer, an archeologist who worked for the Smithsonian, and a friend as well. They had gone to the same college, graduated from the same class. Surely he'd know qualified people to send the job req to.

Bruno returned to browsing the job req. The plan was to recreate the Popol Vuh (the Mayan creation story) as a dramatic play, in the Actun Tunichil Muknal cave in Belize. Nat Geo would be filming the venture. The job required an experienced guide who could lead them into the cave as well as act as lead archeologist. Accommodations would be paid for. The crew would be staying at BIFA, the Belize Indigenous Foundation of Art, located in the jungle. Although it looked perfect, he'd have to turn it down. From a professional stand-point, the job was more for adventure guide than archeologist. He made a mental note to make sure he forwarded the email to his brother, who owned a guiding outfit in Belize.

He continued reading the email and saw the list of people who had been hired. That was when he saw her name. Janine Jankowski was listed as the work-study hire. He set the phone down and angled his neck, first to the right and then to the left, trying to crack it.

He rubbed his face. Janine was one of Rex Martel's students. She was a non-trad student, in her early thirties, and the lead on a site that Bruno busted last year. Unfortunately, Rex and Janine were never prosecuted for the illegal dig. Rex should have gone to jail and lost his professorship. They both should have. The aftermath stung. People had taken sides. Boundaries were drawn. How the Sam Hill did she get the job? Ever since the FBI bust, Professor Martel and his crew were on a black list, at least in California.

The waitress set the burger in front of him. He thanked her and lifted the bun off his burger to make sure it was right. There was pickle, mayo, tomatoes, onion, melted cheese. It looked delicious. He put the bun back on and picked the burger up. Just before sinking his teeth in, an idea came to mind. And it required getting the Popol Vuh job.

CHAPTER FOUR

Claire

Claire stood outside the gallery after the disastrous video. In shock, there was a distinct sense of both heaviness and lightness, like being trapped in a lava lamp. Lights appeared bright but were far away. Noises were loud but muted. Random elbows knocked into her as people walked around. Amaya's video had posted. She knew that from the constant pings on her phone. She turned the phone to silent. She'd been fired. She didn't have the money for Lucia. She'd lose the shop. She'd lose the contract at Barneys. She was done.

She found herself sitting on the front steps of the NYC Public Library near one of the lions, and surmised his name to be Leo. She hit her thighs three times and stared up at the black sky. *Why. Why. Why couldn't anything go her way?* She'd been on top of the world. And now? She told Leo the Lion that she was serious about getting off her duff, off the steps, and heading into the street where she might get hit by a bus and end it all. Only one thing stopped her. She was afraid she might survive. Being a ward of the state once was enough. Twice was far too many.

Stop being so dramatic. From a passing millennial who was

smoking, she managed to bum a cigarette. She put it between her lips. When he put the flame up, she leaned forward and inhaled. Coughing hard, she instinctively tossed it on the ground.

"Don't waste my time and smokes if you can't get it right," he said before turning around in disgust and walking off.

Nothing was going right. *Go home.* Claire got to her apartment, sat on the couch and turned on the TV. In the darkened room, the Roku menu appeared incredibly bright. She flipped through the Popular Right Now section but nothing seemed worth watching. She tossed the remote on the coffee table and checked her phone. There were text messages, tweets, phone calls, Instagram hashtags, even Facebook mentions. #BroPicParty had taken the art world by surprise, and by the end of the night #JaqueFail was trending. New York City, big as it might be, reacted like a small town with hot gossip. She turned her phone off and curled up on the couch.

When she woke, the room was sunny. She'd fallen asleep and woken up with a stress headache. Claire checked her phone. It was eleven o'clock in the morning. She looked through her social media accounts, and was still getting hell for Amaya's video. No one even tried to stand up for her. Her so-called friends had scattered like nails across a concrete floor. She wasn't surprised. Proof again that people were a disappointment. She didn't delete her accounts, nor did she comment or post. There was no point. Nothing she said or did mattered.

Today she owed Lucia eighteen thousand dollars. She looked at her missed calls to see if Lucia had called. Nothing from her. Margot from the shop had called, probably wanting to know why she hadn't opened the doors. Claire didn't know what to tell her, so she didn't return the call. The Barneys' sales rep had called too, she skipped the message. Her logic told her to act, that it was imperative, but it was like she wanted to burn it all to the ground.

On Sunday morning, two days past Lucia's payment date, she checked her missed calls again. Lucia had not called. She thought of their conversation in Brooklyn at the shop. Lucia had suggested getting a personal loan. Maybe she could still apply for one. She had roughly seven thousand in the bank. She'd need twenty-one thousand to pay Lucia. Surely, as the owner of a shop and with good credit, they would say yes. A white-hot ping of hope sparked inside of her.

She got up and opened her laptop. On her bank's website was a marketing slogan, 'See how we can help you achieve your goals.' She smirked, but still, surely the bank would approve her application. She was a successful business woman. She found the business loans and lines of credit, clicked on the link and filled out the required information. Once she submitted, she got an email that said, "Due to system outages, we will not be able to review your loan until Monday. Thank you."

"Ugh," she said, pushing the computer off her lap. She stood and paced the room like a trapped animal. What was she going to do? She had to wait.

On Monday, she woke up at six a.m. She checked her email every minute, sometimes every thirty seconds, and other times she kept clicking the refresh button. At eight thirty-six a.m., she got a generic email from her bank. 'We're sorry, but your loan request has been turned down due to insufficient collateral assets. You may try again in five to ten business days.'

She called the bank to talk to a real person about the

declined loan. The rep wasn't authorized to talk through the process, so Claire talked to the manager and then the manager's manager. She was finally told that the most she qualified for was five thousand dollars. It was explained that after the subprime loan defaults, the bank had revised all lending policies.

The flame of hope spurted and burned black. After hanging up, her head was pounding again, a pulsing beat in her frontal lobe. The only way to make it stop, to feel better, was to take Xanax. She took one and slept the rest of the day.

FIVE DAYS AFTER THE EVENT, a Wednesday, her routine became simple: couch, bathroom, kitchen, back to couch. She made tea. Getting involved with a loan shark hadn't been the smartest decision, but it had been the only way to fund her dream. She had been so sure the gamble would pay off. She'd run the numbers. Opening the store would catapult her financial status. They were going to respect her. She'd be on her way. If only she had gotten a bank loan earlier to cover the monthly payment. If only she'd done things differently. *If I promise to never be sarcastic again...* She stopped right there. Bargaining with a higher power got her nowhere. It didn't work when her parents had died, and hell if it would now.

CHAPTER FIVE

Claire

Claire had used the last of her spaghetti noodles. She needed to go to the grocery store to buy food, but was afraid Lucia would show up and do something horrible to her. Where was Lucia? Why hadn't she shown up? Maybe that was a good thing? Had she forgotten about her? No. Lucia wouldn't forget. But Claire was frustrated with her scaredy-cat self. If this was it, if she was going to get knocked off, well, it was better than starving and drowning in anxiety.

Claire took a shower, got dressed and walked to the grocery store. On the way home to her apartment in Midtown Manhattan, she carried a canvas bag of clearance produce, cheap vodka and pasta. The route took her by a series of high-end antique galleries. To her surprise, there was David, the other sales associate from Apfel, standing on a street corner.

"Well, well, well. Look what the cat dragged in," David said, looking her up and down. It wasn't sexual; he was gay. She knew he was gauging her, judging her.

"What do you want?"

"I'm not stalking you," he said. "I was at this antique gallery, negotiating on a very rare piece for a client. Well, anyway, I just happened to be thinking of you. And then, you appeared."

"That's weird," Claire said. "Were you thinking about how pathetic I was that night?"

"Actually, I was thinking you might be interested in an opportunity," said David. Their relationship had always been direct. Neither of them was put off by the straightforward manner of communication and often laced it with either sarcasm or tidbits of sweetness. "Come with me for a drink. I want to talk to you."

"I appreciate your concern for my welfare, but it's all right. I'm fine."

"The hell you are. Amaya's video was scathing. And truthfully, you'll never work in art again. The least you can do is take a free, sympathetic drink from me."

"Fine, I'll accept your charity. What strings are attached?"

"What happened to your country charm? You're more New York than I am now, except I was born and bred here."

"David," Claire said, not wanting to participate in the banter.

"All right. Why don't you follow me and find out? I'll be happy to share with you."

She lifted her full grocery bag. "What am I supposed to do with this?"

He shrugged. "This is New York. No one cares." He nodded down the street. "Let's go."

They walked to a nearby neighborhood bar that recently updated the décor with new lighting and a fancy quartz countertop, but she could still smell stale beer and old cigarette smoke. She was out of place in her jeans and a day-old t-shirt, even though she had thrown on a scarf and decent jacket.

He ordered a martini for himself and a vodka tonic for her. "I remember your favorite drink," he said, looking proud of himself. The waitress placed the drink on the standing table.

David pulled out a credit card and handed it to her. Inside the billfold was enough crisp one-hundred-dollar bills to equal at least a thousand dollars. A surge of jealousy arose in Claire, fast and hot. *If only if only if only.*

David retrieved a business card and laid it face-down between them on the table. He took a sip of his martini. "This is really good. I like the rosemary garnish."

She took out her lemon twist speared with basil garnish and set it on a napkin. Maybe she could ask him for the money? She'd need the request to come up organically though, so now wasn't the time to ask. "Thank you for the drink."

"You are very welcome, darling," David said. "Cheers." He lifted his drink to her and they clinked glasses, the sound hard and sharp. "I'll get right to it. I have a friend who is interested in you."

Claire raised an eyebrow.

"Not like that, Claire! What kind of man do you take me for?" He tapped the business card on the table. "On this card is the name of a gallery who is interested in your art talents. I remember you told me once, long ago, that your field brought you into contact with archeologists?"

"Yes," she said, taking a sip. Along with art history, she had majored in anthropology. She had college friends who worked in the field. *Where was this conversation leading?* She had a feeling it wasn't going to be good.

"My contact wants to expand her clientele and cannot get her hands on the, shall we say, appropriate antique and archeo-logical items needed to make a name for herself."

"Oh?" Claire had an idea where this was going, but she wanted David to spell it out for her. She didn't want to approach the gallery with any misunderstandings.

"It's been difficult to get said items with appropriate pedi-gree, so she's looking to implement a new source. Maybe one that could be verified by an expert, but perhaps lacking certain documentation."

She removed the basil from a toothpick. "In many countries, it's illegal to sell artifacts that have not passed through the national antiquities board. Is that what you are looking for?"

"With your art expertise and possible contacts, there might be a mutually beneficial relationship. The pay is amazing. You'll be compensated well. If you get the right item, you could easily get a hundred thousand, if not more."

Good God, was David involved in this? It wasn't because he needed the money. He must like the adrenaline rush of skirting the law. And truthfully, he did have a touch of affluenza. *Is this what it meant to have money?* Instead of answering her own rhetorical question, she asked, "What's your cut?" She took another sip of her drink and considered, for the first time, black-market trading.

"I get four percent. Would you like me to set up a meeting?"

"Is this the only option for me? I'd be the perfect person to hire back at Apfel. I'd draw in the crowds."

"None of the good galleries will hire you. I've already checked a few sources," he said, lifting his drink to her with a sour look. "We're not a circus attraction. This is high end art. Surely you can appreciate that." He gave her a fake smile, but condescending. She returned the same smile.

"I'll take the card into consideration," she said, reaching for it. "Any interest in helping me with a starter loan?"

David put his hand on top of hers. "How much do you need?"

"Fifteen thousand."

"I can't, Claire," he said, shaking his head, as if he were truly sorry. Which she did not believe he was for one second. "Besides," David continued, "I'm offering you something that is much more valuable. I'm doing you a favor. I am helping you."

"I can see that. Thank you." She flicked his hand off the card and picked it up. She briefly glanced at it, noting the individual's name and the gallery. She'd heard of black-market trading before, and she'd heard rumors of galleries and people involved in the business, but this was the first time she'd ever had anything concrete in her hands.

"You'll be fine. Besides, I know you. That plucky spirit of yours will save the day."

She stood, swinging her purse over her shoulder and picking up the bag of groceries. "I do appreciate the information. Do I need to call you before engaging?"

"No, not at all," he said. "I'll be informed downstream."

"I see. Thank you so much."

"I'm so sorry this happened to you. You didn't deserve it." He stood to kiss her cheek. It was a kiss from Judas.

She squeezed his hand and smiled. "I'll see you around."

CHAPTER SIX

Claire

Her apartment was a ten-minute walk from the bar. She buzzed herself in since there was no door-man. The lobby was decrepit. The mailbox area was a mess. Warnings to stay away from Amazon packages were taped to the wall. The elevator was out of service, and she'd have to walk up six floors. The stairwell was hot and dry. Sweat beaded on her forehead and the backs of her knees. She saw no used condoms, so that was good.

The hallway to the apartment was carpeted, but concrete showed through worn patches. Decades of suppressed kitchen smells commingled with dry rot. Before the gallery party, she was able to ignore the crap conditions. They were a means to an end while she sold paintings and started her own boutique. Now, her surroundings depressed her. Maybe she was destined to fail at every turn. Maybe she was cursed.

She locked the front door by turning all the deadbolts. She leaned her back against it and slid to the floor. On her desk was a contract cancellation email from Barneys that she'd printed out. 'We have decided to no longer pursue this avenue of development.' The contract had wording that if either party wanted to rescind agreement, they could do so at any time. The termination fee was subtracted from any upfront costs that were incurred, so basically, she got nothing. Maybe she should have answered the phone when the Barneys rep had called, but it was too late now. What was the point? There was no way to get out from under her new reputation. And Margot quit.

All she had left was six thousand four hundred and eighty-two dollars in her bank account. The late fee to Lucia was five grand a day. It'd been five days since the due date, and now she owed an additional twenty-five thousand dollars on top of the thirteen thousand monthly payment. What was she going to do? She couldn't get that kind of money. Not anymore.

She pulled a bottle of cheap vodka out of her grocery bag. Getting drunk was as good a solution as any. She unscrewed the top and took a swig. The sharp booze nipped the back of her throat. She took another. When she felt lighter, a little more ambivalent, she considered her immediate future.

Claire would love to entertain David's offer, she thought with sarcasm. In order to secure an high-value object, she'd have to make an initial investment. She'd have to buy a plane ticket. *Where would she go?* She'd have to find the items. *What items?* If, by pure miracle, she stumbled onto a high-value artifact, she'd have to sneak it through customs into the U.S. She didn't have established connections that she trusted to success-fully engage in a black-market job. Well, that wasn't entirely true; she did know a few people. Except she didn't want to risk their friendship, not after what had just happened to her.

Her phone buzzed. She retrieved it from her back pocket and unlocked it. A little tipsy from the vodka, she had to squint her eyes to see the screen. The incoming text was from a private number; she knew it was Lucia. Her heart raced when she clicked on the message. The text indicated a date, time, and address, and ended with the initials LO. The reservation was six days away. Why had Lucia waited so long to contact her? Claire took another swig, then capped the bottle. In six days, she'd owe her an additional thirty grand.

Claire laughed. Then, she looked at her phone and read the message again, and lost it. She laughed so hard that tears flowed freely over her cheeks as she put the phone on the coffee table. Her financial situation had gone from terrible to absurd. When she met Lucia in six days, she'd owe a grand total of sixty-eight thousand dollars. And Claire didn't have the money. For sure Lucia was going to kill her.

Sighing, she intended to pick up her phone, but instead picked up a Men's Journal magazine that was on the corner of a coffee table. Her ex had subscribed to it when they were in college in DC, and she'd continued it. Riding a motorcycle in Mexico or climbing the highest peaks around the world sounded fun. This month featured a picture of cave diving with a caption "Mayan Archeology Goes Under Water."

Underneath the dramatic picture of an underwater explorer wearing scuba gear—a headlamp illuminating his or her way—swimming through dark blue-green waters of a cave with Mayan sculptures in the background was a caption, "Amateurs swimming through unexplored caves finding new treasures." She continued to read, "Due to the explosion of amateur cave divers in Belize, there are now an unsubstanti-ated number of artifacts being documented incorrectly, without the context of appropriate data such as depth or nearby geologic formations. The worst of it is many items go missing and end up on the black market."

What?

Maybe there was a chance she could do this. The only real offer she'd had since being sacked was douchebag David's: an offer to set up a clandestine relationship with a shady gallery—

the Reade Street Gallery—to sell black-market artifacts. In order to do that, she'd have to call Xander, a friend she knew from college. He was an archeologist. The least she could do was call and see if anything was available.

She scoffed and tossed the magazine. The chance that her old college friend Xander Moore would have a job ready and waiting was ridiculous. *You have to do something. Call him and be done with it so you can move on.* Technically, she wasn't getting him involved if he didn't know her plan. She got up and sat at her desk. She unlocked her phone. The room was stuffy, condensed, so she moved to open the window. No fresh air came into the apartment, but the faint roar of traffic was louder.

She was just a girl looking for a job. She found his name in the contacts list and pressed call. Hopefully, Xander wouldn't answer. He picked up on the second ring. "Hey, Claire. You caught me at the perfect time. I was packing up to head home. What's up?"

"How's life as a married man? I can't believe you married the girl who dumped mashed potatoes all over you. Ha. How is Cheyenne?" Claire had been visiting DC and eating lunch with Xander when this crazy woman had marched up to their table and tipped Xander's meal onto his head. It had been impossible to miss the heat between them. Claire wished someone cared enough for her to… she nixed the thought. She didn't want *mashed potatoes* dumped on her head.

"The wedding was beautiful," Xander said. "We had so many damn pastries. Cheyenne and her little bakery team were unbelievable. I had to actually tell her to stop making desserts. Which reminds me, you need to come down and get your pie."

"Not that I don't want to, but my life just exploded up here."

"I saw that. The video. That was rough. You get fired?"

"I did. In spectacular fashion. I already cried and now I'm ready to move on."

"Wait. *You* cried? I don't believe it," Xander said. "I'm sure you'll get back on your feet in no time. I swear, the way you pull projects together out of thin air, it's like a miracle."

"Thanks," she said. The compliment was a balm. "I need a job. You got any leads? I was thinking this could be a perfect time to pursue my field of study. Anyone looking for an out-of-date anthropologist?" She laughed weakly.

"Actually, that's funny. Hold on. Let me see if there's something for you. I was just about to leave, but it's no big deal. I've gotta turn my computer back on."

"You should get home to your lovely wife. I don't want to waste your time."

"Just hang on for a few minutes. Where is that email?" he said under his breath.

"Take your time." She turned the Men's Journal pages to a spread on other activities to do in Belize, and there was a picture of a woman diving off a hand-hewn wooden dock into a sapphire blue sea. She'd love to do that herself, but she blanched at the bikini. She hadn't worn a swimsuit since everyone could see her scar, a thick, bulbous disfigurement that ran from the base of her sternum to just below her belly button. She always thought it looked like a third-world country's oil pipeline, jagged and dark brown. It was from the emergency surgery after her dad had swerved to avoid an oncoming car that had lost control in the rain. The rest of that night had been blank until she woke up in the hospital. That night, everything changed. Her parents had died.

"Okay, Claire. I found the email about the job. I got an email from Bruno Canul. Do you remember him?"

She couldn't tell if Xander was being sarcastic or serious. How could she forget *Bruno Canul?* Former boyfriend. Ex-lover. An image of his face passed through her mind. His dark, coffee brown eyes, his fantastic smile. After college, they went separate ways. He was offered a job in LA. She was offered an intern position with the Metropolitan Museum of Art. It seemed a lifetime ago. She looked at the magazine in her hand and shivered. She hadn't thought of him in months, years really, and now?

"We had a couple double dates back in the day."

"Yeah, ha. A couple of dates. That's funny. Anyway. He's the lead archeologist on this new event the American Museum of Natural History is doing. They need an anthropologist and a program manager. I hope it's not too late—you'll have to verify with this guy, umm, Christopher Shali, of the American Museum of Natural History. It's probably below your usual pay grade but sounds like you might be in dire straits. You interested?"

As a program manager she'd have appropriate credentials to mail items through customs. Moving them to the Reade Street gallery wouldn't be too difficult. She pushed aside fleeting guilt of wishing she had taken an earlier path to become an anthropologist, the path that included her and Bruno together. "Program manager is below my pay grade, but I got nothing else. Girl's gotta eat. Can you send me the details?"

She could hear him clacking away at his keyboard. "Sure," he said. "Wow. This sounds kinda cool. You'll be in Belize for ten days. Nat Geo's going to be there, and they'll be filming a live rendition of the Mayan creation story inside the ATM cave. Okay. I sent you the email."

Xander bid goodbye and hung up. Claire read the email on her laptop. Program manager. Foot in the door position. She could have been a curator by now, working at the Smithsonian with Xander, if Bruno hadn't gone to LA. If she hadn't moved to New York. Maybe working for Nat Geo. Maybe on the cover of Men's Journal. Well, she might not get the job. Regret never saved a life, so she sent her resume to the museum. She never thought she'd see Bruno again, and couldn't help but remember the last time she saw him. A bittersweet goodbye at the door. The last kiss. A hug. There had been a chance for her to stay, but she said goodbye.

CHAPTER SEVEN

Claire

The reservation with Lucia Occhipinti was at an exclusive Italian restaurant located in Greenwich Village, off Thompson Street. Even though it was early evening, the summer heat hadn't cooled. Hardly anyone was outside: a woman in a business skirt who wore tennis shoes, and a construction worker with a dingy hard hat.

The twenty minute walk did nothing to calm Claire's nerves. Too soon, she was in front of the restaurant. A sign was lit up with a red neon "Carbone," and in the unforgiving sun, the neon was barely visible. The paint had been peeled off the sign intentionally, to create the impression of post-World War II resiliency, even though the place opened last year.

She opened a heavy, carved wooden door and walked inside. The cool dark of the restaurant was a solace against the heat. She took a breath and tried to relax her nerves. The maître d' was on the phone. While Claire waited, she looked herself over in a nearby mirror. There were no wrinkles around her eyes, but she could tell the Botox needed a retouch. She probably didn't need it, but she liked to err on the perfect side. Back in Ohio, somebody might describe her as a boring white girl in her late twenties. But here in New York City, she had creamy skin with just the right amount of cheeky tint.

Keep your wits. She had sold art at the best gallery in New York City. Not just any high-end art gallery, but *the* gallery. So what if the fiasco had left her unemployed? She'd seen confidence and fake bravado win out more times than not. That was her plan. Appear confident, even though she wasn't. Claire didn't have the money, but she had a plan to sell black-market items to Reade Street Gallery. Perhaps she hadn't sourced the items yet, but she had begun machinations to do so.

She puckered her lips and kissed the air. The red lipstick was Instagram perfect. She had chosen a pair of wide-legged capri pants paired with summer heels. Her outfit was crafted to speak style, but not couture. Rugged, but not brute strength.

The maître d' wore a burgundy suit with wide-peak lapels and a spunky tie designed by Zac Posen, a brilliant young American fashion designer. The maître d' finished his call and signaled her to follow him, which she did. As he led her towards the back of the restaurant, she knew the checkered tile floor was inspired by *The Godfather*. She knew these tidbits because it was her job to know these things. A sales associate at the Apfel Gallery had to appreciate eclectic details of who, what, where, and how much in order to sell paintings that started at a million. She had learned early on that people didn't want to buy things; they wanted to buy feelings, and the better they felt, the more they paid. Lucia was probably the same.

The maître d' led her through a narrow doorway into a semi-private room. It seemed darker back here. The walls were stained mahogany brown, though she didn't believe the wood was actual mahogany. The art was minimal, abstract and bold. Patriarchy lived here. There Lucia was, sitting at a small table, sipping a glass of red wine. Even though Claire was on time, early in fact, Lucia had arrived first.

There were stories about Lucia, but Claire resolutely told

herself she didn't believe any of them; at least, that was how she kept her calm. Besides, few people in New York City were actually who they said they were. The host pulled out a chair and Claire sat. The waiter, without asking, filled a glass with red wine. She didn't drink red—tannins bothered her, but she wasn't about to speak up. Instead, she took a sip of her wine as to appear self-assure. She evaluated Lucia as she would a potential client and forced herself to meet Lucia's gaze.

"Thank you for coming. I apologize for being early," Lucia said politely.

Usually in New York, business happened before niceties. The tone threw Claire off, as she had come ready to bargain hard. Now, she'd have to take a different tact. "I appreciate your inviting me here. I've been meaning to try this place out," said Claire.

"My grandfather took me to a place like this when I was a kid. Before Brooklyn was Brooklyn, if you know what I mean. Where did you grow up?"

Claire shifted uncomfortably in her seat.

"Please relax, Miss Townsend," Lucia said with a kind smile. "It's only a conversation—small talk."

The waiter returned to ask if any other beverages were needed. "Please get my guest a glass of white wine. I had forgotten that she is not a fan of red."

Claire swallowed hard and nodded. How did Lucia know her preference for wine? Maybe it came up when they first met.

"Please be sure to give her the best white zinfandel, Gianni, you know the one I'm talking about."

With a prompt nod, the waiter disappeared.

"I believe it was your aunt who raised you back in Ohio. That small town near Columbus, what was the name? I'm sorry, it's on the tip of my tongue. Something that starts with a T? Help me, please?"

Claire held very still. It was as if the room were suddenly much smaller. How did she know this? Rumors of Lucia came with stories of missing family members and chopped off fingers. Her breath came faster. "Tipp City. Near Dayton."

Lucia sipped her wine and then swirled the glass, contemplating the movement. "You worked at Foodtown grocery as a checker." She set down the wine. "That's funny. You're not a farm girl. No cows or corn in your past. Something of a rarity, being from Ohio." She picked up a menu, the only menu, opened it and looked at the options.

Claire tried not to appear startled. Since she had arrived in the city, she had rewritten her past. She hadn't told anyone the truth. No one in the city had doubted her when she told them that she had grown up on a farm. Or when she said her parents were alive and well, happy, living a charmed life on the farm raising chickens and goats. The waiter returned with a glass of white wine and set it in front of her. She hesitated before drinking it, afraid to touch the glass.

Lucia looked up from her menu. "It's just a glass of wine, dear. Really, this is a civilized dinner. We aren't brutes here."

Claire brought her hand to the wine glass and slipped the stem between her fingers. The globe of the glass fit neatly in the palm of her hand. A wine connoisseur would instruct her immediately to remove her hand from the globe—she shouldn't warm the delicate white wine with the heat of her hand.

"I suppose most people believe Ohio is full of farm girls," Lucia said. "Living with stereotypes must be tiring at times, having to correct people and tell them the truth. Your parents died in a car accident. You lived with a family friend first for a few weeks and then your mother's sister for what, ten days, and after that your father's brother. You almost made it out, but then no one wanted you. Foster care for a year and a half.

Eighteen months and two weeks, to be exact. It must have been hard."

Claire tried to smile, fighting back the urge to run out the door, out of New York, and get away to avoid this turn of events. But she stayed put. Lucia would find her. She realized then the reason Lucia hadn't called or contacted her for two weeks—she was stalking her prey. The wait was fun for her. Claire got the feeling she liked to watch.

"What would you like to order? The eggplant parmesan is so dramatic, large and in charge. But the vongole… Oh, Claire. These little baby clams are from South Carolina that you swallow whole. And the Montauk littlenecks. Divine."

"I'll have whatever you're having," said Claire. All this polite conversation was meant to relax her, as if she could lower her guard, and she struggled to stay alert.

"Now see, that is just disgraceful," Lucia said, lowering the menu. "I know you are a particular person, so please make your own choice." She handed Claire a leather-bound menu.

Claire met her eyes. One thing she had learned when the stakes were high: boldness had a currency. "You're right." She scanned the menu. "Thank you, Lucia."

The waiter approached the table with a small notepad and a pen. He held the pencil in his had firmly even though the index and middle finger were missing. She studied his face and noticed a fading scar near the base of his throat. Claire jumped a little but tried to make it look as if she'd been lost in thought and refocused on the menu. Was this Lucia's handiwork? She glanced across the table to see if there was any hint of anger or violence in the other woman, but could find none. Lucia was eerily calm.

"Claire, are you ready to order? Ladies first."

She ordered a Caesar salad and the Dover piccata. Lucia ordered minestrone soup and the linguini vongole. After the order was taken, Lucia closed the menu and set it at the edge of the table. Claire met her gaze, knowing if she got scared, she might as well be dead.

"My grandfather used to come to a place like this. He worked for the mafia back in the day, when it was romantic, I suppose. When violence was raw and powerful, and you did whatever the boss said. But I run my business with a modern touch."

"How so?" Claire asked. She took another sip of her wine and tried not to down the whole glass in one sitting. She'd get out of this mess somehow, even though she had no idea where the money would come from.

"The biggest failure of my grandfather—who was a capo—was to kill off someone who didn't pay." Lucia paused for a moment and seemed to consider Claire. "You know what a capo is, right? It's the person in charge of the soldiers. How is the white? Are you enjoying it?"

"Yes, thank you."

"I wanted to get you something crisp but not too fruity. The oak overtones are nice, yes?"

"It's wonderful. Thank you." Her country girl act would cut no water with Lucia, nor would her socialite city-girl persona. The waiter returned and placed a salad in front of Claire and the soup in front of Lucia.

"Thank you, Gianni," Lucia said. The waiter slightly bowed. "So, my grandfather was a capo. He ended up in jail. Someone snitched on someone, and well, there you have it. He's made. He died in Rikers. They refused his parole request. The probation board said that he had committed too many… atrocities."

The hair stood up on the back of Claire's neck. She had the street smarts to play, but she had never played on a street like this before. The flight instinct consumed her whole body, demanding that she run, but she forced herself to sit still and breathe as if she were in a *savasana* pose. Besides, where would she run to?

"And my father, it just ruined his life. He tried to keep the family out of the business. He had a good job, non-union. Non-mafia. Made sure I went to school and got good grades. I have a knack for numbers, you know. But my father didn't do so well. I think he had witnessed too much." Lucia frowned lightly as if the words were too dirty to say. "He struggled."

The room felt cold. Claire clenched her jaw, unwilling to let words scare her.

"I have to say, he did lift me up and out. I attended the University of Chicago, majored in finance, and was able to get a job working on Wall Street. Oh, Claire," she said, shaking her head, "the money is ridiculous. It falls around you like a cosmic shower from the gods. If I believed in the gods of my ancestors, I'd say Jupiter loved me. But I got bored. And lucky for me, the Fates intervened."

"How so?" Claire asked politely as she took a bite of her salad. A part of her recognized the high quality of the food— the brightness of the lemon counteracting the garlic as the coddled egg mellowed everything together. She wanted to enjoy the taste but couldn't.

"I'm sorry," Lucia said without a trace of sarcasm. "I've been hogging this conversation. I apologize for that. It's not often I tell this story. I do appreciate your listening." She took a careful sip of her soup.

"I'm listening." Claire smiled and cocked her head before tapping her earlobe.

"Suicide. I was home visiting for the weekend. I suppose the demons were too much. He went on a drunken rampage, beat my mother with a baseball bat. Maple. He tried to beat me. At the end of the night, he put a gun in his mouth and pulled the trigger. He got the aim wrong, though." Lucia met Claire's eyes. "I had to finish the job."

The noise in the restaurant seemed a bit louder, the clash

of dishes in the kitchen, the murmur of people laughing and talking, the uncorking of wine. Lucia whisked her hands together as if saying she was finished with the whole thing.

"So I changed my life. I didn't like the long hours on Wall Street, anyways. The parties they'd have at the office. Bringing in booze, escorts—it was ridiculous; hedonistic, really. Boring old bottom row of the Maslow pyramid. I, however, needed more. I needed to focus on my life's dream."

"And what was that?" Claire asked with a quiet voice.

"Oh, Claire. Such a pleasant guest. Thank you for letting me indulge. The first was to embrace my grandfather's roots. Rejecting them caused too much pain for my father. But I realized that I could embrace my family's legacy. The second part of my dream is to change people's lives. I could transform them. I could be like Oprah or Liz Gilbert. I have that power."

Claire scratched her neck, just under the ear, unsure of how she should respond. *How did she have that power?* The waiter came out and removed the plates. She glanced at the missing fingers and back to his face, but the waiter's expression was neutral.

"You see," Lucia continued, "I came up with a business model that embraces my past and yet respects the future I want to build. So yes, I loan money, but what I really, deeply want is to inspire people. If you can do that, if you can inspire me, you walk away."

"Or?"

"Or you can pay me two hundred thousand dollars. Cash. For being late and all. It's quite generous terms, considering."

Claire didn't dare move. The waiter returned with dinner and set the dishes quietly in front of them. Linguine for Lucia and the Dover for Claire. She parsed out the sum: one hundred thousand for the principal. One hundred thousand for interest. The late fee no longer mattered.

Lucia motioned to the entrees. "After you."

The Dover had been baked with its head on. Claire lifted the fork and knife, trying to find a place to cut the body while ignoring the dead eye.

Lucia leaned in toward Claire as if telling her a secret. "I love to watch people motivated by the right criteria. Human beings will go to incredible lengths, do these *amazing* things because of fear. Oprah uses positive thoughts and 'believe in yourself,' but that doesn't motivate the same way a good scare does. I mean, how many more dream boards does the world really need?" She gathered linguine and twirled it on her fork. "But watching people make real change? That's incredible. It's like front row Broadway but so much better. And you? I see great promise in you."

"Thanks, I think," Claire said, trying to maintain a neutral expression.

Lucia took a bite of the linguine, keeping her eyes on Claire. She looked away. It seemed impolite to watch.

"I've been wanting to ask you, if you don't mind. What is it you want out of this life? And don't be trite with some cliché answer."

Claire sat up in her seat. She repressed the urge to look shocked. Why would Lucia care what she wanted? Lucia just wanted her money or this deal, some kind of messed up thing to inspire her, whatever that meant.

"Dig deep. What do you want? I'll know if you're lying."

Instead of trying to charm her way out of this, she had to tell the truth. Claire closed her eyes. She had arrived in New York with three goals of being wealthy, famous, and traveling the world. Selling art at Apfel was a start, but the contract with Barneys and her boutique was supposed to solidify the path to fortune and fame. But that had failed. Even so, it hadn't changed her goal. She opened her eyes and met Lucia's scrutiny. "Money, fame, and travel."

"That's a good start. But banal. And you've already failed at all of that. What do you really want?"

Claire shifted uncomfortably in her seat. The last person she wanted to be honest with was Lucia. But she had to. She knew that it helped. "I want to be free. I don't want to be dependent on anyone. You, the Hermanns, David. Everything I do, I have to hustle."

"Why do you want to be free? What are you trying to break away from?"

Claire took a sip of wine while she thought. Her mind was racing with answers to satisfy Lucia. She couldn't give some bullshit answer like she was at a happy hour eating a fancy canapé. "The stink of poverty. Rejection. Never having to depend on anyone else."

"You came to the city hoping to erase your old life? Find a new one?"

Claire fell back in her seat as if the words had pushed her and said nothing. She nodded almost imperceptibly, and then with more purpose. She'd wanted to get away and was willing to do whatever it took to smash the memories of her teens. No one had made her feel loved, not since her parents had died. When she let her guard down, only pain followed. Now, she left first. She had even left Bruno, her first real love, and was never sure if that had been the right decision.

"Money and freedom is a little cliché," Lucia said, "but I like your honesty. That's a nice start. I have faith in you. Can I offer you some advice?"

"Okay?"

Lucia had a sip of water, looking off in the distance as if she were thinking. "When it gets to the nitty gritty, you'll have to choose. Think about what you *need*, not what you *want*."

Claire's mouth dropped open slightly, and she quickly closed it, upset that she'd let her poker face slip.

Lucia expertly stabbed one of the clams. "I like you, Claire.

This is going to be fun. I have a feeling you are going to do something great." She popped the clam into her mouth and swallowed it whole.

The waiter walked by, and Lucia stopped him. She put her fingers in front of her lips like a flower bud, kissed them, and spread them wide. "Oh, Gianni. My meal is perfection. Give my compliments to the chef, please. Why aren't you eating, dear? Dover isn't an obvious choice at an Italian restaurant. Perhaps it's a little too much?"

Claire looked at the plate and stared at the fish head. The dead eyes blackened. She held the knife in her hand and pointed it towards Lucia. She'd instinctively taken a defensive position.

"Claire, Claire, Claire," she said. "Your actions are so, so predictable." Lucia held her spoon up. "But this? Consider the spoon. It's an effective tool. It's becoming my favorite, although to be honest, I try not to become attached. But the spoon? It can be used for the eyes. The nose," Lucia said, making a small but hard upwards motion that sent a ripple through Claire's spine. "I love the way it sprays, like art. And if it's done right, the gut, the balls too, but I suppose that doesn't qualify for you," Lucia said, as she paused to look down, as if she could see under the table, "unless I were to get creative…."

Claire placed the knife on the table.

"This is a promise." Lucia nodded at the spoon and set it between them. "You might have the stamina to last a while, but that's part of the fun. For me, at least."

And like the last number that fit in a Sudoku puzzle, Claire understood. There was no negotiation. "What are your terms?"

Lucia met her gaze. "Thirteen days."

Claire took a bite of the fish. She wasn't able to taste it but somehow knew it was the best fish she had ever ordered. "Why thirteen?"

"Many people think thirteen is unlucky, but in Italy, it's associated with the great goddess. It's supposed to bring prosperity and life. A lot of Italians love thirteen when gambling. And today might be your lucky day. Unfortunately, the late fees ate up all your existing payments and added a bit on."

"Lucky is thirteen days to pay you two hundred thousand dollars?" Claire asked.

"That's correct. Two hundred is the full sum. Don't fret. You have options. The spoon. *Or you can do something great.* It's a chance to turn water into wine. *Transmutation.* I hope you pull it off. Me personally, I cannot wait to see how you resolve this little issue."

"Transformation," Claire said. "People transform. Things transmute."

"Are you correcting me? Brave girl. People, things, it doesn't matter," Lucia said. "I prefer the word transmute. The word transform seems so, I don't know, formulaic."

"Any chance on a payment plan? I mean, you are a modern business woman. A dead body pays no bills."

"That's boring, Claire. Be innovative."

Claire couldn't speak. She had convinced people to part with millions for pieces of art, but when it came to saving her life? Her jaw suddenly locked tight.

"I like you, so we can start the count tomorrow morning. You have thirteen days. It's a chance to turn water into wine. Otherwise...." She lifted the spoon from the middle of the table and twirled it between her fingers like a baton and said nothing more.

*A*fter dinner, Claire walked back to her small apartment. She wasn't sure how she made it home, because all she could hear in her mind was Lucia's roaring laugher. Horns honked, tires screeched, but she wasn't sure if it was general noise or if she'd crossed without looking. The only thing that kept her tethered to reality was the London plane trees with leaves waving in the breeze and the sharp blue sky. She had to pay Lucia Occhipinti two hundred grand in thirteen days.

Or turn water into wine, *whatever that meant.*

Inside her apartment, Claire bolted the door. She was a little tipsy from the wine. Instead of feeling carefree, like a good glass of wine would do, edges of nausea rose in her belly. She wasn't safe. Once the windows were locked and she double-checked the door bolts, she scanned the room.

With a hard laugh, she realized that the crappy door wouldn't stop anyone. The fire escape was a perfect way for someone to climb up and get inside. The windows could be unlocked easily or the glass broken. There was no way to protect herself, not here. Her heart raced. Her breath came in faster. She used to get terrible panic attacks after her parents died, and she felt one coming on. She rubbed her face, trying to distract her mind. If she could catch it before she actually hyperventilated, she'd be okay.

Her throat tightened and spurred the panic. Her breath ragged, no longer her own, she was dizzy. Nothing looked right, so she closed her eyes and curled on the couch. A few minutes later, her stomach cramped. She wanted to open her eyes and go to the bathroom, but she couldn't, her body overwhelmed. Sweat beaded, then dripped off her face. She was cold, and huddled. Her teeth chattered.

Fifteen minutes later, her heart finally slowed. Her breathing calmed. The storm had passed. With that, she got up and pulled the cheap vodka out of the freezer. The attacks were back. She thought she'd gotten rid of them. Of course, she shouldn't drink alcohol after an attack, but maybe if she didn't get involved with a loan shark, that would help too. After a deep sigh, she poured the vodka into a glass and downed it. The crisp liquid woke her up, and she realized she'd forgotten to take a Xanax to help quell the attack. She considered it, but dismissed the idea. She needed to run through her options, not be passed out on the couch. She needed to figure out a way to raise two hundred grand.

The legal ones made her laugh. She couldn't sue Lucia. The mere thought made her chuckle. Besides, she was a ward of the foster care system, she knew what "legal" meant. If she called the police— she laughed out loud—there was no proof that Lucia had done anything illegal. If she alerted the authorities regarding the Reade Street Gallery activities, she still had no proof; no crime had yet been committed. And she'd still owe Lucia money. Claire would end up in the East River, sooner rather than later.

Poor man's vodka tonic (tap water, vodka, no ice) in hand, she crossed the studio apartment and checked herself out in a full-length mirror. She posed with her lips slightly parted. She squeezed her small breasts together, and evaluated her cleavage. Two problems. First, they barely touched each other. Second, the giant ragged scar ran between her breasts. She wasn't the epitome of luscious and sexy, not to mention that her breasts were barely A cups. Even if she full-out prostituted herself, there was no way she could make that kind of cash in thirteen days. Her stomach clenched. *No.* She'd gotten through life without having to put out, and she wasn't about to start now.

She felt a headache coming on and pinched the bridge of her nose. Back in the kitchen, she opened her fridge and pulled out a plastic bottle half-full of mango-flavored seltzer water and added it to the vodka. Any flavor had to be better than what she had. The bubbles popped as water met alcohol. She took a sip and scrunched her face at the sharpness. Not a good mix, but she didn't have anything else.

She sat on the table and opened up her wallet. The card David had given her fell out. If she found the right item, she could easily make two hundred grand. It'd be easy enough if she could just get the pieces to fit together. In Belize, she'd be in the right geographical location to stumble upon a good piece. Mayan artifacts were popular. The program manager job would get her items past customs. She knew, from working at the Apfel Gallery, that shipping protocols made it difficult if she had to work on her own.

She stared up at the brown-stained ceiling, wishing for a better solution to appear. The plan to sell items on the black market, aside from it being illegal as hell, meant she had to use Xander Moore. That man, sweet as he was off limits, was a real friend. Not a friend like Amaya, the art blogger, who posted the #JaqueFail video.

A third idea popped into her head. Run. Cut up her credit cards and disappear. How hard could it be? Canada? Too cold. Central America? She had a passport. She'd been to

Guatemala with Bruno when she was in college to study Lake Titicaca, but that was a remote area and she'd lost touch with the residents there. She wasn't sure if she could hide without knowing the language or logistics. If she did run, Mexico seemed an obvious choice.

Mexico City scared her. She didn't want to accidentally get killed in some drug transaction or by a stray bullet. Plus, she didn't speak Spanish. Touristy American towns might be a good start. Puerto Vallarta? Cancun? Acapulco? Baja? She'd drop off the grid. A hippy idea of selling jewelry on the beach wearing a flowy skirt came to mind. If she could hustle New York, a sea of Americans in beach chairs ought to be a piece of cake.

She mentally reviewed her list of friends who had Mexican contacts. She had former clients, but they were business related, not a ring-the-bell-and-show-up-in-the-middle-of-the-night kind of friend. And if Lucia ever "got to them," they would tell her in two seconds where she'd gone.

Plus, she couldn't just fly to Mexico, or take a bus or a train. If Lucia knew what grocery store she clerked for when she was sixteen and private items from her emails, Claire had a gut feeling that Lucia could get ahold of any information she wanted. If she ran, she could not leave an electronic trace. No credit cards. No email transactions. Cash only. If she was going to run to Mexico, it had to be disguised somehow, or Lucia would find her. The death Lucia described was awful enough; she didn't want to actually piss her off.

Claire didn't have the know-how to pull a stunt like running and reasonably expect it to work. She grabbed the vodka glass on the table and drank every last drop. She bit back the aftertaste and exhaled. *Better get a real plan going before I get drunk.*

Nothing new came to mind. Frustrated, she got up and changed into comfortable clothes. Ordered Chinese food. Back on the couch, she picked up the Men's Journal magazine and thought of Bruno again. They had dated for a year. He had gone on to fulfill his dreams of becoming a professor, whereas after her internship at Metropolitan Museum, she was offered a job at Apfel Gallery in New York City as a sales associate. The commission and a base salary earned her more in one month than he'd earn in a year. She hadn't thought twice about taking the job.

Had she stayed the course, she'd probably be in some dusty museum doing dusty things. She'd dated others after him, but once the passion burned off, then so did her interest. She never found anyone she could be herself with. No one wanted to hear her real stories; they all loved the sweetness of a country girl in the big city. They wanted to hear about her success as a top art sales associate, her new dreams of a boutique in Brooklyn. The rising star. The American Dream.

If she did end up selling artifacts on the black market, her old friends, her "before New York friends," would disown her. She'd lose the few people in this world who knew her, who shared authentic times with her.

The best option she had to pay off Lucia was to find and sell an object on the black market. She'd go to Belize and maybe hook up with an amateur diver and get a high-value artifact up to Reade Street. With the museum job, she'd be able to skirt the customs check. If she did all that, quickly and quietly, Xander would never know.

The plan was weak, at best, but she didn't have any choice. She had to pay Lucia. There was no mango water left, so she tipped up what was left of the vodka in the bottle and finished the last of it. The alcohol burned the back of her throat. *Bruno.* She'd get to see him again. She didn't cheat, but she hadn't known how to let him in. It hadn't mattered. It was the past, she couldn't change it. She chucked the bottle in the trash, liking the sound it made as it clattered against the metal sides.

Her eyelids drooped, and she fought against closing them. She was so tired. It was the middle of the day. She lay on the couch. *Let me close them for a minute.*

❧

HER PHONE RANG. She bolted straight up. She found it on the coffee table, and saw the number, unsure of who it was. She swiped the green answer button.

"This is Christopher Shali from the American Museum of Natural History. May I speak with Claire Townsend?"

"This is her," she said, suddenly sober. Her head throbbed from the cheap vodka. She went into the kitchen and turned on the electric kettle.

"I'm the curator for an exhibit at the Natural History museum. We need a program manager for the Belize job," he said. "We'd like to hire you."

The *no* she wanted to say rumbled in her mind, but she held herself back.

"I'll be honest with you. The other candidate cancelled at the last minute. Since you worked for the Met as an intern a few years back, you're basically vetted. We can fast track you."

They had picked her because she was the last man standing. The sudden blow to her ego came swift, but it also shook her up. "Program manager position, right. I understand from the job description that I'll make sure everything gets done. I'll take care of the artists and coordinate with a work-study."

"That's correct. Two world-renowned artists will work on art and costumes. Five Mayan shamans from Belize, Guatemala, and the States are coming. You'll be in charge of making sure everyone works together. Can you handle that much personality?"

"Yes. And I'll be shipping the art work and costumes back to the museum?" she asked.

"That's right. Afterwards, we'll display the costumes and the art in a special exhibit. People can watch the Nat Geo video."

"I have experience with art galleries to assure that objects are packed properly and the right paperwork to get through customs."

"Great," Shali said. "We're excited for this project. It's a 'live' exhibition to recreate the Mayan creation story *Popol Vuh* in the ATM cave as it might have been during the Classic Mayan period. We have special permission from the government of Belize. Nat Geo will film the event."

"What's ATM stand for?" She moved across the living room past the wallpaper rolls to a window. All she could see was a red brick wall of the neighboring building. She shut the paper blinds so only muted light came through.

"Actun Tunichil Muknal. It's a cave in Belize," he said, as if she should know. "Are you in pretty good physical shape? You'll need to swim through a river or two."

Claire put her hand on her throat, touching the base of her old wound. Even wearing a long sleeve swim shirt didn't cover all of it. Technically, she wasn't afraid of water, she just hated people to see it. She hated answering questions when people asked. She didn't say anything to Shali about her water phobia. She kept her mouth shut. She needed this job.

"A guide will take everyone floating through a cave river and a Mayan temple. He's also an archeologist. Bruno Canul. Be sure to pack accordingly."

Hearing Bruno's name filled her with trepidation as well as excitement. She hadn't seen him in years. And on top of that, Claire had never done adventure. She'd get jazzed after reading a copy of her Men's Journal but always stopped short of booking a trip. She never had time. Her life as an Apfel sales associate and running her boutique left the days crazy full. "How many days will I be in Belize?"

"Ten days. We'll pay you five thousand plus expenses. You're gonna earn every penny."

"Can I have time to think about it?" Claire clenched her jaw. Maybe there was another way? She didn't *really* want to see Bruno again, did she? Letting old feelings resurface seemed ridiculous. She should be focused on getting the job, not getting excited about seeing an old boyfriend again.

"Frankly, I didn't want to hire you."

Great. Another rejection. She wasn't asking for a lot, just a little time.

"I saw the video," Shali said with a sigh. "But you seem to be in luck. Xander Moore called me up yesterday. Said he forwarded the req to you and wanted to make sure we considered you for this position. He says your organization skills are beyond the natural world. He also mentioned the degree in anthropology and said you were good." His pause seemed calculated to wait for her to respond, and when she didn't, he let out another aggravated sigh. "The flight leaves tomorrow. If you don't want it, I need to know so I can find someone."

"I'll take it," she said and confirmed her email address so he could send her the information and e-tickets.

As soon as they were off the phone, she opened the email from Shali. Someday, she'd have to find a way to thank Xander. She clicked on the list of people who she'd be working with. *Bruno Canul.* He was probably married with kids by now. She could cross him off her list of complications.

Darren Ruiz was a prolific artist—majored in mostly native, Latino, some indigenous—and specialized in art as well as pottery. With a loud sigh, she involuntarily squeezed her hands together. She had worked with Darren before at the Apfel Gallery and hoped maybe, just maybe, he wouldn't recognize her. He was a pompous ass then, and he'd be insufferable now.

Ruth Ann Zylstra was a famous Academy-award-winning

costume designer with Latin/Mayan roots. The wiki article gave a generic description along with a few photos of her work and her profile.

Janine Jankowski was a work study coming from Citrus Valley College out of Los Angeles. Yay. At least there was one person beneath her on the totem pole, so to speak. No need to look her up. She'd get to meet her soon enough.

The tea kettle had finished its cycle with a ding. She loved how fast they were compared to boiling water on the stove. She retrieved a mug along with a package of green tea and promptly made a cup. While she waited for it to cool, she pieced together a plan to secure an item to sell.

At least she wouldn't have to buy a plane ticket any more, the museum would be paying for the flight. While in Belize, she would need to find someone naive, an amateur, preferably someone into cave diving. On Google, she searched for and found a recreational archeology website, and for the cost of membership, was sent a list of all individuals interested in Belize. There were only fifteen names, along with contact information.

Underwater cave diving might be the latest fad, but she knew from working at museums and galleries that water degradation would certainly be high. But any item would be better than what she had, which was nothing. She downloaded the list onto her phone with plans to email everyone later that evening.

She took a sip of the tea. The water was hot and instinctivly, she pulled back. Lucia's words came to mind. *Water into wine.* Like some kind of change, a transmutation. Could she really get out of this whole mess by changing? *Inspire her?* But what did that mean? Was she supposed to become worse? Like Lucia? Was she expected to do something horrific like killing someone? Or was she expected to give up her own life to save someone? Claire would rather find enough money to pay off Lucia.

She picked up the business card David had given her. Reade Street Gallery and Boutique. She poured the hot water into a cup and set a green tea bag into the water. She sent a text.

Claire Townsend here. David recommended me. I'm in. Cash on delivery.

Two hours later, she received a text back: *Deal.*

As soon as Bruno Canul got off the flight, he felt at home. He'd come through the Philip S.W. Gordon airport in Belize so many times he'd lost count. The airport was small, only six gates that he was aware of, and had the comfortable notion that everyone knew one another. The gate area was lively, like a street side café. A range of people were in the airport: from adventure types wearing zipped up khakis to honeymooners in love holding hands. Faded travel posters on the wall promised an "UnBelizeable Time" and "Belize it or not… I'm Beautiful" beaches.

He wanted to eat first and then check email. He grabbed three meat pies from the deli and a Coke. After finding a seat at a tin table, he bit into the meat pie. The dough was flaky like a good, crispy, pie crust. The meat was flavorful; it reminded him of his mom's, although he'd never tell her that.

Bruno's phone email app pinged with a notification of fourteen unread emails. He read the one from Christopher Shali regarding the final crew list and shuttle pickup. The program manager position still didn't have a name listed, but she would be flying in from Miami at four thirty p.m. She was from New York City. He thought briefly of Claire, an ex-girlfriend. He had loved her, but she had decided to move to New York instead of coming with him. The breakup had been rough; he still thought of her every now and again, but it was a long time ago.

Bruno took another bite of the meat pie and washed it down with a swig of soda. He had to focus on things that mattered now. Like Janine. He couldn't believe she got the work-study job with her reputation. Bruno knew she was involved in black-market sales with her boss Rex Martel, but he couldn't prove it. He nearly busted her for the illegal dig, but Rex's fancy lawyer got the FBI charges dismissed. Through the grapevine, he'd heard that their employer, LA Citrus Valley College, was actively trying to get them dismissed, but hadn't any luck.

Was she here to truly work or did she have a plan cooked up? This time, he'd be ready. He unrolled an 8x10 hard-copy map marked with twelve X's. He'd gotten the unmarked map from his mom, who was a commercial real estate agent in Belize. The X's represented a short list of places she might be interested in if she were to start an illegal dig. He circled the critical points in red on his map. He wished there was more he could do, but at this point, he could only watch Janine.

"Bruno? Is that you?"

He recognized the voice but wasn't sure who it belonged to. He looked up, and there was Claire Townsend, five years older and looking more attractive than what he remembered. Her hair was shorter. She was in great shape, petite, and if his memory served him right, a firecracker. He felt a deep longing. Her skin was beautiful and smooth like an alabaster stone.

"I never thought I'd see you again," she said. Her hazel eyes regarded him with something more than curiosity.

"It's good to see you." He stood to greet her with a hug and cheek kiss. Her perfume, a mixed scent of grapefruit and rosemary, was the same. A wave of familiarity washed over him. The way her skin felt on his. He wanted to wrap his fingers in her hair and kiss her, really kiss her.

"I'm the program manager for the Popol Vuh gig," she said, her cheeks turning a shade of pink.

"I thought you sold art? In a gallery?" How had he missed this? Had the email mentioned her by name?

"Trying a new career. I haven't had the best luck the last few weeks."

"Are you okay?" He reached out to touch her arm. The barest touch felt hot to him. Still, after all these years, he had a natural inclination to protect her, to comfort her.

She rubbed the spot where he touched her. "Where'd you get that?" she asked, looking at the plate of meat pies on the table. "They look good."

"Over there at Le Petite Café. You may be tempted to try the jalapeño Johnny cakes, but I prefer the meat pies. I'll walk you over?"

"It's all right, I can see it from here. I'll just be a few minutes. Watch my stuff?"

She parked her roller bag next to him. She slung her purse over her shoulder and walked away. He hadn't realized how much he'd missed her until now, but he crossed his arms. He was here on a mission. They needed to keep things professional. They broke up for a reason. When he got the job in LA, he didn't want to say goodbye. He cared about her, he really did, but they wanted different things.

He cleared the map away and checked his watch. Janine was arriving in less than twenty minutes, and he needed to be mentally prepared. Bruno didn't want to be overly antagonizing. He wanted to seem aloof, but not so aloof that it raised her suspicion.

Claire returned to the table with two meat pies, a Diet

Coke, and a package of Oreo cookies. She lifted up the cookies. "On vacation everyone needs the one thing."

"I remember the Oreos. You got some on every road trip we took."

"You remember that?"

"Yeah, especially the time we went to West Virginia for rafting. That bridge, Class IV rapids. I told Alberto about it. Still one of my top ten." The night they spent in a rustic cabin with nothing but candlelight. The way her hair drifted in his hands, the way her body… his balls tightened and he fought back the urge to reach for her, to reclaim her right then and there.

"He still a guide?" she asked.

"Who?"

"Your brother?" Claire said.

"Oh yeah, him." He nodded. "He'll be working with us to help guide everyone in."

Claire sat and then unwrapped the tin foil from her pie. She took a bite. Her eyes closed and an expression similar to joy crossed her face. "Oh, wow. Now I see what you're talking about."

"Marie makes the best."

"You're not kidding. I haven't had an empanada that good in years, and I live in New York."

He laughed. She still had the same way about her, the same energy, and he wondered why she was here. Whatever it was, it had to be bad to leave the city. "I'll show you around. Belize has some great food."

Claire checked her phone. "Fifteen minutes before the rest of the team gets here. Janine Jankowski is coming from LA Citrus Valley College. You know her?"

"Yes, I know her. I also know her boss Rex Martel," he said, trying not to let anger seep into his voice. "Why are you asking?"

"I just saw that you were both from LA, so I was curious."

From the innocence on her face, he surmised she hadn't picked up on his stiff response. "We're colleagues."

It would be unprofessional to tell Claire the events over the past few weeks. He'd be sure to tell her, when the moment was right, to watch out for Janine. All she had to do was Google Janine's name, and she'd learn that Janine had been arrested for her involvement with an illegal dig. What Claire wouldn't see, though, was his name in the article. McNally, his liaison at the FBI Art Crimes division, had pulled a few strings and kept his name out of the news.

"I suppose I should look them up, but I was hired yesterday. Literally got my plane ticket less than twelve hours ago."

"Did you apply for this job?"

Her movement came to a standstill. "Xander recommended it to me," she said. "Actually, I got fired from Apfel Gallery. A viral video went south. Really bad. Please don't Google it."

"That's terrible."

"Then I lost my shop." She frowned. Her forehead crinkled. He'd been right about why she left New York; it was bad.

"When it rains it pours," he said, kicking himself for such a thoughtless response. "Sorry, I don't mean…."

"It's all right. What am I going to do? Cry about it?"

He was taken aback by the sharpness of the words. "Did you go to his wedding? Xander's?"

"No, I wasn't able to." She looked away sheepishly. "I was too busy."

"I couldn't go either. I heard it was a lot of fun, though. It would've been nice to see everyone." He was about to say he would've asked her to dance, but a tall woman had appeared at the table. The woman he'd been expecting all along, Janine Jankowski.

"Bruno," she said her arms crossed over her chest. "Surprised to see you here."

He tried not to puff out his chest, to keep a relaxed demeanor. "Janine." McNally had told him she used to be a CIA operative and had quit the agency to pursue a degree in archeology. He'd told him the agency hired non-descript people to work for them, but Janine was not in that category. The woman could have been a supermodel even though she was closer to his age than a standard college student. She was at least six feet tall with brown hair to the middle of her back.

Claire stood and stuck her hand out. "Hi. I'm Claire. I'll be the program manager. You're Janine, right? The work study?" Claire glanced from Bruno and back to Janine again. "Do you two know each other?"

"I guess you could say we do. LA is a small town, after you've lived there a few years," Janine said.

"We know each other in a professional capacity," said Bruno. He held out his hand for a handshake. "Good to see you again, *Janine*."

"You too, *Bruno*," Janine said, her eyes hard and small as she returned the shake.

Claire turned to Janine and then back to Bruno. "Um. Okay. Darren and Ruth Ann are arriving soon. If you want to eat, there's a café across the way. I'd recommend the meat pie."

"How much time do I have?" she asked, breaking eye contact with Bruno to smile at Claire.

"They should be here any minute." Claire lifted her watch towards Janine. "But the shuttle doesn't get here for another hour."

WHEN IT WAS TIME, Claire got up to meet Darren and Ruth Ann at the gate. Soon, she came back with only one person.

Darren Ruiz was older, in his early fifties, with graying hair and thick-rimmed black eyeglasses. A compact man, he was short with a square jaw. He wore Levi's and brown cowboy boots with a designer button-down shirt.

"Ruth Ann was held up," said Claire. "She'll be coming in on the next flight. Unfortunately, it arrives much later tonight, so we're going ahead. BIFA will coordinate a new shuttle for her. Darren, I'd like to introduce you…"

"Janine, I believe," Darren said, shaking Janine's hand, using the opportunity to look her up and down before shifting his attention, "and Bruno?"

Bruno held his hand out and Darren returned it with a firm shake. Bruno didn't like the way the other man leered at the women, and if he continued, he'd say something. After gathering their luggage, they went through customs. He took a couple quick glances at Claire. She seemed different than what he remembered. Grown up maybe? More mature? Jaded? *What did she think of him?* He shook his head. It shouldn't matter. He had work to do.

The shuttle back to Belize Indigenous Foundation of Art (BIFA), where they were staying, would be ready for them at five thirty p.m. Janine's job description was to work with locals and courier projects between Belmopan, the largest city near the art compound, and Belize City. She had rented a car and said her goodbyes, letting Claire know she'd meet them at the art compound.

Outside, it was close to five p.m., but the sun was still out and the skies were a sea blue with wisps of clouds. Tall, skinny palm trees dotted the horizon. The air was cool and refreshing instead of muggy. Porters and drivers greeted each other warmly and told jokes. Tourists who had never met said hi to each other. Bruno found the driver waiting for them on the sidewalk. A young man with a pronounced native Mayan hook nose held up a sign with a computer printed paper: MEETING BIFA.

"Welcome to Belize," he said in a booming baritone that assured a good time. "I am your driver. My name is Ed."

A white commuter van was parked street-side. Claire got into the first passenger row. Bruno got into the back seat. As he passed Claire, he leaned in closer than he'd meant to. The proximity caused his heart to beat a little faster. Darren got in last, and Claire tried not to acknowledge him, but he placed his hand heavily on her shoulder. "You sure screwed up Apfel."

Bruno was about to check Darren, but he knew Claire was strong enough to handle it. He watched as she gave him the side-eye, but otherwise ignored the statement. Ed informed them the drive would take roughly two hours, and they were headed to Belmopan City. They drove through the Stann Creek district and onto the Hummingbird Highway.

"If you didn't know," Ed said with a thick accent tinted with British tones, "Belize was first British Honduras before they won their independence on September 21st, 1981. That is why we speak English. Refugees come in from Guatemala, so you'll hear Spanish. By the ocean are the Garifunas, who escaped slavery. We have mestizo and the Mayans, too. We are a small country, but we have a big heart for everyone."

CHAPTER TEN

Claire

Claire was the first one in the van, and patted her backpack to assure the cash she brought was still there. The money was needed upfront to buy artifacts. Although, what kind of artifact could she buy with six grand? If she was able to make that happen, if she was able to make two hundred grand in thirteen days or transmuted for Lucia, it'd be a miracle.

When Bruno got into the van, she felt the warmth from his skin. She couldn't help but think about him, the way they used to be. A kernel of heat flared up in her. She closed her eyes; the memory of how he touched her came unbidden.

"You sure screwed up Apfel," Darren said, his voice jolting her out of her thoughts.

Claire turned away and ignored him. Of course Darren had recognized her—she'd been crazy to think otherwise. He was a jerk, exactly as she remembered him. He wasn't worth the stress, and she didn't care what he thought, so she let the words roll off.

Instead of joining in the small talk, she watched the scenery go by. The landscape was a horizon of bold clouds and the ground a mass of jungle trees and grass. She saw white clapboard houses and clotheslines with sheets hanging in the back yards. The vehicles—mostly smaller SUV's and trucks—were older than in the US. The word function came to mind, certainly not beauty. They were poor, but not poverty-stricken.

Within two hours, they arrived at the Belize Indigenous Foundation of Art (BIFA), a compound near the Sibun National Forest Reserve in the middle of the jungle. She got out of the van and stood near an open pavilion with a thatched roof made of palm branches. The pavilion had one wall large enough to have a fireplace, a mounted TV, and a podium with a scattering of comfortable chairs and tall café tables.

Bruno exited the van as she watched. His eyes were dark brown, and his five o'clock shadow had appeared. The scruffiness was attractive. The man had aged well. He was lean and muscular, built like a soccer player, still a babe. If she remembered properly, his strength came from mountain biking. He certainly hadn't let himself become a fat and lazy professor, nor was he some pompous professor. All the reasons she'd fallen for him years ago still held true.

A small woman, her hair in a neat bun, her belly very pregnant, greeted him. She had to be eight months along, at *least*. Maybe she was carrying twins?

"Delia! My God! Last time I saw you, I had just heard the good news," Bruno said, greeting her with a kiss on the cheek. "Now look at you!"

Delia shrugged sheepishly and rubbed her belly with maternalism. "I've got three weeks left, according to the good doctor."

"You look wonderful. How's Frank handling it?"

"Och. Muy bien. He's gotten used to having a grumpy pregnant lady in the house."

She motioned to the others then, and with a broad smile,

directed them inside the pavilion. Janine was already inside since she'd taken the rental car. She rested on the love seat.

"My name is Delia Gamboa. I am the art director here, and welcome to BIFA! Please, be free to sit. Someone will bring bottled water."

A young woman entered the pavilion with a small tray of neatly wrapped damp washcloths. Claire took one for herself. She wiped her cheeks first, then her hands, and watched to make sure Darren was offered one. She didn't want him reporting her, and she figured Bruno could take care of himself.

Delia handed out pamphlets with a layout of the art compound printed on the back. "The BIFA location is often rented out for art excursion tourist groups. Two cabins were assigned to Darren and Ruth Ann. Here's your key, Darren," Delia said, handing him a white plastic card. "Bruno is staying off the property. Claire and Janine will be sharing the guest room in the Art Lodge."

Claire looked to Janine, who shrugged her shoulders with a smile, as if she were mildly interested. But Claire was concerned. She needed privacy. She needed uninterrupted space to count and hide her money, to plan black-market trading, to consider an escape route.

"As for food," Delia continued, "options are fairly limited. We have a basic kitchen and a dining area in a building behind the pavilion. The Grove House, a farm to table restaurant, will be hosting us for lunch and dinner. It's a twenty-minute drive located at the Sleeping Giant Lodge. Or you can go to the nearest town of Belmopan, about forty-five minutes away."

Ed brought in the luggage and Delia introduced him. He worked for the Sleeping Giant Lodge down the road and would be their main driver. "Don't worry," he said with a hearty chuckle, "Sleeping Giant has some of the best bartenders in the country."

"Now then, let's get settled," Delia said, after Ed left. "Your luggage will be delivered to your room promptly. At eight thirty, please meet back here in the pavilion for the Meet and Greet." She lifted her hands to let them know the open air building they stood in was the same. "Appetizers will be available."

Claire looked to Darren and asked, "Will you be all right? Do you want someone to help you find your room?"

He brushed her off, saying he'd be fine, took his suitcase and started towards his room. When she turned around, Bruno looked upset. "Do you want me to say anything to him?"

"Oh, him?" Claire said, glancing towards the door he'd just walked out of. "No. He's just that way. I don't want him to say anything bad about me to Shali."

"All right," he said. "I'll see you later tonight?"

"Sure."

As he walked past, he accidentally brushed against her. There was a shock; a tiny but bright electric current ran through her body. He stopped in his tracks and turned around to look her in the eye. The intensity made her stomach drop. He swallowed hard, his Adam's apple bobbing in his throat. She bit her lip. "I'm... I've... I'll see you later," he said, and turned tail out the door.

Claire sighed, resisting the urge to go after him. Instead, she headed towards Delia and Janine, who were talking about the compound.

"Shall we?" Delia said when she saw her, and led them towards an outdoor trail, paved with flagstones. Giant palm leaves hanging overhead.

"Here we are, the Art Lodge," Delia said, introducing them to the space.

Inside, there was enough space to set up five people and their easels. The area was well organized and clean. Delia pointed towards the back of the lodge. "The paper is handmade using a technique based on ancient, pre-conquest Aztec and Mayan paper." She explained that even having a recipe was incredible since so much information was destroyed by the Spaniards. The brushes were handmade by students using select quality hairs from local animals like the jaguar, the tapir, even howler monkeys. There was a manual pottery wheel in the corner, which Darren had requested specifically.

"Do you know when the shamans are coming?" asked Janine.

"Tomorrow afternoon," Delia said. "You'll be working with locals to create the costumes. Claire, you'll be working with Bruno. He'll be the one to make sure we get through the ATM in a safe and secure manner. He's also working with National Geographic, making sure they set up the cameras properly, as to not damage anything inside the cave." She walked towards the back of the studio where a basic kitchen was setup and a two-top bistro table nestled into the nearest corner.

Delia swung the bedroom door open. Claire saw one large room, split in two by a set of bookshelves and cupboards. The room was not at all what Claire had expected. She'd anticipated her own room. To be fair, the partition gave quite a bit of privacy—she couldn't see into the other room, but she could hear. Each side had its own closet, a queen-sized bed, and a large window which looked out into the jungle.

"We'll see you tonight, yes?" Delia asked, but did not hesitate for an answer. "In addition, let's meet tomorrow morning at nine. I'll hand over existing schedules and other logistics."

After she left, Claire entered the kitchenette and filled up the electric tea pot with water. "Would you like some tea?"

"Sure." Janine sat at the bistro table. Claire plugged the kettle in and turned it on.

Janine rummaged through a wooden box of tea bags on the table. "What can I get you? There's green, English breakfast, peppermint?"

"I'll take peppermint. I need a pick me up."

"Me too. That flight was brutal. LA to Phoenix and then a red eye to Miami. Miami to Belize. I'm exhausted." Janine removed the plastic packaging from the bag and met her eyes. "I'm just going to say it. Claire, when I first saw you, I nearly dropped my bags. You look almost exactly like my sister."

"Oh? Is she in LA with you?"

"No, she died," Janine responded without emotion. "Cancer. She wasn't my blood sister—foster care—but she was my real one, if you know what I mean." A faraway look came over her face as she slapped the tea bag gently against her palm. "Fifteen maybe sixteen years ago now, we were still teenagers. I miss her. She wanted me to go back to school, do what I love. So I did."

"My parents died too," Claire said, surprised at her candor. She hadn't expected to talk about them with someone she'd never met. It felt easy, like they'd been friends for a long time. "I was in foster care too. No one wanted..." Claire stopped, mid-sentence. Tightness gripped her chest, like she couldn't breathe.

"You too? Are you okay?"

"I'm fine," Claire said. She caught her breath.

"Out of curiosity, how did you get involved with the project?" Janine asked as she handed Claire the teabags.

"My friend Xander. We went to the same college where I got my degree in Art History and Anthropology. I used to date Bruno back in college, can you believe it?"

"And now both of you are here? Life is so funny sometimes. I had something like that happen in Chicago. I was waiting for a flight and a girl I knew in high school walked off the plane. I mean, that's crazy. Nobody believed me, though."

"I do," Claire said.

Janine gave her a small laugh. She placed the teabags into

respective cups and handed them to Claire. "Then what? After college, you…"

"I was an intern briefly, then I worked for Bjorn and Annika out in New York with the Apfel Gallery and had my own shop in Brooklyn. But, uh, that ended. Now I am consulting for the Reade Street Gallery and working as a program manager for the museum."

Janine stopped what she was doing and cocked her head when Claire had mentioned Reade Street Gallery, but said nothing. Did she know the gallery's hidden purpose to dabble in the black market? At the airport, Bruno had acted weird around her. *What was it about her?*

"Anyway," Claire continued, making a mental note to Google Janine that evening, "this project came up, and it was an opportunity for me to be a part of something historic. And a free trip to Belize."

"I know, right? I wanted the experience for my resume. And a free trip as well," she said, winking. "I'm a senior this year. Non-trad student, I had a career before coming here. I used to work for the CIA, if you can believe that. I quit, a year before graduation. My majors were art history, politics, and Russian Literature. Not a big job market, so when the CIA came a callin', I answered." She paused, and Claire watched her brief moment of silence, wondering what memories she was reliving. Janine looked at her with what seemed to an expression of sadness and maybe even regret. "I had to quit," she continued, "but I can't put CIA on my resume. They won't verify my position, standard policy. No one would believe me if I did. Anyway, with a seven-year gap on my resume, no one wanted to hire me so I enrolled at Citrus Valley. Besides, my sister's dream was to see me with a college degree, so I had two reasons to go back."

The electric kettle buzzed. Claire would definitely be Googling Janine and Rex. She filled the cups with the hot water and handed Janine the cup by the handle. "Careful, it's hot."

Janine took the body of the cup with both hands, but didn't flinch at the heat.

"Do you know Darren?" Claire asked, wanting to add she thought he was a jerk, but stayed quiet.

Janine set the cup down. "He's a creep. I've met him around LA, on the art scene, but he's harmless."

"That's true. More bark than bite." Claire added a splash of milk to her tea. "I'm pretty tired. Do you mind if I take this back to my room?"

"Sure," Janine said. "Can we walk together to the pavilion when it's time? There is something I'd like to ask you."

AFTER HER SHOWER, Claire went to the room and pulled the privacy curtain closed. She put on a bra and underwear. She traced her finger along the top of the scar. Her suitcase on the bed, she retrieved her wallet and took out the money, organizing the crisp hundred-dollar bills into piles of a thousand, and separated out five thousand dollars to hide.

The utilitarian room had two hiding choices: under the mattress or in the dresser. Neither choice was great. Unable to decide, she ran a hand through her hair. She circled the room once more. There was a small sink and mirror in the room. Claire considered wrapping the money with a rubber band and hanging it down the drain with a string. In foster care, she had mastered the technique. She wrapped the money into a tight wad and secured it with rubber bands she brought, but the whole thing was too big for the sink drain.

The ceiling didn't have any tiles that she could pop open. The heating register was old fashioned and she didn't have the tools to open it. She stopped in front of the dresser. She didn't have duct tape to hide it under a drawer, the masking tape in the art room wouldn't be strong enough. And so, she put the three-inch-thick wad in a sock and hid it in her hiking boots. The rest of the money she put back into her wallet, and the wallet back in her tote. Claire took a sip of her tea; it had cooled enough so she could have a proper drink.

Claire took the towel off and dressed in a pair of shorts and a t-shirt. Laying on the bed, she unlocked her phone and checked her emails. She'd sent fifteen emails out to amateur archeologists, hoping to connect with someone in Belize. In the email, she had asked if anyone was participating in a dive, if they were finding any objects, and so forth. No one had responded to her query.

Disappointed, but not surprised, she moved on. Claire needed more information on Janine, and Googled her. The first hit was an article about an illegal dig. Rex, her boss, had been the subject of an investigation by the FBI Art Crimes unit. He was accused of illegally digging Native American artifacts near Joshua Tree National Park in California. The article indicated that, according to other witnesses, Janine Jankowski had taken several items with her. When no other artifacts showed up at the school, her apartment was searched. The missing objects, the journalists guessed, had been sold on the black market, but there was no proof.

If the article was true, Janine might be here using the "work study" as some kind of cover, but really scouting for something a little more nefarious. She should at least ask Janine what she was doing here. She might tell her the truth. They could partner together.

CHAPTER ELEVEN

Lucia

*L*ucia sat back in her chair and, for a few minutes, relaxed. Her office was in a new development off the Brooklyn pier with a view of the Hudson River and the lower west side. She liked being able to swivel around on her ergonomic chair and see horizon, water, building, and sky in every direction out of her floor to ceiling windows. Man-made smashed between nature. There was a single knock on her door. Lucia said enter but didn't turn to see who it was.

"Boss," said Tony, one of her top henchmen. "Claire Townsend is out of the country. A plane ticket was purchased for her by the American Museum of Natural History. She left for Belize yesterday, for a job. You want me to follow up?"

"Anything else pop up?"

"Her bank account was emptied. Not closed. There's six hundred and twelve left in the account. She took $6,382 with her across the border."

"Smart. She got through customs without getting stopped." Lucia turned around to face Tony. On her desk, she had a Stealth MacBook and nothing else. She preferred a single laptop, even though she had a complex network that could bounce signals all over the world. Her connections included a direct hack into airline, bus, and train systems. She could easily get phones tapped, cloned, or GPS'd. A former client helped to build her network, and did an incredible job, and in thirteen days. With the right motivation, of course.

On her laptop, she could type in someone's name, and a dataset summary returned information such as the names and addresses of relatives and friends, children, if any. The dataset included a financial summary bank and credit card statements, 401k's, stock portfolios, the works. She had the option to remotely activate a GPS locator on phones, take a picture, and turn on voice recordings.

But what she found after her first year of being a loan shark was that people were sadly predictable. She had an algorithmic program that responded with statistical physical responses and scenario outcomes on an individual, but what good was it when her estimates were spot on? For some reason, she had a feeling about Claire. Sometimes an individual acted with innovations and miracles happened. That was what she lived for. To *see* the moment.

"Boss? What do you want to do?"

"Any other conversations we should be aware of?" she asked.

"She's been added to the museum staff as a paid employee. Program manager."

Lucia laughed. Poor Claire. She was once the top salesperson for an exclusive German art gallery, getting ready to sell wallpaper in Barneys, her boutique was about to go mainstream, and now she was a lowly manager for the American History museum. What a sad trajectory. Had Lucia not forced her hand, Claire would still be in her apartment wallowing. But look at her now, on her feet, in Belize, traveling already. She was happy with Claire's actions. Instead of being completely paralyzed by fear, she was moving forward.

"Go to Belize, Tony. Make sure she knows we are watching. A level two warning should do that. And double check that the GPS locator works; they have spotty issues there."

"Sure boss. Anything else?"

"You're the best. Glad to have you on my team."

Tony gave a brief, single nod, then left the office. Lucia swiveled back around and scanned the view again. She found a street between two buildings and watched the constant flow of people walking down the sidewalk. Her eye followed the view up. The space between the buildings grew narrow as she looked up to the blue sky, but the lack of raptors in the city surprised her. With all the pigeons around, why didn't hawks circle the city?

CHAPTER TWELVE

Claire

At seven forty-five, Claire and Janine walked to the pavilion for the welcome presentation. Glossy palm fronds hung over the trail. Cicadas buzzed in the distance. She wondered what question Janine wanted to ask her as they engaged in small talk. Ever since she had learned of Janine's possible involvement in the black-market trade from the Google search, Claire had so many questions. Was Janine here to find artifacts? Or to sell them? Would she be interested in working with her and the Reade Street Gallery? Should she even ask? They barely knew each other. Could she trust her?

When they arrived, Janine said her goodbyes and sat on a couch, promptly pulled out her phone and appeared busy. Janine never did bring up her question. Claire was confused, but figured she'd have to do something about it. She didn't have the luxury of time. She'd simply ask Janine if there was any interest in working with her and the Reade Street Gallery.

Claire surveyed the round room of the open-air building. Darren stood near the back with a beer in hand, talking to Bruno. Ruth Ann Zylstra, the costume designer, had arrived, and was standing by herself. In her early fifties, she wore her hair in a tight bun near the base of her neck, which allowed the chunky turquoise necklace and earrings to be more prominent. Claire introduced herself and asked if she needed anything.

"You look like someone interesting," Ruth Ann said with a smile that reminded Claire of innocent trouble. "Come with me to get a drink."

"We're excited to have you, Ms. Zylstra."

"Not as glad as I am to be here. I can't tell you how boring LA has been. A slump, darling. I've been in a slump." At the drink table, Ruth Ann pointed to a bottle of red wine, "Right there—that will cheer me up." Claire retrieved the open bottle and poured her a glass. "Ruth Ann, I'd like you to meet Janine."

"Cheers," Ruth Ann lifted her glass and so did Janine. "Let's hope things warm up around here. I need some inspiration."

Darren approached the three of them. "So, Claire, how are you going to bounce back in New York?"

Claire cocked her head and filled a glass of wine. She handed it to him with a wink. "Darren, you know I can't tell you."

He smiled sheepishly, then walked away. Claire tried not to be exasperated.

"Don't worry about him. More bluster than a barking dog." Ruth Ann took a sip of her wine then straightened her back and jutted her chin out. "No matter what happened, you can go back to New York any damn time you like. It's a big city with a short memory. Or move to LA. Do whatever you like."

The last place she wanted to be was New York. But LA had a nice ring to it. Claire gracefully ate a canapé, then checked her watch. The presentation was starting in a few minutes. She suggested Ruth Ann and Janine find a seat before excusing herself. She hooked up her laptop to the BIFA projector. The words American Museum lit up on a screen in front of her. Bruno was setting up a stand and placing a headdress on it. It was a beautiful crown, the base made of solid gold, and accented with jade pieces and seven rubies at least three or four carats each. Bright feathers lined the back of it for a dramatic display of the sun.

Claire eyed the piece, but dismissed the idea of taking it. She'd never do that to Bruno. Delia was at the podium. "Welcome everyone. I'll get right to it. We'll start with Claire and the American Museum of Natural History. Then I'll talk about the art school, introduce the main artists, then introduce Bruno and Janine, and last we'll have a Q and A session. Claire Townsend, please come up and introduce yourself."

Claire took out a piece of paper which she had written her speech on during the flight. She adjusted the microphone, angling it closer. She hadn't spoken in front of an audience in a while, and nervous adrenaline filled her body. She glanced around the room and her eyes settled on Bruno. His dark brown eyes were intent on her, and she felt calmer.

"Hi guys. I'm Claire," she said, and read off the paper. "The reason we are here is because the American Museum of Natural History will be filming an authentic rendition of the Mayan creation myth, the Popol Vuh, inside the ATM cave. Our goal, by working with the local shamans and amazing artists like yourselves, is to produce an authentic reproduction of the Classic Mayan origin story of how the world was formed." Confident, she put the paper back in her pocket. "The Classic Mayans sang and danced as a way to express themselves, so Ruth Ann here is going to create jewelry that functions as musical instruments. The instruments will be an organic part of the dance. Is that right, Ruth Ann?"

"Yes it is, darling. And making music is a first for me too, which there aren't very many these days."

A chuckle went through the crowd.

Claire smiled before she continued, "The ceremony will be performed inside the Actun Tunichil Muknal, or as we call it, the ATM, a cave Mayans considered sacred. Darren will make five ceremonial unglazed ceramic pots for each shaman to break. Delia will be our partner to assure access to local volunteers, supplies, and the shamans. Bruno and his brother will guide us to make sure we're safe and don't harm the cave or its original artifacts. Bruno?"

He came up to the stage and Claire handed him the microphone. His fingers clasped it through hers. "Oh," she said under her breath, the warmth of his hand surprising her. "Thanks. I mean, here."

His smile radiated through her, and a ripple went down her spine.

"I'm here in two capacities." Bruno started as she sat in a nearby chair. "First, I'm an expert guide. My whole life I've been in these caves one way or another." He met Claire's eyes. "I can navigate through them with my eyes closed."

Heat flamed through her body, and she felt it rising to her face.

"Second, and equally as important, I'm an archeologist and history professor at California State University out of LA. We were storing a piece for the Museo Popol Vuh out of Guatemala, and when they learned what we were doing, the shaman community got together and decided the lead shaman for the Popol Vuh, who will be playing the role 'Heart of Sky,' should wear the headdress. Ruth Ann will be making similar headdresses for the twins of the story, two boys who travel to the underworld and defeat terrible demons in order to bring the sun, moon, and stars to life."

A murmur that went through the crowd. The participants knew that museums never let anyone use their items for re-creations, and so this made the event doubly special.

"If I may?" Delia said as she came forward. Bruno gave

her the microphone. "This project is bringing the community together in a new way," Delia said, slightly out of breath. Being pregnant apparently didn't leave much room for the lungs. "The lead shaman will be working with the Chilam Balam books as well as the text from a fifteenth century Spanish scholar along with local renditions to build the screenplay. Janine Jankowski is here to help them, and her capacity will be as a director's assistant and work study, under Claire Townsend. I'd like to introduce her. She's from LA Citrus Valley College."

Janine waved to the group. No one would ever mistake her for having a sunny personality. There was something about her, hard and street smart. Was she really in the black-market trade? If she was, getting involved with her—if there was even anything to be involved with—would be complicated, but doable. Better than stealing from Bruno, anyway.

"This event, the Popol Vuh taking place in the ATM cave along with the museum quality headdress, is unprecedented. The icing on this project is something almost of a miracle. Oftentimes when a story about the past is re-created, we can find things from the present day, remnants of the old life. Tell them the story of your family, Bruno."

"Ah yes. The Chilam Balam books, of which there are nine, are detailed account of eighteenth century Mayan life and contains political information along with some myths, including a story that describes the destruction of an old world and the creation of a new one, a Popol Vuh of sorts. Now, the books also describe an account with a king Hunac Ceel—a power hungry king—who wanted to sack Chichén Itzá. He hired protection from Tabasco, Mexico: the Canul family. My ancestors."

On the screen behind him was a picture of a wall-painting on stone. The image was a proud Mayan man sitting on a throne carved from rock. "This is a photo of my ancestor in the Temple of Warriors at Chichén Itzá, just north of here in Mexico. He is sitting on the jaguar throne. These days, my family and I, we do what we can to preserve the Mayan history, to be protectors of the Mayan tradition. It is the reason I chose archeology. This project is close to my heart."

Claire could see Bruno as a protector. It'd be cool to have his familial history be a part of the exhibit. They could title it 'Living ancestors of Ancient Mayans.' Christopher Shali, the museum curator, would be interested; how could he not be? They could go to Chichén Itzá to take pictures of the jaguar throne. Archeology only makes sense with anthropology.

Claire paused for a moment. Chichén Itzá was near Cancun. Could this be a way for her to enter Mexico and make a run for it? Claire's hand covered her mouth. She could have Bruno drive her up to visit the site. Then she'd run. It sounded so easy.

The problem was, once she ran, she wouldn't know where to go. Running wasn't a great idea; Claire had known this when she considered the solution in New York, but was it better than placing her hope on the random chance of finding an artifact worth two hundred thousand dollars? She hated being undecided, but until she had more information, problem solving would be by the seat of her pants.

Bruno clicked a button on the small black remote in his hand, and her attention returned. On the screen, there was a picture of several people on inner tubes in a dark cave. Head-lamps were the only source of light. In the picture, Bruno had on swim shorts with a life vest. *Those biceps.* Even in the dark, he looked good. "Tomorrow morning, we're visiting Xunantunich, a Classic Mayan temple to understand how they lived. Later in the week, we'll explore the Cave of the Dead, shown on the picture here, to help you get a sense of what it was like for the Mayan shamans. We want you to understand how they viewed the context of beliefs regarding birth and death. Finally, we will go into the ATM to perform the Popol Vuh."

"Thanks, Bruno," Delia said. "Tomorrow, please be here at eight a.m. And be sure to wear the right attire; swim suits, swim trunks, water shirts, whatever is appropriate. Until then, enjoy the food and wine."

Everyone stood to stretch, all eight of them. She really didn't want to wear her suit tomorrow. People would see her scar, they'd stare. They'd want to ask, but polite conversation wouldn't allow for it. With a deep breath, she was able to curtail the beginnings of a panic attack.

The crowd moved to the drinks and appetizer table. Claire was adding a few cubes of cheese to her plate when Darren came up next to her. She was about to turn away when he said, "No more free cheese for you in New York."

"New York has a short memory. I'll be fine." Was he going to be a jerk the whole time?

"Theodore Paul Frederick Champlin won't forget," he said. "I heard the reverberations of it all the way out in New Mexico. And here you are. A *program manager*."

Ruth Ann appeared at the table, and motioned to Darren. "Oh come on, give her a break. Everyone has a little skeleton in their past. I'm sure you can appreciate that?"

He turned to her, and instead of glaring, he smiled. "Me? Skeletons? I like a woman who knows repartee."

"That, darling, is something I am very good at. Do wait by the fireplace, I'll bring you a glass."

As soon as Darren was out of earshot, Ruth Ann whispered, "Darling, I think Bruno is coming for you. He is ravishing. If only I was twenty years younger." She took the glass of wine from Claire that she had just filled. "Let me have that. I'll give it to the beast," she said as she turned away and walked towards Darren.

"How do you like Belize so far?" Bruno asked.

"It's beautiful. I forgot how much I missed the jungle when we..." she said, referencing a trip they had taken together in Guatemala. Realizing that she might have brought up their past without wanting to, she tried to change the subject. "I was wondering what you said about Chichén Itzá. Canuls on the jaguar throne. That's pretty amazing."

"Yeah. My family is considering DNA testing to find other Canuls."

"I'd love to see the *Temple of the Warrior*. How come this story isn't more prevalent? About the ancestry?"

"They told the children Mayan royalty was a fairy tale to guard the truth from the Spaniards. Modern Mayans don't believe it's real. We are trying to change that, to reclaim our heritage."

"Any chance we could go up there to see it? It has relevance to the project. The museum would be interested in the connection, especially on a project of this nature." Technically it wasn't an outright lie. She was sure Shali would appreciate the Chichén Itzá angle to add depth to the Popol Vuh exhibit.

"I'm not sure I want to add that aspect to the exhibit. It might detract from the Popol Vuh."

"Consider it?" she said, meeting his eyes. "I think Shali would love to add a modern angle. We could bring the Nat Geo guys along. They might want a few shots for the magazine."

"All right," he said, clinking the edge of her glass, "I'll consider it. But only on one condition."

"What's that?"

"Tell me why."

Claire's mind raced from getting fired at Apfel, to Lucia, to wanting to run away to Mexico. She feigned ignorance. "I'm not sure what you're getting at," she said. "I want to see the paintings. It would be cool to show your genealogical roots as part of the exhibit. I'm the anthropologist here, you know."

"That's all?" he asked again, smiling broadly. "What about us? You and me again? Road trip."

"Maybe I'll share some Oreos with you," Claire said, genuinely laughing. He sounded just like he did back in college, happy, excited. A warm glow spread through her, surprising her in its intensity. Why did she choose New York all those years ago? How did she get so far from her original goals?

She'd love to go on a road trip with him, to see what could happen between them, but if he drove her to Mexico and she ran, he would never believe that her attraction—her feelings for him—were real. He'd believe that she was using him. *Her feelings don't matter.* She was here to solve a problem. The Lucia problem.

"It's really good to see you again, Claire," Bruno said.

"You too." With a swig of her wine, she tried to relax. *Don't lie to yourself. You still love him.* Instead of feeling like she'd secured another solution in resolving the Lucia problem, she felt scattered, as if she had too many irons in the fire.

"Are you okay?" he asked, holding his hand out to her.

She wanted to take his hand, to believe everything would be okay. Instead, she rubbed the back of her neck. She shrugged and said with a hint of false bravado, "Just a little jet lagged. I'll see you tomorrow."

CHAPTER THIRTEEN

Claire

The next morning, Janine, Claire, Bruno, Darren, and Ruth Ann piled into the commuter van. Ed, the driver, started the eighty-kilometer drive to the Xunantunich Mayan ruins. They were not exciting from an archeological perspective, Bruno explained, except for a few panels and a stucco frieze found under some rubble. Other Mayan sites were more impressive, but Xunantunich was closest to BIFA. "That doesn't mean what you are about to see isn't impressive, though," Bruno said.

Claire wanted to add to the conversation, share something cool from an anthropological perspective since she had studied it in college before moving to New York, but nothing came to mind. She was tired from a night of restless sleep. They turned off a two-lane highway and into the small village of Benque Viejo del Carmen and approached the Mopan River. It wasn't a large river, roughly eighty feet across, but it was deep. The olive-green water was tame and full of fish and turtles.

At the entrance of the Mayan site, run-down shacks sold cheap trinkets along a makeshift boardwalk. The buildings were occupied with Guatemalan refugees drinking their morning coffee. The other side of the shoreline, the destination, was covered by leafy trees that hid iguanas and chirping birds. Ed drove onto a flat wooden boat with a tin roof. The hand-cranked ferry would take twenty minutes to cross.

Claire stepped outside of the van. The air was a bit muggy, but there were no mosquitos. The rest of the crew had opted to stay in the van. From an open window, she could hear Bruno giving a basic overview of the Preclassic Mayans in Belize, their trading routes and alliances.

"Why do you suppose the Mayan civilization fell?" Darren asked. "It sounds like they could have banded together instead of all that fighting."

Darren sounded genuinely interested, but whether his interest was in the Mayans or Ruth Ann was hard to tell.

"Good question, darling," said Ruth Ann who seemed smitten by him. An interesting development.

"Sure," said Bruno. "There's new proof of a catastrophic drought throughout Mesoamerica. Societies—in times of disaster—tend to act suspicious and act in accordance. Survival of the fittest. The kings were power hungry. Instead of banding together to fight a common enemy, they fell apart deciding who would be king of the new empire."

The ferry ride jolted to a stop when it arrived on the other side of the bank. Claire got back into the van, and they drove another hour on a bumpy, dusty road. Ed pulled into a nearly empty dirt parking lot. Nearby was a museum and visitor center which looked like an Old West town with faded wooden structures and covered boardwalks. The sign was a rescued 1x10 plank with the word Xunantunich burned into the wood. The place was deserted and quiet. They spent a half hour or so at the museum, reading about the cultural aspects of everyday Mayan life as it related to the ruins. The artifacts on site were archeologically valuable but worthless to Reade Street.

Once the ad-hoc tour was over, the group started uphill on

yet another dirt road towards the ruins. A morning fog had settled within the canopy of cieba trees, which seemed unbearably tall to her. The canopy branched out from the trunks like an umbrella, blocking the sun. A strange vibration quivered through the air. The crew tentatively glanced at each other. There was a sense of foreboding, of dangerous things yet to come. Ruth Ann stepped carefully and slowly, her eyes never leaving the trees. Darren stayed in front of Ruth Ann, his shoulders and arms tense, ready to defend. Janine didn't seem perturbed by the sound, but rubbed the inside of her wrist.

A loud, ominous shrill echoed through the leaves, as if an invisible supernatural force was coming. The fog intensified the noise. It was coming at her, from all angles. It reminded her of the music that plays just before a bloody murder in a B horror movie. A sound that warned you to run and don't ever you dare look back. Claire felt it in her chest and held her hands to her heart. Suddenly, she wanted to leave, to run.

Bruno took her hand. Scared, she instinctively withdrew it, but he held on, and squeezed three times. That was something they used to do when they had dated. Whenever she was nervous or scared, Bruno would squeeze her hand three times. He was one of the few guys she ever trusted with her whole story. She told Bruno that her mom used to do that when she was little to give her courage. If she'd been afraid of something, first day of school or wanting to go on a waterslide, her mom would squeeze her hand with the message that she was safe, that she was loved. The first time Bruno did it was on the rafting trip in West Virginia. She'd been scared of getting into the boat, and he'd squeezed her hands.

"Howler monkeys," said Bruno, gently dropping her hand to talk to the others. "Howlers are represented in the Popol Vuh. One of them is the hunter's son, representing writers and sculptor; the other symbolizes magic."

"Guys like me, right?" said Darren. "I never knew I was a

howler." The statement generated a murmur of laughs from the group. Claire could have sworn she saw Ruth Ann turn red.

"Magic?" asked Ruth Ann. "What kind of magic?"

Bruno shrugged. "The monkeys are incredible creatures. When they howl, their jaws open wide and their sharp teeth are bared. It's most impressive."

"Sounds terrifying," Ruth Ann said.

As they walked on, the clouds cleared. The sun came out erasing the shadows; the howler monkeys moved on. The group remained quiet until reaching the outskirts of the site. The original buildings were constructed on flat grounds. A series of crumbling, grayish-black buildings made of stone were sinking into the earth. Bruno pointed to the right, to a rectangular building on the outskirts, and said it was a trading center. To his left, he said was the Pok-A-Tok court.

They walked across a grassy plain that used to serve as a plaza and stopped at the Pok-A-Tok court. Back in the Classic Mayan days, this court was used to play a game which modern society would recognize as a form of basketball.

The court was a rectangular grass field about half the size of a basketball court. Bordered on two sides were forty-five-degree gray-stone walls. In the center of each wall, there was a flat, circular stone with a hole in the center that looked similar to a basketball hoop. The goal of the game was to get a hard rubber ball into the rock hoop. Claire couldn't imagine the dexterity needed to win. The hoop was at least six feet halfway up the angled wall, and it was positioned vertical instead of horizontal. Losers were most likely beheaded. When death was on the table, a person could do amazing things. This, she knew.

"In Popol Vuh, the twins go to the underworld. Jealous gods cut off their heads and used them to play the game which they believed was Pok-A-Tok. In a cunning maneuver, the twins replaced the heads they were using as a ball with pumpkins and put their own heads back on."

Claire shuffled her feet. The story Bruno was telling made her uncomfortable.

"Ahead you'll see El Castillo." Bruno pointed to the largest building on the ruin. The façade was crumbling, and revealed river stones stacked one atop the other like a brick wall. "The square form of the building architecturally resembles a castle rather than a pyramid, hence the name."

They walked towards the building, and Bruno pointed out some of its key aspects. "The frieze on El Castillo is in beautiful shape, well-cut at one time, and fairly clear, but the edges have crumbled. The symbols and hieroglyphics represent the sun god Kinich Ahau."

She followed Bruno but lagged behind, and was the last one in the group. On the backside of El Castillo, she saw steep stairs cut into the stone of the temple which led up at least two stories tall.

"At the top, El Castillo has possible ceremonial sites for human sacrifice," Bruno said. "Let's go up."

The steps were gray-stone and narrow, barely enough room to stand on. A person could fall here. Her throat went dry, and she swallowed. Claire wasn't sure if she wanted to go. She used to get panic attacks right after her parents died, when adrenaline kicked in, when she was scared. They'd tapered off the last few years, but had come back. Since the most recent attack in her apartment, she was afraid another one might happen again. *I am not going to live like this.*

"Are you okay, Claire?" asked Janine. "You look a bit peaked."

"I'll be okay," Claire said tentatively, "but will you walk behind me?"

"Of course."

The group had started their ascent. Claire was next, and

Janine behind her. The steps were steeply unnatural to human measure, so she leaned as close as she could against the wall as there were no handrails. She watched her feet and lifted her knees high. Claire found a rhythm that worked for her; step up, lean to the wall and breathe, step up, lean to the wall and breathe. Just as she was about to take the last step, a shadow crossed her feet. Claire looked up to see a hawk swoop low. Her concentration broke, and she slipped. Janine caught her from behind before she lost her balance. Once she was stable, she clung to the wall with her eyes closed.

"We're almost there," Janine said.

Claire turned; with an exhale, she took the last step and then quickly walked to the center of El Castillo, the safest point possible and away from the edges. Janine came up behind her and touched her forearm. "Don't worry. You're safe."

"I don't believe you," Claire said with the barest of smiles. "I'm fine. Let me catch my breath."

Ruth Ann and Darren headed towards them. "Is everything okay?" Ruth Ann asked. Darren just stared, no doubt, she was sure, thinking of something horrible to say.

"What are you doing, Janine?" Bruno said as he approached.

"Give her a break," Claire said, harsher than she'd intended. "She was helping."

"Okay, okay," he said, backing off and holding both hands up in surrender.

"I'm going to go down," Claire said. She was on the verge of a panic attack and did not want to have one here, on the top of a Mayan building. Where human sacrifices were held, no less.

"We'll come with you," Bruno said.

"No. No need to. I'll be fine. Bruno, finish your spiel for the Popol Vuh, it's important. I'll be at the Pok-A-Tok court."

"I'll go with you," Janine said. "You'll need help."

"Are you sure?" Bruno asked, touching her shoulder.

"I'll be fine," Claire said, turning into him. He gave her a warm hug. The touch of his skin, the pressure of his chest against her, relieved her anxiety.

"Thanks, Bruno," Claire said, "I'm good now. She turned to Janine, "Let's get me down."

Bruno gave Claire a long glance and she nodded to him, as if to reassure him everything would be all right.

Claire walked to the edge, keeping her eyes focused on Janine. She tried not to shake too much, to stay in control of her body, but adrenaline spiked, causing her heart to beat erratically. Claire took quick breaths, Lamaze breathing, and focused on her feet and the stairs and worked her way down.

"Whoa," Claire said when they reached the bottom. Her hands shook. She was embarrassed and rubbed her palm to calm herself. "Can we walk?"

"How long have you been afraid of heights?"

The two women walked toward the ball court where Mayans played Pok-A-Tok for life or death. "Yeah," Claire said, "I'm not really afraid of heights. I get panic attacks. Not to be rude, but can we change the subject?"

"I think Bruno likes you," Janine said as if it were the most obvious thing, with a teasing smile. "He's *hot*."

Claire stiffened at first. She didn't want to talk about Bruno, but then she looked at Janine's smiling face and softened. "Okay. You're right. He is hot."

"Do you like him?" Janine asked.

"I don't know. I mean, I do," Claire said, lifting her hands as if she were helpless, "but I'm going back to New York City. He lives in LA. And besides, I already dated him."

"That's right, I forgot you mentioned it. How'd you meet?"

"Back in college. If it didn't work then, it's not going to work now. The airport was the first time I'd seen him in five years." She rubbed her forearms and couldn't help the smile that appeared on her face, even as she tried to keep it from happening.

"You never know. Life is funny sometimes," Janine said. "It's cool that his family, his ancestors, are Mayan."

"I think Shali would appreciate that angle. The Nat Geo guys could film inside the warrior temple. I asked Bruno if we should go up to Cancun."

Janine nodded. "Shali would love it. A cross between anthropology and genealogy."

"Yeah," Claire said, knowing now was the time to move the discussion towards the black-market trade. She wasn't sure if she should trust this woman she'd met less than forty-eight hours ago, but options were sparse. "Speaking of galleries and museums. I wanted to ask you something about the Reade Street Gallery."

"What would you like to ask?" Janine said, stopping to sit on a short stone wall. Behind her was the slanted wall of the Pok-A-Tok court, carved with Incan symbols and a stone hoop.

Claire tried to appear nonchalant while assessing different ways to ask. "Maybe you've heard about their reputation?"

"I have," Janine brushed the front of her neck. "Does Bruno know you have connections to Reade Street?"

"No," Claire said, stepping back. Bruno would detest her if he ever found out she was making a deal to sell artifacts. He'd think she was lower than pond scum. But she needed this deal to get the money and pay Lucia. This was *her life* she was dealing with. "God, no. Look, I don't have a lot of time."

"I do," Janine said.

"Fine. What do you want to know?"

"Do you trust the gallery?" Janine asked.

Claire walked along the edge of the Pok-A-Tok field. She swung her foot and kicked the grass. "Can you imagine having to play a game for your life like that?"

"That *is* life," Janine said flatly. "What about Reade Street? Who do you know there?"

"My contact came from someone unexpected. An old coworker, David, who worked with me at the Apfel Gallery. He gets a cut, so he's vested."

"A cut of what?" Janine asked.

"Cut the bullshit. You said you knew about Reade Street."

"I *am* interested in Reade Street. But I need you to articulate what you are looking for."

"I have a gallery interested in selling artifacts. If you have any, we should discuss business."

"It's possible," Janine said.

Claire kicked a small rock and it bounced against the stone border Janine sat on. "An article I read about you described a man named Rex. What's your relationship with him?"

"He's my boss."

"Is he going to cause problems? I'm sure he's under watch."

"True. But he was never proven guilty."

"Do you think anyone is watching you? Are you a liability?"

"No. I used to work for the CIA. I *know* how to be discrete. It's why they didn't arrest me."

Claire nodded. Her words rang true. She had been questioned by authorities, according to the articles she read, and let go after being arrested. "Do you have any items at the moment?"

Janine regarded her before speaking. "I will know tomorrow morning."

Claire knew it was risky to trust Janine, but she only had eleven days until Lucia's money was due. If she said no to the opportunity, there might not be a second chance.

"You're ready to negotiate?" Janine said, standing, and taking the offensive position.

Claire stuck out her hand, "I am."

Janine shook it. "If all goes well, clear the schedule for Tuesday morning." She was about to say more when they heard the rest of the group walking towards them.

"Hey ladies. Why are you shaking hands?" asked Darren. "You going to play Pok-A-Tok?"

The few laughs they got covered the tension between her and Claire. Bruno didn't seem to like what was going on between them. His arms were crossed and he looked upset.

"Sure. Bruno?" Janine asked. "You got a ball we can play with?"

CHAPTER FOURTEEN

Bruno

After the Xunantunich tour, Bruno had plans to have a drink with his brother Alberto. As everyone was unloading at BIFA, Claire announced to the group, "I know everyone has different schedules this afternoon. Lunch is catered and waiting for us in the dining room. Don't forget to be here at the pavilion at ten tomorrow morning. We will be tubing the River of the Dead."

Claire said her goodbyes to the group, and he watched her closely as she passed by Janine. He could have sworn a knowing glance passed between them. They both acted weird at the Pok-A-Tok field and were quiet during the bus ride home. He'd ask Claire about it later, when she was alone, but right now, he had a chance to ask Janine. "Got a minute?" he asked as he got out of his Jeep.

Janine turned slowly. She had on gold aviator sunglasses; he could see the reflection of his Jeep in her lenses. Tall and athletic, she was gorgeous, in a glossy magazine way. Brown hair fell to the middle of her back.

"I want to ask you something," he said. Normally, if he saw anyone shaking hands, he wouldn't think anything of it. But this was Janine, and he felt an overwhelming need to protect Claire. From what? He wasn't sure. He almost said 'never mind' and got back in his Jeep, but didn't.

Her face was a solemn expression. Instead of asking what he wanted, she raised her eyebrows and sighed, as if he were an annoyance.

"Okay," he said, drawing out the word. "I was just curious why you and Claire were shaking hands today. Are you guys going out later?"

"We shook hands. Not a big deal."

But it was a deal, wasn't it? It was that kind of handshake. "Don't do anything you'll regret."

"Why do you care about her so much?"

He stepped back. Why did he care? Claire had left him. She had wanted other things. But he didn't want Janine to know about their history, he didn't want her to see how it affected him, use it against him, or worse, use it against her.

Janine stepped close to him, so close that he could smell her perfume, musky and cloudy. She leaned in. Janine lowered her sunglasses to the tip of her nose and looked over the rims. "Your pupils are dilated, Bruno. You're breathing fast. I'll bet your heart is racing. Oh my, Bruno. You want me." She smiled ever so slowly, cat-like.

"Get the fuck away from me," he said, almost falling. "Nothing like that. Claire and I go way back."

She pushed her sunglasses back up and smirked.

"Stay away from her," Bruno said. "You're gonna get your due, Janine. Karma is coming."

"Sorry," she said, putting her sunglasses on. "You're going to have to do better."

Bruno glared at her. He got back into his Jeep and pulled away, leaving a cloud of dust. He checked the rearview mirror; she was waving to him, her lips curved upward into a sadistic smile. He squeezed his steering wheel and focused on the road ahead of him. He should let it go. But he couldn't. He stuck his hand up in the air and extended his middle finger.

PRESSING THE PEDAL HARD, Bruno flew down the highway. Once his heart rate slowed, he eased off the gas, getting hold of himself. He hadn't been sure before, about Janine, but now he was. Whatever she was up to likely included Claire. And knowing Janine, it was something nasty. He hadn't thought it important, but now, he was wishing he'd gotten McNally to spill everything he knew about Janine.

He drove into the small village of Belmopan. The main road was so old, the blackness of the asphalt had leached out, and a layer of dust had settled on top, so thick Bruno wondered if it was even a road still. He parked next to a roadside shack named the Cool Bar. Drug deals between locals took place behind the building, mostly weed, sometimes cocaine. Across the street, a young girl rode bareback on an unkempt brown horse that looked too lazy to be wild.

The place was jungle-weary, too much water and sun. The floorboards were faded gray from the sun and soft from the rain over the years. There were no plate-glass windows, only wooden shutters. Alberto drove up in an open-top Jeep, much like the one Bruno had, and his sudden stop sent dust into the bar. The bartender waved an angry arm at him. "Come on, Mon! It's getting inside!"

"Sorry, mate," Alberto said to the bartender before approaching Bruno. "How's my Irish twin?" joked Alberto, his palm open for a handshake.

Bruno stood and clapped his hand, pulling him into a hug. "Doing well, my brother, doing well."

"You dating, my man?"

Bruno hated the question, something Alberto asked every

single time they saw each other. Instead of answering, he said, "Glad you're helping out with the Natural History Museum."

"It'll be an interesting job, for sure. I can't wait to hear the singing in the ATM; that space always seemed like a huge amphitheater when the water's low."

The bartender brought out two cold Belikin beers and set them on the table. Both Bruno and Alberto knew that the Cool Bar served only one drink, so they hadn't bothered to order.

"I'm glad Shali agreed with my suggestion to hire you."

"Me too," Alberto said, lifting his beer to take a short swig. "Mom says there's a private property headed towards closing. The owner wants to find caves. He has plans to open up his own adventure touring company on site. Throw up a few zip lines. That kind of thing."

"Yeah. They like to do that. Where's this one?" Bruno asked. He had pulled out a notebook to write the address and planned to check it against his map later.

"Off Hummingbird Highway, near the others, north. They did aerial photographs and might have found something interesting. The external geology of the land doesn't suggest caves."

"This is Belize, limestone capital of the world. Doesn't need to be a mountain to have a cave."

"You should have gone into geology," Alberto responded with brotherly sarcasm to the professorial answer.

"Mom was the agent?" Bruno asked, ignoring the jab. Their mother owned one of the top real estate agencies in Belize specializing in commercial sales, specifically large acreage or resort sales. Certain owners realized they could cut development costs and streamline project schedules by quietly scouting the land for artifacts and destroying evidence before actually building hotels.

The Canul family kept an eye and an ear out for those people looking to make an easy score, and they had managed to keep their true intention a secret within the community. If anyone knew that the Canuls were out to prevent archeological theft, word would get to the commercial developers and landowners and they'd be out of business. Their strategy was to remain unknown—like Robin Hood or Batman.

"Yeah. She's the real estate lead," Alberto said. "The new owners close on the property next week but won't start excavating until the first of the month. They want to find a cave but avoid NICH until the last possible minute. Luckily, I heard about it before they went off to find their own archeologists."

"They want to push off NICH? Sounds sketchy."

"Mom said they took out an adjustable rate loan, which means they have three months before interest rates recalculate. Last I checked, rates have gone up three quarters of a percent. The owners want movement and completion. Not the NICH, which usually promises delay."

"Three months commercial turn around? Should be doable from my perspective." He took a sip of his beer. "I can get on the property to take the appropriate pictures and site information. I'll reference it with archeology data from surrounding areas. Shouldn't be a problem to get the NICH involved."

Bruno realized he didn't have time to check all the properties out on his list, and he'd need Alberto to help. "I wanted to tell you. Janine, the woman involved with Rex in the illegal dig, is on this job."

"And you're just telling me now?" Alberto said, a look of surprise on his face. "I know you like to take care of things on your own, but this is big."

"Yeah, I have a list of properties that she might target. Could you and some of the crew scout the area?"

"Yeah, of course. I'll come by tonight," Alberto said. "Felicia wants to know if you are staying in Belize after the museum gig is over." Felicia was Alberto's wife.

"Sure, I can. Wanted to let you know, Claire is in town."

"Hell, Bruno. What else are you holding out on? She left you for New York City," he said with disgust.

"We both made choices. Her situation has changed."

"To what end, bruv? I do not wish to see you like that again, Bro. That was way too hard on you."

Bruno took a long swing from his beer and leaned over the table. He was uncertain about his feelings for Claire. He was attracted to her. He was concerned about Janine's "friendly" interest in her. "She was hired on the Popol Vuh job, and she's working with Janine. Feels like karma. Like I'm supposed to be here, with her, good or bad."

"Then you must honor this feeling. Is she working with Janine?"

"I hope not. I can't tell yet, but I need to know."

"Be careful."

"I'll be okay," Bruno said.

"A flood starts with a single drop."

Bruno pursed his lips. Was he going to spy on Janine through Claire? He hadn't thought of it earlier. He didn't want to use her, but he needed to know what Claire was doing in Belize.

CHAPTER FIFTEEN

Janine

*J*anine did not like having to ride in a van with so many people. On the drive back from Xunantunich, Darren raved about howler monkeys symbolizing artists and simultaneously flirted with Ruth Ann Zylstra. Ruth Ann flirted back. Most likely, they were having sex. Or were about to. Janine didn't know if she'd be able to use the situation to her advantage, so she mentally filed it away. Bruno didn't say much, but when he looked in the rearview mirror, his gaze met hers. Instead of giving him a self-satisfied smirk, she turned to watch the palm trees fly by.

At BIFA, Ed parked the van. Claire made an announcement and headed in. Bruno was walking towards her, and she could tell he wanted to talk. She definitely did not want to converse, so she riled him up instead. It was too easy, she thought with a laugh. After he left in a cloud of dust, a vibration rippled from her phone. A text message informed her that a package was ready in Belize City, at a shipping and mail center located next to the cruise ship ports.

She checked her watch before heading to the Art Lodge; it was only one p.m. That would give her enough time to make her appointment if she left now. Janine called Claire over. They talked about Bruno, and Janine could see Claire really liked him, but was nervous. Her tell was big hand gestures. As Claire set up an easel, Janine said, "I've got to run to Belize City. I need to pick up specialized supplies coming in from the States and deliver them to one of the shamans."

One thing she had learned in her former job as a clandestine CIA agent, was that every lie should be truthful as possible.

"Sure. Did you want to go to dinner with us? I need a final count."

"No. I'll be back around eleven p.m., so don't wait up for me."

"I'll make sure Delia knows so she can alert the evening security guard."

"Thanks," Janine said. Before leaving, she grabbed a change of clothes and popped them into a large tote, along with her Pelican camera case. After starting the rental car, she punched an address into the GPS. The drive was uneventful. She passed by a quiet village of plain single-family homes that housed refugees from Guatemala. Children in faded but matching hunter-green and white school uniforms walked towards a cheaply built school. In Belize City, she found the shipping center by the ports. A clerk handed her a box sent from LA Citrus Valley College which contained items needed for the Popol Vuh event.

Janine drove to the shaman's house and dropped it off. Once she finished her errands, she did not go back to BIFA. Instead, she entered a new address into the GPS and started down a two-lane highway. Lumbering trucks with wooden rails passed her, and the sweet smell of oranges emanated from nearby orchards. Just before sunset, she pulled into a jungle resort.

The hotel was beautiful. It was the kind of place where

staff went out of their way to smile at the guests and engage them in questions. She had wanted a place in Belmopan, something less visible. Another CIA clandestine rule: Never be noticed. Blend into the crowd. Be plain. Be forgetful. Rex, her boss, had insisted that convenience was more important, and since he was paying, she had no choice.

The front desk receptionist was peppy, asking all sorts of questions. Was she interested in any excursions? Did she want turndown service? Did she want the meal package? Janine responded promptly: she was excited to be here, no excursions, no meal package, and all she wanted to do was sleep in her room, order room service, and swim in the infinity pool. "I have a job interacting with a *lot* of people so I've come to get away from that." Wink wink. The receptionist nodded with her knowingly.

Janine asked if a package had been delivered. The receptionists returned with a FedEx box and then handed her a key card. Janine thanked her and left. Once she got to her room, she placed the 'do not disturb' sign outside the door.

She closed the curtains, blocking the view of a lush jungle valley. As a former operative, Janine knew how to be discrete. She had expertise knowledge in drug and art related transactions. After retirement, agents were often hired by the wealthy to perform tasks such as influencing key witnesses on important trials to being bodyguards.

Rex Martel had hired her to do a job. Janine placed the Pelican case and FedEx box on the bed. From her tote, she laid out a pair of capri hiking pants and an athletic shirt. The secret hotel room was a way to give her the privacy she needed to communicate with him. They had a call scheduled in three hours at nine p.m. her time, eight p.m. in LA. Janine had arrived early to review her plan and adjust it as needed.

She opened the black, hard plastic Pelican case. It was waterproof, which was beneficial, and she had used it as a weapon before. It contained a DSLR camera, a bundle of hundred-dollar bills secured by a rubber band that equaled twenty-five thousand dollars, two passports with different names and credit cards to match, new sim cards, a packaged straight-hair bobbed blonde wig, a dental insert to change the shape of her profile, binoculars, and an assortment of recording devices. She had considered getting a gun, but this was a job of subterfuge, not coercion.

Rex had hired Janine to frame Bruno to look like he was stealing artifacts and selling them on the black market. The hope was to get jail time, but realistically the goal was to ruin his reputation.

'*Like he did to me,*' Rex had said. Janine knew this was a job based on Rex's desire to hurt Bruno. It was personal to him. Which meant he would make decisions based on emotions rather than logic.

After the incident with the FBI in California, Janine wanted to quit working for Rex. She didn't want to hurt people anymore. She didn't like being angry and making stupid choices. But he wouldn't let her go, something he reinforced with a threat: *If you don't take care of that asshole, Bruno, I'm handing the FBI all the evidence, which implicates you, Janine. And only you.*

That would be the end of any normal career she had hoped for. Rex had promised her that if she did this job, and did it right, that he would walk away. He promised to destroy all the evidence he had of her involvement with the California dig.

Not that she trusted Rex. If he screwed her over, he'd pay.

She thought about ghosting Rex, going off the grid. Except a new life with fake papers required inordinate amounts of time, planning, and diligence. She did not want to be looking over her shoulder. No bullshit life. No double entendres. No hidden secrets. And frankly, she was afraid of Rex. She'd watched him become increasingly obsessed by revenge, hiring bodyguards to protect him from unseen enemies, disparage students with stinging, blunt criticism, verbally assaulting her. By itself, the actions didn't amount to much, but together, the events painted an angry man.

Her former line of work had taught her there were two types of people: killers and non-killers. She had seen the change happen before, and Rex had the classic symptoms. Even though he hadn't executed anyone that she knew of, she knew he was sociopathic borderline psychotic, and his anger was growing such that it wouldn't take much to push him over the edge. If she left, he'd be furious. Most likely, he'd hire someone like her, to go after her. It was easier to do the job and move on.

With a groan, she scratched the back of her neck. *How did she end up here?* She hadn't quit the agency to work for a schmuck like Rex. After quitting the CIA, getting a job was difficult. As a clandestine officer, she was not allowed to put her job experience on her resume. Technically, she could, but who'd believe her? The CIA didn't verify employment.

She ended up with a shitty job selling art at a low-end beach gallery in Marin County and enrolled in LA Citrus Valley College, taking a class or two in archeology. Just like her foster sister would have wanted her to. RIP, Jenny. Fuck cancer. After months of boredom and the same damn question asked by the same damn tourists, she began to miss the money, the adrenaline, the rush of her former life. When Rex, her professor, asked her to "work" for him, she said yes and brushed aside the guilt.

In hindsight, the Bruno job was going down a path she hadn't expected. She'd found herself livid over Bruno, taking easy jabs at him because she was pissed that he arrested her. *How could she have been so stupid to get that close to being caught?* The reality was, Bruno was one of the good guys. He didn't deserve what was going to happen to him. This type of manipulation

—someone using her feelings of anger and retribution for their own purpose and gain—was why she'd left the CIA. *Ugh.* She covered her eyes and rubbed her temples.

This was the job. Instead of thinking about who might be impacted, she focused on the elegance of the plan, how the tiny parts fit together. She pulled out her laptop and plugged in a thumb drive that contained research, and reviewed the existing plan she had to make Bruno look guilty of a crime related to artifacts.

When she started this job nearly six months ago, there were several options. A museum heist was too risky considering all the technology and manpower she'd have to bypass. The juice was not worth the squeeze, as her sister Jenny liked to say. And she couldn't simply place a stolen high-value artifact in his office and call the police with an anonymous tip. The cops would have to know the items were stolen, and they had no way to do that unless a crime had occurred, like a museum heist, and she was back to square one.

Janine had considered selling artifacts to the black market in his name. Her concern was the pesky issue of circumstantial evidence. She needed context. In order for this job to be successful, she required a scenario where all the key pieces fit with one another. When the illegal artifact was found under his name, extenuating circumstances must confirm Bruno's guilt. It made sense to have the crime happen outside of the US, where it would look like an attempt to hide something.

She knew Bruno was from Belize, and had done a generic search on artifacts in his country. On Google, she'd found an article about farmers who were accidentally digging up Mayan artifacts. She knew from experience that commercial developers often bought large tracts of farmland. It was common practice for these companies to hire professionals to come in, excavate and destroy artifacts in order to avoid government oversight. Undeveloped farmland with commercial possibilities was exactly the kind of place to frame Bruno.

She knew from Bruno's dossier that his mother was a real estate agent. If she could plan an illegal dig on a property listed by his mother, that would be perfect. Janine had searched through real estate listings using Mrs. Canul's website. She found two properties that fit her requirements.

Before deciding on which property to use, she switched gears to learn about government oversight and ways she could get Bruno arrested. The NICH, or National Institute of Culture and History, managed all artifact and archeological works within Belize. They had begun to crack down on intended or unintended disruption of Mayan artifacts by creating a new law: upon the closing of a real estate deal, NICH conducted an in-person land survey to identify if any cultural impact or artifacts were present.

So, she'd need an illegal dig on one of his mother's properties that was close to being sold. She had called the number listed on the website and let Mrs. Canul's assistant know she was interested in the two properties. The five-hundred-acre parcel of undeveloped land for sale located in northern Belize was under negotiation. If she was serious, she should come in to take a look.

That was when her plan came together. There were five components: She'd plant Mayan artifacts, supplied by Rex, on the parcel of land. Second, record his mom—and anyone else related to Bruno—coming and going on the property. Third, sell three or four high value items that Rex would supply, to a known black-market antique gallery and list Bruno Canul on the customs declaration form. Fourth, watch the NICH find everything on the land survey and arrest Bruno. Fifth, when NICH performed an investigation of Bruno Canul's activities and found the customs declaration of items sold to a black-market dealer, that was all the corroborating evidence she'd need to assure Bruno's reputation was damaged, if not destroyed. This scenario was the most likely to get him arrested, too.

Her partner, Sal—a former CIA op—had been dispatched a month ago. He'd placed a motion-sensitive camera with the goal of taking video and still pictures of Bruno and his mother on the property. He had found the perfect place to start an illegal dig, somewhere with dirt road access, but still remote. It would look like Bruno was excavating the land for his mother to facilitate a quick sale.

She needed Bruno to be in Belize when NICH surveyed the land, otherwise he'd have plausible deniability. She had gone to the LA Citrus Valley College campus job center and found three Central American jobs. The Popol Vuh open requisition was from American Museum of Natural History and located in Belize. Since her reputation was in the shithole at the moment, she found an adjunct professor, gave her a sob story about clearing her name and that she needed this job. The professor helped make sure she was hired by Christopher Shali as the work study. Then, Janine emailed Bruno the Popol Vuh job requisition from an anonymous email ArtifactsForYou-Too@google.com and made sure her name was listed as the work study. Nine days after she sent the email to Bruno, Shali sent out an updated roster to the team with his name on it.

In order to assure that the NICH "discovered" the illegal dig, she needed to identify the appropriate authorities on the NICH team. Small countries often worked like small towns, and on a hunch, she checked the list of board members. Delia Gamboa, the woman who ran BIFA, was on the board. A bribe may or may not be required, and it was the reason for the twenty-five grand in her Pelican case. But with Claire, she might not have to bribe Delia.

The planning had taken three months to do, and she was in the final tweaking stages. Famished, Janine stopped to order room service for dinner. Roasted chicken, roasted potatoes, and a house salad with no dressing, no dessert, and a Diet Coke. After hanging up the phone, she got back to work.

The last part of her plan required an intermediary person between Bruno and the black market. This was a person Bruno interacted with, and also had ties to illegal trading. Janine's research had come up empty and she had planned to forge customs documents with a bill of sale to a known black-market trader. It was weak, but sufficient. She got lucky with Claire Townsend.

Former girlfriend. Connections to the black market. She was pissed off about having to work this job. She used to sell high end art. So far, Claire's personality appeared to be smart and stubborn. Claire was amenable; a streak in her wanted to please people. She was falling for Bruno, and for Janine, that could be a bonus—or deterrent, she'd have to see. Bruno seemed interested in rekindling *something* with his ex. The FedEx box on the bed contained hard copies of information on Claire—her financials, professional, and background. Within a few hours, she'd know exactly how to position Claire.

Leaning back in her chair, Janine felt dirty. She liked Claire, a lot. She reminded her of Jenny; that was the hardest part. It felt like she was betraying her dead foster sister. Would Jenny be okay with her actions if she knew it would her get away from Rex?

There was a knock on the door. Room service. She put the tray on the nearby dresser, unable to eat. Instead, she went into the bathroom and stripped. Janine flipped a switch for the steam shower. Cloudy air filled the large, floor to ceiling glass. It was everything BIFA was not with relaxing, warm steam and room to move.

After the shower, Janine got dressed. She picked up the FedEx box and set it on the table. In order to generate circumstantial evidence that would make Bruno look guilty, she needed to connect him to a black-market sale. Claire Townsend was a former lover, she had current interactions with Bruno—professional and possibly romantic in nature. She had ties to the black market through Reade Street Gallery, and she'd have the appropriate customs credentials to ship items from Belize to the US.

Could Janine get her to put Bruno's name on the manifest sheets? *Let's see.* Janine opened up the FedEx box. Inside were three manila folders with typewritten labels: CLAIRE FINANCE, CLAIRE PROFESSIONAL, CLAIRE BACKGROUND, and one bio sheet on DAVID JACKSON. Inside was a handwritten note on a Hilton Garden Inn San Diego stationary. 'Pictures on thumb drive.'

The note was paper-clipped to a copy of Claire Townsend's checking account, detailing a series of deposits. Nearly a year ago, Claire had eleven deposits of nine thousand in cash. *Total: one hundred grand. Interesting.* Claire had mentioned that she owned a shop, was this money used to fund it? There were no other angel investors listed, no bank loans, no venture capital infusions, only cash deposits. From her experience, nothing said loan shark more than small incremental deposits of cash. Did she have monthly payments? Indeed, there were another series of thirteen-thousand-dollar withdrawals during the first week of the month.

Janine did the math and figured the interest rate was just over fifty percent. *Definitely loan shark money, or my name isn't Janine Jankowski.* There was no payment in June. Looked like whoever she was paying, she was late. *How much trouble was she in?*

The remainder of her financial paperwork consisted of copies of paychecks from Metropolitan Museum where she had worked as an intern and a copy of a paycheck from Apfel Gallery. *No apparent illegal activities before the loan shark.*

Janine popped in the thumb drive. There were pictures of Claire from boarding school, but nothing before. An old picture of her and Bruno posed on a professional-looking river raft that had been shared on a social media site. *Aw, cute.* A series of promotional pictures from Apfel Gallery, and then numerous hashtags referring to her at #JaqueFail. She found the video and it showed her getting fired.

Claire was in Belize because she was desperate. She didn't have the money to pay the loan shark. Janine rechecked the bank records and saw no thirteen thousand dollar withdrawal after May. Her immediate assumption was she owed around one seventy-five, maybe even two hundred grand now. Getting Claire to sign Bruno's name on the customs declaration would be easy.

She set down the FINANCIALS file and picked up the PROFESSIONAL one. She read a short article in the Brooklyn Times describing the new tenet of a specialty boutique. *Seems Claire went to the loan shark to start up her store instead of saving her money. She's impetuous.* The article stated Claire's parents were alive and well on a farm in Ohio. *What? Claire told me she grew up in foster care.*

Janine wanted to verify Claire's history. From the BACK-GROUND file, she found a set of printed court records. The death certificates of Claire's parents. The will. According to the Brooklyn Times, her parents were alive. *A lie. Claire has no qualms about fibbing.* Her senior year, she attended a moderate boarding school with a scholarship. Janine flipped through the remaining papers: her college degrees (Art History, Anthropology), a copy of her apartment lease in New York City.

Even though Claire had told Janine the truth, she had lied in public several times. If she'd lied to such an extent before, she'd do it again to save her life. Claire could definitely be turned. And Janine would use the financial leverage against her.

When Claire had mentioned the Reade Street Gallery, Janine knew exactly what Claire was after. Janine knew this as she had tried to find an inroad to Reade Street with the Native American pieces from Rex's dig, but had been turned away. She'd heard dealers speculate that Reade Street Gallery sold valuable black-market items to high end clients, but they'd never been caught. She set aside the hard-copy data on Claire, and picked up the sheet titled DAVID JACKSON. He was the sales rep that had worked with Claire at Apfel Gallery. She glanced over the sheet and it confirmed that he did work for the Reade Street Gallery as well; of course, discreetly. Claire's sources checked out. Janine was confident they'd fit perfectly in her global plan.

The gallery Janine had scored on the West Coast was fairly known to accept black-market trades, but operated with discretion. She didn't want to use them because her name was on a watch list in California with the FBI Art Crimes. But, if she could get Claire to move the items through Reade Street, sign the paperwork, and sign Bruno as the guarantor, it'd be the perfect corroborating evidence that he was black-market dealing. *Bingo.*

Janine had three items that Rex had scored for this job. They were being stored at a warehouse in Belize City, and worth at least half a million. She opened a document on her laptop that included a hierarchical view of the players: Bruno, his mother, Delia, and Sal. She added Claire's name and a picture of her to the document. If she could get them romantically involved, the documentation for customs would appear even more damning. She imagined the newspaper title: 'Bruno Canul and his lover illegally selling Belizean artifacts.' She'd get Claire to sign and date the customs paperwork and be sure to include Bruno Canul as the archeologist on record.

That meant she'd have to be nice to Bruno. She kicked herself for being such a bitch with him earlier today. In no way did she want him to have an inkling of her motive; hopefully it wasn't too late.

Janine tracing her finger over a picture of Claire with her head down, working on a document. She had an intense expression that reminded Janine of her foster sister. Jenny was the smart one, always studying. She loved chemistry and physics in high school, before the cancer diagnosis. Her dying wish was for Janine to get her degree. Janine would help Claire get the money and save her from the loan shark. In a weird way, saving Claire was an opportunity to save her sister.

THE PHONE RANG and Janine answered without hesitation. "Yes."

"What's the update?" Rex said with his usual bluntness.

"I performed a review of the individuals onsite and one person stands out. Claire Townsend. She's the project manager for the Popol Vuh event, working for the museum."

"Get to the point," Rex said.

Janine's mouth opened slightly. She knew he was abrupt and impatient. She didn't like the quality. She pursed her lips and shook her head. Finish the job. Move on.

"It's a long story, but to summarize, she has a black-market connection for us. She can sign the documentation which implicates Bruno. My secondary plan in place will assure the customs document is found by the Belizean government. The contextual situation points towards him as a guilty man as well."

"You trust that Claire is legit?"

"Yes. Background checks were performed on the players. Her story checks out. I'll need an additional forty grand for her though, to supplement as a signing bonus and to promote good will between ourselves and her." Even though Claire had never asked Janine to secure additional funds, Janine wanted to ensure she had enough money to pay the loan shark, that that no harm would come to her.

There was silence on the other end. Rex always had something to say; he had no filter, nothing that stopped him from saying what he wanted to say. There was a desire to fill in the quiet space, but she resisted the urge.

"What's her deal," he said, to the point.

Janine swallowed first, then licked her lips. His response was making her apprehensive; she was reluctant to get her involved, but she needed to get Claire the money. *Finis coronat opus: the end justifies the means.* "She's Bruno's ex-girlfriend and is down on her luck. She's got a gallery in New York that will take consignments."

"And I trust you've verified the information?"

"I did, with my contact in San Diego."

"Ah yes. I see."

Janine didn't like the quiet. It meant he was thinking, which usually meant he was about to go off on a tangent. She needed him to stay focused on the plan. He'd already made her get a room at a resort hotel, which could compromise her ability to stay hidden, and now she had the feeling he was about to go off script again.

"Perhaps you could explain how she will be involved?" he asked.

Janine explained that she'd show Claire the goods on Wednesday, they'd ship the items to Reade Street Gallery in the New York using Claire's name as the guarantor and Bruno's as the lead archeologist on the customs form—thus connecting the two as players in a black-market scheme. Once the authorities found out, Bruno's reputation would be finished. Jail time was a real possibility, for both him and Claire.

"All right," he said, in a tone that sounded far away, like he was thinking of other things. She had just delivered a pitch-perfect scheme and he sounded less than interested. What was going on?

"It'll work. I'll expect a call from you after the shipment." And then he hung up. Janine pulled the phone away from her ear and looked at it. What was he going to do?

The Pok-A-Tok meeting had put Claire on edge, and she wanted to be alone. After the Xunantunich tour, Claire reminded everyone to meet at the pavilion the next morning and headed for her room, hoping Janine wouldn't follow. In the shared bedroom, she paced, her focus on the greenery outside her window, then suddenly stopped. What was the point? She wasn't going to hide here. She wasn't afraid of Janine. She had problems to solve, and decided to get to work.

She entered the main Art Room with her clipboard and a checklist of questions to make sure the project was running on its targeted schedule. Darren sat at the pottery wheel with a finished clay pot. Ruth Ann praised the smooth curve and shape. They hadn't noticed her come in. Was Darren actually blushing?

"Hey, Darren, nice job," Claire said.

"Thanks." He looked a little startled. Ruth Ann seemed amused. He ran a wire under the pot to remove it from the wheel and lifted carefully. It was a shame they had to be broken. At the end of the Popol Vuh, each shaman would break the lip of a pot, an effigy to death. When the Hero Twins won their freedom from Hell, they sought retribution from the underworld. Instead of killing the lords and demons who tortured them, they spared lives by symbolically breaking the pot. She thought of her own life, wishing for a brief fantasy, imagining Lucia breaking the lip of a pot in exchange for money. The outrageousness of the idea made her laugh suddenly, the sound causing Darren to trip over his feet and he nearly lost his balance.

"What is wrong with you?" Darren asked, standing with his feet firmly on the ground. He made it to a drying rack fit with special heat lamps. "Have you lost your mind? I almost dropped it."

Claire glanced at the container and a hot flash of anger rose up. She had a sudden need to smash the pot, to start over, to fold the clay back into itself. Was that what she needed to do? Did she have to destroy her old life before she could start something new?

"Hey!" Darren said. Claire rubbed her face. The idea felt too big, too overwhelming.

"Claire!" Darren said.

She met his eyes.

"I've got three done. They'll go on the dry rack for two days, then into the kiln."

Claire shook her head, trying to remember what she had to ask him. She rubbed her eyelid and asked, "Did you say a day to dry the pots?"

"Two days. Then into the kiln. All the pots should be fired and ready in five days. I've made extras just in case they crack during the drying process." Darren picked up a sizable lump of clay and kneaded it.

She made notes to update the project plan. After the event,

the pots would be shipped to NYC. Claire could use this shipment as a cover for any black-market items she wanted to bring into the States, but realized the timing was off. Claire exhaled sharply and wished things with her and Janine would firm up so she could plan accordingly. "Thanks, Darren. How about you, Ruth Ann?"

"Moving along beautifully. The headdresses for the twins are finished, and now I'm making a jade and shell belt for the lead shaman. When he shakes his booty, music will be made."

"I guess he better shake his booty then," Claire said with a laugh. "Does the headdress look like the one Bruno brought?"

"Similar, but not nearly as opulent."

"Thanks," Claire said and looked to Janine. She was coordinating with local artists to make background sets of paper to create a sun and a field of corn. *I have to do this. I need her.*

"Come here," Janine said, "I want to show you this." She held a large brush over the paper and had a big smile on her face. "We experimented with bioluminescent plankton and made paint from it."

"It's supposed to be historically accurate," said Claire.

Janine didn't pick up on the annoyance, or if she did, she didn't act like it. "We can't scientifically or historically prove whether they used or not, but this source material came from the ocean, right here in Belize. Why wouldn't they use it?"

"Who told you about bioluminescence here? Did you just know?"

"Delia told me. There's a brochure near the front desk in the pavilion. We started talking about it, and one of the guys said he could make a paste from it."

"Figures," Claire said, adding with a laugh. "It's an interesting angle. Let's do it."

"Great!" Janine said. "I'll write up a piece for Shali on the possibility that Mayans used luminescent marine life found near Hopkins Beach, and give him the details. By the way, I wanted to let you know that I have to leave at two. Errands to run."

"You'll be back for dinner?"

"Nope. Don't wait up for me. I'll be back around eleven."

LATER THAT AFTERNOON, after Claire emailed Shali with the latest project schedule and the luminescent paint, she went to the pavilion to relax. BIFA was quiet. Darren and Ruth Ann were conspicuously absent. Delia had gone home for the day.

Claire grabbed a bottle of water and sat on the couch with a book. She heard a vehicle pulling into the parking lot. Shortly, Bruno sauntered in, wearing shorts and a Belikin Beer t-shirt, and he carried a small backpack. "Hey, there you are."

His dark hair and brown eyes reminded her of honey; there was always something sweet and lovely about being in his arms. She'd been attracted to him the first moment she laid eyes on him, all those years ago. He had a few new lines around his eyes, but, if anything, aging only made him more handsome. More solid.

She was hot all of a sudden, her skin electric, her senses on fire. She wanted to run her hand up his neck and into the back of his hair, to touch him, but quelled her reaction. She couldn't let her emotions get the best of her; she needed to be in control.

"Listen, I was free this afternoon, and it's hot out. Do you want to go swimming? There's a place not too far from here."

"Sure. I'll need to change, though," Claire said hesitantly, hating the thought of anyone seeing her scars. "Can you wait for me?"

"Of course," he said, plopping on the couch next to her. "Hop hop. Up and go." He gently nudged her with an elbow.

Claire went to her room to change. She took the shirt off, and stared at her defect, the scar. Tiny white dots ran parallel to the bulbous snake of keloid tissue, where there had been stitches. She had named it The Accident. Friends in college told her it was no big deal, to not care so much, to 'c'mon man, just wear a regular swimming suit.' But it was huge to her. She put the swim shirt on and looked in the mirror. The maroon-ish-brown tip peeked out of the shirt. She touched it, but there was no feeling. Scar tissue didn't have nerve endings.

Bruno had already seen it, and the knowledge calmed her. She put on a pair of swim suit bottoms and sat on the bed. Since she'd been in Belize, he had treated her like nothing had changed. She wanted to be that person again, to be better than who she was at the moment. Spending time with Bruno was a good thing. Maybe he could help her become the person she was supposed to be.

Claire finished dressing by putting on a pair of hiking pants with a half-leg zipper, running shoes and a New York Yankees baseball hat. In case she needed to change from the wet clothes, she grabbed a pair of underwear, a bra, and a purple t-shirt along with a towel and put it into a backpack. From the fridge just outside her room, she filled her water bottle and went back to the pavilion.

They walked to the Jeep. The day was hot, mid-nineties, and not a cloud in sight. She could see herself with him. Free from panic attacks—being adventurous, exploring, hiking. Claire stepped on the running board, grabbed hold of the roll bar and propelled herself into the Jeep. "Where are we going? Or is it a secret?"

He leaned in towards her and whispered, "It's a secret." She could smell him, an odd mixture of metallic climbing gear and the fresh smell of oranges. She liked feeling carefree with him. He regarded her with surprise then laughed. "Don't look so worried. You'll be safe with me, that's for sure."

That smile. Brushing her hair back, she put on her seat belt. "Are you sure I'm safe with you?" she asked, teasing.

He patted her thigh protectively, then sat back in the driver's seat, turning the key. "We're going to the Tiger Cave, named after a dog who chased a cub into a cave."

"A cave with tigers? Is that safe?" Claire said, being coy. She glanced at her thigh, where his hand had rested, and wanted more, but held back from reaching out to hold his hand.

"It's been a long time since any jungle cats have been around here, because people have scared them away. Do you have your swimsuit on?"

Her hand flew to her throat. "Yes," she said, uncomfortable, and suddenly aware that she was sweating.

"I know about your scar," Bruno said, placing an index finger under her chin. "Look at me, Claire. You're safe with me." He met her eyes, then kissed her on the cheek, and then the other. The way he touched her was like she was something precious to him. The brush of his lips on her skin was comfortable, and yet new and exciting. "I'm serious."

Claire slipped her hand into his. "Are you sure about this?"

"No," Bruno said and curled his fingers around hers, "but I need to know about us. After we swim, I have empanadas and veggies at my place. A couple beers, too. You ready?"

"Sure," she said, squeezing his hand three times.

"That's my girl," he said, rubbing his thumb against the back of her hand. "Let's go."

Bruno drove through the small town of Belmopan and onto the Western Highway. As the greenery passed, dread began to fill her. She wanted to tell him the truth, to tell him about Lucia. Reade Street Gallery. Janine. She was sinking deeper into this whole mess. Bruno could be a lifeline. She could turn this around, be a better person, with his help.

Just then, Bruno hit a bump in the road, and she lurched forward. "We're almost there," he said. "Just up ahead."

He turned into a dirt parking lot with a boundary of fallen logs. An old piece of particle board had the words Blue Hole burned into it. There were no other cars around. She grabbed her backpack and jumped out. Palm trees and red flower orchids grew wild around them, shading the area. Claire grabbed her fleece jacket, a little chilled. Bruno motioned her over and sprayed her with mosquito repellant. "We'll do a short walk, maybe five-ten minutes. Then we'll go into Tiger Cave. It's more of a tunnel, and leads to the swimming hole."

"Oh cool. So we'll start here, then walk through the cave and end up at the Blue Hole? Is it hard to get back here?"

"Nope. The tunnel is sort of U shaped. It's a thirty-minute walk back."

"Sounds great," she said, following his lead down the path. "Isn't there another place called the Blue Hole?"

"Yeah, the Great Blue Hole. But that's off the coast. It's underwater," he said, laughing at his own joke. "We're going to a swim-hole. We call most of them blue holes, and only the locals know how to get there."

"Ohio was kinda like that," Claire said, admiring the dense jungle flora. It was so different here than anywhere she'd ever been before. "'Take the first right at the Johnson farm, but that was sold to someone else fifteen years ago, but it's still the Johnson farm. Then drive a mile and take a left at the house with barking dogs.' Everyone knew what you meant."

"Yeah, Belize is the same. I'm glad you got out of there."

"Me too," she said. There was so much more she wanted to share with him, how awful it was, how lonely, how she was always on her guard. "I convinced the state and my stupid relatives to let me go to boarding school. I met friends. Then college. Obviously, that's where I met you."

"That's what I admire about you. When we dated before, you never said 'I can't' or 'it's too hard.' There was always a way out." He held her hand, intertwining his fingers into hers. "I'm sorry you had to go through that."

"It was nothing," she said and shrugged it off. Bruno pointed out the jipijapa plant, which looked like a palm tree without a trunk. "The hearts and the young shoots are good. Here, let me show you." He plucked at the base of the plant and pulled two shoots, handing one to her.

She popped the shoot into her mouth, like Bruno had. "Oh, wow, that is good," she said, liking the crisp flavor, and found it similar to celery.

They walked quietly until they came upon a cave with a narrow opening in the limestone. Bruno gave her a headlamp. She put it on, and clicked the lamp switch. In order for her to fit through the narrow opening, she had to take off her backpack and squeeze her way through. Light bounced against the rocky walls, creating angular shadows. The ground was damp. Once she was on the other side, he handed the pack to her through the rock, and then pushed his pack across too.

With just the two of them, she bonded to him, like they were the only people in the whole world. She wanted to be near him, to have the warmth of his skin against hers, to taste the saltiness of his lips.

He must have sensed her need and took her hand. She dropped her pack and pushed it to the side with her foot, and he dropped his. He leaned her against the wall. Water seeped into the back of her shirt, cold against her hot skin; she arched her back, pressing herself against his muscular chest.

She touched his cheek. The roughness of his skin and the smell of limestone, her back against the hard rock, turned her on; wetness dampened her panties. Her heart pounded; she swore it sounded like drums. Bruno kissed her, his tongue licking at her lips. The headlamps clanked against each other, and he pulled hers down, around her neck, and did the same to his. She leaned back against the cave and parted her lips, waiting for him, inviting him. He bit her lip and kissed her fully, running his hands through her hair, his need apparent. He pulled back with purpose to look her in the eyes.

"We have a history together," he said, his chest rising and falling with heavy breathing, "but I want to wait. Not here."

She wanted to stay and kiss him, let his hands rove over her body. But there was pleasure in waiting. A promise that she knew was soon to come. Bruno picked up her backpack and helped put it on. She did the same for him. The gestures were sweet; she felt loved and cared for. He unclipped a helmet from his backpack and gave it to her, then put his own on. Claire readjusted the headlamp and clicked it on. Her body calmed, but there was a muted electric buzz humming through her.

They walked into the cave. A rivulet of water trickled through. They held hands sometimes and kissed each other, sweet kisses that were full of joy, awkward with the helmets obstructing their natural path, laughter welling up in both of them.

Ahead, six-foot-tall boulders blocked the path. Bruno illuminated the natural foot and handholds in the rock, expertly guiding her through. She put one foot into the rock. He was behind her, holding her waist. She should be having a panic attack, her body should be shaking, her mind should be on the verge of panic, but she felt none of that. She was entirely and completely safe in his capable hands. She climbed up to the top of the boulder, turned to face him, and offered her hand to Bruno.

"Keep going," he said. "On the other side, lay on your belly and slide down. Slowly. You'll feel a couple of handholds."

When she got on the other side, she put her hands on her knees, breathing hard from effort, not from panic. The distinction made her smile. She made sure to give Bruno light from her headlamp as he made his way over the boulder. Once he got down, he gave her a hug, then stood back. She squinted and he turned his headlamp light up towards the ceiling. "I swear, Claire, you're so beautiful." He stood there, looking at her with this funny expression and a half smile.

Had he lost his mind? She was in a helmet, with no makeup, her clothes damp and dirty from the boulder climb. She scrunched her eyebrows and looked pointedly at her body, "This?"

"Yes. You are beautiful. We're almost there," Bruno said, taking her hand. They walked on. Sunlight filtered in, and soon enough, they didn't need headlamps anymore.

Hanging vines blocked the cave exit, and the smell changed from that of damp dirt to vegetation. She pushed the vines out of her way and walked into the jungle. It was warmer so she took off her fleece jacket and wrapped it around her waist. "That cave is cool. It doesn't really have an ending to it."

"Kinda like life, I guess," Bruno said.

"Yeah," she said. The people Claire had surrounded herself with in New York would have wanted to take a selfie and pose with duck lips and their tongues out in order to increase the amount of fake internet points. They would have whispered behind Bruno's back. Said he was too kitchy, too sentimental. Whatever. She was glad he was around. She liked being genuine.

They walked through the jungle for half a mile, and they entered a clearing with the swimming hole on the far side. Wooden steps led to the edge of the pool with a makeshift dock sturdy enough to stand on. Excited to get into the water, she set her backpack on the ground and took off her pants. Tiny silver fish swam. With her swim shirt and bottoms on, she lunged into the water. The bottom was a mixture of sand and rocks. Smiling to herself, she was okay being in the swimsuit. Bruno knew her truth, all of it, and she didn't need to cover up or explain herself away.

"It's only five thirty, two more hours of light," Bruno said, taking off his shirt.

Whoa. She admired his body, the sleek pectorals, the defined biceps as he tossed the shirt to a space near her backpack. He let out a whoop then cannonballed into the water. She held up her hands to avoid being splashed.

"Hey you," she said when he came out of the water, with a slightly admonishing tone.

He put his arms around her and lifted her in the buoyant water. She easily wrapped her legs around him. His skin felt like silk against her thighs. He kissed her on the throat, sweet kisses, and went lower on her neck until he got to the scar. Without hesitating, he kissed the top of it, a single intentional kiss. Then he looked at her, deep into her eyes. His expression was serious as if he was silently telling her something important: I see you.

She pulled herself in for a hug and away from his eyes. This was a mistake. She let go of him, unwrapped her legs and swam for the dock. She shouldn't be here.

"We're going to jump," he said, swimming after her.

"We are?"

"There's a ledge up there, you can kind of see the footpath."

"That tiny ledge way the hell up there?"

"Ha. Yes. I've done it a million times. C'mon," he said. "Follow me."

"I am not going to jump." She looked up at the ledge again, judging the height to be about ten feet from the water. Certainly not cliff diving by any stretch of the matter, but it was still too high. Her heart pounded, fast and heavy; she tried to quell the fresh panic attack. Breathe. Breathe. "No way. I don't want to."

He stood on the deck. "We'll jump together."

"We can do that?"

"Sure. I've jumped here, this spot, several times. I'm practically an expert."

Although she did not feel superhero brave, she decided to jump with him. She ignored her rapidly beating heart, she ignored the voices in her head telling her to run. They walked to the backside of the swimming hole, and he carefully stepped through the gravel towards the ledge. Claire was right behind him, stepping into the same spots.

"When you get up here, don't look down. Stay focused on me."

She heeded his advice. When she slipped, her arms flailed. She caught herself and stopped sliding, but now, she couldn't move.

"Look at me. You're fine. A little scare, nothing more."

"Right." Claire said, breathing through.

"Eyes on your feet. Two more steps and you're on the ledge."

She took one, then two steps. She made it to the ledge. She was next to Bruno.

"We're gonna go fast now." He took her hand. "One, two, three!"

Bruno gently tugged her hand, and instead of resisting, she jumped. At first, she was terrified, but then the fear slid off her and she was free. The force of the jump naturally separated them, and she sliced through the coldness. Her feet touched the slick rocky bottom. She pushed upwards and sprang out of the water. She brushed the hair back from her eyes. Her fear was gone, turned by the adrenaline into joy.

"That was great! You did great!" Bruno said. He swam over to her, lifted her chin and kissed her on the lips. The look in his eyes, though, made her calm inside, like nothing could go wrong.

"Let's do that again," she said. "I'm okay by myself." She got out of the water. At the ledge, the fear wasn't so great. This time, she jumped with confidence. She let out a big whoop as she launched herself into the air. When she came back up, there was Bruno, smiling a crazy big I'm-proud-of-you-smile.

"It's starting to get late," Bruno said, checking his watch. "Ready to head to my place to eat?" he asked, a smile playing at his lips. Claire's body responded, an overall tingling.

"I've got to call Delia, let her know I'm not coming back for dinner."

"Sure," he said. They got into the Jeep and she made a quick call to Delia, who said they'd manage on their own. Just as the sun was starting to set, they got back on the highway. The roads were relatively deserted; a British lorry and a beat-up Toyota truck with surfboards in the back passed them. Bruno turned off the highway and onto a dusty road with banana trees, row after row of what looked like short palm trees.

He parked in front of a small, white clapboard house. A dirt bike was parked in the carport, along with a mostly inflated raft boat, a series of organized life vests standing up on end, helmets, and headlamps. On the porch was a bowl filled with water and a floating citronella candle.

"Let's eat inside," he said. "I'll toast a few empanadas."

"Are they as good as the ones in the airport?" Claire asked as she entered his house.

"Better. I made these ones."

Claire marveled at how clean everything was, though out of order. On the bookshelf, there was a stack of leather-bound notepads. A few framed pictures of him and his brother when they were ten, maybe eleven, and of his family randomly scattered on the shelves. Rugged looking leather gloves were next to a philosophy book. She wondered if that was intentional or not. On the walls were panoramic pictures of different archeology sites. Books on Mayan archeology lay on the coffee tables, the pages filled with sticky notes and a National Geographic magazine focused on underwater cave diving and archeology.

"That's interesting," Claire said, lifting the Nat Geo magazine, remembering the Men's Journal copy. "I read about this in Men's Journal."

"Now that advanced scuba gear is available to the masses, more and more people are getting involved," Bruno said.

"That's good, right?"

"Not really. I get it, I've felt the adrenaline when you find a new place. These amateurs stumble upon an 'undiscovered location' that hasn't been seen by man in a thousand years. When you're the first, the euphoria is like a drug. Not quite as good as sex," he said with a wink, "but damn close. The problem is, these amateurs, be they men or women, aren't trained professionals. They don't know how to preserve a site so it's archeologically sound. A lot of them end up taking stuff that doesn't belong to them, accidental black-market traders. They think a shard here, a pot there, means nothing. But it's devastating."

She should tell him the truth. *Right now. Tell him everything.*

"I'm going to get us beer," Bruno said and headed to the kitchen.

"Sure." The moment had passed. It went by so fast, she was sure there'd be another chance to tell him. She'd say something then, she swore to herself she would.

She heard the fridge open and the clinking of glass. "Where'd you… I thought you were right behind me. Get in here."

When she came into the kitchen, he handed her a beer.

"I'm going to toast the empanadas. Go outside, sit on my deck, enjoy the view. I'll be out in a bit."

"Sure," she said, and made her way outside. She sat at the teak table and took a long sip of her beer. The deck overlooked a small riverbed that curved through the back of the property. Vibrant blue butterflies floated through the area.

She found a lighter near the citronella candles and lit the wick. She rustled her fingers through her wind-dried hair. The sound of uptempo jazz music came through the screen door, and the smell of empanadas permeated the air. Claire closed her eyes and let her head fall back.

Bruno came outside while they were cooking. He patted her arm and sat beside her. "This play is going to be incredible. The ATM is a Belizean treasure. And the cavern is perfect sound-wise. To actually be in this Mayan holy place, to perform this ceremonial dance, is unbelievable. I still can't believe the NICH is letting us do this."

"They have been very, very insistent that we are to be extremely careful to disturb nothing. Just so you know, I have read every single rule, and we are in compliance."

"It's a lot. Glad to see you on top of it. What do you think about the others? Ruth Ann? Janine? Darren?"

"I think Ruth Ann and Darren might be," Claire paused, "you know, taking things to the next level."

"Ha. I wondered," said Bruno. "He seemed pretty aggressive with you at first. Now he's not too awful, at least not grumpy."

"He's always been a jerk. The kind of guy without a filter. Glad to see Ruth Ann bring him some happiness."

"And Janine? You're sharing a room together, right?"

"It's not too bad," Claire said. "There's enough privacy. I can't see her, but I can hear her."

"Hopefully she doesn't snore," he said. "She easy to work with?"

"She doesn't snore," Claire said, "and she is pretty easy to work with. Hard worker. She does her job." *Now. Tell him now. Tell him everything.* She was about to open her mouth and blurt out the truth, but stopped cold at the consequences. Bruno rejecting her. Bruno telling Shali. Her reputation going from trashed to ruined. She took a sip of beer instead. A quiet metallic ding rang through the air.

"You sure? There's nothing else going on?"

She was in the middle of her drink, and she lowered it and set it on the table. "Is there something I should be worried about?"

He shrugged and got up. Within a few minutes, he returned with two plates with two meat pies on each one, a handful of lettuce with sliced cucumbers and what appeared to be balsamic dressing. "That was fast," she said.

"This is amazing," she said after her first bite.

"I'll get the dishes," she said, starting for the kitchen.

"Wait," he said, catching her before she went inside. He sighed, put the plate back on the table and took her hand. He guided her so that she was sitting on his lap.

She wasn't sure what was going on in his mind: was he accepting her? Did he believe her? Did he trust her? She pushed the thoughts away, dropped her shoulders and closed her eyes, letting his warmth envelope her. She nuzzled the underside of his ear with her nose.

"How did I ever find you again?" he asked. "I have to say, this is weird and familiar at the same time."

Claire laughed, the feel-good laugh of being appreciated, being loved, being in the arms of a man who wanted her.

It was too late to tell him now. She was in for the ride, wherever it led.

"Tomorrow is a big day," he said, releasing his arms from her. "We're floating the River of the Dead."

"Yeah. I'd love to stay too, but responsibilities," she said, not finishing the sentence. A twinge of sadness came over her, but she didn't let him see it. "Come on, then," she said, trying to smile. "Back to BIFA?"

He brought her in for one more kiss. Once they stopped, he stayed close, kissing the tip of her nose, then her forehead, and rested against her.

Nothing would ever be the same between them.

CHAPTER SEVENTEEN

Claire

At BIFA, Claire walked through the pavilion and to her room. She dreaded sharing; even though it had been separated with furniture and a privacy curtain, she wanted to be completely alone. While she was in the shower, she scrubbed her skin with a washcloth, but the water made her skin feel slick rather than clean. Afterwards, she went to her room, got dressed, and sat on her bed.

Things were getting worse, not better. Was there any other way to handle paying Lucia? She didn't want to hurt anyone, especially Bruno. If she worked with Janine, and he ever found out, he'd never speak to her again. The thought of it made her physically ill. She could still run, have someone drop her off in Belize City, take a bus to Mexico, and be gone. With determination alone, she could make it. Desperation made impractical plans effective. She had to do something. Thinking was driving her crazy. She decided to write Bruno a note, even if he never got it.

With that, she retrieved a piece of paper from the desk and wrote. First, she apologized for getting involved with him again, for not being the woman she could be. Then, she apologized for being unable to do the right thing. Finally, she asked for his forgiveness. She folded up the note and held it in her hand, about to set it on the desk, when she heard a sound.

In her doorway, a man stood in the shadows. Claire backed up. The chair scraped against the tile. He stepped towards her, his shoulders wide, his stance aggressive. He held a gun in his right hand, and it was pointed straight at her.

Claire gasped and grew still.

"Sit down."

She froze. She glanced at the chair, then back to him, and couldn't move, couldn't take her eyes away. Time slowed. A blink seemed to last minutes. She was going to die. He pointed the gun towards the seat with a menacing frown. She didn't hesitate this time and sat in the chair.

"What's in your hand?" his voice quiet as he moved in close. He was a foot away, and the gun was pointed point blank at her head.

"A note."

"Give it to me," he said.

Claire lifted her hand slowly, and he snatched the paper out of her shaking fingers. He read it aloud, laughed, then tucked it into a pocket.

"Lucia knows you are in Belize. The deadline is nine days." He placed the muzzle against her temple. She shrank away, but he made sure the gun stayed on her. "This visit's a friendly reminder."

"I'm getting the money," she said.

"We know. Working with Janine?"

"Yes," Claire said, opening her eyes. "How do you know?"

He moved the gun between her eyebrows. She gasped, then shut her eyes.

"Don't run to Mexico. That's not very bright."

"Oh," said Claire. She wanted to look him in the eyes, but was afraid of what she might see there. *Was this it?* Was he going to kill her? Should she try to knock the gun out of his hands and run for it?

"Don't," he said. Then, he shifted the gun and rubbed the side of it against her face, dragging it along her cheek as if it were a caress. "Last I heard, Lucia won't kill you, but wants to recoup her money by auctioning you off. She knows some fucked up people out there."

Auction her off? The blood drained from her face. It was one thing to be scared for your life, it was another type of dread completely to know your life would never again be yours. Claire resisted the urge to call bullshit. There was no doubt that Lucia would make good on this threat.

"Last guy? He liked'm both. Men and women. Kept them in a horse stable all locked up, like they were his prize animals to ride. Took'm to Siberia, did crazy shit with them. Body parts were missing. Weird scars. Mirrors everywhere, so they could see everything. Bat shit fucking crazy."

What the actual fuck?

"Lucia gave'm a spoon to hold on to. Those sad fuckers smiled when I shot'm."

Fear unsettled her belly with a nausea and spread through her. She swallowed hard. There was no other choice but to work with Janine. Paying Lucia was the only way out of this mess.

"I'm getting the money," Claire said. "You'll get the money."

"If you don't, we might bring Bruno with you," he said. He chucked the side of her chin hard with the barrel of the gun. Her hand rose to her face. From his back pocket, he pulled out a sterling silver spoon and twisted it in front of her face. "There's transmutation too, don't forget that."

She didn't reach out for the spoon. He dropped it and the metal clattered against the tile. Just as quickly as he had appeared, the man had disappeared out the door. Crickets chirped outside. They were loud, louder than she'd ever heard.

The creak of a door sent her heart-rate back up. She stood and craned her head to listen. Light footsteps. Was it Janine or was that guy coming back? She looked frantically for a weapon. The only thing she could use was a metal folding chair. In one swift move she picked it up, ready to launch it at the door.

Then, the familiar tinkling of bottles tapping each other as the refrigerator door opened was followed by a loud sigh.

"Janine? Is that you?"

"Yeah. I'm just getting an apple," Janine said. "You want a beer?"

Claire set the chair down. She rubbed her forehead and caught her breath. She shook out her hands and kicked her feet in the air to get rid of the extra energy trapped in her body, then picked up the spoon. The letter L was engraved into the handle. Claire was about to tell Janine what had just happened, but then closed her mouth. Everything in her body revolted against the act. If Janine knew that she was wanted, that a loan shark was after her, she might back out of the black-market deal. Worse, Janine would use the knowledge to draw her in deeper to the mess she was already in. "I'll be right out."

Claire sat at the bistro table. She was still trying to catch her breath. Her heart had slowed. Even if she wasn't going to say anything, just having her around made her feel safer.

"Are you okay?" Janine asked as she pulled two Belikins out of the communal refrigerator and handed Claire a bottle opener. She popped the cap off both, handing one to Janine. "I have three objects to move. They need to ship out Tuesday morning. The total value is about five hundred K, but you'll have to verify that."

She had nine days. She could feel the panic starting, in her belly, in her heart.

"Claire? Tuesday morning?"

She immediately did a time calculation. If they mailed the items Tuesday, it would be Day Five with Lucia's countdown. That could work. Panic's sense of impending doom began to fade. She'd expedite the air shipment to three days. Two days with customs. Upon arrival at the Reade Street Gallery, they usually assessed and paid within forty-eight hours. That was thirteen days. She'd be back in New York on Day 12. As soon as she had the money, she'd drop it off with Lucia. If there was a way to close the gap by a day, she'd do it.

"I'll make sure the schedule is open. As far as I know, it's a free morning. No excursions," Claire said. "What are the percentage breakdowns?"

"You'll get thirty-four percent. That's the best I could negotiate. About a hundred and seventy K. I'll get twenty percent. What's Reade Street charging?"

"The seller pays five percent and we give up fifteen percent," Claire said. "Wait. A hundred seventy doesn't get me what I need."

"There's a finder's fee of thirty grand. I'll make sure you get it."

Claire nodded. "Free and clear?"

"Free and clear." Janine tipped her beer towards Claire, the glass clinked.

Claire pursed her lips and rubbed an eye. All she could see was Bruno's face looking at her, asking her if Janine was up to anything. As loathe as she was to participate in the process, a cold, black gun had just been dragged across her face. And now, not paying meant something worse than death. She needed the money. "I'll email Reade Street Gallery to let them know we have incoming."

She hated the idea of putting her name on any documentation. If things went south, she'd be the one they came after. From shipping high end art, she knew small hacks to keep customs at bay. She'd have to disguise the objects, maybe even mark them as imitations. "It's worth half a million, right?" Claire said. The amount shouldn't tip off customs; many of her shipments had ranged in the multi-millions. But it wasn't fry change either; the amount would place the crime as a felony if she was caught. "It'll be better on the customs form if we describe the objects as imitations. Will that be a problem?"

"Whatever it takes," Janine said. "As long as we get the artifacts to New York safely and sold."

"Cheers to that," Claire said.

CHAPTER EIGHTEEN

Claire

The next morning, Claire awoke. She sat up in bed. Nothing looked familiar. The curtains didn't look right. She squinted at the cloth. A pair of blue butterflies fluttered by the window. She'd never seen that bookshelf before, and yet it was so familiar. She scrunched her eyes. The answer was almost there, right there. When she saw her reflection in the mirror, she knew exactly where she was.

Belize. Today she'd float on the River of the Dead. She worked for the American History Museum. Shali was her boss. Tomorrow she would be a criminal. She remembered the cold gun on her face. The threat of being sold at auction. *Shit.* She had ten days left to pay Lucia. She rolled her shoulders back and did her best to be prepared to face the day.

She dressed in her long sleeve swim shirt and trunks. The memory of jumping off the ledge with Bruno came to her and she smiled. The kiss. His hands on her back, the taste of his lips. She felt reckless. Excitement and longing made her uneven, uncentered, unable to do the job she meant to do.

She swallowed hard. Claire was no schoolgirl anymore. She didn't have the freedom to fall in love with whoever she wanted. She shouldn't drag Bruno into her mess. He knew too much as it was. *It's too late.* Claire ignored the voice in her head. She got up and dressed, wanting out of the room and to get to work.

Claire stopped at the water fountain in the pavilion to refill her water bottles. Soon, she'd be on her back on an inner tube, floating on the River of the Dead straight to Xibalba, the Mayan underworld. No big deal she told herself, it wasn't real. There was no underworld. Religion was a form of story-telling, a narrative in which people tried to understand spiritual issues. Hell doesn't exist, she tried to tell herself. Demons were made up. She turned to put the bottles in her bag, nearly knocking over Janine. She yelped and jumped back.

"Did I scare you?" Janine asked.

"Yes, you did. But it's all right. Hey, want a water?" Claire asked, holding up a bottle, trying not to feel so discombobulated.

Janine had on a sporty-looking see-through swimming suit cover that draped over her perfectly fitting white bikini and a pair of athletic shorts. Her hair was up in a messy bun. Claire ran her hand along the front of her long-sleeve shirt, along the route of her scar, before consciously realizing what she was doing and dropped her hand away.

"Hey Claire," Bruno said, striding towards her. He gave her a quick shoulder hug. Bruno had on a pair of dark blue boarder shorts and a t-shirt. "Janine," he said. "You want a hug too?"

Janine turned away like she didn't hear him. He laughed and went to go talk to Ed, the driver.

Claire took a moment to look at Bruno. If none of this had happened, if she had never taken that loan, would she have ever seen him again? He turned his head and found her watching him, and gave her a confident smile while tapping his watch.

Claire nodded, understanding it was time to get things moving. "Welcome, everyone," Claire said. "Thank you for getting here on time. As you know, we are going on these tours to better understand the ancient Mayan people and their complex views on death. The Popol Vuh is a story about new beginnings, and it has everything to do with death. The first half of the story describes the hero twins defeating the gods of the underworld. The Cave of the Dead is a place that Mayans believed was 'in between' the living and the dead. They believed it was an entrance to hell. And we are going to float inside of it. Bruno?"

"Thanks, Claire. The cave we're floating in is part of an elaborate system that doubles as a river with tributaries. Water levels can rise and lower based on rain fall. The only art that survived in the cave," said Bruno, "are things that withstand the test of time. In the Cave of the Dead, water would have eviscerated any clothing or baskets that might have been used during the holy ceremonies."

"Often from an anthropology perspective," continued Claire, "we cannot understand a culture by collecting artifacts and framing it in our culture. We begin with *their* beliefs. Mayans had many gods. Most modern religions only have one. What did *they* think about time? They perceived it differently, in cycles. Try to forget preconceived notions, if you can."

A general murmur of acceptance came from the crew, Ruth Ann, Darren, Bruno, Janine, and Claire.

"Are the shamans going to join us?" asked Darren.

"No, due to group size," said Bruno. "Just a few added logistics. The 'Cave of the Dead' tour is roughly a mile hike into the jungle. Technically, we enter St. Herman's cave, but around here, no matter what cave you enter, we tour guides call it the Cave of the Dead. Does everyone have on swimming attire? You will get wet," he said, looking around. "Use the handholds in the cave as we descend to the river; it gets slippery and steep at times. To set expectations, this isn't an exciting Class A river. I don't know why people expect it to be rough, but the river is a slow-moving body of water with a slight undercurrent. Even so, stay on your tubes."

The group looked around at each other.

"Any more questions?" Delia asked, scanning the room. "No? Okay."

"Let's go then!" said Bruno.

The crew got into the air-conditioned van. They followed Bruno, who led the way in his open-top Jeep. The drive wasn't far, fifteen minutes or so on the Hummingbird Highway, then Bruno turned into a parking lot marked by a hand-painted sign that said Blue Hole National Park. It was a different location from where Bruno had taken her yesterday. *He wasn't kidding when he said every place around here was called the Blue Hole.*

The grass lot had a few fallen logs used as a marker for parking. Clean, but it was deserted. They were surrounded by broad palm fronds, ferns, and tiny leaves poking out here and there. There was no sense of horizon, only the jungle-forest in front of them.

Out of the van, Ed handed out yellow life jackets along with a helmet and a headlamp to each person. Bruno handed out inner tubes, which had about a four-foot diameter, and she had to use her whole arm to carry it. They started on a dirt path to St. Herman's Cave; she was alone. The inner tube wasn't hard to walk with, but it was awkwardly big.

Ruth Ann was behind her. Bruno, Janine, and Darren were ahead. The ever present chorus of crickets acted as a drone-like background to their crunching footsteps. The vegetation was dense; seeing beyond the green was all but impossible. A film of sweat beaded on her forehead.

"Hi, darling," said Ruth Ann, patting her shoulder as she caught up to walk together, "did you get a good rest last night?"

Claire let out a breath of air slowly. The unnerving sense fluttered away. "No. How about you?"

"My bed is lumpy." She held her hand out as if to stop Claire from trying to solve the problem. "Darling, really, let's not waste your time replacing my mattress with another of the exact caliber. Besides, I have found another solution." Ruth Ann looked over at Darren, a secret smile lighting up her face.

"Sooo," Claire said, dropping her voice to a conspiratorial whisper, "do tell."

Ruth Ann turned to her, and with a sly wink, said, "Nothing to tell, darling. Nothing to tell. This jungle out here is something else, don't you think? These wonderful palm trees, all this green."

"Yes. It is beautiful, and a little claustrophobic."

"I suppose if you're used to wide open spaces. It's just so green compared to the desert, droughty LA. The lushness is an absolute delight."

"How's the jewelry coming along?"

"The belt I've made will not only keep your pants on, but will keep you entertained. Darren has been such a patient model for me."

"Darren is helping you out?"

"Yes, he's quite charming, you know. I mean, I know he can be awful sometimes. He doesn't share his sweetness with the masses, darling—he's got too much of that male pride wrapped in a machismo taco—but I'm telling you he can be very agreeable."

"I wondered about you two," Claire said. "You seem to have a way with him."

Darren had slowed to walk with Ruth Ann and Claire. The connection between the other two practically shimmered in the hot jungle air between them. Claire blinked the sweat out of her eyes.

Bruno had stopped up ahead and waited for the rest of

them to catch up. "Watch out for the leafcutter ants on the ground." Everyone looked down at the black ants carrying bright green leaves that towered above their heads, like a sail on a boat. The creatures marched a path of relative straightness, single file, and on a mission.

"Now place yourself in the shoes of an ancient Mayan shaman who lived a thousand years before us. And remember the story of the Popol Vuh. The ants helped to feed the Hero Twins as they were stuck in Xibalba, directly translated as 'The place of fright.' When you read the story without the context of leafcutter ants, it's an interesting detail, but when you see the actual ants marching with the leaves, the story takes on a different shape, a new meaning."

Claire stepped over a row of unending ants—she could see no beginning and no end to the line. "This would be proof to Mayans that the Popol Vuh is a real story, that it has context in their world."

"The Mayan belief system is that hell is literally accessed from earth," Bruno said. "How do you think people reacted to that, in art, society, one another?"

"Something must die before a new life can start," said Janine. "We see it in nearly every culture."

Claire paused. She'd heard this before, but it never meant anything to her. She thought of Darren's finished pot and how she wanted to bash it in, to lump it back into a giant mass of clay. "Temples and pyramids were built to honor death." Claire said the words, as if they had finally dawned on her, "And we can see where life springs from death, the relationship between the two." A eureka sensation flooded her entire being. *Something in her life had to die before she could begin anew.* It had gone from a question to a statement.

What? What had to die? Bruno? Did she have to die?

"It might be why the Mayans had so many gods," Bruno said. "Part of the Mayan religion that survived has to do with gratitude and giving thanks to the small and big things. Maybe when faced with so much constant death, they knew how to appreciate life."

"That might be why they added the dancing jewelry," Ruth Ann said. "Life is so much more vibrant, the colors, sounds, all of that."

Claire was still trying to free herself from internal words that haunted her. Talking about death in such a logical, professorial manner seemed strange when she knew how complicated it really was, how absolutely devastating it could be. On the other hand, she loved this dialogue. It reminded her of why she took anthropology in the first place, the act of trying to understand other cultures and place it in a narrative.

"Are there any booby traps out here?" called out Darren. Claire had always seen him in jeans and a long sleeve button-down, and it struck her odd to see him in swim trunks and an athletic shirt.

"No. Only burial tombs are booby trapped. We're halfway there," Bruno said. "Let's keep going."

Ruth Ann and Darren walked with Bruno, shifting their large inner tubes under their arms. They asked Bruno more questions about the Mayans.

Janine and Claire hung back. When the rest of the party was out of ear shot, Janine shifted the tube to her other arm and leaned in close. "Did you clear the schedule for tomorrow?"

"I did," Claire said. A distinct sense of dread settled on her. She wished that she could run ahead, tell Bruno everything, but that action would result in only one ending for her. Death. *Maybe worse,* she thought, shuddering at the memory of a cold gun against her face.

"Plan on leaving the compound around nine a.m. And be sure to let Delia know that both of us will be offsite."

"Of course," Claire said, annoyed at Janine's instructions.

She was the project manager—supervising time and people was her expertise. The path veered around a bend and started downhill. The temperature cooled. Tiny light-brown birds darted from one side to the other while colorful butterflies fluttered through the open air.

She didn't know there was a cave opening until she was right in front of it. The entrance was naturally hidden by shiny palm leaves and hanging jungle vines. There were no visitor signs and no off-limits signs. There was no building to take tickets, just the path and the cave. They stepped down manmade stairs carved into the rock, descending at a forty-five-degree angle. A rope fence provided a natural hand-hold. Claire took each step with caution, her confidence growing.

Halfway there, she stopped to turn around and look at the opening. Cragged stalactites were backlit against the curve of smooth-edged leaves, and when she looked beyond the oval shaped cave, all she saw was white light. She loved this place, immediately and deeply. She understood now why the ancient Mayans believed that caves led to the underworld, but instead of dread, she felt a sense of peace and elation.

As they walked further into the cave, natural light faded. Headlamps came on. The light bounced against the smooth but low ceiling and returned odd-angled shadows. Little lizards scurried along the walls, but Bruno assured them there were no snakes or other wildlife to be afraid of.

After another fifteen minutes of walking, they came to the river. The still water covered the bottom of the cave. A sense of reverence came over her. She stepped into the water. It was cool, but not cold.

Claire set her tube in the water. Bruno held her tire as she got on the tube. It was awkward as she got in, but at least everyone had the same experience.

Then Bruno held the tube for Janine, to steady it, but she didn't want him to. "I'll get it myself, thanks."

"I have to hold the tube," he said, meeting her gaze with pure professionalism. "Insurance purposes."

"Fine," she said and placed her feet outside of the tube, then sat in the middle.

"This particular cave system is extensive," Bruno said. "The water flows through several caves and exits out to a variety of jungle streams. There's a current in the water, even if it doesn't appear to be so. People can and do die here, so stay on your raft. I'll be walking through the water, guiding you. All of you need to stay connected. Claire, you'll be in the lead. Ruth Ann, you're next. Put your feet on top of Claire's tube. Darren, you follow her, and Janine, you'll be last."

Ruth Ann, Darren, and Janine had followed his instruction, and they were connected. Bruno pulled her towards the center of the river until he was waist deep. Part of her wanted to move her leg closer to him, but she didn't dare; she didn't want anyone to see how she felt about him.

Bruno walked through the water, pulling the trail of tubes. He pointed out the difference in stalactites (icicle formation at the top of a cave) and stalagmites (upward growing mound of minerals formed by water dripping, usually from a stalactite), most of them black or dark gray. Then he pointed up, and asked everyone to look up, to see the holes where vegetarian bats lived.

I'm not looking up, in case a bat poops on me. WTF, Bruno?

Along the way, they floated in the dark, random flashes of headlamp lighting up the cave walls. Claire heard other groups behind them. The sound was faint, but not ominous. Ahead, she saw several child-sized gray-white limestone stalagmites and stalactites.

Bruno stopped the group. The water was up to his neck, and he asked them to direct the headlamps to where he pointed. "Water that drips from stalactites is considered holy," he said. "The Mayans stored it in containers and may have made fermented wine from this water. Drunkenness, smoke, and eating mushrooms were considered a holy way to practice divination. To connect with the rain god."

Claire had expected everyone to chuckle at the inebriation comment, but the group was silent. Bruno waded further down the river. "Please turn off your headlamps for a bit," he said, "and close your eyes. The Cave of the Dead is a place between living and death. Imagine yourself an ancient Mayan, in this space, and let it inspire you for the Popol Vuh."

There was no sound except for the drip-drops off stalactites, a faint rushing sound like a spring bursting forth, and the flap of bat wings above them. Claire had the strange sensation that she was no longer a spectator, and somehow she was a part of the cave. Her body felt alive; sounds were crisp. Faint echoes seemed to vibrate against her skin; the smell of damp rock was strong. Was this what death meant? Could accepting death be a calm endeavor rather than a frantic and chaotic response to loss?

Bruno said to turn on the headlamps and in front of them was an immense limestone foundation. "This is known as the Crystal Cathedral," he said. "It's a monolith the size of a semi-truck without a trailer and is made of three distinct stalagmites."

The chalk-white color was a sharp contrast to the darkness of the caves, as if it had bubbled up to spite the shadows. There was a sharp pain on her chest. Her scar felt like it was burning. She rubbed her chest hard with the palm of her hand.

Bruno turned towards her, the headlamp blinding her. She blinked hard and shook her head.

"Claire?"

"I'm okay," she said, the sensation fading.

"Good," he said. "Okay everyone, remember what Delia said about no artwork surviving? This is why. It's so wet in here that anything woven or painted disintegrated long ago. Earlier archeologists found a few broken pots along the riverbed, but they've long been removed."

"Do you think they killed anyone here?" asked Ruth Ann.

"No evidence that they did, but the Mayans did like their human sacrifices," Bruno said.

They floated through the rest of the cave and the crew was fairly quiet. Bruno spoke softly about the sparse plant system, described some of the fish that swam in the water. They passed a few more intriguing geologic formations, but nothing as grand as the Crystal Cathedral. Then, at a certain point Bruno made a U turn and led everyone back the way they had come. Soon enough, they were at the start of the expedition.

"That's it, ladies and gentlemen," Bruno said. Claire got out and the water was knee deep. Each person picked up their inner tube and followed Bruno out of the cave. Claire walked behind everyone, wanting time by herself. The others seemed to be energized by the experience, but she felt stillness, as if her body had synced to the measure of the water. They were well ahead, but Bruno slowed to be with her.

"Everything okay?" he asked. "You seem a little shook up."

Bruno was so incredibly sweet and sensitive to her emotions. Guilt washed over her. If only she could freeze the moment and stay there forever. She didn't want him to know what a horrible, terrible mess she was. She was about to say something banal like 'I'm fine,' but a memory struck her. In her mind's eye, she saw darkness and sudden flashes of blinding white light. She was in the back seat of her parent's car; the blue faux-leather seats were cold. She reached out for Bruno and put her hand on his shoulder, steadied herself.

"Claire?" Bruno unbuckled her helmet and dropped it to the ground.

The sound seemed distant, far off. Her breath was erratic. She remembered being in the hospital bed. The smell. That awful antiseptic smell. That moment she woke up, 'Mom?

Dad?' No one answered. She yelled, 'MOM? DAD?' They never came. A nurse ran into the room instead. Nothing was ever the same after that. Physical therapy. The funeral. The thud of flowers on the casket. She couldn't breathe, couldn't breathe. Her heart raced. She wanted to run. To escape. But there was nowhere to go.

Bruno placed his hands gently on her cheeks. "Look at me."

Claire opened her eyes. She locked onto his dark brown eyes. and immediately felt safe, anchored.

"Four breaths in…"

She was connected to him. Somehow, he gave her strength in the way he looked at her.

"And four breaths out…"

She exhaled fast, almost hyperventilating, and pushed his hands away to cover her eyes. Like a movie clip, she could see the last memory of her family. Claire had just told a joke. Her dad was driving, and had turned around to smile at her. Mom was laughing in the passenger seat. Everything after that was blank until she woke up in a hospital room. The worst moment of her life.

"Claire, look at me." He gently removed her hands and maintained eye contact. "Exhale slowly."

The anger, the frustration, the eagerness to forget her old life welled up inside her. "It's been ten years, I should be better by now," she said, trying to shake him off, to keep him away. "It's nothing. Just a dumb memory." She didn't want Bruno to see how affected she was and looked away.

He lifted her chin and she found his eyes again. "Breathe, Claire. Count of four." He smiled and put his hands on her shoulders. "One, two, three, four."

The measured breathing actually calmed her down.

"The wreck. It was my fault. I killed them." After she said

the words, she slumped into Bruno's arms. She'd never said it aloud before. Bruno was not deterred.

"Look at me, Claire. You did not kill them. That cave has a profound effect on people. You're not the first. Breathe in through the nose. Count of four." He squeezed her shoulders firmly. "Your parents are watching out for you, I'm sure."

"What? Like a pair of guardian angels?"

"Death isn't… final," Bruno said. "Four more breaths in."

"Death *is* final," she said. Her heart was no longer racing, and her breath had stabilized. "It's better to tell the truth."

"In chemistry, they teach you that nothing can be lost, nothing can spontaneously disappear. I believe the same is true for souls."

She was about to spar with him, to say angry, hateful words. Instead, she looked into his eyes and felt like a steel beam bolted her to the earth. She was solid, connected. She hadn't felt like that since her parents had died. Holding onto him, she felt rooted. Her shoulders relaxed. "Thanks, Bruno. I mean that."

"Anytime," he said, intertwining her fingers in his.

Don't love him. Don't love him. Don't love him.

"Is this what you want?" he asked, lifting her hand. She knew he was asking about them.

"Yes," she said simply. She was tired of thinking, planning, scheming. She leaned into him, and he placed her hands on the side of his cheek. Claire forgot about Lucia, the failed boutique, her botched career. She wanted to kiss him, to lose herself in him.

"I want you to know, I see you," he said, gazing into her eyes.

"What do you see?" she asked.

"There's something different about you now."

He had an uncanny way of making her feel as though her

heart and soul were bare to him. His hands moved around her waist, and he brought her in. She lifted her chin, and he kissed her lips. She could taste the sweetness of honey, and opened her mouth. His tongue swirled with hers; the sensation of floating came to her. She felt a sort of stupor, as if she'd finally awaken from a hard sleep. He pulled back and kissed the tip of her nose.

"Let's catch up with the rest before they miss us." He gave her a quick, chaste peck on the lips and took her hand as they walked to the van. "I want to see you again."

"Ask me proper, then."

"Will you, Claire Townsend, go out on a date with me, Bruno Canul?"

Claire couldn't help but laugh, not out of jest or judgment. She loved the way he asked her. He was the same way with her that he'd been so long ago. That same confidence. Great kisser. Looking at the ground, she didn't answer him right away. She should say *no*. She should walk away. Instead, she met his eyes. "Yes, Mr. Canul. I will go on a date with you."

"There's a special place I want to show you. This evening?"

She thought of all the ways to turn him away, but instead blurted out, "I'd love to. When?"

"Around four? That will give us enough time to have dinner and see the sunset." He took her hand and they walked through the jungle paths, stepping over the line of leafcutter ants.

"You'll pick me up at BIFA?" she asked. Maybe he could help her. She could tell him about Lucia on the date. *Seriously?* She couldn't ask an old boyfriend for two hundred thousand dollars to get out of a bind. What if he tried to save her and ended up getting hurt, or worse, killed because of her? *Great way to start a relationship.* Work with Janine. Get the money from Reade Street. Pay Lucia. Leave New York behind forever and start a new life with Bruno. He'd never know.

Bruno squeezed her hand three times, then dropped it as

they approached the crew in the parking lot. Once inside the van, she looked out the window. Bruno had driven separately and was in his Jeep. He waved goodbye to her. For once, just once, maybe her life would work out the way it was supposed to.

Stop daydreaming. Life doesn't work that way.

CHAPTER NINETEEN

Claire

The group drove to the Sleeping Giant resort for lunch and returned to BIFA afterwards. Claire had been quiet most of the time; the rest of the group was chatty. Bruno wasn't there. He had gone off to work with his brother. As Claire got out of the van, she found herself woozy. Maybe she needed a nap? She went into the Art Lodge, but realized she had too much work to do, especially if she was going out with Bruno tonight and then taking off tomorrow morning with Janine.

She found a Diet Coke in the fridge. She snapped open the top and drank half of it in less than five minutes. She felt refreshed, the caffeine giving her a boost. Claire turned on her laptop to work. She opened up the program where she populated a report showing milestones completed and budgetary constraints. Right now, her project was in green status; no delays or over-expenditures had occurred. The project was moving ahead nicely, everyone played well with each other, and nobody had an outrageous spend request. Part of keeping the status in green was a verbal check with her teammates.

Three shamans worked on ceremonial dance steps for

different stages of the play. They told her they were nearly finished and would easily be done in a few hours. Janine was in conversation with local artists as they added final touches to the background art. She made notes on her project plan. She appreciated Janine's efficiency and ability to be direct with others. She was a good communicator and hard worker.

Claire was looking for Darren and Ruth Ann when they both came into the Art Lodge. Her hair was freshly combed. He was practically beaming and actually looked happy. *Interesting.* They were trying to act as if they had no interest in each other, but he kept looking at her, and Ruth Ann giggled.

Ruth Ann led him to her make-shift studio, near an open window. She lifted up a waist chain-belt made of semi-precious stones, tortoise and conch shells that could be a belt or doubled up and worn up as a necklace. Ruth Ann put it on and shimmied her hips. The jewelry made a tinkling clinking sound. Darren watched her appreciatively, and when Ruth Ann stopped dancing, she blew him an air kiss. Darren turned a shade of beet red. Romance was a funny thing that way. You never knew what would turn a person's head.

CLAIRE SPENT the rest of the afternoon working on the project financials. She'd populated an ROI and expense reports, then fixed data errors. When she checked her watch, it was three thirty. The afternoon had flown by. In her room, she changed into a pair of shorts and an athletic t-shirt. Looking at the setup of her room, she was uncomfortable leaving her getaway money unprotected, especially since the recent event with Lucia's man. She took a thousand dollars out of her wallet, put it in a billfold, and placed it in her backpack, along with a change of clothes in case the weather changed or something.

In the pavilion, she waited for Bruno, barely able to sit still.

She was excited to see what he had planned. He pulled up in his Jeep looking like some kind of adventure god. His dark hair was loose and wild from the wind. The t-shirt covered his perfectly sized biceps. His strong thighs were apparent in the shorts. Whenever she was with him, everything felt perfect.

"Claire?" he said, standing up in the driver's seat, one arm across the roll bar.

"Will this work?" She pulled against the fabric of her pants. "It's a short hike, right?"

"You look great." She got into the Jeep and he kissed her cheek before sitting. In spite of the overall sense of calmness, Claire was a bit off kilter, knowing that sooner or later it would all end.

"Shall we?"

They got into his topless Jeep. He started it up with a roar and off they went, down the Hummingbird Highway. The wind was in her hair and she ran her fingers through it, letting it blow wild before pulling it up into a ponytail.

They stopped for dinner at a juke joint off the side of the road with handmade signs on cardboard. Only a small space at a standing family-style table was available. The crowded restaurant forced them closer. He had turned towards her so she had more room, and she stood in his protective space. His chest was only a few inches from hers. Her hip bumped into his every so often, from her natural sway.

Even though they were surrounded by people, it seemed like they were the only two. He ordered tamales, telling her they were made from an ancient Mayan recipe, along with 'salbutes,' which reminded her of street tacos. They were handed two Belikin beers they had ordered while they waited for the food.

"I'm excited to be here. I'm hoping to get my career back on track," she said. Once the words came out of her lips, she cringed, but tried not to let him see.

"What happened in New York?"

"A lot," she said, wanting to tell him the story. "After we parted ways, I tried to make inroads back to anthropology. I interned for six months with the Met, gave tours of the Mayan Experience: The Art of Death—I'll never forget that name. Anyway, I catalogued pieces. It was amazing, but the money sucked. I got the job at the Apfel Gallery, and it was too demanding to do both."

"Didn't you say something about a shop you owned?"

"I did," Claire said. She looked at him earnestly. *At least tell him a little bit of truth.* "I got fired from the gallery. That money funded the shop, and well, I lost it."

"Does this have anything to do with the video Darren spoke about?"

Claire ducked her head. She didn't want Bruno to see that she was mortified. And pissed. Five minutes before that video was taken, she was on top of the world. About to sell a million-dollar painting, earn her monthly payment to Lucia, sell her fancy wallpaper to Barneys. Even hearing about the video made her heart race.

"After the fallout," she said, pausing to find the right words, "I had to figure something out. Xander helped me get this job."

"So you didn't really want a change, it was forced on you?"

He had a knack for finding the truth. "Sometimes, it's the only way people can change," she said, thinking of the conversation between her and Lucia in NYC. "I was really close to paying off a big debt and having it all. You should have seen my shop. I even had a contract with Barneys to sell a 'Claire Townsend' exclusive wallpaper design."

"What about your friends? Didn't they help you?"

"I haven't had friends like Xander and our group since college." She was hesitant to even call her New York City acquaintances friends. They were social media influencers whom she had connected with and shared a goal of boosting likes and shares. To be fair though, she probably wouldn't have offered to help if one of them was in trouble. She didn't like that about herself.

"They just left you hanging? No one did anything?"

Claire shook her head. "Loyalty is skin deep." She hated saying the words. They described her exactly. She pulled at the neck of her shirt and half smiled.

"But then the video happened? Why was it so bad?"

"A perfect storm. This guy was hitting on me, but I didn't like him. Then people got upset because the artist wasn't there. Things got out of control. And everyone left, a literal stampede. This woman, Amaya, had a video camera, and she posted it. I was fired by my boss, and the whole world got to see it."

"That's messed up," Bruno said.

"Yeah. Shit out of luck. Thirty grand down the toilet. And the guy who was hitting on me... turns out he's friends with the purchasing agent at Barneys. I lost my contract."

"That's terrible. High-end art sales are competitive, but that's brutal," Bruno said. "Now that you're here, doing a little anthropology, what do you think about staying in the field? Or do you want to go back to art?"

"I don't know," Claire said, wondering what would happen with Lucia. "Maybe I'm sick of the East Coast."

"Come out to LA?"

"There's an idea," Claire said, but immediately dismissed it. Superficial as it was, she missed the NYC life. The parties, the dancing—it was fun. Although, looking at Bruno, she reconsidered. Was living in New York City with fake friends and a humongous bank account a goal she wanted? When her parents died, she had no recourse while in foster care because of money. All she wanted was a good time, to forget, and most importantly, to never, ever have to worry about money again.

Could Bruno offer her something more substantial than NYC?

"It's like you get a chance to start over. A Popol Vuh of your very own."

"I don't know about that," Claire said sheepishly. He didn't have the whole picture. To start over without any debt to Lucia was a dream away.

"How are you and Janine getting along?" he asked.

She didn't answer.

"I want to make sure she isn't dragging you into anything. Did you know about the bust in LA?"

"She told me," Claire said carefully.

"Did she tell you that I was the one who informed the FBI?"

"What? No."

"I work as a consultant for the FBI Art Crimes division. There were rumors first, then I obtained photographic evidence of the dig, but we weren't able to get enough evidence to convict Rex or her."

"Oh," Claire said. *Tell him!* After the visit with Lucia's man, she couldn't tell Bruno about Janine. She had to avoid any conversation regarding the black-market deal she was getting into, and knowing Bruno was the one who helped arrest Janine only worsened the situation.

Tell him! She took a long drink of her beer and considered telling Bruno what she knew about Janine. The problem was, she had no real evidence. Nothing documented between her and Janine. She could deny everything and call it heresy. Bruno would hate her for her involvement, and the deal between her and Janine would disappear. And Lucia would come after her.

"How does that work?" she asked, genuinely wanting to know. "Being an FBI Art Crimes consultant?"

"Basically, if I see something, I say something. I watch over some of the more sensitive parts of our National Forests, out by Death Valley. We're not on any active leads."

The reply made her nervous. Before this question, she had plausible deniability. Now? If she didn't tell him, and he found out about the black-market trade she did with Janine while working with him, she'd have no recourse. In for a penny, in for a pound. "Are you here to watch out for Janine?"

He looked uncomfortable. "Look, Claire. I don't know what she's said to you, but watch out. She's a chameleon."

"Janine said she used to work for the CIA, in the clandestine department, but quit. Did you know she went back to college because of her sister?"

"I knew about the CIA. But I didn't know she had a sister."

"Not a real sister. One from foster care. She died, though, a while ago."

"I didn't know," Bruno said. "Tough break. I hope she makes her sister proud."

"I hope so too," Claire said, holding up her beer. "Cheers."

"Cheers." Bruno checked his watch, "Oh, hey. It's almost five thirty. Finish up. We have to catch the sunset."

Bruno and Claire got into his Jeep. They drove on the highway for a half-mile before he turned onto a dirt road that led into an obvious orchard, the trees lined up in single file rows. "This is an orange grove," he said as the dust clouded behind the Jeep. The road was flanked by row upon row of small trees with a densely packed crown. Bright spots of orange popped out of the green leaves. The air was pungent with sweet citrus. Leaves shimmered in the fading sunlight. He parked, got out, put on a backpack, and came to her door. He held out his hand and she took it as he guided her.

They walked down a narrow trail between a row of orange trees. "The trees are so much shorter than I imagined."

"Easier for the picking machines," he said. "Did you ever

talk to Delia or the Nat Geo guys about going to Chichén Itzá? We've got a free day coming up on Wednesday."

She'd completely forgotten about Chichén Itzá and looked at him funny. "With everything going on, I forgot to mention it to Shali. Something else came up. We have a lot to do for Popol Vuh timelines. And it's an eight-hour drive, not to mention going through customs."

"All good points," he said, and stopped to narrow his eyes on her, "but it's not like you to forget. We can go after the Popol Vuh. We have some time then."

"I'll check with Shali. But my flight leaves the next morning."

"The timing doesn't seem to be working out," Bruno said with a shrug.

They walked through the orchard for five minutes until they reached a jungle-forest mix. Deciduous cieba trees stood tall like open umbrellas against the squat, broad-leafed jungle shrubs. Sunlight came through the leaves, leaving patterned streaks of light on the shadowed ground. The air was warm, lightly humid. They stopped in front of a low bush with small, compact yellow flowers. He picked a small bunch and moved her hair back, sliding it over her ear.

"These flowers are called rudas. They bring good luck and good fortune." With a smile that could melt a thousand candles, his fingers brushed along the underside of her jaw. "Yellow looks good on you."

His words, along with a soft breeze through the leaves, quickened her heart. Claire was naturally attracted to him; she always had been. She swallowed hard. Chirping birds accentuated the conversation with cicadas humming through the air. After a short walk in, there was a rock outcrop that went almost straight up. Claire thought it might be a hill that eroded away.

Thick, ropy, Tarzan-looking vines had grown from the top

and over, hiding the trail. Bruno pushed them aside, and they headed up. The elevation was slight, so she wasn't scared. Green and black geckos scurried around, up the rocky sides, down the tree trunks, and a pond-green frog stood absolutely still. After maybe ten minutes of hiking, they reached the top of the outcrop. To her surprise, there was a double-decker gazebo.

A mountain range rose beyond the valley. While she didn't want to go right to the edge, she was thrilled not to be having a panic attack. Bruno pointed out the different butterflies, the Belizean blue butterfly with nearly iridescent wings amongst the five other types that floated in and out among the leaves. She was enthralled by something so delicate among the density of the forest-jungle.

"What mountain range is that over there?" she asked, turning to him.

"They call it the Sleeping Giant. Do you see its head? Just at the cusp of the valley? Follow it to the left and you'll see the belly. My family watches over this valley. We try to protect the old Mayan sites."

"That's incredible. But… is that a good thing? I mean, shouldn't you be telling the archeological groups?"

"We do, but there are so many out there. I cannot tell you how many times a site is compromised by grave diggers, greedy treasure hunters looking to sell an artifact to the highest bidder."

A distinct glow of embarrassment burned hot up her neck and cheeks. Bruno wasn't looking at her, he was still gazing over the panorama. She wished she was on his side, but there was no way she could tell him everything.

"We have to take care of these places like it's family."

"That's not how family works," Claire said, her voice sharper than what she intended. She knitted her eyebrows and shook her head.

"Sure it does. What are you talking about?"

"The world doesn't work that way, Bruno. My parents died when I was sixteen years old. I got passed around relatives, ended up in foster care. Family doesn't give a shit."

Bruno's eyes softened. She could drown in them. For a moment, she let go and believed in his world. It was a good place. Family mattered. Except that wasn't reality. She backed up and regarded him suspiciously.

"Everything in this world is connected, Claire. I genuinely believe it. There is a reason you and I met again."

"It's called *a job*," she said, crossing her arms. "You and I both have one. That's how you explain it."

He let out a belly-roaring laugh. "Ah yes. Let us believe for a moment that there is no magic in this world. That everything is logical and has its place. Life would be so empty, so boring."

"That's how the real-world works, Bruno. Magic is… a pipe-dream."

"I don't think you truly believe that, not deep down. Take a hold of my hand? I'd like to show you something."

"Hold on," she said, her heels dug in. "Why would you want *me* to care about magic or goodness in the world?"

"Why wouldn't I? You are in front of me. We have this moment."

Claire looked over the jungle and regarded the lines of the mountain against the sky. "Let's go back," she said. "This is ridiculous."

"Trust me," he said, pulling her close, but he made no move to kiss her. He squeezed her hand three times. A slight shiver traveled along her back, but she could not give up her steely resolve. She didn't want to be swept away. She needed something real, something that didn't disappear at the slightest hint of danger, someone who was willing to tell her the truth. Someone willing to be her truth. "This better be good."

"I promise you, it is." He kissed her on the forehead, then

took her hand. They walked down the rickety stairs of the gazebo and towards a landing in front of the rocky outcrop. The smell of oranges was light, surrounding her, enveloping her in sweetness. He stopped midway and asked her to close her eyes. She cocked her head in uncertainty.

"Trust me," he said.

She closed her eyes and felt him behind her. He lifted her arms so they were out in the air to form a T. Having her eyes closed made aware of her body. The slightest breeze came upon her, and goosebumps popped up all along her arms.

"Open your eyes," he whispered into her ear. His breath was warm against her skin. "Don't move, just look with your eyes."

A dozen iridescent blue butterflies had landed on her outstretched arms. She gasped in amazement.

Bruno put his arms around her waist. The warmth of his body was against her back. The butterflies lifted for a moment, but then settled back down on her. He whispered, "The Mayans believe that the butterfly is a symbol of two worlds. Half of their wings represent the dream world and the other half represents the physical You need both to fly." He turned her forearm so that her wrists were facing upwards. The butterflies moved with her arms, and a few fluttered away.

"Incredible," she said. "How do you know about this?"

"I found this place as a boy. Made me believe in magic."

She closed her eyes again. Completely relaxed, she forgot everything except for the knowledge that butterflies surrounded her, the bright blue color, the soft feet upon her skin that felt like nothing at all.

Bruno had come around and was facing her. "You are so beautiful right now."

She opened her eyes. "You haven't changed, do you know that? Still handsome as ever, and I love that devil-may-care sense about you."

He leaned in. "Come to LA with me."

Claire lifted her chin in invitation, and he understood her intention.

"May I kiss you?"

"Yes."

He closed his eyes and moved towards her, his lips touching hers. She put her arms around him, the butterflies taking flight. He wrapped his hands in her hair and pulled her to him, his lips soft yet strong. He bit the bottom of her lip and released her. She sighed with content.

He touched her bottom lip with his thumb. "Let's go back up," he said, taking her hand and leading her to the stairs. "I have one more surprise for you."

This time Claire didn't hesitate, and she took his hand. He led her up to the gazebo. They stood at the edge of the railing to watch the sunset over the valley. White wispy clouds faded into blazing oranges and reds. The music of the jungle, random beeps of tree frogs and the bird brattle, made her feel alive. She wanted to kiss him again, to press her body against his. She leaned in to him, her chin lifting towards his face.

He kissed her. She opened her mouth to him, letting herself be free, letting go of concern. His tongue dipped in and swirled. He tasted of beer and something sweet. The kiss knocked them off balance. She steadied them by placing a hand on the railing and taking a step back. She placed a hand on his cheek, the stubble rough under her fingers. "If you could do anything, be anywhere, what would you do?" she asked.

"This, right here. I'm living it. I always wanted to be an archeologist. I have a good family. You are in my arms."

He dropped his hands around her waist. Their lips met again. Her tongue dove in and out, tasting him, teasing him. "I want you, Claire," he said, placing his whole hand on her breast, over her thudding heart.

Overwhelmed with desire, she couldn't speak, and nodded instead. Bruno picked up his backpack. They walked back to his Jeep holding hands and kissing. She felt wonderful, but with a weight in her body that she ignored. *Tell him*, it whispered, but she was too full of pleasure to pay attention.

She got into the passenger side and waited. When he sat in the driver's seat, Claire clutched his shirt and guided him towards her. She kissed him, hard, with driving need, the desire to forget, the want to be someone else. His mouth met her measure, biting her lips, his tongue lashing. She used the roll bar to pull herself up and away from his mouth and stood over him. He placed his hand on her hips. Holding onto the padded bar, she leaned over so her breasts were in his face.

Bruno lifted her shirt and pulled her bra cups down. With one hand, he twirled a nipple, pinching and squeezing. She arched her back with desire. He held her shirt back with his hand and took a nipple into his mouth. The sharp angle of her body only allowed him to take in the tips, teasing and delicious. She moved her body over him, building decadent frustration. Claire changed position, pulled her nipple out of his mouth, and straddled him in the driver's seat. His dick was hard and throbbing under his shorts. She moved suggestively, rhythmically pressing his hardness against her covered wetness.

His eyes were intense with unabashed, animal desire. Claire took her shirt off and tossed it on the passenger seat. Bruno wrapped his arms around her and she leaned back. He lifted her breast to his mouth. He bit the tip of her nipple, then blew on it, like he was blowing out a candle. The warmth of his breath against the taut nipple shot electricity through her. Her core was on fire, her panties wet. He pressed his palm against her chest and slid his hand down her body, along her scar.

Her muscles tensed. He stopped to wait for an answer. She nodded. He placed his hand on the front of her thighs and then slid it under her shorts, cupping her mons over her underwear. She moaned as fresh wetness covered her labia. She grabbed the roll bar and lifted herself. Roughly, he pushed aside her underwear and slid two fingers into her.

Unable to stand the intense pleasure, she pulled her hips back, but he wrapped his arm around her bottom and held her tight against his hand. She gasped as he slipped another finger inside her, pressing inside as far as he could, trying to touch her core. She cried out, her back arching, her body electrified with pure pleasure. His palm pressed against her pubic bone, against her clitoris. His fingers moved inside her, spreading her. She looked to the sky, feeling free, like she could fly.

He withdrew his hand. "I have to stop or I'm going to take you right here."

Claire's chest was heaving. She didn't want to quit; she was ready for him. The sky grew dark, but a sliver of sun was left on the horizon. He helped put her shirt on after she had re-adjusted her bra. She wanted to stay and keep kissing, let his hands roam over her body. He caressed her breast one more time. "That doesn't mean you're going home."

She laughed, a pure release of tension and joy. Claire moved to her seat, and Bruno started up the Jeep. There was a delicious anticipation in waiting. He turned onto the highway and after only a few minutes, turned left onto a dusty road.

"I didn't realize we were so close to your place" Claire said.

Bruno smiled and put his hand on her knee. He drove down a pot-holed dirt road, each bump sending a thrilling pulse of desire through her, then they pulled up to his house. Everything was familiar this time, the motorcycle in the car port, the adventure guide equipment. Vibrant blue butterflies floated through nearby trees. Claire smiled. Maybe Bruno was right. Maybe there was magic in the world. Maybe there was goodness. Hope. Love, even.

"Are you hungry?"

"No," Claire said, getting out of the Jeep.

"I am," Bruno said as he rounded the vehicle. He took her hand. "A beer, and we can share an empanada."

"All right," she said.

He walked into his house, and she trailed him into the kitchen. He turned his iPod on to Latin jazz, then grabbed two beers out of the fridge and a lime, setting them on the counter. He motioned to Claire and pointed out a kitchen drawer. She got out a can opener and a steak knife. She popped the metal cap off the beer and used the knife to cut the lime into small wedges.

By this time, he'd retrieved a paper plate with a tin foil wrap from the fridge. He uncovered it and placed the plate into a toaster oven. *Tell him now!* She opened her mouth, to say the words, the truth, but silence followed.

"The empanadas take five minutes or so to warm up."

"Okay," Claire said, and handed him his beer with a wedge of lime in the top. She watched him push the lime into the bottle and sucked the juice off the tip. A small smile lit up her face. She was excited, knowing what was going to take place that night, the way he would touch her. He took a drink of his beer, then set it on the counter. He put his arms around her, embracing her. "I'd forgotten how much I missed this, missed you. It always comes back to us, doesn't it?"

She pushed him back gently. "What are you saying?" she asked.

"I have feelings for you, strong feelings." He cupped her face with his warm hands, looking into her eyes. "I am here for you. Are you here for me?"

She took her shirt off rather than speak. She slipped off the straps of her bra, the cups still covering her breasts. Her scar was exposed, thick and shiny between them. He touched the top of it, starting at the base of her clavicle. She hunched her shoulders instinctively, trying to protect herself.

He removed his hands and pressed on the tops of her

shoulders to help her relax. "I care about you, Claire. This scar is a part of you."

Tears welled in her eyes.

"I never forgot you," he said, taking his hands off her shoulders and placing his fingers on the top of her scar. "This is part of you." He traced it to the middle of her stomach. "I think it's beautiful."

An involuntary laugh escaped her lips. "Right."

"I'm serious, Claire." He placed his hand flat against her chest. "It's beautiful because it's you."

She took his hands in hers and squeezed three times, a lone tear trailing down her cheek. He brought her hand to his face, kissed the center of her palm, and placed it against his heart. She looked deep into his eyes to see if there was any doubt, any fear. She wanted to know if his words were just words, but she did not see hesitation. Only acceptance and love.

He put his arms around her and pulled her close. She could have sworn her heart would explode with the love washing over and through her; it was so strong it threatened to overwhelm her. She wanted to touch every part of him, to know the warmth of his skin on hers. The toaster oven dinged, and Bruno kissed her on the tip of her nose, pulled away and got the food out.

He wiped a steak knife on a nearby kitchen towel and cut the empanada in half. She got two forks out of the same drawer as the can opener and set them on the counter. He cut a piece and held it up to her. She opened her mouth, and he fed her. She closed her eyes and swallowed. This was the life she wanted. It was possible, it was available to her, but only if she told him the truth. Only if she was willing to risk losing Janine's deal. Only if she was willing to risk Lucia's wrath.

He fed her again and then took his own bite. She had a sip of beer, and they did this until the empanada was finished. Without a sound, he took her hand and led her to the bedroom. The room was as neat as his house, clean, but with a change of clothes on the ground, a pair of biking shoes left near the closet. The bed was on a metal frame with no headboard, and the pictures on the wall were Belizean Tourism twenty years past. There was a desk but no chair to accompany it.

Bruno pulled her towards him and their bodies met, arms around each other, lips kissing, licking, biting. He tried to undo her bra, but was unable to separate the clasp. His breathing was shallow; she could see naked desire on his face. "Truthfully, Claire? Don't laugh. I'm nervous."

Claire's heart melted into a thousand pieces and she threw her arms around him, kissing his earlobe, his cheek, and running her hands through his hair. "I'm here for you," she said, reaching behind her back and unclasping the bra. It fell to the ground. She stood in front of him, uncovered. Her nipples were hard and sensitive to the air. He took her in his arms and they tumbled onto the bed, a jumble of legs and arms, kissing each other deeply, as if to leave nothing unexplored.

He untangled himself to stand up. She propped up on her elbow and gazed at him. He took off his shirt and his shorts, leaving red plaid boxers on. She hooked the waistband of her shorts and wriggled out of them, lifting them to him with her toe. He tossed them to the side.

Bruno kneeled on the floor before the bed. He grabbed an ankle and firmly pulled her towards him. One leg went left over his shoulder, the other leg, to the right. Her pussy was inches from his face. With both hands, he spread her wide, using his thumbs to part her slit.

The anticipation was driving her wild. She wriggled her hips again, hungry for him, wanting his touch to release her pleasure, to set her desire free. With his eyes on her, he pinched her clitoris. She leaned her head back and closed her eyes, trying to angle her body closer to his touch.

"Look at me, Claire. I want to see your face when you come."

Claire met his gaze and found him watching her. He rubbed her clitoris back and forth, pinching the nub, swirling it in his fingers.

"It's you, Claire."

Looking in his eyes, she fell into dark brown pools, a place where love and pleasure lived. He moved his thumbs into her opening, rimming her, gentle but firm, taking pleasure in her slow agony. Her body quivered and she tried to close her eyes, to let the pleasure consume her. He stopped moving. "Keep your eyes on me."

She was on edge, every nerve in her body alive and tense. She wanted him inside, to fill her. Claire lifted her head to make eye contact. With a smile, he moved his thumbs and spread her, stretched her. A wave of pleasure rose from her core up her spine, and she arched her back, but kept her eyes on his. They were bonded, connected, and she felt as if she were jumping off the ledge into water.

He pressed three fingers inside her, pulsing his hand. She moved her hips in unison with him. He grunted with each movement, pressing harder into her, filling her, his sound animalistic. He kept eye contact with her, wanting to give her pleasure, but taking what was his. She squeezed the sheets with her fists and lifted her chin into the air. Her body stiffened as an intense wave rolled through her. He pulled his fingers out, and suddenly his mouth was on her, sucking her clitoris hard as if drinking her in, needing and wanting only her. The sensation threw her outside of herself, and her whole world went black. She came hard, shudders wracking her body.

When she stopped shivering, and met his gaze again, he placed his three fingers into his mouth, licking them clean. "Your taste is mine."

The words invigorated her, made her feel special. He stood

and put a knee between her legs, against her throbbing pussy. She moaned. His free hand moved along her scar and over her belly.

"I need you," Claire said, sitting up.

She yanked his boxers down. His uncircumcised cock sprang free. The skin was flushed, and his penis had a natural curve to it, magnificently long with a wide girth.

"I want you." She wrapped her fingers around his dick and pulled the foreskin back, exposing the tip. With her other hand, she cupped his balls. She sucked the head into her mouth, using her tongue to circle the tip. He groaned and leaned back.

Claire tightened her grip and pumped her fist along his shaft, licked and teased the tip. His ass muscles tightened as he groaned, thrusting towards her. He was getting close.

He pulled out of her mouth before he could come and stood proud, his slick cock between them. "What do you want?"

"All of you," she said, squirming with uncomfortable pleasure, wanting release, wanting him to take her, to be deep inside. She moved to the middle of the bed and pulled her knees up. Bruno's eyes dropped to her pussy. He swallowed hard before grabbing a condom from his nightstand. He opened the package and rolled it on. He moved on top of her, his hard cock sliding against her wet slit. "Is this what you want?"

"Yes, oh God, yes," Claire said, letting her knees fall, and she lay back on the bed.

The tip of his cock opened her, and then, as he came into her, he spread her wide. A low mewling escaped her lips as the pain and pleasure increased exponentially. He moved inside her slowly and completely until he was rooted.

Suddenly, he took her shoulders and rolled over so she was on top. Claire started laughing, with glee, with unabashed happiness. She met his eyes again and adjusted herself. She leaned back, letting him stretch her with the new position, carnal ecstasy shooting up her spine. Bruno groaned and closed his eyes. She moved her hips in a circular motion, feeling the whole of him inside her, moving the taut edges of her opening against his hardness planted firmly inside her. Every movement sent titillating charges through her body.

He placed his hand on her hips and moved her rhythmically over him. Her breasts bounced hard, faster and faster. She cried out, a wave of pleasure coming through her, until she was struck still by passion. He flipped her over again, so they were missionary style. Claire could barely breathe; her pussy throbbed violently, sensitive and wet. He plunged deep into her. Her body clenched around him, and a howl escaped from her mouth. He grunted and thrust into her again. She felt the instinct, the animal inside him, entering into the heart of her.

"Come inside me," she said, matching his rhythm, squeezing him to her, taking and giving until they both came in unison. All she saw were tiny bright pinpoints of light.

Breathing hard, he collapsed on her, his cock still pulsing inside her. He looked into her eyes, saying nothing. She inhaled as he exhaled, loving the smell of his breath. Without a doubt, she loved him.

Bruno pulled her in close and kissed her forehead. "I want to stay like this forever."

Claire ran her fingers lightly up and down his back, thinking of the blue butterflies fluttering away when they kissed that afternoon. Without him, she would be lost. He got up and held his hand out to her. They walked naked to the bathroom. They took a shower together; he helped to wash her body, she his. Afterwards, in the kitchen, he made a charcuterie plate with cheese.

"I have to tell you something, Bruno."

"What?" he asked, concerned.

"Someone is after me."

"What are you talking about?" he asked. Every part of his body was in position to defend her, a wide stance, his fists clenched. "Who is after you?"

Claire took a deep breath. She knew it was a lot, and that she hadn't even given him warning. "Back in New York, I borrowed money from a loan shark. I owe her two hundred thousand in seven days."

Bruno didn't say anything at first. His mouth opened and then shut. He poured two glasses of water as he seemed to consider her words. "What happens if you don't pay?"

"She will kill me."

He scratched the back of his neck. "She is going to *kill* you?"

"Yes. That's basically what she said." Claire tried to stand very quietly, but her hand was shaking as she thought about her last dinner with Lucia, that dangerous calm she emanated, the spoon between them.

He brought her inside his strong arms. "It will be okay, Claire. Let's talk this through. Is that why you wanted to go to Chichén Itzá? Did you think you could run?"

She sighed with relief, thankful to be with him. "Yes. There's another way to fix my problem." She let go of his hand and picked up the glass to take a drink. She nearly told him about the endeavor with Janine. She knew his opinion on people who sold on the black market. Bruno would hate her for working with Janine, no matter what the reason. Right then, she decided that she would not pursue a deal with Janine or Reade Street Gallery, but she wasn't going to tell him, either. "But I'm not going to do it that way."

A thread of guilt snaked through her. She was only being half honest with Bruno, even though technically, it was only a lie by omission. "I don't know what to do."

He didn't ask her what the other plan was. Instead, he

kissed her on the forehead and said, "You are safe here, with me."

"You don't understand, Bruno," Claire said as she pushed him away. She reached for the glass of water, but spilled it. "She sent someone to Belize. He was in my room at BIFA. He had a gun. I don't think you get how much danger I'm in. Or that I could be putting you in danger too."

"What are you talking about?"

"One of Lucia's henchman came to Belize and put a gun to my head. Reminded me that I had a certain amount of time. If I don't pay her, I will be killed." She set her hands in her lap and looked at him. Did she really think Bruno could help? "Do you have *two hundred thousand* dollars laying around? No."

"Why didn't you tell me about this earlier?" he asked. "Ugh. Never mind. Why did you take the money?"

Claire took a deep breath. "You know my shop? I knew I could make it work, I just needed a little bit to make it really great, but no one would give me a loan. I didn't have any collateral, no assets for the bank to use. No one would co-sign for me. I don't have family. So I borrowed a hundred thousand from Lucia. I knew I could make the payments. I made great money at Apfel."

"And then everything collapsed when you got fired, right? You lost the sale, you didn't have the money to pay him."

"Her."

Bruno looked confused.

"The loan shark is a her."

Shaking it off like it didn't matter, Bruno said, "The amount doubled because you were late on payments? Jesus. We'll figure this out. I know people. I work for the FBI. As a consultant, but still. You'll be safe."

"No FBI. I trust you, but not them. They won't take care of me."

Bruno looked as if he were about to say something, then stopped. "We'll come up with a plan. My mom has money, I have some saved up. We will figure something out with the FBI," Bruno said. "I can't do anything right now, but let me ask around tomorrow."

"I trust you. The FBI, though? They'll use me like a dirty rag and throw me away."

Bruno said nothing, and instead unclasped his necklace and held the jade pendant in his hand. "I want you to have this." He put it in her hand. "It's a Mayan protection pendant. A jaguar."

"I can't accept this." There was no way a pendant was going to save her, but a warmth bubbled up.

"The reason I give you this necklace is because in you, I see the jaguar. You are strong. Don't forget who you are."

She inspected the pendant, regarding it with the keen eye of a professional. She bit her lip and tried not to cry. Bruno put his arms around her and hugged. His cheek brushed up against hers. She loved his rough, unshaved skin against her soft skin, being drawn to him. She rubbed the pendant one more time to linger in an honest moment between them. Bruno took it from Claire's hand. He circled his finger in the air, and she turned her back to him and lifted her hair.

He clasped it around her neck and whispered in her ear. "We shall plant ancient words." He placed the necklace over her head. "It is planting." He lifted her hair and let the necklace settle. Turning her around, he placed a warm palm over the pendant and met her eyes. "It is root-beginning as well."

"What is that from?" she asked.

"The Popol Vuh. A story of beginnings."

CHAPTER TWENTY

Claire

Claire had slept well in Bruno's arms, a heavy, dreamless sleep. That morning, a knowing had come over her. No matter what happened, all would end well. They woke up early and made love again, slow, sweet, intentional. They walked back to the Jeep. They held hands, only separating when they had to. Whatever it was between them, she understood it. Around Bruno, she wanted to be a better person. She was going to do the right thing, no matter what it cost. She was in love.

Bruno pulled up to the BIFA compound around seven a.m. and leaned in to kiss her. "I'll make some calls and let you know. I'll see you tomorrow."

She walked through the pavilion and onto the trail that led to the Art Lodge. Through the still dark jungle, the smell of cool leaves calmed her. Headed towards her room, she had fifteen minutes to figure out how to tell Janine she would not work with her. As she entered the Art Lodge, something was amiss, but Claire couldn't pinpoint why. The crispness of the air seemed off, but how could that be?

In her room, her suitcase was on the ground, clothes were

randomly tossed, her toiletries had been emptied into the sink. The bed upended. The dresser drawers were on the bed. The money was gone, she was sure of it.

"Where have you been? We've been looking for you."

"Oh no," Claire mumbled under her breath.

"It happened last night, while I was with Darren and Ruth Ann at dinner," said Janine. "I tried to call you, but it went straight to voicemail."

"My phone died. I didn't have my charger," Claire said, avoiding Janine's question as to where she had been.

Claire sat on the bed and covered her face with her hands. The money hidden in the sock was probably gone, but she didn't want to look while Janine was still there. Luckily, she had brought her wallet with her on the date and still had a thousand dollars.

"You did this, didn't you?"

"No, I didn't. What? Are you crazy?" Janine said. "I was out at dinner. Ask Ruth Ann or Darren."

Janine sat on the bed next to her and patted her thigh. "It wasn't just you, you know. My stuff was scattered around, too. I had a few hundred dollars in cash stolen. But worse? They stole the headdress, the one on loan from the museum."

Claire's stomach flipped. Bruno had gone to a lot of effort to get that piece out on loan. When he heard the news, he was going to be devastated.

Could it have been Lucia's henchman, the guy who had put a gun on her face? She wasn't sure.

Claire pushed Janine's hand off her thigh. "Why are you doing this to me?"

"Honestly, I didn't do it," Janine said. "I swear."

Claire was unable to read her face, unable to tell if she was lying or telling the truth.

"Rex is in Belize City today. He wants to meet you after."

The smile on Janine's face was accompanied by a triumphant glint in her eyes.

"I can't work with you, Janine," Claire said.

Janine stood and put her hand on her hip. "How are you going to pay back the loan shark? Is wittle Bruno and *love* going to save the day?"

"How do you know about Lucia?" Claire asked.

"I know things, Claire. Unlike you, I don't gallivant around halfcocked. I did my research."

"Screw you," Claire said, feeling reckless. Maybe love would save the day. Even if she didn't believe that the FBI would take care of her, at least it was something honest, something truthful. Doing the right thing was the point.

"If you think for one second that you're getting out of this, you're wrong," Janine said. "Loan sharks never go away. They'll kill Bruno in front of you and not blink an eye."

The jaguar pendant Bruno had given her lay heavy on her chest. The way he looked at her, seeing her as a good person… That was the person she wanted to be. She wanted to believe it would end well, that somehow she could solve the Lucia problem without having to commit a crime, without having to lie to Bruno. There had to be a way, even if she didn't know what it was. "I'm out," Claire said. "Find someone else."

"You and I both know that love doesn't save the day. Your parents died. Life is hard and full of crap choices. You remember foster care? If it was anything like it was for me, you know in your bones that love doesn't save the day. The reality is that money always wins. Money is the only thing that assures safety. Love will disappoint you. Every. Single. Time."

"No it won't," Claire said, trying to hold onto the feeling she had that morning with Bruno. She could change. Everything would be fine. But she could sense it floating away, drifting just out of reach.

"What is Lucia promising if you don't pay her back?" Janine asked.

"Nothing good," Claire said, refusing to say more than that. She remembered the dark night that her henchman was in her room, how he knew she was planning to run to Mexico, how he dragged his gun across her cheek.

"Then you know. You know what you have to do. Falling in love with Bruno will not save you. You have to depend on yourself. You cannot trust that he will do the right thing for you. In the end, you'll do whatever it takes. I know how strong you are."

Claire turned to Janine with her mouth agape. "Get out."

"We're leaving for the warehouse in fifteen minutes. Be out front."

CHAPTER TWENTY-ONE

Claire

*E*verything Janine had said was true. *You have to depend on yourself.* Bruno didn't have the means. Neither his mom or Bruno's brother would shell out two hundred grand for her. Running away was out of the question. But she had to think bigger than just herself. She changed into a clean pair of hiker shorts and a shirt.

Right now, the FBI wasn't going to save her, but that equation could be changed. The time had come for her to play offense instead of reacting. If she wanted to make a deal with the FBI, she needed information. She'd need proof that Janine and Rex were part of the black-market scam. That meant she'd have to find out where the warehouse was. She'd have to know what they were shipping. Uncover any other facets of Janine's plan. She was sure that Rex and Janine had something nefarious planned, but it was only a gut feeling at this point. She needed real evidence.

Claire didn't have time to tell Bruno what was going on, and regretfully wished she could. It wouldn't matter in the end, though. If she got him the information—if she told him the truth—she might have a chance with the FBI's help. But no one was going to believe her without proof. She set the GPS on her phone so that she could get the exact address; it was possible they used the warehouse as a holding zone. Once she had the warehouse address, she could start identifying the source for the artifacts and any other players involved. Maybe she could even take pictures of the warehouse or record conversations. Then she'd go to Bruno as soon as possible.

Love could save the day, dammit. Love and a little ingenuity.

Claire didn't have a voice recorder on her phone so she downloaded an app. She decided to put it in her backpack and leave the recorder on, rather than fumble with it while she was with Janine. She'd ask Janine to stop in town to purchase a burner phone, so she could take pictures and send them to Reade Street. Claire strode out to the main part of the Art Lodge. Janine stood at the café table. "Tell Delia we're leaving for the morning and we'll be back."

Janine nodded and set down her coffee cup. Claire saw a tiny smile at the corner of her mouth, like she was being smug. *Let's see how you smile when I'm finished with you.* Janine had gone off to tell Delia of their plans to head into town for the morning. She didn't care what excuse she gave her.

"Let's go." Janine and Claire got into her rental car and drove towards Belize City. On the way, Claire had nothing to say. She wondered briefly if Janine would turn evidence on Rex. Could she use the memory of her sister, or did Janine even have a sister? Was that a lie to get her sympathy? Had Janine been playing her all along?

Claire turned on the radio and reggae music came on. Not her usual fare, but the steady beat helped her focus.

They stopped at a department and food store called Brodies, the Target of Belize, as Janine called it. Claire purchased a burner phone with text capabilities in order to send pictures to Reade Street Gallery. Hopefully, she'd be able to text them covertly to her phone as well. After that, they drove on the Philip Gordson Northern Highway into Belize City and navigated to the industrial side of town.

Janine parked in front of a white warehouse with three white silos and a commercial driving ramp. The sides of the silo were decorated with graphic art of oranges. Claire guessed she was in a factory that used to squeeze and bottle orange juice. These details wouldn't matter, though, unless she couldn't get the GPS reading for Bruno.

Janine got out and struggled to slide open a heavy warehouse door. She was only able to push it wide enough for the two of them to slip in. It was bright inside; the place was lit with industrial lighting, but there was no sound of hustle and bustle. An abandoned warehouse? *Better for the recording.* "Is this whole place full of artifacts?" Claire asked. There was no answer from Janine. Who owned the building? Was it owned by a shell company? Did Janine have any stake here? Wooden crates with random black letters were stacked on top of each other, floor to ceiling. She couldn't quite make out the writing. The floor was concrete, and a cut-wood smell from the crates permeated the space. She wanted to take the burner phone out and take pictures, but she'd told Janine specifically the phone would be used for Reade Street.

Janine led her through the maze to the center of the warehouse where a man was standing next to a rectangular metal table. "This is Sal."

Sal was short and fine-boned. He reminded her of a Cirque du Soleil gymnast. His mannerisms were precise, and not once did he acknowledge her. She wanted to ask his last name, but didn't dare.

On a nearby table were three items. Claire set her backpack on the table and aimed it just right.

"You can't put that there," Sal said.

Claire moved it to the ground and positioned it the best she could. "Do you have any gloves?" she asked to either Sal or Janine.

"Sure," Sal said, with a knowing glance to Janine. He handed her a pair of leather work gloves. Claire was about to say she preferred latex gloves, but the looks on Janine and Sal's face clued her otherwise. She checked the leather to make sure there was no oil or other residue then put them on.

While she wasn't an expert, she'd use her experience working as an intern to determine validity and her art appraisal experience to get a price range. It wasn't perfect, but she wasn't worried; the goal was to find a range of pricing rather than specifics.

"The first item is a circular hand-carved limestone ball court marker. I see here it's carved with a kneeling captive in the center." She picked it up for a closer examination. Her Mayan knowledge from college days was rusty, but she knew enough from working at the Met to know the item was authentic, but she had to work through specifics to let them know she knew. "It's heavy enough," Claire said. "The material is stone. I've actually seen people bring in papier-mâché or cement and try to pass it off."

Claire turned the item over in her hand. She hadn't seen this kind of valuable artifacts since she'd worked at the Met. "The quality is very good. These carved symbols around the perimeter looked to be a Mayan time or date stamp, and the word pet, which means 'to encircle.' This Pok-A-Tok marker is an incredible find, very rare to find one whole."

Sal seemed to have a question on his face as to why that would be true.

"Careless thieves," Claire said to him, "usually are in a hurry. They tend to remove the markers with a blunt object. I'm not sure on price ranges, but I'd set the piece in easily at one twenty."

"Why aren't we getting auction prices?" asked Sal.

"Reade Street only pays market value. We will never see an auction." Claire set down the stone marker. She took out the burner phone and took pictures from different angles. She tried to get Sal and Janine in the pictures, but was only able to get their lower bodies, since angling the camera any higher would tip them off.

"What's she doing?" Sal asked.

"Pictures to the gallery for pre-pricing," Claire said.

The gloves were making it hard to take pictures, so she took them off. The fresh air felt good against her hot fingers and she closed her eyes. Suddenly she had a memory of being with Bruno last night, the way his skin felt against her, his smell.

"Are you okay?" Janine asked.

"My hands were sweating. I wanted to cool them off. The last thing I want is to accidentally drop something."

"You just had a weird look on your face."

Claire shook her hands to cool them faster. She turned towards the table and moved on to the second item, a large jade carving of some type of god. She lifted it up, "Ten pounds of jade, at least. It doesn't have the usual markings of being 'jade plated.' The head was designed with solid, strong lines. There is quite a bit of finer detail here, so that means this carving was done for someone in the wealthier class."

Claire put the gloves back on to examine the head, held it back to get a view of it, then held it close. "I think this is Kinich Ahau, the sun god. I only remember because the god was watermarked on Belizean currency. Anyway, I'm not sure on the specific time frame, but the amount of jade would make it worth a small fortune. Given the delicacy of the carving, the market price is a hundred."

Claire set down the jade head. There was at least a half million on the table, if not more. Whoever was sourcing these objects was good, and probably worked for a museum. That was something she could tell Bruno.

She started assess the third item, a knife with a rag wrapped around the handle, as every edge was sharp. Claire looked over the rag first, to make sure that it was clean. "Sal? Can you get me a clean rag for the knife?"

"Sure," he said, then looked to Janine.

"Don't look at me, you're here more than I am."

"Check the janitorial closet," said Claire. "There's usually something in there."

Sal left straightaway and returned in a few minutes with a rag.

"This is a curved knife made of igneous rock—obsidian." She held the knife towards Janine, "See how shiny it is?" She angled the knife to let the light reflect off it. "The technical term is 'eccentric carving.' That means this knife was used by the shamans for holy ceremonies. This volcanic rock chips easily, so crude tools were not used to make this. The original maker had to be an expert, a skill set far beyond flint knapping. I'd value this knife around one eighty, two hundred."

Claire gently laid the knife on the table. The last thing she wanted to do was accidentally chip the fragile edge. She removed her gloves and took several pictures.

"We have everything you'll need to package the items here. Our courier will leave in roughly two hours," Janine said.

Sal nodded and swooped his hand toward another table that contained shipping boxes, tape, and packing materials. "When you're finished, I'll need the paperwork filled out, and we'll send it with the courier." He made eye contact with Claire finally and handed her a sheaf of papers. "We're doing this old school. You'll need to fill out this paperwork for customs by hand."

"The package needs to go through customs tonight," Janine said.

Claire looked confused. She wasn't expecting to ship and package everything herself. She thought about protesting, but decided to use the moment to hide the customs documentation. "Fine," Claire said. She started to fold the papers up.

Janine grabbed Claire's wrist gently at first, then slammed it on the table. She picked up the obsidian knife by the rag handle and pressed it against her pulse. "The paperwork needs to be filled out."

Sal took the paperwork from Claire and unfolded it. He lay it on the table. Janine slid the knife against her skin and Claire cried out.

"Okay! Fuck, I was just going to do it back at BIFA."

Janine let go. Claire squeezed her hand around her wrist. A rivulet of blood appeared on her skin and dripped off, onto the table, barely missing the customs paperwork.

Claire saw the rag used to clean the obsidian knife and wrapped it around her wrist. *Dammit.* She had hoped that it wouldn't come to this. She'd hoped that maybe she'd talk her way out of signing the papers, to get Janine to sign it instead. Claire considered turning around and walking out, but Janine stood over her, the knife still in her hand. *Shit.*

She flipped through the papers. A couple lines for signatures were marked with an arrow sticky note showing where to sign. Sal held a pen in front of her. Claire leaned over filled it out, using the credentials Shali had given her for museum work. When she was finished, she double scanned the information again, to commit it to memory, then handed the papers back to Sal without a word.

"All right," he said, "Let's get this baby packed and ready to go."

Shit. Shit. Shit. The paperwork was filled out, with her name on the documentation. How the hell would she ever convince Bruno that she was going to tell him everything, that she hadn't done this to save her ass, but to give him information? Even with the cut on her wrist, would he believe her? *Shit.*

"The boss wants to meet you, so before we head out, we're making a quick stop. We'll get the finances squared away."

CHAPTER TWENTY-TWO

Janine

Janine was pissed at Rex for sending someone to rob BIFA. She knew it; she was certain he'd been planning to do things his way all along. But if he didn't keep her apprised, shit would hit the fan. Claire had come back that morning, after having sex with Bruno, and decided that love would save the day. WRONG. Love ruined everything, assaulted logic, turned a good plan into a mushy one. Reluctantly, though, she had to admit the perfectly timed robbery had returned Claire from la-la-love-land to reality.

She'd been able to get Claire to the warehouse, but stronger persuasion was required to finish the paperwork and get the packages off to Reade Street Gallery. Honestly, she knew how closely Claire paid attention to detail and was surprised she hadn't seen Bruno Canul's name listed as the originating archeologist. Janine finally had what she wanted: documentation that Claire and Bruno were involved in a black-market scheme.

For the second part of her plan, Sal had to finish up the fake dig located on the northern Belizean property that was for sale, deposit a few relevant artifacts in the vicinity and broken pottery in the sifter. Then, she'd anonymously email the archeological board, the NICH, with pictures of Bruno and his mom on the property, and of the fake dig. Bruno would get arrested, his reputation would take the hit, and she'd finally be free of Rex. When hell broke loose and the NICH began an investigation into the stolen artifacts from the property, she was sure they would find the customs documentation with both Claire and Bruno's name, and then the investigation would take a new turn.

Janine didn't like what she had to do to Claire, but she shook off the feeling. The whole reason she was doing this was to help Claire, to save her, to get her the money to pay Lucia. She couldn't save her sister's life, but maybe she could save Claire's. Sadly, that meant she had to hand her over on a silver platter to Rex. *Finis coronat opus: the end crowns the work.*

Rex had texted Janine he wanted to meet Claire. Janine rolled her eyes as she re-read the text. Another tangent. Ugh. Micro-managing was going ruin everything. Claire had served her purpose, and it was best to not get her involved more than she needed to be. Janine checked her phone. Rex had sent her the address of his AirBnb in the text messages. The ride to Rex's hotel was quiet, the tension between them thick.

CHAPTER TWENTY-THREE

Claire

Claire wanted out of the car. She wanted out of Janine's face. She wanted out. The only thing calming her was the knowledge that she had the warehouse address and could tell Bruno where it was.

"Here we are," Janine said and pulled into a parking lot of a gated resort community. "Follow me." They walked on a cement sidewalk through a well-manicured garden of red heliconias until they crossed over a modern aluminum bridge to the presidential suite. Jungle leaves framed the entrance. Janine punched in a key code unit at the door. A buzzer sounded, and they walked in. They took the elevator up to the third floor.

The suite faced the ocean and had floor-to-ceiling windows with no curtains. Rex sat on a white leather couch. She'd always coveted those. Thought it meant something special. He held a cut crystal glass filled with something amber. He tilted his head to the side. "You must be Claire," he said, the tone deliberately edged between statement and a question.

"I am," Claire said. She pointed to a photograph series that was a microscopic view of a butterfly wing, set in three frames. "I like the pictures."

He ignored her. "Janine," he said, holding up the glass in greeting. "Take her phone with the pictures on it, please."

"I haven't sent the pictures to Reade Street yet," Claire said, keeping the burner in her pocket.

"What are you waiting for?"

Claire clenched her jaw. "I don't have the phone number. It's on my other phone."

Rex looked to Janine, and she said, "It's to get an estimate. Perfectly valid." He nodded.

Claire took off her backpack and retrieved her cell phone, swiped it open, and took steps to get the Reade Street Gallery phone number. Then she picked up the burner phone, entered the number, and sent the text. Since she had to give the phone to Janine, she didn't dare send any pictures to her phone. *Shit.* At least the voice-recorder app was still running; all she could hope for now was a decent taping.

"Give the burner to Janine."

Claire handed it to Janine and put her own cell phone back in her backpack, placing it in a pouch to keep it from rolling around.

"So, Janine tells me you need help. That true?" Rex leaned forward and rested his elbow on the the arms of the couch.

Claire looked at her feet.

"Well? Do you want our help or not?" asked Rex.

She looked at her feet, then asked, "Can I get a drink?"

"Sure." Rex waved to a nearby cart with amber liquid in a large, cut-glass container and several matching glasses.

"I do need help," Claire said as she poured herself two fingers of the amber liquid and brought the glass up to her nose to smell it before sipping.

"You know you'll have to earn that help," Rex said. "I'm not some benevolent uncle."

She looked at the butterfly picture behind Rex and closed

her eyes. *The weightless feet of butterflies on her skin.* "I don't know if I can help you."

"We'll find a way," Rex said, taking a healthy sip. "Ask Janine, she'll tell you how easy it is."

Janine seemed unhappy, but covered it up with a pleasant enough smile. There was a second white leather chair across from the couch and Claire moved towards it.

"Don't sit," Rex said. "We are not friends."

"Oh," Claire said, sounding surprised.

"I need an answer."

"What exactly do you need me to do? I've got a buyer for your items. I'm using my museum credentials to bypass customs. What else do you want?"

"If you want the money to pay this, uh, Lucia, if you want that black-market deal to go through, you'll have set up Bruno Canul. Put the final piece in place."

Claire had taken a step backwards and into Janine. She steadied her, and Claire shook her off. She set the drink on a nearby table. "I'm sorry, you want me to *what*?"

"Set up Bruno Canul. I don't care who I burn to make it happen. Your connections with Reade Street? Janine? You? I'll burn it all to the fucking ground, as long as Bruno takes the fall. There's a commercial property up north that's being staged by our good friend Sal. He's already got pictures of Bruno and his mom walking on the property. Circumstantial, but good enough. You are going to take the museum headdress that Bruno brought on loan for the Popol Vuh and make it look like Bruno was going to sell it. All you have to do is fill out the customs documentation and ship the item to Reade Street. You'll also be the one to contact NICH and let them know what Bruno is doing. Janine?"

Shit.

Janine would not look at her. "You already signed the customs documentation, and unfortunately you didn't read it carefully. Bruno is listed as the lead archeologist," said Janine. "Back in the warehouse, we have numerous Mayan artifacts, but we want to assure that whatever artifact we plant on the commercial property is the right one. You'll make sure that happens."

"Why would I work with you?"

"The loan shark. You'll need to give me information on how to pay her. Your life will be saved, but unfortunately Bruno will be arrested, and so will you."

"So I get to trade jail time for Lucia? Why would I do that? And how do I even know you'll pay off Lucia? You could betray me again."

"You'll have to trust me. It's only a few years in a minimum-security prison with nonviolent offenders. Nothing hard core." Janine walked over to the table and opened up a leather briefcase. "Once Bruno's been arrested, I'll give Lucia an account number and password for the commission you earned as a middleman for the… activities."

"And of course, if you tell Bruno or anyone else, you lose every single dime," Rex said.

Claire didn't move or say anything, but had a set look on her face.

"Well?" said Janine. "What are you going to do? Do you want the two hundred grand? Do you want Lucia off your back?"

"What I want apparently doesn't matter. I'm curious, though," Claire said to Rex. "Why me?"

"Janine called me and told me about your *situation*. When we realized you could provide the selling part of the black-market setup, that meant less culpability for Janine and I. We saw the opportunity and took it. If you don't do it, your loan shark lady will come find you. The beauty of this tangential plan is that it costs me nothing."

Claire ran to the bathroom. Janine followed. Claire put her

hands on the rim of the toilet seat and threw up. The yellow bile contrasted sharply against the white ceramic. When she finished, Claire turned the tap on and washed her mouth out. Their eyes connected, and Claire had to stamp down the raw rage and hurt raising hard and course inside her. Claire grasped the side of the sink wishing she could tear it out of its mooring and throw it in Janine's face.

"Get her out of here, Janine," Rex said. "Disgusting filth. I have to call housekeeping now."

CHAPTER TWENTY-FOUR

Claire

Claire rode back to the warehouse with Janine, refusing to look at her. She pretended to be tuning Janine out by playing music through her earbuds, but she was really listening to the recording she'd gotten on her phone. Only a few words came through, but most of them were jumbled. With every one of them, her dream of catching Rex and Janine in the midst of their scheming were ruined. What a spy she'd make.

Her heart was broken; she'd betrayed Bruno. It was done. Without proof, there was no way out. How had she not seen Bruno's name on the customs document? How had she fallen so easily into Janine and Rex's hands? The items meant for Reade Street Gallery were gone, already shipped.

Sal had set up the table with a series of artifacts that would be placed at the fake dig, and she was supposed to pick the best ones. At a second table was the fancy headdress that had been loaned to Bruno from the Museo Popol Vuh out of Guatemala. Even though she didn't have to steal it, just looking at it filled her with dread.

Claire selected three items from the first table, unable to

hold back a scowl: a ceremonial pot, an atlatl, and a set of broken pottery pieces. Now that she knew Rex and Janine's whole plan, she realized it had cost her dearly. Bruno might not ever believe that she never intended to take part, even though she had gone to the warehouse or that she hadn't wanted to sign the documentation, even though the ink was now dry on the paper.

Claire and Janine made it back to BIFA in time to have dinner with Delia and the group. Janine accepted the invitation with a smile, like nothing had happened, like everything was the same. Claire declined. In her room, she dropped the clothes she wore onto the floor and wanted to burn them. She put a pair of yoga pants and a t-shirt. She desperately wanted a place where she could think without being bombarded with adrenaline and judgement, fear, or bravado and pulled the covers over her head.

Claire lay on her back. She'd been through foster care, in a similar situation, and had gotten out. Claire reviewed her position with cold logic. Janine would be watching her the next few days like an errant child, making sure that she did everything she was supposed to do. That was how Frank and Judy Smith had treated her, the second set of foster parents.

He was the scariest son of a bitch she'd ever met. He never hit her, but violence was always close to his skin, constantly threatening. Nothing was hers, he reminded her, from her clothes to her friends; he wanted control over it all. Frank had gone so far as to put a security system up in the house with cameras monitoring her every move. Even the bathroom. She had learned to take a shower, dry off in the tub, put on a robe, then change in her closet.

The foster home setup couldn't be legal, but she was hesitant to say anything, afraid her CPS counselor wouldn't believe her. While she worked on a plan, she found ways to appear compliant, but in every way she was not. Claire's goal was to get out; she didn't care what happened to the Smiths. A friend at school bought her a burner phone. Another friend gave her an old camera. She established contact with the boarding school of her choice and was accepted with a full ride scholarship.

She documented everything for two months and kept a secret journal. When she had sufficient evidence, she went to the case worker and gave her a choice. Either she went to an attorney or she was granted the autonomy to go to boarding school. The caseworker marked the right boxes—or whatever it was, Claire didn't know—and she said goodbye to the Smiths.

Looking back, she wasn't sure why the caseworker let her go—whether it was due to her kindness or just an overworked woman avoiding the aggravation of more court dates, lawyers, and a pissed off boss. What mattered was her planning, her tenacity, and letting go of the idea that someone would take care of her. She had learned the hard way that she'd have to be the hero of her own story. It was time she bucked up. She needed a similar plan.

The problem was, the proof she had pointed to her and Bruno as the guilty party. She had no proof of their innocence.

Unlike Janine, who was guilty, but appeared completely innocent. At least Claire knew she was nothing like Janine, but then she stopped cold. *Or was she?* Claire had desperately wanted out of the Lucia situation, and was willing to participate in a black-market scheme, but she reasoned, she did not make choices to actively hurt people, like Janine had. *Reade Street Gallery doesn't count as a choice? Getting involved with someone like Janine? Signing the customs documentation?* The truth was, she was still making bad choices. Her jaw clenched. She was a piece of shit, that was what she was.

Tell him. She hadn't planned on getting a conscience and having the desire to make the right decisions. She hadn't planned on falling in love. Claire was uncomfortable in the bed; she'd been trying to find a place where her body could relax, but there was no respite. The constant adrenaline was wearing her down. Janine manipulating her with such ease. Rex treating her like trash. This was not a life she wanted. She threw the covers off, feeling as if she'd been drowning.

If she lied to Bruno and let Janine's set up go as planned, she would get the money, pay Lucia, and be alive. But every day after that would be complete hell, knowing she had betrayed the love of her life. If she told Bruno the truth, he'd hate her, they'd never be together again, and she'd probably be dead. Or worse, auctioned off. She shuddered as an image of spoons and horse stalls came to mind. Was her life worth more than his reputation?

The jaguar pendant Bruno had given her lay on her sternum. Claire rubbed her thumb over its head. Being with Bruno made her want to be a better person. The issues with Lucia, Janine, and Rex? She had dealt with worse. The death of her parents. Being in the foster care system. Fending for herself at the boarding school. She could find a way out of this. Since her parents had died, her whole life had been about what she wanted, what she needed, and look where it had taken her. If she kept making the same choices, where would her life end? Surprised at how deeply calm she was, the answer was clear. She loved Bruno. She would tell him about Janine and Rex's plan no matter what it cost her.

Maybe she didn't deserve forgiveness, but she had to act in a manner that allowed her to forgive herself. If she told Bruno the truth, *everything*, there was a slim chance that he might forgive her. She'd be free from Janine's grasp. She'd have to give up the two hundred grand. She'd have to face Lucia, and probably Rex. Most importantly, though, she wouldn't die a fuckup.

Telling Bruno the truth was the last thing Janine expected. Working with Bruno was counter-intuitive to self-preservation, and Claire doubted Janine would believe she'd take that risk. Claire sent him a text saying that she needed a ride to Belmopan to pick up one of the shamans for a dress rehearsal of the Popol Vuh. Could he pick her up at nine a.m.?

She set an alarm on her phone and then heard Janine come back after dinner. Anger radiated from Claire's very core, and she directed it through the bookshelf and into Janine's side of the room. Soon, she heard snoring and gave up her glare.

THE NEXT MORNING, she woke up before the alarm. She must have fallen asleep from sheer exhaustion. She got dressed and was out in the Art Lodge. Janine was already up and laying down grass mats, what they would be using as a stage for the Popol Vuh. "Bruno is picking me up, we're headed to Belmopan to pick up Martin, the shaman."

"It's a little early, the rest of them won't get here until noon."

"Bruno and I wanted to have breakfast together," Claire said, winging it.

"Don't even think about telling him."

"Why would I?" Claire lied, because she was going to tell him no matter what.

"Telling him will get you killed," Janine said. "And just so you know, if I get wind that you have told anyone about anything, I'm out of here so fast your head will spin. You won't have the money to pay Lucia. No one will corroborate your little story. The evidence will look like you and Bruno colluded to sell items on the black market, and your finger pointing will be viewed as self-preservation, not truth."

"I know that," Claire said. "Do you think I'm stupid?" She walked off and headed to the pavilion to wait for Bruno. Once she was out of Janine's sight, she leaned against a wall. Her breath came in heavy, jerky. Her mouth dry. When Bruno drove up in his Jeep and she saw him, relief coursed over her. She got in and gave him a kiss. "Hey, can we go to your house first? There's something I want to talk to you about."

"Sure, anything else?" he asked suggestively.

"No," Claire said seriously. "We have to talk."

"Is everything okay?"

"It will be," Claire said, letting out a breath of air, finally able to breathe normally.

Bruno took her hand and gave her a kiss. "It will be."

At Bruno's house, she sat on the futon couch. Here, she felt safe. She swallowed hard, afraid to tell him the truth.

"You want coffee first? I have a pot brewed from earlier this morning."

"Sure," she said. "Black. No sugar."

He left for the kitchen. Next to the couch was a side table with a lamp and a framed picture. She picked it up, and it was a picture of him at a dig site, the jungle in the background. He was sitting on his haunches, proudly holding up a complete pot. His entire professional life was about preserving heritage. If he was framed for a black-market dig, it would devastate him. Seeing the pictures bolstered her, gave her a specific reason why she had to tell him. Because she loved him. He didn't deserve any of this. When she told him the truth, it wouldn't matter if he yelled at her. It wouldn't matter if he never wanted to see her again. What mattered was that she did the right thing. For Bruno.

He came back with two cups of coffee, gave one to her, and sat on the couch. There was a way to tell someone a truth bomb. A process of unfolding information as to elicit the best response. She wanted to tell him in a smooth way that would lessen the barb. She was about to take a sip of her coffee but set it on the table instead, afraid that she'd lose her nerve, and blurted out, "Janine is planning something bad. She is setting you up. Something black market, and she's going to frame you for it."

His eyes widened and he set his cup down. His shoulders dropped, as if he were disappointed, but not surprised. He stood and turned to face her. "How do you know about this?"

This was it. She had to tell him the truth.

"Claire? How do you know about this?" he asked, gripping the edge of the couch.

"She told me."

"Janine did? Why did she tell you?"

"Because," Claire hesitated, and wanted to tell a little white lie to absolve her part so that he would still like her, but she didn't. "She wants me to do it."

He stood and loomed over her. The movement was so swift and sure, she found herself mesmerized by the action. She held the coffee cup in front of her as if she could block his anger, wishing she could lie to him to make herself look better, but she vowed only to tell him the truth. All of it.

"Why? Why would you do this?"

"Remember I told you about Lucia?" she said. "How I owe her two hundred thousand dollars? She's going to kill me if I don't get it to her."

He shook his head, as if trying to comprehend the severity of the stakes. "You just told me that I was about to be betrayed and… I'm not sure what to say… I don't want you to get hurt, Claire," he said, still shaking his head and looking confused, "but I need the whole story."

"A coworker in New York gave me the number of a gallery that buys artifacts that… uh, you know, were not cleared by the archeology board. I didn't think I'd hurt anyone, though, that's the truth. I just wanted to sell the items, save my life, and be on my merry way. I didn't expect you to happen."

Bruno's black-brown eyes darkened, but other than that, he

looked neither pleased nor displeased, happy or unhappy, sad or disappointed. "And then what happened?"

"After I met Janine," Claire said, "everything snowballed from there. She had some items that needed a buyer. The amount I would get would cover Lucia's payment. I shipped them up to Reade Street using my museum credentials."

"Did you ship them before or after we were together?"

Claire met his gaze and said, "I'd changed my mind about everything. I planned to go and find information about the warehouse and then tell you everything, but when I got there, they made me sign the papers."

"Before or after we were together?"

"After, but you have to understand, I only went to gather evidence. I wasn't going to intentionally implicate you on the document." Bruno had to believe that was driven to such measures. Her actions were not who she really was. At least, not who she wanted to be.

"Why didn't you tell me everything when you told me about Lucia? I could have helped you."

"I wanted to fix it by myself. I didn't want to get you involved. I mean, I hadn't seen you in years, and then to expect your help to pay a two hundred thousand dollar loan seemed, uh, presumptuous. I thought I could sell a few items, pay Lucia off, and move on with life. I'm so sorry, Bruno. I had a gun on my face two days ago. Janine held a knife against me, this crazy sharp obsidian knife." Claire held up her arm, wrist out, to show Bruno.

He rubbed his thumb over the thin red line. His expression seemed a mix of sadness that he couldn't help, and frustration that she didn't ask.

"I have eight days left to pay Lucia. She gave me thirteen days to pay, and today is number five. I was going to sell the artifacts, and it'd be a done deal. But I met Rex last night, and he said in order to earn the money, I had to betray you, I had to set you up. And I can't. I love you. I've never stopped."

She could see different emotions crossing his face: anger from being betrayed, wanting to comfort and protect her, confusion over the sudden uncertainty between them.

"Come on, Claire." He shook his head, as if trying to clear it. "How are you and Janine connected?"

"Well," Claire said, trying to piece together the events without sounding laborious or desperate. "I told her about Reade Street Gallery. She knew the gallery's reputation and said she'd be interested in a partnership. That was how it started—I just wanted to sell a couple items to make the payment to Lucia."

"Oh?" Bruno said. "A couple of items?" His questions made her nervous.

She wanted to tell him everything and as quickly as possible, to get it over with. But she only had one chance. She absolutely wanted to tell him everything, but also let him know that she wasn't aware of having to betray him until yesterday.

"How am I involved?" he asked.

"They put your name on the customs document as the archeologist, and I signed it." At his look of surprise, Claire said, "I didn't know it was there. Janine had a knife on me when I signed it. I didn't read the whole thing."

"Is that all? Is there anything else? How does the theft at BIFA come into all of this?"

Claire was on the verge of crying, but she held herself in check to tell the story. "There's some property up north. Something that your mom is involved with, a commercial property. They've got someone out there creating a fake dig. Pictures of you and your mom. Rex wanted me to assess a few pieces, to make sure they are the right ones for age, location, that sort of thing. The plan is to lay out the items on site. I had to ship the headdress you got from the museum to Reade Street Gallery, and then I'm supposed to call NICH and tell them that you and I are selling artifacts to the black market. You'll look guilty, and they'll arrest both of us."

"Shit. We were out there a few days ago looking it over. Does Janine know you're here?"

"She knows we are in a relationship," Claire said. "She knows I'm physically here, but she doesn't know I'm telling you everything; she doesn't think I would risk my own death. You know that's what I'm risking here, right? I'll be killed if I don't get the money to Lucia. I wish I could…"

Bruno rubbed his face in his hands. "God fucking dammit. And the theft? Was that Janine?"

Claire shook her head. "I really have no idea who did that. Maybe Rex? Maybe Janine? Maybe Lucia? Honestly, Bruno, I don't know who took the headdress."

He pulled her into a hug. The warmth of his skin, his smell, calmed her, but she wondered if it was the last time he'd touch her with this much care when he let her go. "I'm calling McNally," Bruno said after an eternity. An eternity in which the gulf between them widened and deepened until it was if they were on opposite ends of the universe from each other.

"Who's McNally?" she asked, her voice cracked with emotion.

"My FBI liaison." He tilted his head to the side as if he were *really seeing* her for the first time. "I told you about him. We need a better plan than wishful thinking. You can wear a wire and he'll help with Lucia. In order to arrest Janine and Rex, we have to catch them in an illegal act."

"What about us?" Claire said as her stomach twisted. She had to resist the urge to run to the bathroom and throw up again. She wanted to reach out and hold his hand, assure him that everything was going to be okay, that she was worthy of love, that she wasn't such a terrible person. She didn't have any words to convince him.

"We have to focus on bringing them in," Bruno said, avoiding the question, avoiding eye contact. "Rex and Janine cannot get away with this. Not twice. Is Rex still in Belize?"

"I don't know. I met him yesterday, in Belize City. He was staying in a house by the ocean, near the docks. Bruno, I can't wear a wire," she said, the words forced through the tightness of her throat.

"Why not?" asked Bruno, finally staying still enough to look at her. "Why are you here?"

"What do you mean?"

"You just told me about this plan with Janine and Rex. We have no proof, and this might be the only way to get it," Bruno said. "The FBI might even help us get the money for Lucia."

"I'm done being involved," Claire said. "I've done enough."

"A wire is the only solution here. If we can, McNally and I will come up with something better, but there's not enough time," Bruno said, looking pained.

"Can I trust the FBI to do the right thing by me?" asked Claire.

"You have to trust me. I'll see if you can get into witness protection. Lucia can't get you there."

"The government isn't exactly great at keeping promises."

"And where has *your way* gotten you?" Bruno asked.

She wanted to throw the coffee cup at him, and stared at him. Couldn't he see that she was trying to do the right thing? She was practically throwing herself at his mercy. But she wasn't going to blindly trust that some random FBI agent—whom she had never met, for that matter—would have any care or concern for her situation. "Do you think McNally is going to front me two hundred grand? No. If I do it your way, I'm dead. Do you get that? But you're right, my way is fucked up. I want to help you. That's why I'm here."

"Then let me help you. We have to do it my way."

He was right. Her way led to destruction and demise, as she'd had the same thought this morning. She was telling him because he had inspired her to be the woman she wanted to be. Because it was the right thing to do, because she loved him. Good God, if only Lucia could see this moment. If she didn't know any better, she'd say she'd turned water into wine.

"You're right," Claire said, exhaling a sigh of relief. It was like everything she'd tried so hard to hold together was being cut loose. "Get in touch with your friend at the FBI and let me know what he says."

"I'll pass the information to McNally. He'll tell me if it's enough to get you into witness protection. We're going to find a way to save you."

Claire looked away. She was thankful Bruno cared enough to try, but she had known the outcome wouldn't be favorable for her. Unable to resist, she had to ask. "What's next for us?" Claire asked. At his astonished expression, she said, "I mean around Janine. We can't look like anything has changed."

He stared at her, didn't move from his spot.

"Yeah, around Janine, we can't be different. We have to look like we are falling in love with each other," Bruno said.

The words hit her like someone had thrown an MMA punch right in her gut. *Look like we are falling in love* was very different than the simpler *falling in love*. Claire looked away from him and at her watch. Only thirty minutes had passed; had it only taken thirty minutes? "We have to get going before Janine suspects something."

Bruno checked his watch too, and then picked up his phone. "I'll send the shaman a text and let him know we're running behind."

With a brave smile, Claire nodded. They walked towards the door together, the space between them awkward. They got into his Jeep, and drove to Belmopan in quiet. She stayed in the Jeep when he went to the shaman's house. When they pulled up to BIFA, the shaman got out, and Bruno stayed with Claire for a moment.

"You headed back home?" she asked.

"Yeah," he said with a weak smile. She could see anger and hurt in his eyes. "See you later."

"Forgive me," she said and impulsively kissed him on the lips and got out of the vehicle before he could respond. This was not the way she wanted it to work out, but it was the way it had to be.

CHAPTER TWENTY-FIVE

Claire

Twenty-four hours later, Claire had accepted that the situation was now out of her hands. She felt empty and sluggish, and wanted to lay down, but she didn't have the luxury. She had to show Janine everything was fine. She was fine. That nothing had changed. She clapped her hands in front of her face three times to wake herself up, to stop herself from feeling sad and overwhelmed. At the communal fridge in the pavilion, she stopped and poured herself a coffee into a go-cup. The coffee was terrible, so she added a little cream to break up the burnt taste.

She took a sip, and the coffee was cold. Claire set the cup on the counter. Today had started out hard, and right now, she didn't need the universe making it worse. "Knock it off," she said aloud to whatever gods were listening, then put the cup in the microwave and heated it up.

Claire had seven days left to raise money for Lucia. There was no time to think about that, either. With a long and controlled sigh, she reminded herself about the present. She would do the best that she could. Claire convinced herself that the hurt and pain would be worth it, that when all of this ended, hopefully she'd still be alive, and if so, she was finally making the hard, but right, choices. She was sorry for the problems she caused, but right now, she couldn't let herself feel regret or sadness or she wouldn't make it through the day. She went to get the coffee out of the microwave, but the cup was too hot to touch.

The full team was onsite and a dress rehearsal would commence after lunch. The Popol Vuh play was the next day already. Shali, the curator and her boss, was arriving on site in about thirty minutes. McNally, the Art Crimes FBI Special Agent, was also flying in, according to a text from Bruno.

The Art Lodge was loud and chaotic. Claire's job as program manager was to make sure that all last-minute issues were handled and surveyed the room. Local actors along with shamans were bickering over who would stand where during the play, but Janine worked with them to cement final movements and choreography.

The National Geographic camera crew were present, but they were missing one of the cameras. The lead photographer was already working with the airlines. Claire made a note to ask Delia about local pawnshops to see if anything turned up there. Ruth Ann and Darren were both finished with their projects; there was a row of Darren's fired but unglazed pots, and the headdresses Ruth Ann made, along with the jewelry, were positioned on cloth mannequins. Check and check. Claire tried not to dwell on the fact that Bruno's headdress was not there, that she was responsible.

Over in the corner of the Art Lodge, Ruth Ann was showing Darren how to work with silver. She sat next to him with a piece of metal in her hands and turned it over slowly. Claire sat back on her heels and watched them. There was something sweet about them, like two unruly kids sitting under the boardwalk sharing ice cream. Ruth Ann said something quietly to Darren, and he laughed with a sound that was actually quite wonderful.

Claire's phone buzzed with a text notification. She got a text from Shali that he would be arriving in the next ten minutes or so. Check. She told Janine that he was on his way, and headed for the pavilion to let Delia know, with the intention of being there to greet him. She sat on the couch to take a break for a few minutes, to think.

Bruno wanted her to work with the FBI without any guarantee that Lucia would be paid. He wanted her to trust a government agency. Just like she had trusted the government to help her after her parents had died, but instead they stuck her into some crazy ass home with control-freak-bordering-on-pedophile-freak Mr. Smith. An overwhelming feeling surged through her; unable to stop it, her eyes filled with tears.

She had to remind herself that she was doing all of this willingly. She'd do what Bruno had asked of her, even though the very thought of it put her on the edge of panic attacks. Claire heard a vehicle drive up and she wiped her eyes, blinking rapidly. If only she had some Visine. She didn't want Shali to see her face like this. She got into the bathroom, turned the faucet on with cold water, and dabbed her eyes. She took a deep breath and returned to the pavilion where Janine and Delia were standing together, talking quietly, waiting for Shali.

Bruno came into the pavilion, and Claire started for him, thinking it was going to be Shali, but then when she saw him and took a step back.

"Hey, Claire," said Bruno, coming in for a hug. He whispered in her ear, "Janine's here."

Claire put on her game face. "Of course." Her stomach dropped like she'd been hit full force by a Mack truck. *Was the hug for real or for show?* Claire looked around to see if Janine saw them, but she didn't seem to be paying attention.

Bruno gave Delia a kiss on the cheek and patted her belly. To Janine, he simply nodded as his greeting. The commuter van pulled up and Shali came into the pavilion. Introductions were made, and then Claire began the tour. They started towards the Art Lodge. Claire expected chaos, the same shouting and yelling, but it was quiet.

The Popol Vuh background had been set up as if it were a live production. The audience would sit on mats of woven grass. The background consisted of handmade paper using an Aztec recipe and painted with swirls of bioluminescent dye. *Light always finds a way,* her mom used to tell her when she was little. The thought warmed and comforted her rather than causing anxiety.

First, Bruno was scheduled to speak to the group about the rules. He explained that Belize had allowed the project to move forward only under incredibly strict guidance from NICH, and they would respect the rules because what they were doing was unprecedented. "The ATM Cave is one of the few experiences where history, archeology, and anthropology all meet. In most archeology sites, something this precious would be closed to the public, but Belize had kept it open for all to experience. Except for the Nat Geo team, do not bring your cameras. They aren't allowed. They used to be, but someone dropped one on a skull and cracked it open."

"Some idiot always has to screw things up," said Janine.

Everyone just looked at her. "It's true," she added defensively.

During the Popol Vuh play, no one was allowed to take off their helmet. Only flashlights and headlamps would be used for lighting purposes. No more than five unglazed pots. Absolutely nothing could be left behind. Filming could only be done where no artifacts were found, and a space had been marked out for them.

"From a safety and technical perspective, Alberto and his

guides will be bringing in the gear in as many trips as it takes to get everything in safely. I will be guiding you all in. The water is extremely low this year. We will traverse two slow-flowing rivers and a small spring at the beginning of the cave. The cave is tough in certain spots, but certainly not impossible."

When all the questions for Bruno were answered, Janine approached the microphone. "Thank you, Bruno. We're ready for a dress rehearsal," said Janine. "Everyone, take your places. Claire? Could you turn off the lights?" asked Janine.

Janine moved the microphone off stage. Claire flipped a switch to turn off the overhead lights. Janine came to the back, and they watched the show together for a few moments. Janine whisper-asked, "Are you okay? You don't seem like yourself."

"Oh? I'm fine. Maybe a little tired. I drank coffee this morning. I might be shaky." She held up her hand as it slightly trembled. "Other than that, I'm fine."

Claire rubbed the jaguar pendant Bruno had given her, and tried to act normal and be a professional. She was doing this for him. She'd take down Janine and Rex because she loved him. She had to be strong. She had to believe something would work out. Janine nodded, then left to sit next to Delia and watch the play. *How could she do that? How could she be so nice to Delia knowing the truth?* Claire knew the answer, because Janine had been nice to her, too.

After the play, the crew gathered everything into water-proof bins that would be used to carry the items into the ATM. The tasks kept her busy, and before she knew it, an hour had passed. Claire went towards the back of the room, and started reviewing her clip board that held the project schedule.

"Anything left on the list for me to do?" Janine asked, as if nothing were different between them. Well, if Janine could do it, then so could she.

"I'm going over my checklist for the Popol Vuh. I'll need to you to verify some things for me. Sound good?"

"Sure," Janine said as Claire pulled out the clipboard.

"Okay, all the backgrounds are finished and packed?" Claire saw that she had nodded and put a checkmark. "You've worked with the shamans, and they have the choreography?"

"Yes. They will bring their own outfits, uniforms, whatever you want to call it, with them in their own waterproof pouches."

"Bruno told me they'll have to take five or six trips to get everything in. Nat Geo people have their own system for cameras and such. The fact we're able to do this is almost a miracle."

"Money makes everyone happy, right?"

Claire stopped running her finger down the checklist, but then completed it. Janine wasn't going to shake her.

"What's with the serious stare?" Janine asked.

"I'm working, Janine. Enough, all right?" Claire said, meeting her gaze. "Shali will want to know everything is ready to go."

"My partner Sal is setting everything up tonight, at the property up north. Tomorrow morning, just before we leave for the Popol Vuh ceremony, you'll need to make an anonymous call to NICH."

Claire sighed and nodded her head. She'd have to make sure that Bruno knew about the NICH component before any of their agents showed up.

"Afterwards, when Bruno comes out of the Popol Vuh, he'll be arrested for trying to sell black market."

"Your sister would be real proud of you," Claire said under her breath.

"What did you say about my sister?"

Claire balked for a moment then thought, *fuck it*. "Your dead sister would be real proud of you."

Janine's eyebrows furrowed, and it seemed as if she'd brought the dredges of hell up. "That's none of your goddamned business. You still need to send the emails out and finish this job. Wouldn't Lucia want you to?"

Claire knew she should look compliant, like she was on board with Janine. "The hell?"

"If you don't," Janine said with a smile that curled her toes, "Rex is coming after you."

CHAPTER TWENTY-SIX

Bruno

The night before the big show, the Popol Vuh crew had plans to eat an early dinner at the Grove House restaurant, located in the Sleeping Giant resort. Bruno didn't want to arouse Janine's suspicion, but McNally was in town and waiting at his place, and Claire needed to be there. It was time to go, and he nodded to her. Claire excused herself saying she didn't feel well. Janine looked back and forth between them and then winked at Claire. Claire smiled brightly and winked back, but Bruno could tell it was fake.

After everyone had left, Claire and Bruno were in his Jeep, driving towards his house. He didn't know what to say to her. He loved her, he always had. They fit together; she was perfect for him, physically, mentally. The few dates they had were intense, and he saw so much good in her.

And yet, he couldn't ignore the fact that he was angry. And hurt. What she'd done had been a huge betrayal to him and everything he believed in. Selling artifacts on the black market?

He gripped the steering wheel tighter. Even he had to admit he might have made similar decisions if his life was at stake.

He had parked in the driveway, and Bruno turned to Claire. "Before we go in, I want you to know I tried to get the money from my family, but it's tied up in other things. We just don't have two hundred grand in cash."

There was no way he could liquidate enough assets to get the money in time.

"That's why I love you." She unbuckled her seatbelt and got out. She walked into the house alone. He hit the passenger seat of the Jeep with a clenched fist. Why hadn't she told him the truth sooner? If her life was in danger, and he had known, they would have had time to come up with a solution that worked. She hadn't trusted him enough to ask for it earlier. As it was, it had been too late.

Or was Claire lying about that, too? Was Lucia even a real person? Should he trust Claire and her version of the events? The only redeeming factor was that she finally did come forward. Hopefully, it was not too late. Hopefully, it wasn't some cover lie to make her sound innocent. He got out of his Jeep and went into his house.

He hoped Lucia was real, because if she wasn't that meant Claire was making it all up. That would be an even bigger blow to his heart. He desperately wanted to believe her, but the modern loan-shark tracking her to Belize sounded made up to him. It was all crazy-making.

McNally was in the living room, standing, with his coat still on. After Bruno informed him of Janine and Rex's plan, he had gotten on a plane straight to Belize.

Claire was sitting on the couch. Bruno introduced the two of them, and they both mumbled that they'd taken care of that themselves. Bruno invited them back to the kitchen for beers and planning.

McNally took his jacket off and pulled out a pad of yellow paper from his leather briefcase. "I'm old school," he said, with a nod to the legal pad. "We'll do this low tech."

He wrote Claire's name in the center and circled it. Around her name, he printed everyone else's and circled those as well. "So you already sent items to Reade Street Gallery with the customs doc signed?"

"Yeah," Claire said.

McNally drew a line between Claire and then to Janine and to Rex. McNally asked questions about all the relationships until they were visually represented. Lucia was the only name with a single line to Claire. Below the picture was a bullet point list of information. 'Janine has pictures of Bruno and his mom on location', 'Located Rex's warehouse', 'Rex in town?', and so forth.

"We can't do a sting, unfortunately," McNally said, tugging at his shirt collar. "We just don't have the time to set it up right."

"What about getting Janine to confess?" Bruno asked.

"Everything is happening tomorrow afternoon. If you say anything, or try to get her to confess, you might tip her off, and she runs," Claire said. "And if she's gone, we have no other witnesses. Aside from Sal."

"Who is Sal?" asked McNally.

"He's the one who has taken pictures of Bruno and his mom. He's the one faking the dig site."

"Tonight?" McNally asked, adding Sal's name to the list and bullet-pointed the items below it. "We need to move on that now. Do you have a description, Claire?"

Claire described him as a smaller man, athletic, brown hair, brown eyes.

"Give me a minute." McNally stood and got out his cell phone. "Hey, Sarah. Be on the lookout for a guy named Sal," McNally said and finished the conversation with his description.

After he hung up, McNally said, "Bruno, let NICH know ASAP. Call Delia, get someone up there tonight. We have to bust Sal. If we can get him, there's a high probability Janine will confess."

"We need more than Sal, though. Janine still has plausible deniability," Bruno said.

"Maybe Janine will say something. Can you wear a wire, Claire?"

Bruno looked at Claire, and she met his eyes. "Yes," she said. "I'll wear a wire."

Nothing could have prepared him for the overwhelming relief he felt when she said yes. She was doing this for him; he knew in his heart the only reason she'd even come forward was because of him.

"What about the warehouse?" Claire asked.

"We've got people on it, but we can't go in if we want to bust Janine, and especially Rex, being in a foreign country and all. None of this information is good enough yet that the Belizean government will help us. If we can bust Sal tonight, maybe. These collaborations take time, and I need to make sure the evidence trail is clean."

"Delia is aware of this business, I informed her this afternoon," Bruno said. "I'll give her another call to see if she can get someone up north. If that doesn't work, my family will know someone."

"Delia's aware?" Claire asked, sounding somewhat surprised, maybe even hurt. "Do I even need to call NICH in the morning? I mean, wouldn't that eliminate some of the headache?"

"At this stage in the game, appearances are everything, so yeah, we need to call NICH."

"We're hoping, praying really, that Janine and Rex don't make the connection that it was you who spilled the beans. If you want any chance to get into a witness protection program, you're gonna need to take down Rex."

Claire rubbed her face and squeezed her eyes shut. "What does that mean?"

"You have to come to LA."

"Seriously?" she asked. "What about Lucia? She'll find me."

"Do you have her full name? That'll help us get a start on finding her."

"Occhipinti. Lucia Occhipinti."

"Thanks," McNally said, writing her name on the legal pad. "The best deal we've got is to get Rex and Janine. If you qualify, we'll move forward with witness protection, and figuring out how to take on Lucia."

"I'm a pawn," said Claire.

"You sure are, ma'am."

The ride back to BIFA with Bruno was awkward. He was hurt that she'd been involved with Janine and the black-market deals, that she'd engage in something he had worked his whole life to prevent. In the BIFA parking lot, she looked at him just before she got out of his Jeep. His eyes reminded her of a tornado; concerned, hurt, angry, sad, and a small center of calm. She swallowed hard and got out of the Jeep, not even saying goodbye, and disappeared into the pavilion.

CHAPTER TWENTY-SEVEN

Claire

*D*ay 10. Popol Vuh—The Mayan Creation Story— was taking place today at the Actun Tunichil Muknal cave. Five days left. Claire bit the inside of her lip. *Stop counting the days.* There was no time to feel sorry for herself, or scared, or angry, or sad. She took out the wireless receiver McNally had given her last night. It was black and about the size of a cigarette box. She'd wear it until they had to leave for Popol Vuh; she couldn't exactly carry it through the rivers, so she placed it between her breasts and taped it. She had just enough bosom to hide the box, making sure the corners didn't protrude.

She headed to the Art Lodge and worked to get the staff organized by the time Janine woke. The Nat Geo camera had arrived late last night. The shamans were getting along, even laughing and joking with the local actors. Ruth Ann and Darren were acting distant to each other. Claire'd hoped they would make it. The teams worked together to have the vans loaded by nine a.m. Claire rode up the Nat Geo van driven by one of the camera crew. Janine rode in a second van along with Shali, Ruth Ann, and Darren. They arrived at the drop off point, a trailhead about two miles out. Everything had to be carried in.

The ATM cave was closed to the public for one day so they needed to be efficient—complete the setup, film the Popol Vuh Mayan creation story, and get out. Bruno was already at the ATM parking lot with his brother. Four vans were on site. Nearby, there was a picnic area with three or four tables and a built-in grill. Up a grassy hill, there was a bathroom with lockers.

The Nat Geo team got out of the van and unloaded their equipment. Bruno's brother Alberto would lead the first crew going in. They had hired guides from Alberto's adventure company to carry in the majority of props, costumes, the ceremonial pots and Nat Geo's specialized equipment. Bruno's team would be leading the museum crew along with one Nat Geo member who would film the team's hike in.

"Remember, no personal cameras are allowed in ATM. We have special permission from the country of Belize to allow the documentary team's equipment," Bruno said, directing his attention to the Nat Geo crew. "Be sure to follow the guide's explicit instructions on where to place items, as we don't want to do any damage to the cave."

Claire watched as Bruno expertly adjusted packs and helmets. He was rugged and handsome as holy hell. He started his way to her, and a warm desire for him flooded through her. The same man who just a few days ago had his fingers inside her, pleasuring her, desiring her.

"Ready to go?" he asked, rather brusquely.

Claire held back tears. The sharp distinction between the pleasure she had with him and the anger in his voice felt as if someone had gutted her. She couldn't breathe, but she refused to cry. She had to hold it together and look as professional as possible. Janine was standing right there.

"Yeah. We're ready."

Bruno reached for the shoulder straps on her backpack. "Your pack is a little loose," he said after a tug. "This better?"

"Much," she said, smiling for him. His unique scent of leather and Old Spice washed over her. It was easier to pretend there was nothing wrong, to pretend that it was only the two of them in the whole world, even if it was a lie. "I'm fine," she said. "A little nervous about the hike. Three rivers?"

"Two. Don't worry, I'll be here. My brother's here. You're safe."

"Right. Yeah. I'm sure it'll be fine," she said.

"Hey, Claire? I have to ride back with Ed," Janine said as she got back into the vehicle. She hadn't closed the door and instead was writing something. "We are missing two boxes with the shaman's instruments along with some of the background materials."

"Just call Delia back at BIFA," Claire said, "and have her deliver it."

"She isn't picking up."

"You can't go back. We'll send someone," Bruno said. Claire knew that he didn't want to let Janine out of his sight.

Janine didn't scoff, or even seem that upset with Bruno, just focused. "We need this box, it has the one of the shaman's ceremonial robes and incense. I'll go and pick up Delia, too."

"She can't come with us on the hike," said Bruno. "She's pregnant."

"Delia told me she wanted to be here when everyone got back. And we'll bring the lunches."

Ed had already started the van. Janine got into the front seat.

"I'm coming with you," Bruno said, standing in front of the door so she couldn't close it.

"You're acting ridiculous. I'm going back to BIFA. *You* have to lead the crew up," said Janine as she pulled the door in, like she was going to shut it.

"You're part of that crew. We can't go until you're here."

"I'll have your brother or one of the other guides take me in. Not a big deal."

"Keep an eye on her, Ed, okay?"

"Sure, boss," he said, and Bruno stepped out of her way.

She pulled the door closed and turned to Ed, "Let's go."

Bruno threw up his hands and turned to Claire. "She's getting away. Did you say something to her?"

"No." Claire retreated from him. "Don't look at me like that. I did not tell her."

"Then why was she so determined to go back?" Bruno asked.

"I don't know. Do you want me to go after her? Stop her? We can take your Jeep."

"I'll call McNally. Besides, he can get there faster than you can," Bruno said. He stepped off to the side. She could hear was his voice, but she couldn't make out any of the words.

The crews were ready to go and assembled at the entrance of the hike waiting expectedly. Before they left, Claire asked him, "What's McNally going to do?"

"I don't know, check out BIFA, try to stop her at the airport. Not much he can do without probable cause."

"What should I do with the wire?"

He gave her a look of incredulous disbelief.

"Sorry for asking. I don't think it's waterproof." What a stupid thing to say. She couldn't do anything right today.

"Seriously? Look, I don't care what you do with it," he said, looking away from her and at the van disappearing down the road. "Shit."

*E*veryone else was at the trailhead, waiting for Bruno and Claire. She excused to remove the device and put it in a waterproof bag. If Janine came back, she'd put the device back on. Except, in her gut, she didn't think Janine was coming back.

"Let's get started," Bruno said, checking the road that led to the highway, the one Janine had just driven on. He shook his head.

Alberto clapped Bruno on the shoulder, "Hey, bruv. What's going on? Do you want me to send someone back?"

"Yeah, would you? I hate to do this," Bruno said, "but one of the guides will have to stay."

"I'll tell one of the guys," Alberto said, not asking for any reason why. He nodded towards one of the guides. "Can you head back in the van and make sure that Janine is okay? Make sure she gets back here."

"If I can't find her?"

"Do the best you can," Alberto said as he handed the guy his keys.

That seemed to satisfy Bruno, enough to focus on the task

at hand, which was to get the Popol Vuh team up to the ATM. "It's a short hike to the first river. When we get there, make sure you keep ahold of the rope."

Bruno led the way. Shali, Claire, Ruth Ann, two of the shamans, and Darren followed him through the forest-like jungle, mindful of the leafcutter ants.

"What's going on?" asked Ruth Ann. "I can tell Bruno is upset. You don't look that great, and why the hell did Janine take off like that?"

Claire's eyes widened, but instead of answering, she said, "I can't tell you right this very minute, but I will tell you later. Why don't you tell me about you and Darren?"

"Oh lord. He is a good lover," said Ruth Ann. "Oh darling, don't look so shocked. As if you didn't know."

"And?"

"Well, he is wonderful here in Belize, but I don't know how he'll be back in LA."

"What do you mean?"

"Well, he's a different man there. He has a reputation as an asshole. I have my own circles. And old habits are hard to break."

"Do you love him?"

"I don't know. We have been honest with each other about it. Neither of us wants to give up on each other, but I—we—aren't sure if we are having a plain old love affair, if what we have will survive the harsh lights of LA."

"Hard to know unless you try."

"It might be easier to break up here, you know; neither of us wants a heart-break at home. Ah. Here we are," Ruth Ann said and pointed to the river. Claire looked over the expanse of a wide, brownish-green and slow-moving river.

"Walk in and hang on to the rope. It's not fast, but it is deep; the water will come up to just under your arms."

She walked in. The water was crisp and cool. The water

level was up to her ribs. She bent her knees and leaned her head back, getting her hair wet. A short hike followed; no one bothered to towel dry off since another river was coming up shortly, and she crossed that one easily as well.

The jungle grew thicker. The walking trail narrowed and began to wind back and forth down a slight decline towards the entrance of a limestone cave, the Actun Tunichil Muknal. At the threshold was a deep pool of water which prevented them from continuing. The color of the water was a light aquamarine, very different from the river. It didn't look ominous like she thought it might. Silver minnows darted in the water. The natural border of rock appeared soft rather than the sharp edge that they were.

There was a ledge wide enough for people to walk on, but it tapered off into the walls. One of the shamans spoke about the symbolic cleansing that they believed was essential before coming into the mouth of the underworld, Xibalba.

"When this cave was first found, the artifacts showed that they celebrated and sanctified the entrance," Bruno said. "This pool symbolically washed you clean before you could enter this holy cave. We Mayans believe god belongs to everyone. Please jump into the water, don't dive."

Bruno went first, Darren was next, Ruth Ann, and finally Claire. The water was warmer than she had expected, and deeper. She pushed herself back up and when she reached air, the first thing she saw was Bruno gazing at her. With a serious demeanor, he rubbed his thumb on the space between her eyebrows. "This holy water will clean out your third eye."

Goosebumps appeared on her forearms, and a wave of goodness passed through her. One of the shamans dipped his index finger into the water and then drew lines on his own face. He motioned to Ruth Ann, and she faced him; he dipped his hand into the water and made the same markings on her face. The shaman called out Claire's name, and she waded over to him. He touched her face with his wet fingers, drawing a mythical and protective charm on her.

Bruno had gotten out of the water, and from the ledge, he held his hand out to her. She took it, reveling in the touch, and pulled herself out, placing her feet on the small rocks jutting out as a natural ladder. He turned Claire's headlamp on and asked her to move forward. He helped the rest of the group out, and advised them to turn on their lamps as well.

The cave was wide enough to let a small river of water through. Flying bats echoed off the walls. The knowledge that she was in a cave that Mayan shamans had come to thousands of years before to participate in ceremony, to appease death, to find answers, made her connected to something bigger than herself, connected to humanity.

They waded through the central river in the cave for about twenty minutes before arriving at boulder-sized rocks blocking the route. Their sharp knifelike edges left an opening just wide enough for a throat to pass through. There was plenty of space above and below the split, but the river came up to the opening.

"This part here is the guillotine rock," Bruno said.

Claire wondered if the rock was cut this way by Mayans or if nature had symbolized the entrance to hell.

Bruno showed them how to grasp the rocks on either side and lift their throats up to pass through the narrow opening. "This part here looks worse than it is to go through. The water does most of the lifting."

Ruth Ann was first, then Darren. Claire hesitated.

"Trust me, it looks way worse than what it actually is," he said and held out his hand.

Claire reached out her fingers. Bruno positioned her hand on either side of the rocks. He left his hand on top of hers as encouragement. "You can do this, Claire."

Claire lifted herself up out of the water until her neck was even with the opening and passed through, barely grazing her neck on the stone as she did so. The experience, although perfectly safe, felt exhilarating, as though she had escaped death.

They waded deeper into the cave, and the water got shallower. Soon enough, it was ankle deep and she shivered from the water evaporating in the cool darkness of the cave.

She distracted herself with the incredible geological formations. The ceiling was impossibly high with mostly white stalactites met by mountainous stalagmites. There was a constant sound of dripping, as water fell from the stalactite cones and built up the stalagmites. She could see why Bruno never stopped caving, why he loved adventure. Regret pinged through her body. Could this have been her life had she chosen to stay with Bruno all those years ago? She could have been happy here, like this.

The excursion continued as they climbed over large rocks, traipsing through a hole in the earth that smelled of wet rock and bat dung. In tight spots, they clung to the sides of the cave as they maneuvered through.

They came across a statue of the Virgin Mary, sparkling against the glare of the flashlights. "They believe that the Spanish knew about this cave and placed an icon here so that the Mayans would believe Christianity had as much to do as the Mayan beliefs."

One of the shamans snickered. "As they have done for hundreds of years."

They climbed up a rock with manmade footholds until they got to a place that opened up like a plaza. The cave floor was flat but for small pockmarks where stalactite water had dripped and no stalagmite had grown to meet it. "This is where the Popol Vuh will be held. There's the team over there, setting up a stage made of grass mats."

The plaza was dark around the edges where the headlamps

could not reach. The Nat Geo team were assembling GoPros on selfie sticks and propping flashlights on cardboard holders. Alberto and his team were setting up the stage, a series of reed mats on the ground. "They are almost finished," Bruno said. "Before we start performing the ceremony, we'll finish the ATM tour and see the Crystal Maiden. Research concluded that the figure may actually be male, but the Crystal Man just doesn't have the same ring to it."

They passed by the plaza and climbed up stalagmite steps that had been worn over time of people stepping on them—looking like a flat mushroom, like a Dr. Seuss drawing, *Oh the things you'll see.*

At the top of the short climb, they took off their shoes. This specific part of the cave was where the bulk of the original ceremonies took place. The 'no shoes' rule was in place to protect the delicacy of the cave. They continued on in socks. The ground was wet, and the top layer was soft from moisture and a bit sticky, like wet clay. On the floor were a series of large, unpainted clay pots. Every one of the pots had a broken lip.

"The Mayans believe that if you chip off or break the pottery, you are releasing the soul. We'll have the new pots that Darren made for us to smash during our ceremony," said Bruno. "Our spirit lawyers, as we call the shamans, along with biological evidence, indicated there was a severe drought the last years of the Mayan Classic period. All of this," he said swooping his hand over the area, "was to appease the rain gods."

Bruno led them even deeper into the cave, and Claire saw a wooden ladder tied together with thick ropes. Bruno, Darren, Ruth Ann, and Claire climbed it and reached a small antechamber. They were at the deepest part of the cave. No markings or symbols identified this area as special or extraordinary, only a skeleton covered with sparkling quartz crystals.

"And this is the Crystal Maiden."

Flashlights illuminated the quartz that had formed over a thousand years. The bones sparkled. Claire closed her eyes. She felt at peace, enveloped in the sacred silence.

CHAPTER TWENTY-NINE

Claire

The crew returned to the plaza-like feature of the cave and set their backpacks on top of a reed mat. Claire worked with Ruth Ann to dress the main characters. The lead shaman wore the headdress Ruth Ann made. Darren handed each shaman the pot that they would break.

Alberto arrived, alone, carrying a box of supplies. He set it on of the reed mats, then went straight to Bruno. Claire saw Alberto shaking his head. She didn't know what it meant, but she was sure it wasn't good.

Alberto clapped his brother on the back, wished him luck, and started back to the entrance. Claire helped the crew setup. Small pots filled with yellow resin, called Copal, were burning around the edges. There were five shamans, each of them with a musical instrument, and they had painted their faces and arms in the Mayan style.

A secondary set of grass mats had been set up for the audience to sit on, which comprised of Alberto's crew, Ruth Ann, Darren, Shali, and Bruno. Claire handed out granola bars, with the strict warning to not litter. Shali approached Bruno, tapping his watch. "What are we waiting on?" he asked.

Bruno looked around and made eye contact with Claire. "Nothing. We can start." He and one of the shamans stood at the front and he rattled an instrument to get everyone's attention.

"Can you turn off your headlamp? We can't see you," said Ruth Ann.

Bruno did as she asked. He was bathed in the headlamp light of others. The glow was soft, almost ethereal, as if were an angelic guide sent to help them navigate the perils of the underworld, Xibalba. "The Popol Vuh teaches us that death is not the end. Popol literally translated in K'iche' to Mat, like the woven mats we brought for you to sit on. Scholars translated the title to 'The book of Mat.' Vuh is the K'iche' word to write. Popol Vuh translates to the mat you sit on while writing the family story."

Could Claire rewrite her family story? Perhaps not the past. Maybe she could have a new future. Unwilling to let reality and pessimism darken her thoughts, she simply hoped.

A shaman said, "Some of us shamans call this book 'The Light that came from beside the sea,' as it is believed to be events that happened before the first dawn, when night is darkest." The shaman held his hands wide over the audience. "With that, we invite you to close your eyes." He paused to let the crowd follow his direction. Someone began to pound a drum, softly and rhythmically. "Imagine a time before, imagine the idea of rebirth, when the gods ran through your blood."

The insistent beat of the drum blended with the tinkling sound of Ruth Ann's music jewelry and reverberated throughout the cavern. Claire closed her eyes, letting the sounds run through her, the damp smell of the cave helping her feel grounded to the earth. She leaned back, unaware that anyone was near her, but then felt Bruno next to her. Claire opened her heart as she turned to him. The drum beat intensified to match the beating of her heart. He met her gaze, but did not smile. For what seemed a long while, they stared at each other, until the drums stopped and they naturally looked towards the stage.

The show was like a mist to her. The twins going into the Xibalba. The twins playing Pok-A-Tok and losing their heads. Finding a way out, beating death, they ended up coming up through the earth, alive, and with the first stalk of corn to feed their family. Hunahpu and Xbalanque, the twins, were transformed into the Sun and the Moon. The sound brought her somewhere sacred, although she could not define where it was. She watched as the Popol Vuh unfolded, as the characters died and came back, as they crawled out from the underworld and lived.

Each of the five shamans held a pot up in the air, and with ceremonial sticks, they shattered the edge of the pot. "It is root-beginning as well," they said in unison.

The words coursed through her. The dampness of holy water was drying on her skin, the pulsating drums, the citrusy and light copal tickling her nose, and the darkness of the cave came together. She knew in her heart—in that inexplicable part which knows certainty—that she would go forth and begin anew.

CHAPTER THIRTY

Bruno

Bruno opened his eyes at the sound of clay pots breaking. He hadn't expected to fall asleep. It was a strange sense of floating, as if he'd been away somewhere and was just returning. When the Popol Vuh was finished, the shamans woke other participants up with a chant in an ancient Mayan K'iche' tongue. Bruno hadn't been the only one to nod off, he noticed as he looked around. Everyone had a sleepy quality to them, as if they had just woken up from a spell of sorts.

Except for Claire. She was awake and wide-eyed. There was something different about her. A change that made his skin tingle with hope for a moment. Then reality crashed in.

There was no way they could be together, not after what had happened, but that didn't change the fact that he loved her. Loving someone didn't mean you could make a life with them. Still. Without thinking of the consequence, he kissed her on the cheek and walked away.

The Nat Geo crew put away their camera equipment, and Alberto roused the guides. Hiking back to the ATM trailhead took an hour of easy walking. The floating sensation dissipated and by the time they got back, he felt solid again. Four vans parked, including the one that Janine had gone back to BIFA with. At the picnic area, Delia was helping set up lunch. Maybe Janine was in the restroom. He was willing to give her the benefit of the doubt until he knew for sure.

"Hey Delia, where's Janine? Did she come back with you?"

"No. I rode back with Ed. Alberto's guide followed us. Is everything okay?"

"It's fine," Bruno said.

"I didn't see her leave though," Delia said with a look on her face that he had seen many times on his own mother: a mixture of concern, consternation, and what-the-hell-is-going-on. Bruno put his hands on her arms and made sure to look her in the eye. "It'll be fine."

Bruno saw Ed coming out of the bathroom, adjusting his shirt. "Ed, what happened to Janine?"

"She said she had to go to her room. I was sitting in the pavilion waiting for her when I heard a vehicle start up. When I looked out the door, it was her, in the rental. I assumed she was just coming back here. Then I got Delia…"

Bruno held up his hand and called McNally. "Janine's gone," he said. "Her rental car and bags are gone according to Ed, our driver. Can you make some calls to the airport? I can check the rental company to see if she's returned the car. Claire will know which one."

"You think Claire had anything to do with this?"

"No," Bruno said. "I don't think she'd about-face that fast, but anything is possible." Even though he loved her, he wasn't ready to trust her. Not when it was something this big. Not when it had been betrayal. "I'll ask her, though."

"You thinking straight?" McNally asked. He said it firmly, without condescension.

"What kind of hell question is that, James? You don't think I'm aware?"

"I have to ask, you know that," McNally said, his voice gruff. "I'm going to search Claire and Janine's room, then head to the airport. There was a flight that took off today around eleven, but we can't ask for the flight manifest unless we have a warrant. Do you have a basic description of the car? The Belize cops might put a BOLO out for us." McNally said.

"A brown sedan is all I know."

"Are you kidding? The most generic and common of all rental cars. Damn it. You last saw her when you called me, this morning right, around ten?"

"Yes," Bruno said, shaking his dried hair with one hand.

"You think she had time to get out of the country?" McNally asked.

"My bet? She's almost back in LA."

"You're on. What's the wager? Breakfast at Big Bear again?"

"Sure. What happened at the commercial site, up north?" asked Bruno.

"Sarah couldn't find anything that might point to you. Delia's NICH archeologists came. He did all the right things; the property is now on the NICH list. You are in the clear."

Bruno breathed a sigh of relief. Rex's plan and Janine's had ultimately failed. "What about that guy Sal? The one Claire mentioned."

"No one was there. Looks like it was cleaned out, though; tire tracks, that sort of thing. We got paperwork to check out the warehouse in Belize City," McNally said. "If Janine's gone, she's in the wind, my friend."

"Were you able to get a bead on Rex?"

"As far as the place that they met, we scrolled through Airbnb. Too many fit Claire's description."

Bruno's fingers whitened from his grasp on the phone. "What about Reade Street? What happened on that end?"

McNally grunted over the phone. "The boss wants to wait

for evidence before he lands Reade Street. Apparently they've slipped away from us before."

Bruno clenched his jaw. He didn't want his name on the customs document. The FBI did a lot of good, but goddamn it, they were slow sometimes. He could understand Claire's reticence with them, with wearing a wire.

"We told Delia to let the customs doc slide, because we need an illegal action to happen in order to take down Reade Street. The document is in holding, and the board knows that it will be used as part of an investigation to clear your name. When the time comes, though, we'll have to arrest Claire."

Bruno didn't want to hear that about Claire; it surprised him when McNally implicated her as the perpetrator. "Any way we can help her with the Lucia problem?"

"First things first. We have to get Rex and Janine first, too, then we'll track down Lucia. Tell her she is coming to LA with us."

When he hung up the phone, Bruno knew he'd have to push McNally to do more on the Lucia front. Somehow, Janine had found out they were going to arrest her, and she was gone. The real question was whether or not Claire had anything to do with it. What else was Claire keeping from him? Had she really told him *everything*?

He glanced over at Claire. He loved her. And he could never be with her.

CHAPTER THIRTY-ONE

Claire

The crew helped pack the vans with the waterproof containers and other items from the Popol Vuh. Claire watched as Bruno got a key from Ed for one of the vans. She got into the passenger seat; they drove on the bumpy dirt road towards BIFA.

"McNally wants to meet, so we're stopping by my place first."

As they arrived at his house, Claire remembered when they had pulled up after the butterfly date. The memory of pleasure clashed against her harsh new reality and she felt pain inside her body, trying to choke her. She steadied her breathing, and the sensation abated. When they were inside, Claire and McNally acknowledged each other briefly. Bruno went into the kitchen and came back with three glasses of water.

"What's going on?" Claire asked.

"Janine is gone, disappeared. Do you know where she is?" Bruno asked.

Claire shook her head no. McNally added that no one had seen Janine since she left BIFA that morning and it was assumed that she was on her way back to the States.

"No one had seen her at the airport," he said and told them Janine had worked for the CIA within the clandestine branch, and was exceptionally good at disappearing undetected.

"She ghosted me," said Claire. "Really?" Why was Claire disappointed? Wasn't it Janine's nature to be a scorpion?

"The gig is over, Rex loses," McNally said.

"I guess I don't have to call the NICH now, huh," she said, half-joking, half-serious. As soon as she said it, she clamped her mouth shut, realizing how callous and stupid it sounded. Luckily, no one had heard her.

"You'll have to rebook your ticket to LA," McNally said. He explained it was voluntary, of course, but they needed her for several reasons: to help bring in Rex or Janine if they devised a plan that required her (as a decoy, she guessed), to keep her safe from Rex and Lucia. The idea of leaving Belize and flying to Los Angeles at the behest of James McNally, FBI Art Crimes special agent, was the last thing Claire wanted to do.

"I'd love to, but I don't have any money. I have to go back to New York; I already have a plane ticket there."

"We have to tell Shali everything," McNally said. "It's time he knew. I'll be by BIFA later this evening. I have a few things I want to put into place first, set some BOLO's with the cops in LA, that sort of thing."

A wave of shame washed over Claire. She had known this was coming, but knowing and experiencing were two different animals. She said nothing, for what was there to say? Claire asked to be taken back to BIFA. She wanted to finish her job before everyone knew. Besides, she needed something to take her mind off the latest events. Bruno pulled into the parking lot. Claire said goodbye to Bruno and started towards her room in the Art Lodge.

"Wait up, I'll walk with you," Bruno said. They stepped into the Art Lodge, which was empty.

"I'll pay for your ticket to come to LA. McNally can get a room at a hotel for a few days while we figure out something."

"Fine. I'll go. Once Shali knows, it's not like I'm welcome back in New York. Will I be safe there?"

"He'll have a car watching the hotel. They'll be looking for Janine or Rex, and we can certainly add Lucia. Look, Claire, a lot has happened in the last forty-eight hours."

"I know," she said, scratching the back of her neck. She didn't want to talk to him right now. She didn't want to be present in the truth.

"I'll do what I can to help you, but don't misunderstand the intention. We are done."

Claire nodded. She didn't cry, she didn't freak out. She held onto the knowledge that this was part of the 'root-beginning' as she watched him walk away.

LATER THAT DAY, McNally had come to BIFA to explain the situation to Shali that it would be in his best interest to release Claire from her contract, and she would be leaving for LA instead of going back to New York. Unfortunately, he could not elaborate. Shali, predictably furious, threw a fit when he found out that Janine was gone as well. Claire tried to calm him, assuring him that the final stages would be fairly easy. As a program manager, she already had a detailed to-do list built out to track the return to New York City, and she gave it to Delia.

Delia gave her a sharp, but seemingly uncertain glance when she took the list and started delegating to the BIFA staff. Claire felt the sting of regret. She could have had a job as an anthropologist, but that was dead in the water. Delia was a wonderful woman; she knew they could have been friends if she hadn't been so tied up in her own pursuits.

❦

Bruno, McNally, Sarah—McNally's partner—and Claire would be flying out of Belize that evening. On the plane, she sat next to Sarah. Bruno and McNally sat behind them. The plan was to set up Claire in the airport hotel and then meet at the FBI offices to finalize plans to catch Janine and Rex. Not once did McNally, or Bruno for that matter, mention Lucia. She tried to bring it up, but as soon as she said the name, McNally refocused the conversation on Janine.

She heard Bruno and McNally whispering behind her on the plane. Her heart and stomach physically hurt. The thought of never touching him again, never holding him, never experiencing pleasure with him made her feel physical pain, like drowning, unable to breathe. She wanted nothing more to do than be in his arms, but that wasn't possible. They were finished.

Claire laughed and Sarah looked at her funny. She'd managed to escape a life-changing tragic car accident that killed her whole family because she had her seatbelt on, because the oncoming vehicle hit the driver's side and she was sitting behind her mom on the passenger side, because it was a smaller car, because it had been raining, because her parents shielded her from the full impact. A million different things that happened in an exact sequence that night and she had managed to survive.

And this was how she chose to live her life?

Her whole life she'd always fought so hard, fought to forge a path ahead, blinded by the goal of wealth. Her solution was to keep moving forward. Tough choices she skirted around, and not once did she ever look back. She wanted nothing to do with the ache of her sadness, to be truthful about how much she missed her mom, or how desperately she'd like to ask her dad to hang a shelf for her. As they taxied on the runway, she looked out the plane window. The glass was cloudy, and everything smudged and faded.

Images flashed through her mind: Lucia's spoon, the henchman running a gun on her face, the look on Bruno's face when he realized that she was complicit. Her hands shook, and she clasped them together to steady herself. And yet, like a spinning coin about to fall on its side, the end was near and now it would be based on fate. Would her choices matter now? Claire slid the window cover closed. A hundred people surrounded her, and yet she was all alone.

CHAPTER THIRTY-TWO

Lucia

*L*ucia was excited to read the updates from Claire's story. In her Brooklyn office, on her desk was a manila folder with the name Claire written on the front in black rollerball ink. She liked the small things to be done by hand; there was a sense of authenticity. She opened the file. The first section was background info, where she grew up, the accident, probate information, foster parents, report cards, jobs, and social connections.

The next few pictures were of Claire coming out of her boutique, at the Apfel Gallery talking to Teddy, the potential buyer for the Jaque Bromanshank piece. *Old news.* She lifted a picture of Bruno and thought him devilishly handsome. An interesting twist had come up with the woman Janine. A chance for her to earn the two hundred grand that she owed. Some black-market art deal.

Most of the time, people who couldn't pay the money back —and were offered the opportunity to change—simply couldn't. They froze in the face of fear, they stalled in frustration, they weren't willing to do what it took: rob a bank, commit a felony, but Claire here had made her own luck. She got the job in Belize, she met Bruno, she met Janine. Then Claire did the most surprising thing of all. She told Bruno everything and refused to betray her lover.

This was the whole reason Lucia offered people the opportunity to change: to see a moment of real transformation. To watch a revolution occur in a person's life was a rare thing indeed.

Would Claire stay true to Bruno, find Janine and turn her in? Would fear win? Or would love?

Lucia wasn't bored, at least. She might alter the outcome, but she hadn't fully decided. When she thought of missing the final events, a sort of angst came over her. She pushed away from the desk and turned to look out the window. There was no reason she should be sad. Lucia made a call, and within thirty minutes, her driver was waiting outside. She would go to LA and see the rest of Claire's success or possible demise in person. A surge of excitement came over her, and she knew she'd made the right decision.

Lucia's driver pulled into the JFK terminal and turned towards the private hangars. Her flight was set to leave in forty-five minutes. The driver pulled up to a Boeing Business Jet BBJ2 which in her opinion, was sleek, but plain. Normally, it wouldn't catch anyone's attention but for the thirty-five-meter wingspan.

The car stopped and within a few minutes, her driver opened the door with a hand and offered to help her out. She graciously accepted and stepped out of the vehicle. A slight breeze blew her long black hair to the side. The stairs were out and the pilot waiting for her. As she approached, he extended his hand as an offer to help her up the stairs. She ignored him.

Once inside the plane, she walked to the back. When she had purchased the plane, she ripped out the existing décor and had Marc Newcomb—*the* airline industrial designer—redo everything. The cabin was upholstered in arctic white with ergonomically placed black lacquered tables. The cabin lighting gave off a purple hue, known to enhance and elevate mood. She felt so clean sitting in it, like a rebirth of sorts.

CHAPTER THIRTY-THREE

Janine

Janine ditched Ed at BIFA and took the sim card out of her phone. She drove to the Sleeping Giant resort to gather the Pelican case which contained the camera, the wig and dental insert, money, fake passports and credit cards. Everything else she left behind. From there, she headed to Belmopan and stopped in Brodies. She purchased a tropical muumuu and a long sleeve cardigan, nurse shoes, a pair of blocky and bright green reading glasses, and the right makeup to create a disguise.

Being in the CIA had taught her how to hide in plain sight. First she cased the location for CCTV's. There were none, and she went into the bathroom. Fifteen minutes later, she came out a brand-new, old woman. In the parking lot, she bent over to pick up a handful of gravel, and when she got in the car, she took her shoe off and added a few pebbles to change her walk. She tossed the remaining gravel back in the lot.

She ditched her car in Brodies parking lot and took a taxi to Belize City. At the airport, she bought a ticket to Cancun on Tropic Air that left in thirty minutes. While waiting for her flight, she created an email address on Google and created an account on a travel website. With her fake passport and credit card, she purchased a ticket online from Cancun to LA. She checked her watch; only two and a half hours had passed since she left the trailhead of the ATM. The Popol Vuh play should just be wrapping up, and she'd be long gone.

She made it to LA without getting stopped, and rented another car with her fake passport. Within a half hour, she sat in a nondescript beige Kia sedan and was on her way to her apartment. When she arrived, the locks had been changed. She called Rex and the call went to voicemail. She'd been blocked. *Fucker.* Luckily, she knew how to pick her lock and was in her place in less than five minutes. All she wanted was a change of clothes and an hour on her computer.

She logged onto her laptop. Rex might have locked her out, but he hadn't raided her apartment. She navigated to a webpage and put in a request. She still had friends in the dark web who would help her out, so she used some of the money from Belize to pay a hacker. Within an hour, she found out Claire was on her way to LA with Bruno and McNally. Janine had given the hacker a heads up to research hotels near LAX. FBI agents tended to book hotels near the airport, and she was sure McNally wasn't going to change his patterned behavior. This assumption was confirmed when the hacker provided the data without a hitch. Claire hadn't even bothered to use a fake name.

She also asked for a dossier on Lucia. The hacker's email came back with a few facts: Lucia's birthplace, college attendance, first job, and that was it. "Look," he wrote, "it's not my business, but she doesn't exist, like on a professional level. If you want my advice, I'd leave her out of whatever you're planning."

Janine thanked the hacker via email and got back on the highway headed towards the hotel and parked. In less than a minute, Janine found what she was looking for: a guy smoking a cigarette in a black sedan parked in the long-term lot. *Classy. Predictable move, FBI.*

She pulled out a package of baby wipes she'd purchased at the airport and wiped the remaining traces of makeup off. Janine was sure that the FBI's only concern for Claire was capturing her—Janine—low man on the totem pole, whom they could use to get to Rex. She didn't know if they were after Lucia or not, and on this, she made no assumption. She was sure McNally didn't have a plan on what to do with Lucia. That was opportunity. It was risky, probably the worst idea she'd ever had, but if her plan succeeded, Rex would be dead.

That son of a bitch had promised that this gig was her last one. When she called him from Belize the morning of the Popol Vuh and told him that they had to abort the mission, he told her to get back to the States pronto to 'fix what she fucked up.' Janine considered taking off and disappearing into the great wide open. She had everything she needed to start a new life.

But he had proof that she was heavily involved in the California dig, the one Bruno had busted. And if she ran, Rex had enough money that he could hire someone to go after her for the next ten years. She wanted her own life back and was going to LA for one reason only, to get Rex off her case.

Within twenty-four hours, she'd lost her home and would not graduate. All she had to do was finish the job for Rex, and then she was supposed to start over again, try better this time. The last little shreds of that life she'd started to honor her dead sister were severed. She didn't give a fuck what happened. Fuck Rex fucking Martel. She had a plan. If all went as planned, Rex Martel would be dead and Lucia would kill him. And she'd be free.

She sat back in the Kia in a generic color, perfect for the job. If she could get Lucia involved, she'd be able to shut down Rex once and for all. What she needed now was an 'in.' Claire.

She reviewed the hotel roster and found the last name Elliot three times. She took out her cell phone and Google-searched the hotel and clicked the call button.

With an affected Southern accent, she said, "I am Ms. Elliot, and I'm staying in your lovely hotel. I have just driven into the parking lot, that back one, you know. There is a man sitting there in a black sedan, smoking a cigarette. He looks dangerous. He's wearing sunglasses, but I don't understand why he would do that when it's not light."

She paused for a moment as the clerk spoke. "You'll send a security guard out right away? Oh thank you. I was so scared I practically ran into the hotel."

Security was always a better, more efficient solution than trying to depend on local police to show up. It took less than fifteen minutes for a security guard to shuffle outside. While he was talking to the FBI agent and the agent flashed his badge, she snuck into the hotel.

Claire fussed around the room. The only clothes she had were those from Belize, and they were dirty. She washed a pair of underwear in the sink using the cheap soap cake and let them dry on the shower rod. Bruno and McNally planned to come back that afternoon. There was an APB out on Janine's vehicle and license plate. The next step was to wait. She had asked McNally if anything would be done to appease the situation with Lucia.

"Not without Janine or Rex," he had said.

"I have two days, did you know that? Until Lucia comes for me," Claire had said. She wanted to strangle him for using that tone, that flippant 'well-you-do-something-about-it' tone. 'Sit tight, we'll talk tomorrow morning' and 'Our hands are tied.'

Sit tight? Our hands are tied? Couldn't he at least come up with something original to say? "If the FBI doesn't help, Lucia will kill me," she'd said. Nothing would make McNally budge.

Claire knew Bruno had tried to do something. He'd made inquiries to his parents and his brother to secure funds from his family, but no one was able to procure that amount of cash quickly. Getting a loan was out of the question, not without collateral. Trusting McNally was the best she could do under the circumstances.

When they left, Bruno looked pained, but hopeful. She wanted to be doing something, solving her problems, but there was nothing to be done. A calming acceptance washed over her. The words "root-beginning" came to mind. She saw then that there was a choice she could make. She could react to the fear, run, fight, or be calm and accept whatever came next.

There was a knock on the door. Claire looked at it strangely. *Who was it?* Bruno and McNally had just left. *Was it Lucia?* Had she realized the situation was futile, and decided to end it early? She looked out the security peephole and when she saw who it was, stood back.

Why was Janine here?

"What do you want?" Claire said. "I have a gun!"

"No you don't. Let me in."

Claire bit her lip. *Shit.* She unlocked her phone and was about to hit Bruno's number when Janine spoke again.

"I have a plan that will benefit both of us. Let me in so we can talk about it."

The only reason Claire was in LA was to help bring Janine or Rex in. If she could keep her there until Bruno and McNally came back, she will have fulfilled her obligation. Claire slid the chain open.

"Finally," Janine said, pushing in past her.

Claire shut the door. What was she doing? Was this a betrayal to Bruno? She exhaled a sharp breath and closed her eyes briefly. She'd make sure Janine stayed until Bruno and McNally came back.

Janine made herself comfortable and was unwrapping a plastic glass. "Did you get ice yet?"

Claire glared at her in disbelief.

"I take that as a no," Janine said.

"You may think I stupidly believe that we're still friends, but we're not. What do you want?"

"In Belize, I was the one who gave you an opportunity to earn two hundred grand to pay Lucia. Why did you have to blab the whole thing to Bruno? Now you're dead. You don't have two hundred grand, and my guess? McNally isn't going to lift a fucking finger to help you."

"I couldn't do it to Bruno," Claire said. "I couldn't betray him like that."

"But it was okay to do it to me? Great morals."

"This conversation is getting us nowhere. I wanted to do the right thing, no matter what. For fuck's sake, I still have Lucia after me. I turned myself in willingly to save him, knowing that Lucia was still out there. Knowing you and Rex would probably come after me."

"Oh la-dee-da. *Love saved me*. That must have been amazing sex," she said, sarcasm swelling with each word. "Well, let me tell you, Claire, love is shit. What's Bruno doing for you now, huh?"

"I didn't do it so he could save me," Claire stammered. She didn't want anything from him; she had told him because she didn't want him to be harmed, because she did love him. "He didn't deserve *your* plan. So la-dee-da. Love DID save me. You want a participation trophy? Tell me what *you* want."

"I want out. I need this crazy shit to end and move on with my life. I want Rex dead. I want Lucia to do it."

Claire wasn't expecting such directness. She'd expected Janine to pussyfoot around her little goal and say a bunch of bullshit.

Janine held up her chin. "What do you say? I'll help you, you help me."

Claire walked over to her window and opened the curtains to see the LAX airport spread out before her. Airplanes were coming in and others going out. People walking, some running.

Somewhere in there was a couple in love, somebody leaving the city for the last time, someone arriving for the first. Red lights blinked. The air control tower silently conducted over the whole thing. Well, what if, in life, you needed to be a little bad to beat the bad guy? Justification and nuance were the only difference between the two.

She thought about what Bruno said about the butterfly, that it represented both the dream world and the real world. She loved Bruno. She gave herself to him; she was willing to stop being the bad guy, even willing to give her life for him. She hadn't come all this way for nothing.

"I am not going to help you kill Rex," Claire said, turning to Janine. "Do something your sister would be proud of. Work with Bruno and me. If you kill him, you'll never stop running. You will be one of them. Besides, maybe you can work out an agreement with McNally."

"If I work with you, I'll go to jail," Janine said, tossing the plastic cup into the sink.

"It's only a few years in a minimum-security prison with nonviolent offenders," Claire said. "Nothing hard core."

"Not funny."

"Here's the deal, Janine. No matter what you choose, you will pay in some form. If you kill Rex, you will never get to go back." Claire said, throwing up her arms. "I don't know why I even care; you were going to throw me under the bus. You wanted me to take the fall for Bruno, you wanted me to betray him. You were using me. Why should I help you with anything?"

"You didn't care who you hurt, you wanted the money," Janine said, and appeared like she was ready to walk out that door.

"Wait," Claire said.

Janine turned to face her and looked her in the eye. Maybe Claire had let fear rule her decisions, but no more. The quicker she owned up to her own shit in this show, the more likely she'd find a solution to the Lucia problem.

"You're right. I didn't care who I hurt. There were a hundred good reasons why, but you're right. What about you? You wanted out too, and instead of making a clean break, you went with Rex. Not once, but twice. We've both had a shit life. Foster care, fucked up parent stuff. But I don't want to see you turn into one of them, a Rex, or Lucia, for that matter."

"I'm not going to jail for it."

"Then you'll pay the piper another way." At Janine's dubious look, Claire said, "Yes. You will have to pay. You'll either be on the run for murder, or be on the run from Rex and the FBI. And if by some miracle, you get Lucia to murder Rex, she'll probably figure it out and come for you. All kinds of shit could go wrong. Or you can talk to McNally and work out a deal."

Janine rubbed her eyes and groaned. "Why did you do this? Why did you tell Bruno? You had it, you were about to make the two hundred grand and be done."

"Are you kidding? Rex would have come calling again. Men like him never stop. You should know."

"Lucia is going to come for you."

"I know." She was scared as shit, and no one had any real solutions for her. *It is root-beginning.* The words were clear in her mind as if someone had spoken them aloud. Instead of panic, she felt her body calm. "I am scared, but death has been chasing me my whole life. I'm tired of running."

"You're just going to let her come in and kill you? Without trying?"

"I'm not giving up. This time, I'm trying to find a solution that doesn't require me killing anyone or shitting all over someone."

"Nobody changes just like that," Janine said, snapping her fingers. "Everyone is scared of death."

"I didn't change overnight," Claire said with a resigned sigh. "But something happened to me with Bruno. Something during the Popol Vuh. I can't explain it. I can't go back."

"What a fucking load of fucking bullshit. *You've changed,*" she said in a sing-songy voice, "What the fucking fuck ever."

"I'm trying to get you to see this another way. Explain to me how you would you get Lucia to kill Rex? I have a phone number for her, but she's in New York. How would she get here? How would you get Rex to meet her? How would you keep the FBI from finding out? And how are you going to make it happen in less than forty-eight hours?"

Janine opened her mouth to talk, but then closed it.

"I bet you have a half dozen other devious plans that are far more complex than working with McNally and Bruno," Claire said. "The easiest out for you is to work with the FBI. I wish there was a magical way to fix this. But we can't go back."

CHAPTER THIRTY-FIVE

Bruno

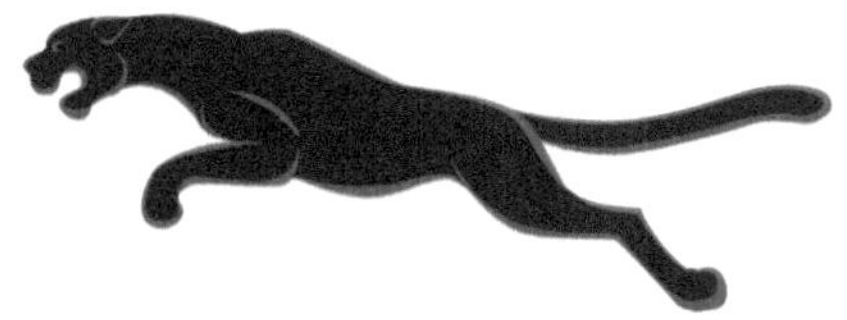

*B*runo had dropped off McNally at his office, who planned to check Rex's tax returns and find as much as he could on Lucia. According to McNally, all they could do right now was wait. Bruno headed back to his home in LA. He was still riding a wave of adrenaline, ready to crush it hard, ride hard, beat the bad guys. The rush of the past few days was hard to rein in and readjust his pace, and still he had not yet taken the time to assess everything that had happened.

Once he pulled into his driveway, he opened the garage door. There was his bike. *No. No, no, no.* A lot of people had left messages about impending deadlines, there was work to do and planning, all this ever-loving planning. He lifted his mountain bike off its hook and popped it into his Jeep. He was tired of preparing, talking, thinking. He wanted to act. What he needed was hard pedaling and a blue-sky panorama of the Mojave Desert.

He ran inside and changed to a pair of mountain biking shorts, grabbed a backpack and filled it with a few granola bars and a bottle of water. Within an hour, he was on the outskirts of LA pulling up to a trailhead. Six minutes after that, he was pedaling hard on a dirt trail, evergreens and deciduous trees whizzing by.

Everything that had bothered him, angered him, frustrated him, he put into the pedals. His body still wanted Claire, ached for her. She was everything he loved—funny, kind, smart. That day with the butterflies had bonded the two of them.

They were kindred souls, and she had planned to gut him. What drove him mad was that even knowing the truth about her didn't change the way he felt. He missed her. He loved her. How could his body betray him like that? How could he still want her? Harder and harder he pedaled, going dangerously fast along the narrow trail, maneuvering sharp turns with agile moves.

He didn't stop pedaling until he got to a lookout and came to a dusty stop. His shirt was wet with sweat. His heart was practically beating into his head, but he was clear-headed for the first time in days. He took off his backpack and retrieved the water bottle. He sat on a flat, dry spot on the ground and looked over the vista. The soft roll of mountains. The edge of the desert. The blue sky meeting the horizon in a thin line.

What to do about Claire?

He got a text from McNally: Sarah ran R and L paperwork. Come to the office.

Without a second thought, he tossed everything into the backpack, turned the bike around and pedaled back to his Jeep. After a quick shower and change, Bruno was at the FBI offices in LA with McNally. Sarah came into the room and handed him a sheaf of papers. McNally flipped through them.

"Good news is Rex is in town. Had an agent who happened to be near LA Citrus Valley College. Says she walked by his office. The door was open and he was just there, nonchalant, working on his computer. Doesn't mean anything. Usually perps get nervous after a failed coup; he might move fast."

"Unless his ego's too damn big and he thinks he's above the law."

"We can only hope."

"You'll find this interesting. We got Claire's bank records with a warrant, because of the Reade Street Gallery business."

Bruno sat up in his chair. He'd learn if Claire was telling the truth or if she'd just fabricated a story to make him feel sorry for her.

"She's got deposits that adds up to a hundred grand and a couple of large withdrawals. It's not definitive, but it paints a picture."

"You think she's telling the truth?"

"Yeah," McNally said, flipping through the sheaf of papers. "Here's Lucia Occhipinti's dossier." McNally sat back in his chair, with a look of disgust. "Lucia's the real deal." McNally dropped the paper onto his desk and used his index finger to point along as he read. "Says here Lucia's a loan shark out of New York City. Some guy owed her five mil. She sold him to a drug lord in a Central American prison camp." McNally placed a finger on the paper. "During the day, they left him in a coffin-sized metal chest in the sun all day, every day. At night, well, he was at their pleasure. He'd gotten out somehow, grabbed a machine gun and killed the whole fucking camp before blowing his brains out. Pictures were posted on a —holy Jesus Christ—posted on a community board at the school his kids went to."

Bruno's mouth dropped open. It was all true. Everything Claire had told him *was true*. He jumped to his feet.

"What are you doing?"

"I'm going back to the hotel," Bruno said. "Now."

IN THE JEEP, traffic on the 405 was shit. He tried to call Claire, weaving between lanes of traffic without moving ahead any faster. She didn't answer. He tried again and it went to voice-mail. Had Lucia showed up early? *Why didn't I believe Claire?* He had left her alone while he was working out his feelings. *Had Lucia come for her? Was Claire dead?* He turned into the hotel parking lot expecting sirens and ambulances. The lot was quiet, normal activity of people coming and going. He ran through the lobby and up the stairs to the third floor. Breathing heavy, he knocked on her door. After a few minutes, he heard her unlatch the chain and open the door.

"You didn't ask who I was first?" he said. "What if I was Lucia? What if I was Rex? How come you didn't answer your phone?"

Claire didn't seem to register the questions and stared at him, so he started slower, "Your phone?"

She seemed surprised as she patted her back pocket and pulled it out. "Oh crap. It's dead," she said, holding it up to him. "I'll get the charger."

"You don't seem to be upset," he said. "This is serious."

When Claire moved out of his line of sight, he saw her. Janine Jankowski stood by the window. His instinct was to rush her, but he maintained control over his body, "What. Is. She. Doing. Here?"

"We had a long talk," Claire said carefully.

"She works for Rex. There is *no way* she has honest inten-tions," Bruno said, raising his arms in the air.

"She wants out," Claire said. "She'll help us get Rex."

"Her last gig was to screw me," Bruno said as he turned to Janine, his heart pounding. She was the reason everything had gone haywire. Janine was not there to help. Janine was there to use Claire, use Bruno, and turn the situation in her favor. He faced Janine. "My reputation. My relationships. Claire. Nothing mattered to you."

"You're right," said Janine. "I did all of those things. And

Rex didn't hold up his end of the bargain."

Claire stood between him and Janine.

He was on edge, and ready to pounce. "I'm calling McNally."

"You should," Janine said. "I came here to convince Claire to help me kill Rex. But instead she convinced me to work with you guys."

"We'd be stupid not to consider the inside information she's telling us about Rex," Claire said, "to get him arrested. And as much as I did not want to work with her, this is our best chance to arrest Rex. And maybe find a solution for Lucia."

Bruno ran his hands through his hair when he realized he'd have to make a gut decision. This venture with Janine was risky, especially if Claire was involved.

"I don't like it," he said, turning to make eye contact with Claire, "but I'll hear you out."

When McNally arrived, he didn't ask questions and pulled out his handcuffs. Janine backed away. Bruno put his hand on his shoulder and asked McNally to stop. "If you arrest her now, Rex is in the wind. Let's use this opportunity."

McNally's lips pursed. "Join me in the hall?"

They slipped into the hallway, and once the door shut, McNally walked down a few doors. "Are you crazy? I don't trust Janine."

Before answering, Bruno let out a breath. "I'm the one she targeted, McNally. I don't trust her either. The problem is nothing else has come up. We have no plan to arrest Rex or help Claire."

"You know Claire and Janine are both going to jail."

He winced, but didn't let it stop him. "Janine is a door prize. Rex is the one we want."

McNally nodded, slowly at first, and then with more sincerity. "You're right. Rex is the main target."

"And if you don't like what she has to say, arrest her," Bruno said.

McNally nodded in agreement. They walked back to the room and Bruno rapped once on the door.

"So, what's your plan?" McNally asked.

Janine was by the window. She held the curtain slightly back and was scanning the lot. She dropped the curtain and turned towards the group. "I've been thinking about one. I need information, though. My laptop is at my apartment."

"Let's go," McNally said. He promised Bruno he'd be back in a few hours. When the door shut, Claire turned to face Bruno. Their eyes met. The air between them grew heavy.

"Do you trust Janine?" he asked.

"I trust she wants out," Claire said. "Janine has said that since the beginning, since Belize."

"You don't think it's a ploy?" Bruno said, stepping back. "To get us to do her dirty work?"

"I prefer to think of it as mutually beneficial," Claire said. "After McNally tried to arrest her today, she knows she's going to jail. What would her angle be?"

"I don't know," Bruno shrugged. He'd spent so much time focused on taking Janine down as a bad guy, he wasn't willing to consider her as one of the good guys. He threw his hands in the air. "You were going to let Janine and Rex ruin everything I had built. Everything."

They faced each other, breathing hard.

"Why'd you do it?" he asked.

She released a sigh as if she'd been holding her breath, then shook her head as if trying to loosen something. "When this started and I missed Lucia's payment in New York City, I was scared. My whole life was over. Everything I knew before. She was going to kill me. *Kill me, Bruno.* I didn't try to get into the black market for fun or to hurt you, or to hurt anyone. I just wanted the money." She broke eye contact with him and looked at the floor. She bit her lip and met his gaze. "I got the offer from Reade Street Gallery. Xander had the job opportunity. All of it was a means to an end. I did it because no one would really would get hurt. I mean, of course, black-market selling harms the archeology community, but no one specific would get hurt. And I'd be alive. But then you came into the picture. I wasn't expecting that at all. When I had to betray you… I couldn't do it."

Bruno's heart pounded in his chest. He didn't know what to say. He knew how awful Lucia was, but he needed to hear her explain the situation.

"Don't I deserve a second chance?" Claire asked. "All that talk about butterflies and metamorphosis, new beginnings? Was that horseshit?"

"No." he said, unsure of how to proceed through the barrage of emotions.

"I didn't betray you," Claire said. "I came to you and told you everything, Bruno. *You* made me see that life could be different. That there are things worth fighting for."

Bruno rubbed the stubble on his cheek. The sharp, short hairs felt good on the palm of his hand. It had been easy to say the words to her when they felt good, when the sun was warm on his skin. "I believe people can change. What I don't know is if I'm ready to forgive you. I can't answer that."

Claire hid her face from his.

"It doesn't matter right now. We move forward." Bruno placed his hand under her chin and turned her face towards him. He kissed her on the lips. It wasn't chaste, but neither was it passionate. She wrapped her arms around his torso. When his lips touched hers, he knew he cared about her. He wanted her safe; he would protect her. But, was he able to love her without reservation?

CHAPTER THIRTY-SIX

Claire

Claire watched Bruno open the door for McNally and Janine, who cradled a laptop in her arms. The four of them had agreed to devise a plan before contacting Rex. Otherwise, Janine assured them, there was no way Rex would interact. "His ego is big, not stupid," she said.

Claire cleared her throat. "Rex knows that I wouldn't compromise Bruno. If I contact him again, won't he think that I am involved with Bruno, and thus the FBI?"

"It's possible," said Janine, "but I don't think so. The FBI never went after Reade Street Gallery, which means, in Rex's calculations, that Claire never advised Bruno of the illegal sale. Rex also knows that Claire owes a loan shark and her life is on the line. Those two facts work in our favor. We can lead Rex to believe that Claire has a strong financial motive."

Bruno turned his head towards Janine and furrowed his eyebrows. "Why does it have to be Claire?"

"I would love nothing more than to see his smug face when the handcuffs go on," Janine said. "If we can come up with a plan to include me, I'm all for it. The problem is he won't let me near him, especially if he thinks you, the FBI, or NICH is on my tail. You'll never get a meeting. You'll never get an arrest. Nada, nothing."

"I agree with Janine," McNally said. "He's pissed at her for bombing the original plan. He knows Bruno and the FBI are coming for her. He changed the locks in her apartment. If we want to arrest Rex, our best option is with Claire."

Claire's mouth felt dry, but instead of getting upset, she was annoyed. The last twelve days had been nothing but fear-driven, and she'd had enough. "I'll do it."

Bruno opened his mouth, about to say something, but seemed unsure. McNally gave her a brief nod. On yellow legal paper, he wrote Claire's name in the center and circled it. Then, he wrote Janine, Rex, Bruno, Reade Street Gallery, and Lucia around her name. Each name was circled and a solid line was drawn to link Claire, symbolizing the relationship between each. The resulting picture looked like a wagon wheel. Under each person's name, Rex listed a fact: Failure to pay loan shark, Black Market contact, Black Market partnership, Former lover.

How could she have been so stupid to give him up all those years ago? Why hadn't she made better choices? What kind of person was she? A panic attack started. Her heart pounded and her breath hitched. She shook her head, unwilling to let the anxiety roll through her body, and inhaled to the count of four.

"You okay?" Bruno asked.

When she looked in his eyes, she felt something strong, something good. She wanted to be a better person, not only for his sake, but for her own. Doing the right thing for Bruno was worth it, even to risk the wrath of Lucia. "I'm good," she said.

Bruno put a hand on her shoulder. "You're not alone."

"Lucia's up there on our wanted list. If we can get her," McNally said, "there's a decent chance of getting you into witness protection. We should devise a plan that includes both Lucia and Rex."

"I have some ideas," Janine said.

Claire felt a twinge of hope, followed by nagging doubt. She ran her hand through her hair and glanced at Janine. "Going after Lucia and Rex is too complicated, and we'll end up with nothing. Let's stay focused on Rex."

"We look at all possibilities," Bruno said.

"The only reason we're considering Lucia is to help you. What do you want to do?" McNally asked.

"Could the FBI just give me two hundred grand?" Claire asked, half-joking, half-serious.

"I looked into it already," McNally said, with an apologetic smile. "My boss wouldn't approve it without a plan to get the money back. This is your chance to come up with a plan."

"Fucking bureaucracy," said Janine, knocking Claire slightly on the arm.

Claire gave a half-hearted laugh. "Right. A plan that will bring both Lucia and Rex into play is just not feasible. The phone number I have for Lucia is probably a burner. Who knows if she'll even answer? And then there's the logistics of getting her to LA from New York. That will take another day. There are too many problems." She pursed her lips and swallowed, trying not to think about what would happen once she missed the deadline. "It doesn't matter. We have to focus on Rex."

He looked uncomfortable with the answer. "It does matter," Bruno said as he scratched the back of his neck. "Lucia won't win."

"The FBI won't help me. I can't get a bank to loan me the money. I'm not going to rob a bank or do something stupid. I don't have friends who can pony up two hundred grand unless they sell their house or cash in a 401k. Even if they did, those things take time," Claire said. "Time we do not have. So for all this shit that I've been through, that all of us have gone through, let's get something out of it."

"She's got a point," McNally said. "Involving Lucia makes it too complicated, given the constraints of time. Let's figure out a solid plan to arrest Rex."

Claire was taken aback by the directness. Instead of getting upset, she smiled outwardly, even though she wasn't happy. The ending was not like she'd expected. She'd wanted an easy sitcom ending, a *KAPOW!* and the hero saves the day. Clearly, that wasn't going to happen.

Of course, she'd like to remove Lucia as a threat, but the options to secure money required a betrayal or descent further into criminal life. That life wasn't worth it and owned up to the choices she'd made. Claire tried not to think about her death at Lucia's hand. Instead, she focused on making good choices rather than reacting.

Janine turned on her laptop. "He's got a warehouse in Malibu somewhere. During the California gig…" she paused. Her eyes flicked from Bruno and then back to the screen. "I found a gallery to sell the items, but Rex did not want to move forward while the FBI was investigating, so we stored them in a warehouse. He wouldn't tell me where it was, but I know it's somewhere in Malibu."

"We can't get into the building without a warrant anyway," McNally said, "even if we knew where it was."

An air of gravity came over Janine. "We *can* get in there if someone is in serious trouble, about to be injured or killed."

"No way we put Claire in danger," Bruno said.

"I reviewed her laptop, emails, and other documents for evidence against Rex," McNally said, tilting his head towards Janine. "Nothing. In order to arrest him, we have to have access to his home or warehouse so we can search the premises."

Bruno forcibly set his hands on the table. "We are not putting Claire in danger."

"Rex doesn't want her dead. Claire isn't in real danger,"

Janine said, rolling her eyes. "He wants to use *her* to ruin you. She's an asset to him alive."

"Let's work the problem," McNally said. "We'll review the facts and walk through a potential scenario."

"Let me," Janine said to Claire. "First, call Rex. Tell him that you have the money from Reade Street. But you have a proposition he should consider. When he asks, tell him that you are short thirty grand and need the money to pay Lucia, the loan shark, and now you are willing to do whatever it takes."

Claire rubbed the side of her face, remembering the cold gun in the dark, but said nothing. She was scared, but determined to do the right thing.

"Why wouldn't Claire take the money she needs from the cut? It's not like they are paying Rex directly," said Bruno, returning to the table, "and it's likely she'll have a cashier's check."

"Good question," Janine looked up in the air, and exhaled. "Tell Rex you're tired of running. The last thing you want is him on your tail. You want payback for me."

Claire took a deep breath, she turned back to Janine and McNally. "Let's say curiosity wins Rex over and I have a meeting with him. Where would that be?"

"Most likely his Malibu house," Janine said. "He'll want to be seen as the good guy. Showing off with a fancy house and money will often convince people of that. But then you'll need to try and get him to the warehouse."

"Don't jump ahead," Claire said. "I'm at his house. I give him the check. It has to be a real check. Galleries involved in the black-market trade don't leave a paper trail; it'll need to be a cashier's check," Claire said to McNally.

"Can you get one today?" asked Bruno. "From a bank in New York?"

"It won't be easy, but yeah, I'll get one."

"It will have to be real check, Rex will call it in before moving forward," Janine said.

"Of course," McNally said. Claire pushed away a twinge of irritation at how quickly McNally agreed to get the money.

"Rex is expecting the total payout from Reade Street Gallery to be about five hundred based on market value of the items," Janine said. "Claire, your cut is thirty-five percent, which we estimated would yield about a hundred seventy thousand. My cut is a little less at a hundred. Reade Street gets five percent from us, totaling twenty-five thousand. Rex gets two hundred twenty-five thousand."

"You really think he'll meet me?" Claire asked.

"After you tell him that I stiffed you and the loan shark payment is due, tell him you're willing to do whatever he wants. You have to sound desperate, but full of self-confidence. Acting a little pissed would help. Also, sound scared about Lucia, but do not let him see you cry or crumble. He responds better to bravado than to damsel in distress."

"Not impossible," Claire said. "If Rex asks me to betray Bruno, how will I do it?" Claire asked, using her hands to put a double quote around the word betray.

"You'll have proof," Janine said. "Show Rex a picture of the customs documentation that listed Bruno as the originating archeologist."

"I will?" Claire asked. She had no such picture.

"Come on guys, try to keep up," Janine said. "You'll get her that picture, right, McNally?"

"Right," McNally added a note to his list.

"When you talk to Rex, tell him will send the picture to the Americans instead. Since Janine left Belize, Rex knows that the NICH was investigating the northern property on behalf of Bruno."

"Rex doesn't believe the NICH will take any claim against Bruno seriously?" asked Claire.

"That's correct," Janine said. "Rex thinks I screwed up the property portion of the grand plan, but he does not know that Reade Street Gallery or Claire are compromised."

"Surely he realizes that NICH would question everyone you worked with, especially Claire" Bruno said, "Besides, Claire already turned him down when he asked her to betray me. Why would she actively seek him out to pursue that choice?" Bruno asked.

"Let's take this part slow and unpack your questions. First, Claire will have to make it absolutely clear to him that she's not under suspicion. Second, Rex doesn't have her on his radar, I am on his radar because I fucked up the actual betrayal piece of it. Third, Claire can present the opportunity to complete his desire to ruin you. And because of her financial situation, he's willing to believe she has motivation." Janine said. She looked from Bruno to Claire. "To answer your second question of why she would actively seek Rex out, he believes Claire initially turned him away because of her *morality*. In other words, Rex thinks Claire has a moral compass and she is willing to adjust her actions to assure Lucia doesn't come after her. He doesn't know that Claire loves you."

"Oh," Bruno said, sitting back as if stunned.

Maybe he finally saw how much she loved him. Maybe he wasn't lost to her. Claire wanted to see the new plan through, a desire to make sure it was done right.

Janine turned to Claire. "You need a black eye."

"A real one?"

McNally sat back in his chair. "You can do that?"

"Sure," Janine said. "Makeup is a wonderful tool."

"Claire won't need to tell Rex exactly why she's motivated," McNally said. "A black eye will do that."

"Yeah, it'll be good. A quick recap? Claire? Give us an overview, to make sure you have all the moving pieces," Bruno said.

Claire stood and stretched her arms. "First, I call him up. I've got the money from Reade Street Gallery, a cashier's check for two hundred twenty-five grand. I'll have Janine's, too."

"So far so good," Janine said.

"Okay," Claire said, "after I pay him, then I tell him I have a proposition. That my life is in danger. I've made a deal with a loan shark and am willing to do whatever it takes to get thirty grand."

"Keep going," Janine said, nodding. "Why don't you cash the check?"

"I don't want him on my ass either. I want all debts cleared."

"Good," McNally said. "Then?"

"Rex will ask what I am willing to do, and I'll say I have proof that Bruno is involved in the black market. I have the customs documentation from Belize. Assume he says yes and now, I'm at his house. I show him the documentation, then he gives me the cash?"

"He'll want you to send the email and then he'll pay you. Make sure to verify that on the phone with him, and that he'll have cash on hand."

Claire nodded, and wrote it down.

"You can't read from there," Janine said.

"I know, but I need it to help me commit all this to memory."

"Soon as you have the money, exit the house," Bruno said. "Get into a safe position."

At the same time, Janine said, "Ask him to go to the warehouse to see if there are any other objects to sell to Reade Street."

The two of them looked at each other with suspicion.

Bruno turned to Claire. "If you think you can get him to the warehouse, do it. But if it's too dangerous, or if you think it'll bring the whole deal down, then call it off."

"Rex will do one of three things," said Janine as she scowled at Bruno. "He says 'Thank you' and walks away. Or he tries to get you to do another job, which is what I think he will do. That's when you go to the warehouse. The third option is that he tries to either hurt or kill you."

"Great," said Claire. "If it turns violent, then what do I do?"

"Get to a safe position. We'll send someone in," McNally said. "We'll be close, watching you."

"Rex is greedy. He'll want to use Claire to further hurt Bruno. He wants to sell the California artifacts. He is not going to hurt her."

"How much danger will Claire be in?" Bruno asked McNally.

"Rex might go off the rails," McNally said. "He has plenty of bodyguards and sometimes wears a gun." He turned to Claire. "Can you keep your cool?"

"I've made it this far," Claire said.

"If you don't keep your cool, we all lose," Janine said. "You can still back out. We can devise a new plan."

"We're not doing it," Bruno said. "Not if you have to risk your life."

"Bruno," Claire met his agitated gaze with a calm demeanor. A sense of strength flowed through her. "We went through the other options. This plan is the easiest, and it's the only one that works."

"If you don't do this, Rex will keep coming after you," Janine said. "He hates you like nothing I've ever seen."

Claire placed her hand on Bruno. "Let's take the son of a bitch down."

"We will do everything to protect her," McNally said. "I personally will be on site monitoring the situation closely."

"You promise?" Bruno said to McNally. "You swear on your life?"

"I promise," McNally said. "Nobody dies on my watch."

CLAIRE CALLED REX. He picked up on the third ring. She said she had the Reade Street money and wanted to meet. He agreed to bring cash if she satisfied the requirements, but wanted to meet in person at his Malibu house the next morning at eleven a.m. After she hung up, she got a text from him with the address. That was a lot easier than she anticipated. When she hung up, Janine gave her a high five. McNally shook her hand, and Bruno gave her a hug. She was in.

A decision was made to let Janine sleep in Claire's hotel room. She couldn't go home. The hotel was booked solid because of a conference. Claire wasn't thrilled with the decision, but didn't push back, either. After the two men left, they talked a little bit, reviewed the plan once more, but otherwise, they both were quiet. Claire spent the evening reading a book on her phone, and went to bed early. The next day, with one day left to pay Lucia, Claire woke up at five a.m.

She'd gone to the bathroom, and after brushing her teeth, looked at her watch. McNally and Bruno were scheduled to arrive at nine a.m. McNally needed to talk to his boss about getting a cashier's check and getting a picture of the customs documentation. Bruno was on task to bring breakfast and get makeup for Claire's black eye. She came back into the room and sat on the edge of the bed.

"You look super tense," Janine said. "Let me help you with a meditation. I learned how in the CIA."

"Seriously? Did you learn the chakras too?"

"Shit works," Janine said with a shrug. "They taught us to meditate before a job. We instructed our assets to do a five-minute meditation before information gathering. It helped them maintain composure. Nothing fucks a gig up like scrambled nerves. Meditating is easy, and there's an app for it."

Janine pushed a few buttons on her phone. A woman's voice introduced herself, and started a fifteen-minute meditation. She was instructed to lay on the bed and close her eyes.

Claire did so. She was guided through a fifteen-minute meditation of imagining herself in a better place and deep breathing. When it was finished, Claire opened her eyes. She was unsure if she'd fallen asleep or not, and to her surprise, she felt calm. Until she remembered where she was and why, but the experience helped get her body out of fight or flight mode.

"You know if you get panicked, you can reset your mind back to a logical state. If you feel the adrenaline, do simple math equations in your head."

"Like five plus two equals seven," Claire said.

"Exactly like that," Janine said. "It's a fast way to switch your mind from an instinctive state into a logical mindset."

Claire shrugged. She knew the advice wouldn't solve her panic attacks, but she couldn't let herself freak out in Rex's company. "Hopefully I won't have to try it."

"Let's get you dressed," Janine said.

Claire riffled through her suitcase, looking for something nice to wear. "All I have is stuff from Belize, dirty clothes. Maybe we should run to the mall or something?"

"If you show up in a fancy silk shirt, something about it will bother him. He won't know what it is, but he'll feel uncertain. And that doesn't bode well for you. The last thing you want is Rex nervous. Just wear a pair of your hiking pants and a t-shirt."

Claire's eyebrows shot up in concern. "You're telling me I should wear smelly clothes?"

"Yeah. You just got back from Belize, and you're looking for Rex. You're staying at a hotel. You're afraid of getting killed by Lucia. When do you have time to do laundry or clothes shopping?"

Claire pursed her lips. She wasn't sure if she agreed, but she was willing to try. Janine was former CIA, she probably knew a thing or two. Claire looked in her suitcase and the clothes she wore for the butterfly date stood out to her. She lifted the shirt and smelled it. There was a faint orange smell mixed with Bruno's musk. She closed her eyes and remembered the blue butterflies as they descended upon her. Going to face Rex was dangerous, but she felt a certainty about her actions, that of all the choices she could make, this was the right one. The feeling stemmed from her gut, giving her a sense of confidence—not bravado—that she hadn't had in years.

"Looks good to me," Janine said.

"Dirty shorts and a t-shirt it is," Claire said with a half-smile. "What was I thinking? Shopping?"

"I know, right?" Janine said.

Bruno knocked on the door and Janine checked the peephole before opening it. He had a paper bag filled with food and a second bag filled with makeup. "Egg sandwiches with cheese and bacon, just like you guys ordered." He handed Claire one. She unwrapped it, but found she wasn't able to eat. Janine wasn't that hungry either, apparently, and lifted the bag of makeup to Claire. "Shall we?"

In the bathroom, Claire sat on the toilet while Janine applied makeup around her eye. They practiced the scenario back and forth while Janine peppered her with questions. Then, without warning, Janine ripped out a few hairs that framed her face.

"Ow," Claire said, her hand on her cheek.

Finally, when she was finished, Janine leaned back with a grin as she examined her artwork. "Pretty nasty if I do say so myself."

Claire's eyes widened as she saw her reflection in the mirror. *Holy shit, that was a shiner.*

McNally had arrived and sat at the table, a cashier's check in front of him. He was busy with his smart phone, sending Claire an email that included a photograph of the customs documentation. Janine took Claire's phone and moved the photo to her download folder. In case Rex wanted to see the picture, it had to seem like she had taken it and stored it. Then Janine deleted McNally's email.

"Recap," McNally said to Claire. "Go."

"I need money to cover Lucia's payment. Thirty grand. I was roughed up by Lucia's men as a reminder of my payment." Claire paused for a moment, and the memory of the henchman against her made her shiver. "I am highly motivated to help Rex."

"Why?" Janine asked.

"My life is in danger. I have documentation that Bruno was the originating archeologist on the Reade Street sale, but I'm having trouble locating it. For the right amount I could look for it." Claire said. "Do you think he'll get the innuendo?"

"Yes. Good job. You have the voice record app on your phone?" asked Janine.

"I do," she said.

"Let's do it," said McNally. "We don't have much time. Only two hours until you have to meet up. I've got the wires." He handed the transmitter to Janine. She held it up. It was small and embedded into a piece of flexible, flat silicone. "The cool thing about these wires," she said, "is that they are virtually undetectable. Place it under your breast, the soft part out, the speaker towards your cleavage. When you're getting patted down, try not to stiffen. The device feels like your boob."

Claire felt the space where Janine placed the silicone wire. "Oh wow. You're right. I can't tell. Can they be detected by one of those wandy things?"

"Nope. The devices are too small. But the radio waves won't travel far. McNally and his team need to be close."

"What's the safe phrase again?"

"If you need us to come in, it's the phrase 'For the love of Pete.'" McNally said. "If you need us to stay put, it's 'Hold on.'"

"One more thing, Rex is going to try and intimidate you," Janine moved towards Claire with an aggressive stance. "He'll stand in front of you, stare you down, that sort of thing."

The movement scared Claire, but she squared her own shoulders in response.

"Demure, but not afraid. Good job," Janine said. "He'll be condescending, too. Rude. Don't let it get to you."

"Right," Claire nodded, remembering their meeting in Belize.

"All right then," McNally said and clapped his hands. The group turned to him, and he used the momentum to shake Claire's hand. "Wait at least thirty minutes or so before you leave. We need to get our setup done before you arrive."

"Will do," said Claire.

Janine gave her a quick hug. "You'll do great. Calm and cool wins the day."

"I'll be there in a minute," Bruno said to McNally and Janine. "I'd like a moment with…."

"We'll wait for you in the lobby," McNally said. The door closed behind them, and Bruno and Claire were alone. He reached out and held her hand in his. "Even though this situation is really fucked up, I wanted to say thank you."

Claire looked at him, unsure if she'd heard him right.

"You didn't have to tell me the truth, but you did. You don't have to risk your life to save mine, but you are. I can't say it makes up for everything, but… I want you to know, I see it."

Claire felt a rush of relief. Knowing that Bruno understood what she was doing was huge. He gave her a hug. "Kick ass," he said, and kissed her on the lips, a strong kiss that seemed to pass his confidence to her. He rubbed her cheek, then walked out of the room.

By herself, Claire took a deep breath. She closed her eyes, and the words from the meditation washed over her. *Live in the moment. Live in the breath.* She opened her eyes and looked in the mirror. She was ready.

CHAPTER THIRTY-EIGHT

Claire

Claire waited outside for an Uber in front of the hotel. She had worn a summer hat to hide the faux black eye. Even though she knew the bruise on her face was makeup, she didn't want people to see her, to judge her. The midsummer day was bright, and the temperature hot, even though it was only ten a.m. She wiped the sweat off her brow, careful to avoid the eye area. When the car arrived, she had the driver confirm who she was, then got in the back seat and gave him Rex's address.

They started on the 405, driving at a snail's pace in the congestion. Once off the highway, the drive was serene. The dry air smelled of sea salt and grass. Chaparral grew wild over the rolling hills of Malibu Canyons. Western sycamore branches hung over the two-lane road, but the view of the ocean was unobstructed. There were no neighborhoods, mostly compounds with a giant house, swimming pool, tennis courts, and jumping arenas with riders on shiny black stallions.

The Uber pulled up to an ornamental-iron privacy gate with a perimeter fence. The driver pressed a buzzer, and a male voice asked for everyone's identification. Claire handed hers to the driver and he held up both licenses to a video camera. The gate rolled away. At the top of the drive, two security men waited in an offensive stance. They were large and muscular, and wore black pants with a white shirt and black nylon jacket.

One of the guards motioned the Uber driver out, but told Claire to stay in the car. The driver seemed nervous as he got out, looking around as if he were trapped. Once the security agent verified he did indeed work for Uber, he was asked to get back into the vehicle. The second guard opened the door and motioned for Claire to step out.

"You may leave now," said the security guard.

The driver took one last wild-eyed glance at the security guard before he slammed the car in reverse and sped off.

"Do you have any weapons?" asked the second security guard to Claire.

"No."

He instructed Claire to lift her arms, then patted her down, feeling the space between and under her breasts. Instead of focusing on the fact that he might find the device hidden underneath the wire frame of her bra, she controlled her breath, as if she were meditating. The way Bruno had showed her in Belize. Four in. Four out. His hand went right over the wire and he didn't stop or say anything.

"May I see your purse and phone, please?"

She placed the phone in her satchel and handed it over. The guard held it under his arms. "You'll get it back when you leave. This way, ma'am."

The first security guard led her inside to the living room where floor to ceiling windows allowed a panoramic view of the ocean. A male butler in his mid-thirties came in. He seemed more than a butler. His demeanor was cold and his build wiry. The way he walked, quietly yet firmly, made her think of old Kung Fu movies. Claire dismissed the thought; he was a butler. He carried a silver tray with a Champagne glass filled with golden bubbly and a sprig of rosemary. She declined. Without a change in his expression, he set the tray on a nearby table and stood off to the side.

"Mr. Martel will be with you shortly."

Against the back wall were pictures of Rex posing with big game kills: an elephant and a lion. In front of the love seat, there were three step stools made from elephant feet. She cringed with disgust. On the floor was a tiger skin turned into a rug. A panel from the wall opened, and Rex Martel strode into the room. He wore safari style clothes, khaki pants, and a poplin shirt with an evergreen fishing vest.

Claire realized that if he had a hidden hallways system in his house, he probably had a surveillance system. She glanced around the room to see if she could identify any cameras. As she was looking, Rex approached and stood in front of her, staring her down. His hard glare evaluated her, judged her. She met his gaze and for a split-second, spooked. Had Janine tricked her? She blinked and in that fraction of a moment, Claire remembered that Rex would try to unnerve her with his physical presence; she and Janine had practiced for it.

"I won't bother with pleasantries. Let's get to it," Rex said.

"First things first. Here is a check for the money from Reade Street. It includes Janine's cut." She glanced to the butler, not knowing why. "May I?"

"Of course," Rex said.

She pulled out the check and handed it to him. Rex did not take it; instead his butler took the check and exited through the unmarked door.

"As I said over the phone, I'm short thirty grand to pay Lucia."

"I remember."

"I have to pay that money back tomorrow, and I am very motivated."

"Your eye?" Rex said with a nod towards her.

At first, Claire had no idea what he was talking about. She was going to ask him to clarify, but then remembered her faux black eye. "A reminder from one of her guys," Claire said. "I don't know what she'll do to me. Kill me, probably."

"I see," Rex said. She couldn't tell if he believed her or not.

"I have something you want. I have photographic proof that Bruno was the originating archeologist on the Reade Street deal. I don't know if NICH cares, but I bet the Archeological Institute of America would care."

"So?" Rex said, seemingly impatient. "It will cost me thirty grand to make it happen?"

"A small amount. I have a picture of the customs documentation."

"Why didn't you cash the check and be on your merry way?"

"I didn't want you coming after me."

Rex didn't seem all that interested. The butler presented him with an amber drink in a cut crystal glass. Rex took it from the tray without acknowledging the man and swirled the liquid without taking a sip.

"I want to show you something first. Follow me."

He led them out of the living room and into a library decorated with a gleaming mahogany desk. Behind it was a plush captain's chair with burgundy leather. "John Lloyd Stevens found the Mayan world," he said, pointing to a book on the corner of his desk. "It's a first edition that introduced the world to the ancient culture." The title read Incidents of Travel in Central America, Chiapas, and Yucatan, Volume 1. "There were others who knew about it, but he documented the ruins first. That's what matters, you see, being first. The papers called Mr. Stevens the 'American Traveler,' can you imagine? Nowadays that kind of sobriquet would be considered banal."

"Right, of course," she replied, unsure of where he was going with this.

He turned towards a few pieces of framed art on the wall. "These are two original drawings from Frederick Catherwood of Chichén Itzá. Frederick was Mr. Stevens' artistic companion when the Mayan ruins were discovered. Can you even imagine this?" Rex asked. "To sweep away the jungle vines—and there, unbeknownst to modern man—is a civilization unheard of."

Claire wished she had taken the Champagne now. Rex was such a dramatic asshole.

"These two men were good men, bringing ancient civilizations to light. In many ways, I am doing the same thing. I am one of the good guys," he said, focused on the ink plate picture, looking serious and at the same time, slightly aloof.

One of the good guys? Claire tried to appear interested instead of appalled. *Was he for real?* She used to cater to this kind of man at the Apfel Gallery, but now she had trouble.

"Let's get to business," Rex said, facing Claire and lifting his glass towards her. "You might have a future with me. But I have to ask first. Why are you willing to do this to Bruno now? Your answer back in Belize was unequivocally no."

Claire didn't say anything at first. She looked out the window and over the Malibu Canyons. The scrub grass reflected dull in the heat. "Moral issues bothered me," she said, turning to look him in the eye. "But Lucia, the loan shark, reminded me that I don't have that luxury."

"Ah. If you would have simply agreed back in Belize you wouldn't be in this trouble. What has changed?"

"Realization of my stupidity," Claire said. "I have a picture of the Belize documentation."

"You'll go on record, submitting the information to the Institute?"

"Yes."

"This is delicious," he said, "to have Bruno's lover turning him in."

Claire maintained a neutral expression; how she did so, was beyond her. "I'm dead tomorrow if I don't. Cut me a check and I'll text you the photo."

"Watson. We're going to see Lorelei. No interruptions."

At the LA FBI office, McNally, Bruno, and Janine sat at a conference room table. Using Google Maps, they reviewed the area around Rex's property in Malibu. McNally marked where they would park, and explained they were far enough away to escape detection, but close enough to catch the radio waves from Claire's transmitter.

Another agent brought in architecture papers that had been filed with the county. Unable to predict Rex's movements within the house, they planned using the documents to help if anything went awry. Janine took pictures of each section, and since she had been in the house, was in charge. Next, McNally geared up Bruno and Janine with a Kevlar vest and black baseball hats along with a pair of field binoculars. McNally's badge hung from a lanyard around his neck, and he wore a black hat with white lettered FBI stitched on the front.

They got into the front seat of McNally's government-issued sedan, and they headed towards Malibu Canyons. On the 405, Bruno watched as the traffic slowed to a twenty mile an hour crawl. The lane next to him was faster, and as he watched people drive by, involved in their own life, he was uneasy and swallowed hard. He never should have let Claire face Rex alone.

McNally navigated to a remote street and parked. They had parked southeast of the property grounds, which gave them a perfect view into Rex's house. The car was hidden by a row of sycamore trees. He rolled the window down and looked through a pair of binoculars.

"The property has a six-foot perimeter fence," Janine said, "but no barbed wire. The best access point is the front security gate; it's not electrified, as far as I know," she said as Bruno watched her scan the fence line. "The gate opens and closes, but if you touch it, there's no shock."

A lone car drove up to Martel's property and stopped at the gate. McNally shifted his binoculars towards the vehicle. "Uber confirmed," he said. "Claire is in the backseat."

From the wire, they could hear the driver talking to security. Within a few minutes, Claire was in the compound, being searched by a security guard, and the Uber driver was leaving the premises.

Goose bumps popped up on his forearms. This meeting wasn't safe for Claire. Rex was a dangerous man. This attempt to get him to commit a crime was not worth her safety. Dread bloomed in his belly and started up his throat. What if Rex didn't care about making another deal? What if he blamed Claire for everything that had gone wrong? Could it be Rex invited Claire to his home because he wanted to hurt her?

Janine was looking at her phone. She had taken a picture of the architectural layout back at the office and was zooming in. "They are headed to the living room to talk. If you look on first floor to the middle set of plate glass windows," she said, pointing.

A voice crackled through the speakers. Claire was being offered a glass of Champagne by a man whose voice they didn't recognize. She declined the beverage.

"Something's off. I don't think Rex wants to make a deal with her."

"What are you talking about?" Janine asked. "Of course he'll make a deal with Claire. He wants to hurt you."

"He'd hurt me more by doing something to Claire. Are you sure he doesn't know about us? That we were together?" Bruno asked.

"He knows that you're together, but I'm positive he thinks Claire was faking it. That she was only using you." Janine avoided eye contact.

They heard Rex enter the room. Bruno wanted to vomit when he heard his voice, knowing he was in the same room with Claire. She'd just given him the check. Okay. Rex started to say he was one of the good guys. When Bruno heard that, he recoiled. His ear was cocked to the radio and as he heard Claire and Rex banter, Bruno couldn't shake the building dread. "Something's wrong. I know it."

At first, Janine looked doubtful, and she shook her head. "We planned for this, we looked at every angle," she said, and looked deep in thought. Then, her expression changed. "Maybe? I don't know. The only thing that matters is what Rex thought. And he thought Claire was dating you to use you, not actually in love with you."

McNally rubbed his forehead. "We need to focus on the conversation *inside*. Last minute changes can screw up an operation. Stick to the plan."

Bruno turned his torso so that he could see Janine in the backseat. "How far is Rex willing to go, you know, to make me pay?"

"Pretty far."

"Like murder far? Or I'll show you how big my balls are far?"

"The latter," Janine said.

"I've lost visual," McNally said.

. . .

Claire

Claire followed Rex down a flight of well-lit stairs to a modest four car garage. They walked past a Tesla Model S, a 1973 Porsche 911T, a luxury Range Rover, and in the very last bay, a plain golf cart. He sat down and patted the spot next to him.

"Hold on, where are you taking me?"

"I want to show you something on the property I thought you might enjoy. Plus we have more to talk about."

The hairs on her arms stood out straight. She wanted to touch the jaguar pendant that Bruno had given her, but she didn't dare, afraid the motion would project fear. And yet, knowing it was there gave her courage.

He unplugged the vehicle, then lowered the sun visor and a set of keys dropped into his hands. He patted the seat next to him again. She got in slowly, with hesitation, not knowing whether or not to trust her gut. How could this be dangerous? It was a golf cart. She'd laugh if she wasn't so disturbed by the situation. He hit a garage door button, and when the door opened, he started the cart and placed it in reverse.

CHAPTER FORTY

Bruno

*B*runo trained the binoculars on the house, searching each of the windows methodically. Janine looked at her phone to view a picture she had taken of the layout. Claire's voice crackled over the speaker, "Hold on, where are you taking me?"

Everyone in the car stopped talking and looked at the radio. 'Hold on' was the code for wait and see.

"She's fine," McNally said. "We stick to the plan."

They listened to Rex's reply, "I wanted to show you something on part of the proper..." The end of his sentence was cut off.

Claire's words sounded different. There was an echo.

"She's in the garage," Janine said. "McNally, do you have a visual yet?"

"Not since she left the living room." McNally trained the binoculars on the four-car garage, but only vague shapes were visible through the frosted glass panels. Suddenly, one of the doors opened. A white golf cart with a canopy reversed out of the bay. They were unable to see faces.

"The passenger appears to be Claire," McNally said,

"based on the color of pants she is wearing. Assumption that Rex is driving."

Janine took the binoculars from him and moved down the path of the golf cart muttering under her breath, "No."

"What is it?" Bruno asked.

"We need to get there," Janine said and lowered the binoculars. "See that building?" She pointed to the horse barn.

"Yeah," McNally said, "that's obvious. It's a stable."

"Next to the barn, Rex has an acre camouflaged with a tarp he bought a few years ago," Janine said.

McNally shifted his focus, and adjusted the focal strength. "You should have told me."

"The last time I was at his Malibu place was over a year ago. I forgot," Janine said. "If he took her there, it could be dangerous. He has a female jaguar hidden under the cover in a chain link enclosure. A couple rhesus monkeys, and wild birds."

"The golf cart stopped near the barn," Bruno said to McNally. He watched as Claire got out. Rex made a sweeping gesture towards the camouflage cover. He could see Rex's mouth moving, but there was no sound coming from the transmitter.

CHAPTER FORTY-ONE

Claire

Claire shook her head. The ominous feeling returned, but she didn't believe it. They were outdoors, on a perfectly normal sunny day. She wanted to check out the perimeter of the property, to see if she could spot McNally and Bruno somewhere, but she didn't want to tip Rex off that somebody was watching them. The cart turned sharply, and she held onto the side as they started down a dusty, unpaved road that lead towards a barn.

"I've got a wild animal sanctuary just over that hill," Rex said. "I'd love for you to see the jaguar enclosure. Have you ever seen the beast in person? If a man ever believed in God, this would be a creature to inspire him."

"Isn't that illegal?" Claire asked. Rex stiffened. She should have kept her mouth shut.

"You should see this jaguar, she is beautiful. She was found wild, on one of the teak tree farms, and I had the opportunity to bring her back."

"Sure, let's go see it." Claire did not want to see the jaguar. She hated zoos, and she hated the thought of this poor animal being trapped. The only reason she said yes was to appease

Rex. She wanted to finish the job. Have him arrested, and go home, wherever that was.

"What I am doing is a good thing, Claire," Rex said. "Poachers often kill animals like this. I'm saving her."

As they approached a large stable, she could see the adjacent field was covered by brown camouflage netting that rested on ten-foot wooden poles. Netting hung down from three sides. Within the covered field was a smaller chain link cage filled with the green of jungle trees and vines, a sharp contrast against the brown field.

The gorgeous black creature slinked around the borders of the cage, which seemed too small for her elegant size. The animal's green eyes darted back and forth, searching the ground. Claire wished that she could free the jaguar. "What do you feed her?"

"Raw meat most of the time. Every once in a while, we put a live goat in the enclosure."

"Is she all alone in there?"

"Yes," Rex said without elaborating any further. "Come with me. We can see her up close." He opened the first gate into the field, and motioned for her to come in.

She stalled at the gate. Something was wrong. "I don't know about this," she said, looking back at the house. She could ask Rex to take her back. Walk back if it came to that.

"There's nothing to be afraid of. I just want to show you this amazing creature up close," Rex said.

She realized that under the tarp, and with the side netting, she was in a spot that made it impossible for Bruno or McNally to see her. "For the love of Pete, you're scaring me." She backed up towards the golf cart.

Rex smiled at her, a creepy 'I've got you' smile and said, "You should be scared."

Someone grabbed her elbow. Watson was behind her, and

he easily subdued her arms. He must have come from the barn.

"What are you doing?" She tried to swivel out of his grasp.

"Careful, Claire. You wouldn't want to get hurt now," Watson said, matter of fact. He pushed her gruffly towards the enclosure. "Let's take a walk."

"Make him stop, Rex," Claire grabbed the gate as they passed into the enclosure. "For Pete's sake, I can help you get Bruno. I have proof."

"Claire, Claire, Claire," Rex said as she struggled against Watson. The butler pried her fingers from the wire mesh and subdued her arms again. He simply lifted her and started walking towards the enclosure.

"You realize that I would never make a deal with you," Rex said. "And give you thirty grand in the process? Did you think I was stupid?"

Watson set her down, opened the gate, and shoved her inside. She hit the ground, hitting her knees hard on the dirt. She ignored the pain and sprang up towards the gate of the enclosure just as Watson clicked a padlock onto the gate. He retrieved the cashier's check from his pants pocket, ripped it up and threw it into the enclosure.

"You're stupid if you leave me in here," she said, nervously looking around, wondering if the cat was already stalking her. "For the love of Pete, get me out of here!"

"What I didn't tell you is that Lorelei here was a cat that the locals were going to put to death," Rex said, standing a few feet away. "She'd developed a taste for human flesh. We haven't fed her today. Good luck, Claire."

Rex and Claire walked towards the cover, and they disappeared underneath the tarp. His stomach dropped. He knew Rex wasn't going to make a deal with her. "We have to get her," Bruno said, his instincts going crazy.

"We wait," McNally said. "There's no evidence of wrong-doing or violence. We could lose the arrest if we go in."

Bruno unbuckled the seat belt and opened the door, then got out.

"Bruno, wait," McNally said. "This is our only chance. If we go in, we might lose the arrest."

Bruno walked to the driver's seat window and leaned in. "You promised no one would die on your watch. Janine said he's taking her to the jaguar cage. Her life is in danger."

"Get in and get your seatbelt on," McNally said, picking up his phone and slid the screen open. He pressed it to his ear.

As Bruno got into the car, he heard McNally say, "Backup request for the Malibu job. We're going in." He placed the phone in the drink cup. "You ready?"

"Hell yeah I'm ready."

McNally threw the gear shift into drive. He sped on the

two-lane road, expertly navigating the hairpin curves. At the security gate, he slammed on his brakes.

Two security guards ran towards the car. Their handguns were out and aimed at the vehicle. McNally opened the door and shots rang out.

"FBI!" McNally said, lifting his badge in the air. "Lower your guns and open the gate."

"I'm going in," Bruno said, "Cover me, McNally."

Bruno didn't wait for a response; he was out the door and running towards the gate. He had a decent chance of scaling it, as long as no bullets hit him. From the corner of his eye, he saw Janine running parallel to him, and not very gracefully. She was trying to attract their attention. It was working. More shots were fired towards her. He home-run slid along the ground until he hit the gate. He looked back to Janine; she was on the ground. Although he couldn't see, the position of her body indicated she'd been shot in the leg.

"Get your guys out of here!" He heard the security guard yell. "You don't have permission to be here. You need a warrant."

"Not when guns are being fired, asshole," yelled McNally. "Put down your weapons and open the gate."

Bruno heard nothing and used the quiet to launch himself up and over the six-foot gate. When he hit the ground, he took off running towards the barn, adrenaline spurring him faster than he'd ever run before.

CHAPTER FORTY-THREE

Claire

Claire watched the golf cart as it wound its way toward the house without her. Watson was in the driver's seat and Rex was in the passenger's. She screamed at the top of her lungs, but no one looked back. She slammed her back against the gate to see everything in front of her. Trying to catch her breath, she pulled out the silicon wire and yelled into the speaker, "For Pete's sake!"

Claire's heart thudded. She couldn't remember the phrase she was supposed to use. Maybe that's why they hadn't come. "Where the hell are you?" Familiar threads of panic rose in her. She closed her eyes, and tried to breathe in like Bruno had taught her, but the fear widened inside her body. If she didn't stop it soon, she'd hyperventilate, pass out, and die.

"Three plus two equals five," she said, opening her eyes. The simple equation was supposed to force her brain to use logic and bypass the instinctive response, but it only slowed the attack. She heard a sound of faint rustling. Was the cat stalking her? Was it in front of her? Her breath quickened and fear ignited her heart pounding again.

"No. No. NO." She wouldn't let the rising tide of adrenaline overcome her. She had to fight it. "Eight plus six equals," she paused, unsure of the answer. The veins in her throat throbbed, but she forced herself to answer the simple equation. Fourteen.

Like a fog clearing, she felt a bit more levelheaded, and scanned the enclosure. No animals were within her peripheral vision. If she was going to get out of this alive, her next decision was crucial. She'd have to decide to bust out of the enclosure or crawl up in a ball and hope for the best.

Claire felt the diamond shapes of the mesh as she pressed her head against it. In order for her to open the enclosure, she had to find the weakest link. She looked up to evaluate the chain link mesh, and upon cursory glance it appeared that the enclosure was solid. Along the posts, she saw metal braces that held the mesh in place. She wasn't strong enough to dismantle them. Even if she could, there was no way she'd turn her back on a black jaguar hungry for human meat.

The silicon wire was still in her fist. She slowly opened her hand and stared at the useless technology. What had happened to Bruno? Did they give her a faulty wire on purpose? Had he, had they all, decided that she wasn't worth saving? She threw it to the ground. There was rustling. She snapped her head towards the sound. None of her thoughts mattered. Her actions would.

She rubbed the jade jaguar pendant Bruno had given her. From the corner of her eye, she saw a black tail curl around a low hanging branch. The jaguar was up in the trees. She heard more rustling, this time on the other side of the enclosure. *Damn, that animal moved fast.* Her best chance of survival was to curl up into a ball. The jaguar might knock her around, but at least she'd be alive.

The enclosure was quiet. Too quiet. Just as she was about to curl herself into a ball to protect herself—a Pok-a-Tok ball, she thought, and almost laughed—she saw the most beautiful and terrifying sight. The black jaguar had climbed the tree in front of her. She was in a graceful leap, her powerful front legs stretched out and the curve of her black claws fully extended, aimed for her throat.

Instinct curved her body into a ball, arms around her head. The full force of the jaguar was upon her, sheer concrete of muscles and sleek fur. The force blew her backwards and to the side. Heat and sharp pain radiated up through her spine, but she wouldn't uncurl. She held on fast.

There was another slash at her torso, and she could hear growling snarls coming from the cat. Her body trembled. Panic wanted her to burst out of the tight roll and run for the gate, but it was locked, there was no way out. She fought every instinct to release her arms from the tuck. The slight sound of rustling trees caused the hairs to stand up on end. She kept her eyes closed. Staying in the roll was a psychological feat of mind over matter. The paws batted her back and forth. Pain shot out from her upper arms and forearms. Wet blood ran down the sides of her arms and body. Instead of letting go, she squeezed into a tighter ball.

I refuse to die.

CHAPTER FORTY-FOUR

Bruno

*B*runo's thigh muscles were on fire as he ran for the barn. The pain barely registered as he had one focus. *Save Claire.* His feet flew over the yellowed grass and he swerved around chaparral bushes. He breathed with his mouth wide open, maximizing the oxygen he could take in, his ribs extending and contracting. He willed himself to keep going.

The barn wasn't far now, but he knew every second counted. Ahead of him, he saw the camouflage cover supported by ten-foot poles. Netting hung from each of the sides. A ten-foot-tall chain link fence with razor barbwire mapped the boundary of the camouflage cover. There was no way he could climb efficiently.

Bruno kept his eyes on the enclosure, trying to find Claire, to assess the best way to get her out of the cage. Sweat dripped into his eyes, and the barn was only a hundred feet away. He could see the side of the jaguar enclosure; it looked like several batting cages connected together.

The only entrance he saw was closest to the barn. He ascertained the fastest path, then modified his route. He was sure the gate was locked in some form, even though he couldn't see it. He didn't have a gun to blast open the gate. He switched his focus to the barn. There had to be something inside he could use, a metal bar of some sort. He changed his path towards the barn with the intention of finding a tool, and that was when he heard Claire scream.

"I'm coming, Claire!" he yelled, uncertain if she could hear him. He dropped his head, and even though he thought he'd collapse, he stayed on his chosen path towards the barn. His ribs felt like they might explode out of his chest, his thigh muscles burned hot, but he wouldn't give up. He had to save Claire.

When he reached the building, he grabbed hold of the door and planned to swing inside the building. The physics were too much for his grip. His fingers slipped off and he rolled on the ground in a move ski bums called the egg beater. When he stopped, he rubbed the dirt off his face, then stood, wincing in pain. He started for the barn; once inside, he heard Claire scream again. This time, the sound made his heart curdle. He had to fight his instinct to run for her. If he couldn't open the gate, he would be helpless, and she would be dead.

Bruno riffled through stuff from the sides of the barn—boxes, food, hay, and that was when he saw a door that led to the saddle room. Inside, he found a red metal toolbox. Throwing it open, farrier tools fell to the ground. He grabbed all the tools, hoping one would work. Another scream from Claire jolted him.

Once he was out of the barn, he saw Claire in an inner enclosure. She was huddled in a ball with deep claw markings on her arms, bleeding profusely. The jaguar was on her back legs, batting her back and forth with her extended claws, like she was a toy to play with.

Bruno stopped at the gate and dropped the tools in front of him to select the best one. He picked up a giant nail file. He slipped it into the lock and tried to jimmy it open, but when he applied pressure to break the lock, the file curled into a U shape.

"Shit," he said as he tossed it. He picked up a tool that looked like pliers and slipped them into the bolt. As he applied pressure, the same thing happened. He tossed the bent handle to the ground. Bruno suddenly remembered a secret to unlocking padlocks. He'd been told by his mountain biker friends who had used it when he lost the key to his bike lock. 'Tap the side, it'll pop open.'

Another blood curdling scream from Claire let loose. Bruno picked up a small hammer, turned the lock on its side, and hit it. The lock popped open without ceremony. He pulled it off and pushed open the gate.

"I'm coming, Claire," Bruno said, "I got the first gate open."

She did not disengage from the ball she had wrapped herself into. At the second gate, Bruno hit the padlock on the side with the small hammer. It opened, and he tossed the lock off. But before going to Claire, he had to figure out how to distract the jaguar. He hoped that they were like black bears, afraid of big movements. He couldn't remember the exact advice he'd been given, but he didn't have time to Google it.

He turned to face the elegant jaguar. The cat's incredibly strong muscles were outlined as she paced in a circle. Every muscle inside his body was ready. He extended his arms wide as he could and waved them around. In a booming voice, he said, "I am your jaguar brother!" Then he made guttural sounds he knew would frighten a horse.

The jaguar bared her teeth at him and hissed. The sound sent ripples of adrenaline through his body. This cat could tear him limb to limb with her four-inch canines. She lunged for Claire, but he stood his ground in front of her, knowing he was her protector. Instead of attacking, the cat stepped backwards with a menacing growl at him.

"Let us be, jaguar sister. We mean you no harm." Bruno waved his arms again, but didn't make eye contact with the large cat. She turned in a figure-eight pattern, unwilling to leave, unwilling to attack. With another loud hiss, she got on her hind legs and swatted at the air. Bruno had enough. He let out the loudest and most instinctive roar he could muster. His chest was thrust out, his eyes wide open, and his stance solid. The visceral sound ripped through his vocal cords.

The black jaguar dropped to all fours and walked away, as if she were bored.

Immediately, Bruno turned to Claire. When he touched her, she began to unfurl. From a quick glance, he knew no major arteries were cut. He picked her up in his arms and carried her out of the enclosure, shutting the gate door behind him with his foot and making sure he heard the latch close. He made it through the second gate and set Claire on the ground. First, he checked the arm wound to see if he needed to apply a tourniquet. The cuts were deep, but not to the bone.

He took his shirt off, ripped it to shreds and wrapped it around to stop the bleeding. Then, he patted her down to make sure there were no other large gashes besides the ones on her arms. He found no other wounds, so he sat back on his haunches and for the first time, took a deep breath of air.

"You came for me," she said, so quietly he almost didn't hear it.

"Course I did. Why wouldn't I?"

Claire said nothing in response. Her eyes closed and she went limp in his hands.

"Aren't you two cute," said a man.

Bruno knew the voice. He looked up. Rex stood there with a smirk on his face. Next to him was a man he'd never seen before, but he had a gun, and it was pointed at him.

CHAPTER FORTY-FIVE

Claire

Lightheaded, Claire thought she might pass out, but fought it off. Her mouth was desperately dry. She wanted water. The smell of Bruno was mixed in with the iron-stink of her blood and sweat along with the animal scent of hay and cat. She opened her eyes and tried to look at Bruno, but the world was spinning. Bruno's brown eyes were a beacon in the haze. She was safe. Her body relaxed, and she closed her eyes, sinking into his arms.

"Aren't you two cute," Rex said.

He'd come back for them. Claire opened her eyes. Bruno was focused on Rex. Watson had a gun pointed at them.

"Why are you doing this?" asked Claire, her voice scratchy and hoarse.

"If Bruno would have left me alone, everything would have been just fine," Rex said, approaching them. "But he wanted to persecute me. He wanted to make me look like a fool. He ruined my professional reputation. He had no right to do what he did, turning me in to the FBI. He is not my judge or my jury."

"You can't be serious," Bruno said as he shifted. Claire was afraid he'd drop her from his lap and tried to reach out, but gasped at the pain and clutched her arm.

"You committed a crime and got caught," Bruno said. "Be a man and own up."

"I'm as serious as the gun pointed at you, Bruno. Yes. You ruined me, and now I'm going to do the same for you."

"You were digging illegally in the national forest and selling those artifacts. How are you being persecuted?"

"America is a free country," Rex said. "My share is worth more than yours, though. I have more money, more power, more equality. Besides, what I am doing is beneficial for Americans. I am sharing Native American history with the highest bidder. How dare you encroach on my right to capitalism."

"You broke the law. The FBI wants you arrested. You're a joke to the archeology community."

Rex scowled at Bruno and started to say something, then closed his mouth. "Who fucking cares anymore. The hell with it," he said, "You will never see it from my perspective. There's no trying to reason with you. Watson, put Claire and Bruno back into the jaguar enclosure. I've had enough."

Watson pointed the gun at Claire, but spoke to Bruno. "You heard the man. Get up."

"No," said Bruno, shifting his position so that he was in front of Claire. "We're not moving."

"You are when there is a gun," Rex said as Watson approached.

Watson closed one eye and zeroed in on Claire.

Every sense she had was alive. She wanted to run, but was frozen. Watson was too close. Sweat beaded on her forehead. He could fire the gun and easily hit her.

"He's a crack shot, Bruno. There's no way he misses at this distance," Rex said. "What body part are you focused on?"

"I've got her heart in sight, sir."

"Claire, you and Bruno deserve each other. Maybe there is hope for you in the afterlife. Go ahead, Watson. Fire at will."

Watson pulled back the hammer until it cocked into place. Claire had always thought that if she were in this situation that she'd be able to talk her way out of it. She felt stoic instead. Bruno got on his knees in front of her, blocking her major organs from Watson's gun.

"This is the best thing I've seen in weeks. Bruno on his knees. Claire looking like she's accepted her fate. But I'm not a tyrant. I don't want blood and guts all over my land," Rex said with a small flourish. "We live in the land of opportunity. I'll give you both a chance."

"What do you mean?" asked Claire.

"I'll let both of you live... if *one* of you comes to work for me, my way. The offer expires in thirty seconds, then Claire is dead." Rex tapped the face of his watch. Watson aimed his gun at Claire.

"That's not a choice," Bruno said.

"Didn't your mother tell you? Life isn't fair. Twenty-five seconds."

Claire didn't know what to say. If she offered to work for Rex, he would expect her to betray Bruno. But if she didn't stand up to Rex, they would both die. If Bruno offered to work for Rex, he would have to kowtow to Rex, a man who was everything he hated.

"Twenty seconds."

No one made a sound. The brush crackled in the wind. Birds chirped in the air. The sky was a clear cerulean blue. At the sound of padded footsteps, Claire looked back to see the sleek jaguar pacing along the fence line. Then she saw Bruno. The muscles in his jaw was tense. Claire adjusted herself, readying herself to stand. Bruno turned to her and shook his head *no*. Then he smiled; it was a sad smile, but if she didn't know better, full of hope.

"I will do it for you," he said calmly. She heard no anger or guilt in his tone.

"No, Bruno, don't."

"Let Claire live," Bruno said, standing slowly.

"I want to hear you say it," Rex said. "That you are coming to work for me. Ten seconds."

Watson adjusted his aim, pointing the gun at Bruno's chest.

"Give me that thing," Rex said. Watson gave him the gun, and Rex aimed it at Claire.

Bruno glared at Rex, and said, "I will work…"

"Not on my watch," McNally said, his voice booming.

McNally and three FBI agents stood by the barn with their guns trained on Rex and Watson.

"Nobody invited you to the party," Rex said, keeping the gun aimed on Claire.

"Seems you should drop the gun. You're outnumbered and outplayed," said McNally.

"All I have to do is press the trigger. I can take one of them before you take me."

"I'm not kidding, Rex," said McNally, "stop moving before we shoot you."

"My lawyers will be here faster than you can say 'I fucked up.'" He nodded towards McNally. "I look forward to seeing your face in court again."

"We have you to rights. Assault. I bet I'll find some very interesting items in the house once we open it up. That animal probably isn't legal. You haven't got a chance."

"Jesus, McNally, you are not a prosecutor, stop talking," Rex said, taking another step and getting within reaching distance of Watson.

McNally fired a warning shot into the air.

"There's nowhere to run, Rex. You can't escape in your golf cart. Play nice."

"Fuck you," Rex said. He pulled the trigger.

The sound exploded in Claire's ear, much louder than she had expected. Deafening.

She squeezed her eyes shut. A hot burning sensation pulsed in her shoulder. And the pain! She was dimly aware of more gunfire, but the numbing buzzing in her ears made it sound distant.

Before she knew what was happening, Bruno was on top of her, pinning her to the ground. She wasn't able to move. She tried to open her eyes, to see the wound, to look at Bruno, to do anything, but her head spun.

She was only dimly aware of more gunshots. She struggled to move, to get up and run away, but Bruno's weight on top of her kept her in place.

"Stay down, Claire. Stay. Down." Bruno sounded so muffled and far away.

Maybe he is underwater, she thought, her mind slipping, and she lost consciousness.

CHAPTER FORTY-SIX

Bruno

The gunfire had stopped. The stink of it peppered the air. Bruno lifted himself off Claire and checked to see if she was okay. Her eyes were closed and her body limp. All he felt was wetness. His hand was covered in blood. Her shoulder was bleeding from the bullet wound. He covered it with his hand and tried to take off his shirt, forgetting for a moment it was already wrapped around her arm.

"McNally!" Bruno yelled, trying to find him. *Was he dead?* The barn was in front of him, and two agents were standing there, talking to each other. "Hey guys, get over here and help me. We need an ambulance. She's been shot."

"Yes sir," the agent said, "there's one coming. They have to come down the golf cart path, to get the gurney in and out safely. They should be here soon."

"I need your shirt too," Bruno said. "Where's McNally? Janine?"

"Absolutely, sir," the agent said. He unstrapped the Velcro sides of his Kevlar vest and lifted it over his head and dropped it on the ground. He took his black FBI emblazoned t-shirt off and tossed it to Bruno. He pressed it over Claire's wound. She stirred and groaned at the pressure. "You're gonna be okay, Claire. Stay with me."

Bruno moved to the other side of Claire to keep better pressure on the wound and so he could see what had happened to Rex. McNally stood over a body.

Rex was dead.

Bruno didn't know how he felt about it. On one hand, he was glad that he didn't have to deal with the situation anymore, but on the other hand, he had reverence for life. Red lights flashed on and off, and the sound of emergency vehicles approached. He looked towards the front drive, but the netting blocked his view. He could tell from the vehicle shape that there were two fire trucks and two ambulances.

Bruno heard the clatter of metal and saw two EMT's coming down the hill. They yelled ahead, "Get out of the way!"

"We'll get that bandaged," the female EMT said. "You, sir, go to the ambulance parked in the driveway." She removed the blood-soaked shirts that had tied Claire's wounds. The second EMT was cutting off her clothes with a pair of heavy-duty scissors.

"We need to take her to the ER to have the bullet removed."

"No way I'm leaving Claire."

"Are you spouse or family?" asked the EMT.

After a long pause, he said, "No."

"Then you'll need to secure your own ride to ER," said the second EMT. "We'll be at Santa Monica UCLA."

Bruno nodded, looking around to see how he'd do so. McNally couldn't go anytime soon, Janine was having her leg bandaged, and the other agents were busy. He'd have to call an Uber.

CHAPTER FORTY-SEVEN

Claire

Claire woke in a white-walled recovery room. An antiseptic smell hit her. A hospital. Her eyes widened. She needed out. Now. She tried to take the IV out of her arm, but searing pain shot through her arm and shoulder. She winced and fell back in bed. Her head was woozy; the smell was strongly rooted in her memory. Her legs trembled with instinctive fear. It was the first time she'd been in a hospital since the accident that killed her parents.

The nurse came to her bedside and read the stats on a machine. "Your heart and breathing are erratic. Is everything okay?"

Claire wanted to ask the nurse what had happened to Bruno, but she couldn't get her mouth to open and speak the words. She couldn't even nod her head.

"It's okay, honey. Take your time. Gunshot wounds always come with PTSD," the nurse said as she wrote something on the clipboard.

Claire watched her carefully. She didn't have a sad face, like she had bad news. Nor was she overly stoic, like she was trying to hold something back. Claire exhaled. She'd been expecting to hear unbearable words. She gave her the smallest of nods.

The nurse went around the bed and check on the two IV's inserted into her arm. "I have good news, you're only here for one more day," said the nurse, "then you will be released. Do you have someone who can pick you up?"

"I need my phone," she said hoarsely.

"Is it in the room?" asked the nurse. "I don't see one here."

Claire couldn't remember where it was. Why didn't she have any clothes? Where was her purse? Her brain was befuddled from the drugs and trauma as she glanced around the room seeing only her bed, hospital equipment, and a chair with nothing on it. There was a window in her room where she could see the hallway. Outside, there was a man in black, sitting on a chair, watching her. He had an FBI badge on a lanyard around his neck.

"You could ask him," said Claire.

"Yeah, he probably knows something. He's here to make sure no one unauthorized gets in. First, let me check the closet for you," said the nurse.

She knew the man at the door was important, but she didn't know why. Then Claire remembered something. She remembered driving up to Rex's house in an Uber, but she couldn't remember if she brought her purse or not.

"Nothing in the closet."

When she first got to Rex's house, she'd given her phone to the security guard. And her purse. How was she going to call anyone? She must have looked agitated, because the nurse stopped what she was doing and came to the bedside. She put her hand on her forearm. "Someone will help you. Don't worry, we'll figure it out. I'll have one of the nurses bring in a pair of yoga pants and a t-shirt for tomorrow."

"Thanks," Claire said, grateful for the kind woman.

"I have to go," the nurse said, "but I'll be back this afternoon." Just as she was leaving, Bruno walked in. A wide grin came over Claire. She was so glad to see him. She loved him.

"You're awake!" He went to the side of the bed and kissed her on the lips. "How are you feeling?"

"Tired," Claire said carefully, remembering Belize, her betrayal. Even if he didn't love her back, she was deeply grateful for him, for standing up for her, for saving her life. "Happy to be alive."

"When you're released, you can stay with me."

"I can? Are you sure?" Claire asked as she met his eyes. Those deep brown eyes that she could sink into forever. She was reminded of safety, of second chances, and blue butterflies floating on the wind.

"Yes, I am sure. Once you're better, we can talk about us."

"I'd like that," Claire said, "but I want to talk about us now. I can't do that to you. I can't burden you if you don't want to be with me."

"We can talk about us. What do you want to ask?" Bruno said with a smile.

She was comforted by this response, confident that no matter what happened, they would walk away with mutual respect. He didn't hate her; she knew this now. "Do you want to be with me?"

"Claire," Bruno sat next to her and intertwined her fingers in his. "I don't know what will happen in the next few weeks. Why don't you heal first and then let's try to get to know each other again?"

Claire nodded. "I like that."

"I have to forewarn you," Bruno said, looking at their hands for a few moments. "You are going to be arrested for selling items of importance to the Reade Street Gallery. McNally says they might not charge you because of your help in bringing down Rex."

"Okay," Claire said, tensing. She hadn't expected Bruno to

tell her, or anyone, for that matter. It wasn't something she'd thought of, but now that it was out in the open, it made perfect sense.

"He'll be by tomorrow to talk to you. We've got a guard posted outside, just in case Lucia decides to come by."

Lucia! Everything came rushing back to her and it was as if she'd been punched in the gut. The deadline was today. She didn't have the two hundred thousand dollars needed to pay her debt. She was still alive, with Bruno, and an FBI guard outside her room.

"Isn't it past the deadline?" asked Bruno.

Claire shrugged in bewilderment. "I don't know what is going to happen. I guess I keep looking over my shoulder until she shows up." She exhaled loudly, wincing. Breathing hurt. "I can't think about that right now. I mean, there's nothing I can do."

"You'll be okay," Bruno said.

"You don't have to save me, Bruno," Claire said. "I'm not your duty. I can take care of myself."

Bruno sat back, and shock registered on his face. "I love you, Claire. Of course I'd help you."

Claire squeezed his hand, "I love you too. You got me out of the jaguar cage. You stood up to Rex." She knew what she wanted to ask, and closed her eyes shut tight, scared he might say no, but then opened them one at a time. She wanted to look right at him when he answered her. "Do you forgive me?"

"I forgive you," Bruno said, squeezing her hand back. "You convinced me you were for real when you went head-to-head with Rex."

He kissed her, the touch of his lips soft as a petal hung with summer rain. Claire settled into the kiss, comforted, and falling for him in a way she'd never thought possible.

When they parted, Bruno rubbed the side of his cheek. "I have something for you." He held his hand out.

The jade jaguar necklace was in his palm. She hadn't even realized it wasn't around her neck, she grasped at her throat. "How did…"

"The ER team had to take it off. The necklace is broken; I brought a new chain." He lifted the necklace, and she leaned forward with a slight groan. He placed it around her neck and clasped it. A wave of relief settled over her.

She cupped the pendant in her hand, and then looked up at him, almost startled. "What happened to that poor animal? They didn't put her down, did they? Is McNally okay? Janine? Is Rex in custody?"

"One thing at a time," Bruno said, chuckling. ""The jaguar's been placed onto a wildlife rehabilitation farm."

"Sounds good for the kitty. God, her nails were sharp," Claire said, touching her bandaged arm.

"You lost so much blood. And McNally is fine. When he comes to arrest you, try not to hate him, he's just doing his job. He says he won't put handcuffs on, but he'll need you to come downtown."

"Is that a real thing, 'come downtown'?"

"Yeah, when the offices are downtown. Rex is dead. McNally shot him after he reached for Watson's gun."

Claire rubbed her shoulder instinctively. "I don't remember any of that." She sat up a little. "And Janine? Is she okay? What happened there?"

"She's actually upstairs. She took a bullet in her thigh."

"How'd that happen?"

"She was coming with me to rescue you, but she got hit."

"Wait? Janine was going to try and save me? Are you serious?"

"Yeah," Bruno said, smiling. "Anyway, she's upstairs, but under watch by the FBI. As soon as she's released, they'll be arresting her."

"That's too bad."

"McNally said they'll probably go easy on her, given her actions over the last two days."

"I want to see her," Claire said.

"Why?"

"I don't know. I just want to see her face. Say goodbye. Closure, I guess."

"You're not mad at her?" Bruno asked.

"I don't know if I am or not," Claire said honestly.

Bruno made a call to McNally. Claire was given clearance to talk to Janine and given the room number. She wanted to go before visiting hours where over, but she didn't have any clothes to wear, just an open-back hospital issue gown.

"You want me to get something for you?"

"See if the nurse has any clothes for me? If not, grab me an extra gown, would you?"

BRUNO BROUGHT BACK a pair of hospital scrubs that were too big for her. The turquoise blue V-neck was so big her breasts were barely covered, and she pulled up the shirt as high as she could. The pants were too long, so she rolled them up.

"I'm going up with you," Bruno said. "No way am I letting you out of my sight. Not with the Lucia deadline up."

"With the guards watching, checking me at the elevator, and when I get there," Claire said, "Pretty sure I'll be okay."

"No," Bruno said. "I'm going with you."

They walked together. An FBI agent escorted her to the elevator and punched the up button. He made sure the elevator was clear, and then allowed Claire and Bruno on. When the elevator doors shut, Bruno kissed her. A sense of deep comfort filled her. She was safe. They rode to the fourth floor. The elevator opened. A female agent was waiting for her at the door. Bruno said he'd wait outside the room for her.

After patting her down, the agent escorted her to Janine's room and let her in.

"Hey," Janine said, the surprise apparent in her voice. "How do you like my bouncer?"

Claire knew she was joking, but didn't know how to respond. "I'm glad you're ok." Claire pointed to Janine's leg, wrapped heavily in bandages.

"I'll live. I wish I had something to offer you," Janine said, pointing to a lunch tray, "but all I have are these stale crackers and chocolate pudding."

"That's okay," Claire said. There was a knock at the door, and Bruno came in. "Hey Janine, glad to see you're doing all right."

Janine nodded with a smile, "I'll live."

Bruno turned to Claire, "I have to go. They found the warehouse and need me there. And I figured you were right, it's pretty safe here."

"I'll be fine," Claire said. "I'll see you later?"

"I love you," said Bruno.

"I love you too."

When the door shut, Janine looked at Claire with both eyebrows lifted.

"Not a word," Claire said, her eyes bright, a smile wide on her face.

Janine picked up a hospital cup and took a noisy drink from the straw. "Okay. Um. So," she said as she looked away, like she wanted to disappear from the room. Then she set the cup down, took a breath and slowly exhaled. "I…" she paused, choosing her words carefully. "You made me think about what I was doing. That's why I agreed to your plan, back at the hotel. I wanted to make things right."

"Your sister would be proud of you," Claire said. "And I'm glad it's over with Rex. I mean, I'm not glad he's dead. Well, I am, but I'm not, and I wish…"

"I know what you mean. It's okay. Is he really dead?"

"That's what Bruno told me. He tried to shoot me, and McNally got him."

"You and Bruno?" Janine asked.

"Yeah. I think we're going to be okay," Claire said. "It'll take time, but we're going to try."

"Oh good," Janine said, a half-smile playing at her lips.

"I want you to know that I forgive you. I mean, helping me out in the end. We won't be best friends, but I wanted to tell you in person."

"Thanks. That means a lot to me," Janine said. "What happened with Lucia?"

"I haven't heard from her," Claire said. "The FBI has someone posted at my room, too. I guess if I disappear, you'll know why."

"I wish there was something I could do," Janine said. "I really tried."

"In your way, I know you did," Claire said. "That's why I'm here."

The FBI agent knocked once and opened the door. "Mitch Horton's here to see you. Says he has official capacity with the fire department." He looked at the cut flowers with a raised eyebrow. "But you can only have one visitor at a time."

Janine smiled at him, a smile Claire had never seen before. "Give us a minute," she said.

The agent pressed Mitch back and closed the door.

Claire turned back to Janine. "Who is that?"

"I don't know," she said coyly. "Someone I met at Rex's."

"He's here in an official capacity? Mmhmm. A fireman?"

"He's different."

"Does he know who you are?"

"I told him everything."

"You just met him," Claire said.

Janine shrugged.

Claire laughed. She had changed, so why not Janine too?

"I'll see you around, then?" Claire asked.

"I'll probably end up in Mendocino selling shitty beach art. Come on up sometime."

"We'll see," Claire said. She waved and watched as Mitch walked into the room, his eyes focused on Janine. The FBI agent accompanied her to the elevator. When the door opened, there was a platinum blonde woman with blue streaks in her hair standing in the corner. She had on black frame glasses and a white lab coat reviewing paperwork on a clipboard. There was an identification card on a lanyard around her neck. She didn't look up. Claire said goodbye to the agent, stepped inside and faced the doors.

A needle jabbed into her neck.

CHAPTER FORTY-EIGHT

Claire

Claire awoke sitting in a chair. She couldn't see; something was taped to her eyes. The edge of the object was blunt, but hard. The rim dug into her skin, but didn't cut. She shook her head and the dynamics felt off, like there might be something more to it. The hardness suggested metal, the shape over her eyes, concave and pressing against her eyelids.

Spoons.

She struggled to move, but couldn't move her arms or her legs. Heavy tape was wrapped around her arms and ankles.

"Hello, Claire. It's good to see you again."

A woman's voice. Unable to see the person who was speaking, Claire tried to shake her head to free herself. She knew who it was.

Claire heard the sharp click of high heels headed towards her. "I'm so sorry to have to put you in this position. If only you had remembered to bring me what you owed. Do you have it?"

Starting from her gut, fear rose into her belly, into her chest, into her throat. Like drowning. She couldn't breathe. She felt trapped in a lake with a layer of thick ice above her. She swallowed, hard and deliberately. She lifted her head up and took short, fast breaths. *Keep your wits.*

"I don't have your money," Claire said, trying not to sound defiant, but also trying to sound brave.

"That's such a shame," Lucia said. "You were so close."

Claire heard clicks around her. Lucia was circling her; the clicks were her high heels against the flooring.

"So you chose love over betrayal? Is that right?"

Claire exhaled slowly to the count of four like Bruno had taught her after the Cave of the Dead. Images of him flashed through her mind. Bruno, when she first met him all those years ago in Anthropology 101. Bruno, at the door when she said goodbye. Bruno, at the airport. His look of unadulterated passion. The look of devastation. The way he kissed her at the hospital. She'd never see him again.

"Don't keep me waiting," said Lucia, who tapped her shoulder right where the bullet had entered her. Each touch sent a stab of pain through her upper body, but she couldn't curl in to protect herself—she was tied to a chair.

"Yes," Claire said simply, accepting her fate. A sense of calm came over her, settling deep inside her. The sense that she had been drowning changed. She was no longer out of control. There was a sense that she'd gotten her head above water. "I chose love over betrayal."

"Take the spoons off, Tony," Lucia said.

A cold knife settled on the space between her eyebrows. She yelped when it was forced upwards and the blinders fell into her lap. She was right, spoons.

"You understand what we are doing here, Claire?" Lucia asked. She was behind her. Claire tried to swivel her head to see Lucia, but was unable to do so. She could, however, see Tony. He was the same man who had put a gun on her in

Belize. She hadn't realized how small he was, the size of a gymnast.

A ripple of adrenaline coursed through her with the desire to run. She shook her arms, the pain from the bullet wound sent shock waves through her body, and she stopped trying to free herself. He smirked, then crossed his arms and stood there, like a sentry guard.

"Please don't do that," Lucia said. "You're making me nervous."

Claire settled. If this was her fate, she might as well accept it with dignity. She had earned this, after all, taking a loan with Lucia, and she had been unable to pay it back. "What's next, Lucia?" asked Claire.

"Please don't bore me with tedious questions."

Claire held her breath and bit her lip. What did Lucia want? She wanted water into wine. Transmutation. Or transformation. Be patient, let her lead. Claire looked around at her surroundings. The walls were aluminum, with metal shelving, and bare. A walk-in refrigerator at a restaurant. She'd seen enough cooking shows to know what one looked like. She assumed the door was behind her.

"For the last thirteen days, I've had someone following you, taking videos or pictures. It's been quite a journey, I must say."

Claire's throat seized up. This was it.

"Remember, I said if you could transmute, that I would let you live. How do you think you did?"

Claire shrugged.

Tony stiffened. His eyes were focused behind her, where Lucia was standing. He nodded sharply, once, then approached Claire. She watched in terror as he raised the back of his hand and slapped her across the face. She whimpered and squeezed her eyes shut.

"I want an answer for every question, a real answer." Claire heard more clicks behind her. Lucia seemed to be pacing.

"Don't act like a petulant teenager. I do not want silence. I do not want to hear pathetic excuses. Let me ask again, do you feel like the same person you were in New York?"

She struggled against the restraints, wanting to protect her face, wanting to curl into a ball.

"Answer me, Claire. Do you need motivation?"

Claire stopped struggling and looked Tony in the eyes. They were dark and cold. He would do whatever Lucia told him to do.

"I'm not the same person," Claire said, unsure at first. "Before in New York, I only cared about what I wanted. Now that I have Bruno…" Claire pursed her lips together and made eye contact with Tony. Hot tears brimmed at the edge of her eyes, but she did not want to give him the satisfaction of seeing her cry. She was afraid they would seem like crocodile tears. She lifted her chin slightly to keep them from spilling over.

"Don't keep me waiting," Lucia said. "Now that you have Bruno, what?"

"Now that I have Bruno, I… I love him. My decisions include him."

"That sounds trite. Shouldn't you save yourself? Isn't that what women want?"

Claire was surprised at the direction of questions. She'd often wondered herself where the line was between 'playing a victim' and asking someone to help. McNally, Janine, and Bruno had devised a plan together. But was Bruno saving her? Was he the knight in shining armor at the end of the book? He had helped her change. His love and his actions, along with her decisions in response, had changed them both. But it wasn't just for him. She wanted to be a better person, but it wasn't dependent on him loving her.

"Well?"

"Bruno and I saved each other. And right now, I *am* saving myself," Claire said. "Bruno has no idea where I am. He might be calling the police, getting the FBI involved to look for me, but he can't save me."

"And how do you save yourself, Claire? What must you do?"

Tony stood and raised his hand, ready to slap her again.

Her heart thudded with renewed fear. "Give me a second to think!"

Lucia held up her hand to Tony. He lowered his hand, but kept his eyes trained on Lucia.

"It better be good."

"Adapt," Claire said, "that's how you save yourself. Stand up, even in fear," Claire said and glanced to Tony. "And find people, good people, to trust, that I can love, that I'm willing to sacrifice for."

The henchman placed a chair between Claire and the computer, but off to the side, like a referee at a tennis match. On the left side was a bucket of Champagne and a small table with a crystal glass. Tony set a small table on the right side of Lucia. On it was a laptop and what looked to be a projector. He hung a white sheet from the aluminum hooks on the back wall. The laptop screen was being projected onto the sheet. A photograph of Manhattan taken from Brooklyn.

From the computer, Tony started a photo slideshow. The first pictures were background info, where she grew up, the accident, foster parents, and pictures of her at boarding school and then college. There was a picture of her and Bruno on a yellow raft. It was the West Virginia rafting trip.

"Imagine if you had stayed. Did you wish that you had?"

"Yes," Claire said simply and met Lucia's eyes. Neither blinked for a few seconds, then Lucia waved her hand to Tony. The next pictures were of Claire coming out of her own boutique, a wide smile on her face, rolls of wallpaper under her arms. Then, a picture of her at the Apfel Gallery talking to Teddy, the potential buyer for the Jaque Bromanshank piece, and the last picture ended with a still shot of a shocked Claire, just after she was fired.

"We've already seen this," Lucia said and tossed papers to the ground. Claire could hear the separate papers flutter as the bulk of the folder hit the ground with a thud. "What's next?"

Tony pulled out a thumb drive from his front pocket and placed it into a USB port. The files were listed in order, DAY 1, DAY 2, and so forth. Within each day was a photo album filled with still photographs and videos. Claire at home, getting drunk on cheap vodka. Claire meeting Lucia. *God, she looked scared.* There was a picture of her and David on the street, and a copy of the text to Reade Street. *Holy Mother and Mary, how did this woman have so much?* Then, there was a picture of her in the Belizean airport with a shit-eating grin on her face as she stared at Bruno. There was a video of her floating on the River of the Dead. A still photo taken though the jungle leaves of Claire and Bruno's first kiss.

"How sweet is this?" asked Lucia rhetorically. "Is he a good kisser, Claire?"

She was struck still by the surveillance. How had she gotten such intimate moments without Claire even noticing?

"You know how this works, Claire. I'm not going to ask you again; I'll have Tony do it for me."

Tony stood, the back of his hand lifted to her at the ready.

"He's an amazing kisser," Claire said.

"Can you describe it?"

"Um? It excites me."

"And?"

"I am connected to him, in ways that I'd never been with anyone else."

"A sufficient answer," Lucia said as she scrolled through a few more pictures. "Oh this one is good. Isn't this when you and Janine started getting into the black-market stuff?"

There was a still of Janine helping her down the steps of Xunantunich.

Claire nodded. "Right after that, on the Pok-A-Tok field."

"Ah yes." Lucia turned to Tony. "We'll come back to the pictures. I want to see video. Tony?"

The henchman reduced the photo album and navigated to the videos. The first clip was of Claire's phone when she had performed a search on Cancun and Chichén Itzá.

"That was laughable, and predictable," Lucia said. "It's a good thing you didn't do that." Lucia took a sip of her Champagne. "I was happy to help out in that regard."

How did she get that video? She must have hacked her phone. Claire had known Lucia would be watching, but only now did she realize how easily she was watching her whole life.

"I have to say, Claire, this was one of the better stories. Most of the time, people are predictable. They get over-aggressive and the knives and guns come out, and most of them have no idea how to handle those weapons. Boring. Some play dead. Others run. But your story intrigued me. You honestly tried to solve the problem. You got to travel! Ahhh. And Bruno, the lost love. Janine, the evil antagonist, or was that Rex?" Lucia sighed, as if a weight had been lifted. "It doesn't matter, it was all delicious!"

Claire's mouth dropped open.

"I love that look," Lucia said. "Now that you know how much power I have on your life…"

Lucia started the next video clip of Claire signing her name on the customs document.

Claire cringed. She couldn't believe what a schmuck she had been; she looked so smug. She couldn't keep watching.

"Don't you dare take your eyes off the video," Lucia said. "That was terrible. You need to own it."

The next video started as Bruno was taking off Claire's top. Claire wanted to look away, but as she watched the video of

Bruno touching her, her body keened and yearned for his touch. She watched as he put his mouth on her, sucking and tasting her. A deep welling of need bloomed inside. The way he moved her legs apart, the way he felt when he slid into her, filling her. Her breath shortened.

"This is really good," Lucia said. "I am not a fan of porn, but voyeurism, and watching two people who love each other, is… wow."

Embarrassed of her naked body on the screen for them to watch, to have her immediate need so blatant, Claire squirmed in the chair. Would she ever have that look of pure bliss on her face again? Would Bruno ever truly forgive her?

It is root-beginning. His words had come to her.

Lucia instructed Tony to move on to the next video, and Claire watched herself tell Bruno the truth about her impending betrayal. She didn't want to watch it, but forced herself to keep her eyes on the video. Lucia swiveled to her with narrow eyes and actually smiled when she saw that Claire hadn't turned away.

"Even then, you didn't tell him the whole truth," Lucia said as they watched Bruno giving Claire his necklace. She stood and approached Claire, lifting the jaguar pendant and yanked it off.

Claire tried to reach for the necklace, but couldn't. Her shoulder was throbbing. She looked to the bandage and it had a dime sized spot of blood on it.

"Skip ahead, Tony, go to the part when she tells him everything."

Knowing she had done it was hard enough. Claire blinked several times, but stopped with her eyes open. Having to rewatch it was painful.

"You did this for love. You saw beyond your own selfishness and told Bruno the truth. You risked Janine, Rex. You risked facing me to save Bruno. You truly changed, didn't you?"

Claire felt release as if she wasn't drowning anymore, as if it were the first time she'd had a gulp of oxygen in she didn't know how long. Her lungs expanded. Tears streamed down her face. Lucia walked up to her with a needle in hand and the jaguar necklace in the other. She lay the spoon on her lap and pooled the necklace into it. Claire met her eyes. They were dark brown, like Bruno's.

"I got to see the rest in person. It was quite a show." Lucia smiled as she lifted the needle.

It didn't matter if Claire smiled or laughed or cried. This was it. Lucia was never going to let her live. She angled her chin up and Lucia stabbed her in the throat with it.

CLAIRE AWOKE. There was no tape on her. The spoons were gone. She could see. The computer was gone. A linen card was on the table, along with her jaguar necklace. She picked up the necklace and rubbed it along her cheek before slipping it into her pocket. Next, she picked up the card. Written in calligraphy were the words, 'The debt is paid.'

The metal door was open. She walked out and found herself in a busy kitchen. Chefs wore white hats and waiters wore black aprons. A dishwasher pointed her towards a set of doors. She walked out and found herself in a bustling restaurant. People were laughing. Some were drinking wine. Others were taking bites of food. She was out of place in a pair of hospital scrubs, but didn't care.

The place reminded her of Carbone's in New York City. The interior was more feminine; the waiters a little less macho, the art a little less severe, and the wood didn't seem as dark. The maître d looked up from his podium and motioned to her with one hand to come forward. He asked her to be patient as he ordered her an Uber to the hospital.

She walked outside to wait for the ride and sat on a park bench. Above her was a street sign, a faux weathered red neon with the word Carbone, made to mimic a sign of the forties. Little did she know, Carbone's was a chain restaurant. The sound of cars in the street sounded strange, and yet the familiarity of it calmed her. Her phone was in a back pocket, and she knew better than to wonder how it got there. She slid open the screen and clicked on Maps. She was in West Hollywood.

The Uber arrived and the driver smiled. She got in the car and checked her text messages. She had expected maybe fifty, but there was only one from Bruno in all caps. WHERE ARE YOU? She checked the time. Only two hours had passed since she had left the hospital. Claire could see the white Hollywood letters in the distance, on the hill. She dialed Bruno first.

"I'm coming home," she said. "I'll tell you everything when I get there."

EPILOGUE

Claire

*E*ventually, McNally arrested her. The FBI gave her a deal if she helped to bring down Reade Street Gallery, but she had to serve six months in jail. Immediately after the court case, she was taken to 'Club Fed,' a minimum-security prison in Cumberland, Maryland. Summer camp it was not.

Claire was issued an ID badge and given a set of prison clothes, plastic shoes, and a plastic covered pillow. Someone monitored her every move. Everything was structured and everyone had a job. She woke up at five thirty in the morning and scooped oatmeal on the breakfast line. Her bunkmate was a Harvard graduate caught falsifying financials to scam venture capitalists in Silicon Valley. Her job was to take out the trash. Talk about irony.

No one raped or attacked her, she didn't get an acid flower on her hand, nor did she experience the wrath from any one guard or officer. She did what she was told, kept her nose down, and generally flew under the radar.

She made peace with herself there, and listened to the advice of her bunkmate, "do your time, don't let the time do you." Her and Bruno corresponded through snail mail. She had sent him a letter every day, and received one from him. The strangest thing happened; the letters became the most intimate communication she had ever written or received. They did not describe any physical acts. The words they shared with each other contained their deepest sentiments, the hardest of truths, and made the most invisible parts of them visible.

Exactly six months later, at precisely six forty-five a.m., a guard came to her cell. She hugged her Harvard cellmate goodbye. They returned her street clothes and she gave back the prison ones. Putting her jeans on felt weird, like they belonged to someone else entirely. The guard produced an inventory list of items she had come in with: a watch, a jade jaguar necklace, and fifty-two cents in change. The items were in a plastic bag, and she had to sign for them. A guard escorted her to the lobby, and then, without fanfare, retreated back into the building. By the time she turned, he was gone.

Claire didn't know anyone in the lobby and walked outside, because she could do so without having to sign in somewhere or let someone know. It was nearing the end of January. Snow was on the ground and the air was cold. She didn't care. Right there, in the middle of the sidewalk, she twirled around, happy to be done, happy to be alive, and truly, she was free.

"You ready to go home?" said Bruno, coming up from behind her.

"Is that where we're going? Home?"

"You risked everything to save my life. *I see you, Claire.* So yeah, let's go home."

"When the dust settles, Señor Jaguar, will you regret coming for me?"

"Maybe," he said, with a grin on his face, "but I doubt it." He took her in his arms. Bruno brought her in close. She leaned her head back and laughed, a big laugh, full of joy, full of love. He kissed her neck and ran his hands through her hair. Her hands slipped under his jacket, touching his muscles, his wonderful skin. The smell of him was intoxicating and warm. There was a hint of oranges still.

Then he stopped and held her back to get a good look. "I love you, Claire," Bruno said. "I missed you."

"I love you too," Claire said, and then whispered in his ear, "You are my home. Take me to the hotel now, ya big stud."

ALSO BY JUNO CHASE

The D.C. Knights Series

Follow the women in Congressman Lincoln Pierce's office as they navigate life and love in Washington D.C. To add a little fun to their high pressure lives, they play a game. The winner of the game gets to go to Washington D.C. with the Congressman for a secret meeting. The game is supposed to be a way to meet some new men while helping them decide who gets to go on the trip.

Read the first six in any order, but save the last for a giant recap and epilogue to all the other stories! Here they are in order.

New to the Game—D.C. Knights Book 1

Chloe's the new intern, but she jumps into the game both feet first.

Playing For Keeps—D.C. Knights Book 2

Katherine thinks she's got things figured out until a sexy scientist tangos his way into her heart.

All In—D.C. Knights Book 3

Madeline has no problem playing games until she meets Ewan a man who knows how to treat her like a woman.

Fair and Square—D.C. Knights Book 4

Lizbeth doesn't have time for games, but she ends up in the midst of a political game no one in Congressman Pierce's office saw coming.

Only Bluffing—D.C. Knights Book 5

Eleanor Winslow and Daniel Prado are from different worlds. Will their love overcome dark histories and ancient legacies?

Game On—D.C. Knights Book 6 — Early Summer 2018

Cheyenne LeFleur lives on the wild side. Will Alexander Moore be able to handle her history, or will he reject her like so many before him?

For the Win—D.C. Knights Book 7

Opal Meyers isn't into playing games—not at work and not in love. When she lands the coveted spot at the Las Vegas meeting, she finds herself caught between the congressman and a rich entrepreneur. Both offer different kinds of love. Which will she choose?

ACKNOWLEDGMENTS

We'd like to thank a few people who helped us get this book into your lovely hands, dear readers. We are part of an amazing writing group who has listened to our ideas, helped us with plotting, and given us some straight feedback. We couldn't have done this without your energy and help-—you ladies rock! Thank you for all your reading time and thoughtful suggestions.

Thank you to Liz and Christy for their editorial feedback and expertise to help shape this story. Liz has this amazing ability to provide just the right kind of feedback that assures the struggling characters remain in line with who they are. Christy provided timely advice that helped to strengthen characters and plot lines. Thank you both very much!

To our intrepid beta readers. Thank you for taking the time to read and give us honest criticism. (Sweet reader, please let us know if you find anything that needs fixing, we'd appreciate it a lot.)

And to our families—our fabulous husbands and children who have supported us in so many different ways and picked up the pieces as needed. We love you!